Praise for Anne Schulman

An intriguing novel.

– Family circle

A blockbuster novel by Ireland's answer to Jilly Cooper.

– Image

Intrigue *is a wonderful page turner.*

– It Magazine

A gripping read.

– Woman

Encounters

Encounters

Anne Schulman

POOLBEG

Published 1995 by
Poolbeg Press Ltd,
Knocksedan House,
123 Baldoyle Industrial Estate,
Dublin 13, Ireland

A catalogue record for this book is available from the British Library.

ISBN 1 85371 458 5

Cover photography by Michael Edwards Photography
Cover design by Poolbeg Group Services Ltd
Set by Poolbeg Group Services in Garamond 10/11.5
Printed by Cox & Wyman Ltd, Reading, Berks.

Acknowledgements

Kate Cruise O'Brien, for her dedication, advice and support.

Patricia Scanlan, for caring and sharing.

Gillian Woolfe, whose inside knowledge of Concorde made fascinating listening.

At Poolbeg Press, Philip, Kieran, Breda, Margaret, Brenda, Nicole, Terry, Gerard, Karen and Bernadette. A wonderful team.

Ruth Bernstein and Hilda Simon, for their generosity and enviable colour giftedness.

Colette, who understands.

Ed Vincent, who always makes me laugh.

Aer Rianta and British Airways for filling the gaps.

Rathbornes, for a most interesting glimpse into the world of candle-making.

The firms who wish to remain anonymous – for reasons that will become obvious – thank you.

Always important, my friends who have shown such patience and understanding.

Lynda, my daughter, who read the book and made wise comments.

My son Paul, who takes my job seriously and encourages me.

And lastly, my husband, David, my best friend and right arm.

Thank you all most sincerely.

Dedicated with love to my mother
Ruth Radnor
who encouraged me to read books
then sat patiently while I wrote them

Prologue

PERSONAL AGENDA

An invitation to relax and share a luxurious weekend break in the company of other bright, single professionals. For brochure write to Box 1034 or telephone 5555 7203

Chapter One

"At least I know where you are now," Jane Anderson muttered as she flung the single red rose into the open grave. The veil, hastily tacked to the small brimmed hat, disguised any lack of grief. Apart from her own close circle of friends she knew very few of the people gathered there. Mostly they were attractive women who had come to offer her their condolences – Hugh's friends.

A mini-skirted girl with riotous, curling, fair hair came smiling towards her. "You must be Jane – his ex," she said. "I'm sorry, we'll all miss Hugh dreadfully."

Jane didn't bother to reply and rudely ignored the outstretched hand.

The bright smile vanished. "He said you were a cold fish," the girl retaliated.

"And which one of his little sting-rays are you?" asked Jane sarcastically as she turned to go. The heel of her shoe sank into the wet grass and her haughty exit became an undignified stumble.

"Let's go home, Jane," Susie urged, tucking her arm through Jane's. "Matt's waiting in the car."

"Did you hear that? His ex indeed." Jane slammed the car door and flung her hat on the seat beside her. Hats always gave her a headache.

"I suppose if he was out on the razzle, he'd hardly admit to being married," Matt volunteered. "Most girls would find that a bit of a turn-off."

Susie glowered at her husband. "Take no notice of him," she snapped.

Jane watched as a stain of embarrassment snaked upwards from Matt's collar; tact was not his strong point.

"It's OK, I know what you meant," she reassured him.

The nearer to Jane's house they got, the denser the traffic became: family cars loaded with uniformed schoolchildren, Porsches and Minis, buses and taxis revving impatiently and filling the murky air with acrid exhaust fumes. Hugh adored his BMW, *had* adored his BMW, she thought suddenly. I'll never see that car again, she reminded herself. "Totally wrecked, only fit for scrap I'm afraid," the policeman had said.

"You two hop out and I'll find a space." Matt broke in on her thoughts. Jane climbed the steps and rested a foot on one of the two large wooden plant pots which contained miniature bay trees. She fumbled in her bag and found the keys to the yellow front door. She pushed it open and breathed a sigh of relief.

"Thank goodness that's . . ." Her words trailed away in disbelief. All around them there was destruction and chaos; broken ornaments, damaged drawers, spilt flower vases, paper strewn everywhere. What was left of a plate of sandwiches had been deliberately trodden into the carpets. Bottles of drink had been smashed against the glass doors of the china display cabinet.

Neither of them spoke. Susie's face was white with anger and, for the first time that day, Jane found she could cry.

The bulky uniformed figure almost filled the doorway. Jane recognised him instantly as one of the two policemen who had come to break the news of Hugh's accident.

"We must stop meeting like this," the policeman said jocularly as he stepped around an overturned plant.

Jane glowered at him and failed to see any humour in the situation.

"Anything missing?" he asked, resignedly opening his official note-book.

"We haven't looked. We haven't touched anything, isn't that the right thing to do?"

He laboriously recorded her answer.

After several more routine questions Jane was reconciled; she was about to become just another unsolved burglary statistic.

The shrill sound of the telephone made them jump.

Susie said, "I'll get it." She listened to what the caller had to say. "I think it would be better if you phone back later, tomorrow in fact," she advised.

"It was the MD from City Secretarial Placements to offer his condolences. He'd like a word with you when you're up to it."

"Thanks Susie, I couldn't bear to talk to anyone just now."

The doorbell rang several times. If she hadn't been so upset she would have found the shocked looks on the faces of her friends quite funny.

Someone ordered Chinese food and, gathering

odd cups and glasses, they salvaged what was left of the drink. Jane felt considerably calmer.

By the time they were ready to leave, the rooms were in reasonable order again.

"You sure you don't want us to stay?" Susie asked again, hugging her friend.

"Positive, a good night's sleep and I'll be as right as acid rain."

Chapter Two

The packing cases were neatly stacked one on top of the other in the empty room. They barely filled a quarter of the space. How on earth would she fill such a large house with so few possessions, find furniture and fittings that were right for it? Seeds of self-doubt began to tease their way into Jane's mind. But in order for her dating agency, *Personal Agenda*, to succeed she needed this *spacious, desirable, country residence*. The location was ideal. Near enough to London for clients with cars, excellent train services for those without transport. She hadn't expected to find the right house so quickly, she'd imagined she would have to spend months, even a year searching for the perfect property. But that first glimpse of the village instantly captivated her.

"For goodness' sake," she rebuked herself. "Stick to your guns and stop fretting. You've made the decision."

I should have done all this before I moved, Jane grimaced as she sat on the floor amongst the boxes and stared at the photograph in her hand. It was less than a year since that night Hugh had wrapped his car, himself, and some girl around a tree. Now she could barely remember what he looked like without the photograph to remind her. She had been grateful when Hugh's brother had volunteered to identify the body, at least she'd been spared that. What do I feel, she asked herself for the umpteenth time – emptiness, detachment, relief? Nine years of charm, lies and excuses – maybe she'd done her grieving.

She turned the frame over in her hand and removed her husband's picture – a handsome, almost boyish face with a lopsided smile – then she slowly and deliberately shredded it and threw the tiny scraps into a black plastic sack beside her.

"Jane Anderson?" a crisp voice startled her.

Jane stared at the apparition standing in the open doorway which lead to the garden.

"That's it, now I'm really going bananas," she decided.

Her eyes travelled upwards over a female figure dressed in buttoned-up boots, their cracked leather ending at the hem of a long skirt which showed just a touch of crisp white petticoat. The loose open coat she wore revealed a jacket nipped in at the waist and finished with a neat collar. Twinkling eyes belied the severely scraped-back hair, adorned by a straw boater trimmed with a fresh daisy. A large floppy bag and tightly rolled umbrella completed the picture.

Jane giggled to herself.

"Sasha Dubois, trainee actress, at your service," the girl announced.

That explains it, Jane thought. At least I'm still of this world even if she isn't.

"Don't worry, you're not going round the

twist," Sasha volunteered as she read Jane's expression. "I like to dress the part. Your advertisement – it held a hint of . . . desperation, perhaps?"

Jane could no longer stifle her smile. "Sort of, exasperation more like."

"I understand," Sasha nodded knowingly. "But help is at hand."

Jane stood up and brushed stray bubbles of polystyrene from her leggings. Her mind raced. If this girl's an actress she's just killing time and not right for me. She'll have no commitment, no dedication.

"I'm not ready to launch myself on the theatrical world yet, if that's what you're thinking. Life is the best training there is for the stage so I intend to give myself another five years' experience – living it," Sasha stated baldly.

She's reading my mind, Jane reflected. Maybe she really *is* Mary Poppins. I need a good strong cup of tea.

Sasha rooted amongst the precariously stacked piles of china in the kitchen sink for two mugs while Jane filled the kettle and searched for a plug point above the littered counters.

"It's an awful mess still, I've had no water and the decorators only moved out a couple of days ago," she apologised.

"Not to fret. We'll have it straight in no time. We need to wash those cupboards, get everything put away. Do we have hot water?"

Jane began to feel control slipping away. "You don't know what the job *is* yet," she objected, "it may not suit you."

"*I* might not suit *you* either."

"True!" Jane laughed.

"Let me tell you something about myself. My real name is May Day – I ask you – would you go on the stage with a name like that?"

Jane shook her head, mesmerised by Sasha's daisy and its nodding petals.

"I love Russian names, hence the Sasha, of course, and Blanche Dubois is one of my favourite fictional characters. I've been called for hundreds of auditions but only managed to get two walk-on parts. So I've decided to wait, practise, develop my own style. I need to work and I'm fed up living alone in miserable bed-sits. I like company. Your ad sounded interesting, and I am *energetic, enthusiastic and entrepreneurial*," she quoted. "Oh! and I'm honest."

Jane was beginning to like this girl. She was outgoing, funny. There was great warmth in those hazel eyes and in her voice now that she'd dropped that clipped tone.

"Tell me about you and the job," Sasha demanded.

Jane hesitated, she was not prepared to bare her soul to a stranger. "The job is . . . undefined. I need someone to help me to run a bureau, well, a residential dating agency to be exact. It's experimental, different. Not the usual computer service or anything . . ."

"Brilliant! I love it," Sasha interrupted enthusiastically. "I can see it all; romance, people falling wildly in love, wedding invitations all over the place."

"Hang on, it hasn't even taken off yet. It may well fall flat, I don't know."

"Why should it? That's very negative, Jane."

Despite Sasha's generous, but obviously inexperienced approval, Jane was grateful to have found an ally. The first since the Great Idea began to germinate. Through the years of her unhappy marriage her friends had supported her totally. They were solidly behind her when she started her secretarial agency and protected her from the growing rumours of Hugh's philandering. But when she told them excitedly about her plans to open a dating agency, they became dubious, apprehensive, then positively discouraging.

"It's downright dangerous to let strangers into your home," Matt argued, in an unusually vehement tone.

"Why?" Jane retorted, "I've been doing it for years – courtesy of my husband."

Their warnings deterred her for a while but the idea stubbornly refused to die. She didn't consult Hugh, he was merely an appendage to her life. The last person she could discuss anything with – they'd stopped communicating years ago. Jane was shocked but somehow not surprised when the police had knocked on her door. They led her to a chair then gently broke the news. Hugh had been drinking, the car skidded out of control in the muddy lane . . . his companion, although badly injured, had miraculously escaped. Jane blocked the girl's name from her mind, it was no concern of hers. She was on her own now.

"I need someone who'll share the work with me," she explained to Sasha. "Someone who'll pitch in and not mind giving up weekends. Weekdays will be quieter of course but at this stage it's all a bit . . . hazy." Jane's voice was unsure.

"No problem, I'm game for anything legal and different. It sounds just my scene."

Instinct told Jane she'd found the right person but she knew nothing about Sasha.

"You'll want references." Sasha's ability to read her mind was unnerving.

Sasha delved in her big tapestry bag and produced a couple of envelopes which she handed to Jane. *Reliable, hardworking, pleasant, trustworthy* . . . the letters of recommendation were unstinting in their praise.

"Let's give it a try," Jane decided aloud.

"When would you like me to start? I can't wait."

Chapter Three

Jane watched as the two men heaved and pushed the second of the big trunks up the stairs. "What've you got in 'ere ducky, rocks?" one of them winced.

"A couple of gorgeous hunks," Sasha answered cheerfully. "Move it my good man!"

"What *have* you got in those trunks?" Jane watched the sweating pair of removal men.

"My life," Sasha said simply. "Clothes, books, photographs and my theatrical costumes."

"How about a nice cup of tea?" Sasha smiled disarmingly at the two men. She whispered to Jane. "While they're drinking it I'll unpack and dump everything in my room, then they can lumber the trunks up to the attic. Keep them talking."

♥ ♥ ♥

"It's a lovely house," Sasha said with open admiration, "you've done a wonderful job."

"I loved the challenge. I was lucky to find such a big house, in good condition and at a reasonable price. The timing was right too – a buyer's market. There wasn't too much to be done to it either. I did have to add bathrooms, modernise the kitchen and redecorate of course."

"That all?" Sasha considered it was plenty.

Jane enjoyed making the decisions after the initial shock of finding herself the owner of a large country house had passed. She'd taken the plunge and used her artistic talent to design the bathrooms and plan the colour schemes. She was modestly pleased with the results. Then she chose the furniture. Hugh's insurance policy cleared the mortgage on their town house and gave her a healthy cash bonus. At least he did something right, she thought bitterly.

Jane often wondered if it was her lot in life just to be tolerated. She'd been an only child brought up with loving indifference. Her parents led their own busy lives and when they died within such a short time of each other, she didn't tell Hugh about their legacy; the town flat in Dublin as big as a house and the tiny but picturesque cottage in the country. There was also a small amount of money. Hugh took no interest in her agency, no interest in her. When she'd dismissed her inheritance as paltry he didn't question it. His own success and activities were all that mattered.

There had been no screaming rows between them, no accusations, no recriminations – just a gradual growing apart. She hated confrontations and so did Hugh. He adored his work as an insurance broker. The freedom suited his adolescent approach to life. Jane withdrew from him and threw herself totally into work. It stopped her thinking, stopped her hurting. There was no shortage of clients for her multilingual secretaries and personal assistants, no shortage of highly qualified people to fill the posts. She'd been approached by other firms to amalgamate or sell out, but she'd resisted their tempting offers. Jane liked what she did, liked the girls and their eager-eyed brightness, their enthusiasm.

They liked her too. She always had time to find out what made them tick. She was sympathetic to their personal problems and painfully aware of their loneliness in the big city. Very few of them ended up "marrying the boss." Several of them were propositioned, harassed, and one of them fired when she'd repulsed unwelcome advances. Jane's mind worked overtime. What would she do in their position, she wondered? How *do* you find the ideal companion in a large impersonal town? On an impulse she gave a dinner party and invited three of the girls she admired most to meet three unattached male friends. The evening was an unqualified success – one serious romance blossomed. Another was in the making. That gave her a real kick and was the spark which kindled the notion of doing for others what she'd failed to do for herself. Although her friends tried to discourage her, Jane stubbornly clung to her faith in the idea.

It was strange how things turned out, she reflected. In the space of a day she buried her husband, her house was burgled and she received the largest offer to date for her secretarial bureau. An omen? Whether it was or it wasn't, she made up her mind the next morning to accept the offer and start afresh. The time was right. She would be thirty next birthday, young enough to make a new beginning.

Sasha stared out of the window sensing Jane's need for solitude. There was an air of unhappiness about this attractive woman. Her eyes were often sad, but she would wait until Jane was ready to tell her why. So far Jane had hardly spoken about her husband or her marriage. Sasha guessed that it couldn't have been happy.

"Let's put my cooking to the test, I'll make us an omelette for lunch. A Sasha special," she said, breaking the silence.

Jane sat quietly. The kitchen was really taking shape, almost finished. It was possible now to find plates, cups and saucers without causing a minor avalanche of damage every time.

"They're coming tomorrow to install the dishwasher." Jane consulted her check list. "And by Wednesday we'll be the proud owners of a washing-machine *and* a drier. Such luxury after that swampy line of clothes in the bathroom."

"Try drying a duvet cover in a bedroom measuring six by six." Sasha rolled her expressive eyes as she vigorously whisked the egg whites and added them to the beaten yolks.

Jane watched her moving easily between the two pans. A wonderful aroma of onions, mushrooms and tomatoes permeated the kitchen.

"Such a change from the smell of paint," Jane sniffed appreciatively. "I've lived on Chinese takeaways and pizza for the last couple of months."

Sasha crossed to the oven and put the frying pan under the hot grill. The omelette puffed up like a soufflé. Quickly she divided it between two warmed plates. Jane ate contentedly; it tasted even better than it looked. Things were going to work out, she was sure of it.

Chapter Four

"How about one of those murder mystery weekends?"

"Umm, I don't fancy that," Jane replied dubiously. "Do we really need a theme?"

"Absolutely. It's a great ice-breaker, besides everybody does this *theme* bit these days."

"Yes, but everyone isn't as extrovert as you are. Some people might find it a turn-off."

"Panic not, we'll come up with something," Sasha soothed. "A barbecue would work beautifully if only we could guarantee the weather. Informal, easy. It's harder to be shy outdoors somehow."

"How would you know? I bet you've never had a shy day in your life."

"Maybe not, but I do recognise it in others." Sasha was miffed.

"What else can you think of?"

"I'm thinking, I'm thinking. In the meantime, pass me that pillowcase," Sasha demanded.

The windows of the bedroom were thrown open to dispel the smell of paint which stubbornly lingered.

Each of the ten main bedrooms was alphabetically named. "More personal than numbers," Jane insisted.

Sasha suggested actors and actresses but Jane preferred the names of trees. They tossed for it and Jane won.

Their combined energy fast turned the confusion to order. They worked well together, sharing tasks, pooling ideas. Jane learnt to keep a straight face when Sasha appeared in the costume-of-the-day. So far she'd transformed herself into Joan of Arc, Cinderella, Nell Gwynne and Catherine de Medici. Men were not forgotten either, Rasputin, Peter Pan and even Methuselah. Her make-up was excellent but Jane worried about the practicality of Sasha's make-believe, as climbing ladders in a long skirt didn't quite fit the modern lifestyle. Neither did the incident when Rasputin's beard got caught in the washing-machine door. Much to Jane's relief it caused Sasha only minor damage. The antiseptic ointment on her skinless chin prevented her from doing anything too stringent in the make-up line for the next couple of weeks.

"I've got it! How about a drama weekend?" Jane suddenly exclaimed.

Sasha's face lit up. "Tell me," she demanded.

"If you'd be willing to use some of your wonderful costumes . . . naturally you don't have to if you don't want to . . ."

Sasha's reply was tentative. "Well . . . yes."

"I'll be responsible for any damage, of course, but I'm sure people would be careful. Those who don't want to act can paint scenery or stage-manage. You'd be in charge of production," Jane bribed.

"Who else?" Sasha asked loftily. "Which play

should we use? One of Shakespeare's? Oscar Wilde? Something more modern?"

"None of them, I thought the guests could write their own," Jane suggested briskly.

"Sometimes, Jane Anderson, you are inspired. I think this is one of those times."

"At least it's different. Do you think it'll work?" Jane arched her eyebrows in a worried frown.

"Too right I do. Even adults like to play games," Sasha assured her, "you'll warn people in advance and it's up to them – take it or leave it."

"We're trying to attract people," said Jane. "Not put them off."

"It won't," Sasha assured her.

They took a last look round the room before closing the door. Spring sunshine streamed through the open windows. This was the bedroom Jane liked best, overlooking the big garden. She had chosen a mixture of peach and cream for the walls and soft furnishings. The fluffy carpet reminded her of milky coffee. She needed to add some pictures and flowers, of course, but that would come later. Sasha's suggestion that they spend their weekend in London combing through the art displayed on the railings round Hyde Park appealed to her very much.

"We might discover a complete unknown. New talent, very exciting," Sasha enthused.

"It could be fun, perhaps we could take in a theatre too," Jane offered.

Sasha needed no urging. "I'll have a look right now at *What's-On* and book seats."

Chapter Five

Charles Graham dumped his shopping in a pile on the kitchen table and pressed the button on the flashing answering machine.

"Hello Charles, it's Carol. We have an American lady who wants to go out to dinner tonight, can you take the booking? Give me a shout before three o'clock. Byee!"

He looked at his watch, two-thirty, plenty of time before he returned her call. Trust Carol, she always allowed him the maximum possible time before she contacted another escort, always offered him the cream of the crop. There were times – like today – when he would dearly have loved to refuse the assignment. But his time meant money and there was never enough of that. He usually enjoyed escorting American women, they liked to have a good time and were prepared to pay for it. Even though the agency took a hefty booking fee, he did well too. Irritably he punched out the office number.

"Good afternoon, *Companions Escort Agency,*" Carol's crisp voice answered.

"It's Charles, Carol, how are you today? I've just got your message."

Carol's voice softened, "Charley, hi! Are you on for tonight?"

He hated it when she called him Charley but didn't allow his annoyance to show. "Why not? Do I know her?"

"I don't think so," she chirped. "She wants to go somewhere posh but not bankrupting. What appeals to you?"

"A table at the Bon Viveur or at Plumbey's, either will fit the bill. What time?"

"She wants a car at the Charters by eight o'clock."

"Not slumming it then?"

"Apparently not, Charley. I'll organise it. Pick you up about seven forty-five? That'll give you loads of time."

"That's fine. What's new with you?"

"Not a lot. Oh! We've acquired a dog. It strayed into the garden last week and made itself at home. It doesn't like the food we give it, doesn't like its bed and doesn't like us over-much either. That's all I need – a dog with an attitude. The sooner it's claimed the better. And that's all the excitement for this week," she laughed.

"I hope for your sake you find the owner soon. Talk to you later."

"Cheers," she said and rang off.

♥ ♥ ♥

Charles glanced at the woman sitting facing him. Her brown hair was perfectly cut, her make-up subtle. But in spite of the glossy effect of groomed elegance she struck him as a tough, ball-breaking sophisticate. He knew her type. This was going to be one of those nights when he hated his job. But it did pay well. Plenty of perks. If the client was generous he could pick up a hefty tip. Some women hinted, others were more blatant – they would like more than a dinner or theatre companion. If he was attracted to them he obliged, if he wasn't he produced his pat excuse. "I could lose my job," he claimed convincingly, "and that would be disastrous for my poor son."

His son was a convenient figment of his imagination. It worked every time. His widowed, day-caring, single-parent story was even more successful.

"How are you enjoying your trip?" Charles smiled.

"It's a downer. I'm here to work. London is getting as bad as New York – crowded, noisy and fast."

"What do you do?" Charles asked in a pleasant voice.

"Trouble-shooter," she answered sharply.

Great conversationalist, Charles thought as she clicked her fingers impatiently for a waiter. "Let's order. Have what you want – apart from the caviar."

"Thank you, Ms Robart," Charles replied sardonically as he searched the menu for the most expensive dishes he could find.

"Call me Sara," she instructed.

"Thank you, Ms Robart," he repeated stubbornly.

Angry colour suffused her face. She *had* been a bit sharp with him, she supposed. But she needed to be tough to survive, women always did. She was used to men trying their macho best to put her down, but in fairness, Charles Graham had been polite. Maybe the fact that she'd had to pay for his company was bugging her.

"Would you like to choose the wine?" Her voice was softer.

"Certainly, would you like red or white, Ms Robart?"

"Look, I'm sorry," she heard herself say. "I didn't mean to be nasty. It's been a long day and I shouldn't take it out on you. Let's have a bottle of champagne – that is, if you like."

"Champagne's fine." He'd made his point, he might as well enjoy the evening.

"Are you married?" she asked as they waited for their main course.

"Widowed with one little boy," he lowered his voice. There were times when he almost believed his own lie. "He is . . . unwell. I look after him in the day-time, my sister takes over at night."

Her gaze softened. "I'm sorry to hear that. I had a boy too." The harshness left her eyes.

"Now *I'm* sorry," he said with genuine sympathy.

"It's OK. My husband was awarded custody," she clarified. "You asked me about my job. I work for Desanto and Lucas, have you heard of them?"

Charles nodded, he was aware that the American multinational company had recently built a particularly attractive circular building in the City.

"When one of our branches shows a downward trend, I'm sent to investigate. You can imagine how my arrival is welcomed! But I'm good at what I do and I've learnt to ignore the popularity angle. At first I loved the travelling but now I'm getting blasé, I suppose. Too many unfriendly, nervous faces, too many hotel rooms, too much packing and unpacking. Sometimes I feel I want to give it all up and move to some God-forsaken Midwestern town back in the States and start my own firm. I've put out a few feelers and . . ."

Charles had heard it all before. It wouldn't happen, these women loved the power they wielded. His mind wandered as she catalogued the details of her life. Tomorrow he was meeting a woman called Jane Anderson. Carol had left a hurried message and telephone number on his answering machine a couple of days ago. He'd returned Jane Anderson's call. Her approach was hesitant, she wouldn't say much except that his name had been suggested as a possible interviewer to vet clients for a dating agency. He was intrigued.

"Would that interest you?" Jane's soft voice questioned.

"Yes, it may well," he replied cagily. He didn't know what his qualifications were meant to be, but he was certainly prepared to find out. It could fit in very nicely with his work. He was getting bored with this escort lark.

Charles Graham rarely came alive before midday. When he was alert enough to focus, he made himself a cup of strong black coffee and took it back to his bedroom. Then he examined his appearance in the full-length mirror. Mostly he liked what he saw. His shock of brown hair was conditioned, groomed and well cut, his even white teeth gleamed – flossed to perfection with boring regularity. But it was his eyes, brown and soulful, that usually melted the hearts of his many well-heeled clients. He worked hard to keep his tall, lean, muscular body in shape, exercising for at least half-an-hour each day. "It's your stock-in-trade," he chanted to himself with every muscle-aching push-up. After that rigid regime was complete, his days were usually free and he spent his time searching for well-cut suits, shirts and ties at bargain prices. Clothes were important to him – the wrapping on the package. He made it his business to keep up with current affairs, the cinema and theatre. He was au fait with the ballet and the opera. He followed the fortunes of each new restaurant that opened and noted the numbers of any that appealed to him. Sometimes he saw the same show twice in a week. Carol usually managed to manipulate clients away from their first choice if it meant Charles would be faced with a second or even third visit to the latest musical. Charles was Mr Perfect in her dull grey eyes and she'd never quite forgiven herself when he'd been forced to sit through *Les Miserables* four times in the space of ten days. New clients excited him. He was as ambitious as the next man. Ambitious to meet the right woman, the one who would provide him with a luxurious home and the trappings of wealth that he so deserved. But for his father, all this would have been his by right.

Chapter Six

Jane Anderson dashed up the thickly carpeted stairs two at a time. Charles Graham was due in a quarter of an hour. She tied back her hair, turned on the shower in the tiny bathroom and stepped under its steaming jets.

How will I know if he's suitable? she fretted. I don't even know what questions to ask.

"Just imagine you're interviewing one of your secretaries, you'll be fine," Sasha had encouraged her earlier that morning.

Did *she* ever have doubts? Jane wondered. Sasha's ability to face everything in life head-on was a constant source of amazement. Nothing fazed her. Jane smiled to herself and tried to imagine what Charles Graham's reaction would be to Sasha. She'd already dressed for the occasion in a severe black business suit and had scraped her gelled hair back from her face and squashed it into a tight bun. She'd perched a pair of steel-rimmed prescriptionless glasses on the end of her nose.

"It'll intimidate him," she laughed in answer to Jane's questioning glance.

Soothing water played over Jane's shoulders as she tried to think of the right attitude to adopt.

What was the point of worrying? Sasha was right, she'd play it by ear.

As soon as they'd chosen the right person to interview their prospective clients, they'd be ready to advertise. Jane felt a flutter of excitement. She would be thirty next week, a new decade in her life.

Jane left her home in Ireland when she was nineteen. Lots of her friends worked in London and she could have shared a flat with any of them. But she was young then, relished the idea of freedom, having her own space. She chose a one-roomed studio apartment with every modern inconvenience; faulty heating, leaky taps, noisy neighbours. She adored it all.

She entertained on a rickety table with three chairs and a bathroom stool, drank too much plonk in wine bars and ate junk food whenever she felt too lazy to cook. She loved her job as a bilingual secretary and added friends to a growing group. Three months to the day after her arrival in London, she'd looked up from her desk into the startling grey eyes of Hugh Anderson. He fell for the softly spoken Irish girl with her gentle manner, heart-shaped face and cerulean-blue eyes. "As clear as the summer skies," he used to say.

He invited her out that night and every night after that. She married Hugh with all the dreams of a young girl. She loved him unquestioningly, hung on his every word, thrilled to his touch. They went about their work during the day, revelled in their shared evenings and made love at every opportunity.

Life seemed idyllic. When had it all started to fall apart? Jane frowned. Was it the night he phoned to say that an out-of-town client needed his advice? Not unusual for an insurance broker. Two weeks later, his advice was needed again. She had a rare night out with her friends and enjoyed it. His late nights became more frequent, his calls less so. It was the telephone calls to their home that fuelled her doubts. Tentative at first and then insistent, the caller always hung up when she answered. What an idiot I was, I believed him when he offered business as an excuse for his frequent absences. It had taken nearly five years of uncertainty before she finally forced herself to face her suspicions.

Susie, her closest friend, insisted that her nearest and dearest must help her celebrate her promotion with a slap-up lunch at Le Parapluie. Five of them gathered in festive mood around the table and toasted her success. Sleepy from the champagne, Jane's eyes dreamily locked on to two flaming skewers carried by a waiter who was skilfully threading his way between the tables. How romantic, she giggled. The waiter stopped at a table and, with a flourish, extinguished the flame. Her heart leapt to her throat. Tucked away in a corner, a young couple released hands as the plates were placed in front of them. The girl she didn't know, the man was her husband. Without thinking, she rose from the table and approached him.

"Hello Hugh, I didn't expect to see you," she challenged.

"Jane!" he replied suavely. "What are you doing here?"

"I was just about to ask you the same question."

Why had *she* felt so foolish, an interloper? Even now her cheeks burnt when she remembered apologising as he introduced the girl. "One of our most valued clients."

With all the dignity she could muster she smiled, said she would see him later and beat a hasty retreat, crashing into a couple behind her.

He didn't phone that night nor the next. She wore sunglasses to work, her eyes ached from the tears she'd shed.

There was no remorse on his part, he dismissed her indignation. "It's just part of my job, flirting with clients. This is the real world, Jane, business doesn't just fall into my lap."

"No, but I bet she does," Jane snapped.

"Grow up," he advised, "if you don't, you'll get hurt."

She didn't bother to tell him that she already was. The chasm between them widened. They rarely spent an evening together, he was away most weekends. They slept in separate rooms and never made love any more. Two strangers sharing the same house. His manner when he did appear was always breezy, friendly. She marvelled at his ostrich-like attitude. Nothing was wrong as far as he was concerned. She tried to get her own back by being abrupt to his friends when he brought them home. But then he really didn't expect her to join in. How many nights had she spent with her fingers stuffed in her ears blocking out their sounds of laughter? And then, it no longer mattered. She was resigned. She thought of divorce but didn't want to prove her parents right. They'd fussed and fretted, didn't like Hugh, didn't want her to marry him. Her father was ailing and a divorce might have been more than he could cope with. Her mother found her father's illness difficult enough, she certainly didn't need Jane's problems too. Jane accepted things for what they were and just got on with her life. Hugh and his friends were drinking more and more. They often came back to the house after dinner at one of the "in" clubs or restaurants and stayed until morning. Sometimes a heavy, strange smell wafted up the narrow staircase.

"Don't be tiresome, it's very *now,*" he sneered when she objected to his friends smoking pot in the house.

She spent a lot of time with her mother after her father's death. Jane had always thought of her mother as an independent woman but, without her husband, she wilted and shrivelled, lost her will to live. Five months later, Jane was alone.

Chapter Seven

Charles Graham surveyed his surroundings with interest. The red brick house, its conical slate roofs jutting protectively over the windows, was large and attractive. It had probably been extended over the years but it sprawled comfortably in the beautifully designed garden. For the last few years of his adult life he'd been a town-dweller. He drew a deep breath to inhale the fresh sweet air. A line of fir trees bordered the house on one side, a fine laurel hedge protected the rest of the grounds from prying eyes. In the well-ordered beds, shrubs, with their tiny tips of healthy colour, were preparing for their showy debut.

"Charles Graham?" The voice made him jump. "I'm Sasha Dubois. Please, come in."

"Good afternoon." Charles recovered his composure and eyed the girl in the black business suit. She could be quite attractive, he thought, although her hair and those ugly glasses did nothing to help. She must be Jane Anderson's secretary. He followed her into a spacious circular hall dominated by a curved staircase. Pale golden light washed the walls. An enormous ceramic bowl filled with spring blossoms stood on an ivory painted table in the centre of the hall. The only other piece of furniture was an ivory and gold chair in a corner. Sasha waited quietly for a moment while he gazed at the flower bed – an indoor garden which followed the contours of the staircase. Miniature narcissi, crocuses and tulips stretched towards the light from the floor-to-ceiling window. The deep gold of the carpet was protected from the soil by a raised wrought-metal fretwork.

"What a lovely feature, so unusual," Charles admired.

"It's wonderful isn't it?" said Sasha. Like a proud mother waiting for a child to walk, she'd watched the bulbs pushing through the soil, eager for the flowers that would follow. "Jane will be ready in a minute, would you like to wait in here?"

He prowled the living-room restlessly and discovered that the glass doors separating the two areas could be folded back creating one enormous space. Sofas and chairs were arranged comfortably around coffee tables. Large vases contained artistically arranged twigs and blossoms. Sunlight poured through the picture windows. He could imagine how the big lamps with their pagoda shades would cast an intimate glow after dark. Charles stood with his back to the room. Through the windows he could see a patio with honey-coloured flagstones, its pergola roof entwined with branches which he recognised as jasmine. Sloping lawns led to the river beyond. A majestic willow, not yet in full leaf, swayed lazily at the river's edge. A sylvan setting, peaceful and tranquil. But this was no bucolic backwater. He'd realised that on the short drive through the pretty village of Dornley-on-Thames.

A curved terrace of freshly painted shops included a delicatessen, butcher and fishmonger. He noticed a chemist, grocer and newsagent. The central point of the village was a pond with its own tiny armada of bobbing ducks. The local pub stood alone surrounded by lawns. The Drake's Inn was festooned with hanging baskets. An enormous old cart, filled with trailing blossoms, rested on black and gold poles in the spacious courtyard. Charles would have liked to pop in to the picture-book village pub for a pint but there wasn't time. He prided himself on being a stickler for punctuality. It was impossible to catch even a glimpse of the mansions behind the dense hedges.

"Would you like to see the garden?" a lilting voice asked.

A slightly built figure walked towards him from the shadows of the room.

"I'm Jane Anderson." She held out her hand. "It's almost my favourite season, everything fresh and new."

"It's delightful, especially to a townie like myself."

"I was brought up with gardens. Then I moved to a flat in London. That was when I realised how much I'd missed them," she said as she turned the key in the door and led the way.

"Me too." He didn't elaborate.

They walked along the path to the river, glancing at each other covertly. Jane reached his shoulder. She was slender and her blue eyes crinkled when she smiled. He recognised a trace of Irish in her accent. Her well-cut beige trousers were looped by a wide, expensive, leather belt and he judged that her cream sweater was cashmere. She'd knotted a matching cardigan round her shoulders.

"I've been very lucky to inherit the gardener who's looked after all this for years," she said waving her graceful hand.

"It must take some doing," Charles agreed.

He was tall and muscular with a pleasant smile, well over six feet tall. The check jacket and cords, worn with a faintly striped shirt, suited his tall frame. Tall men made her feel dainty and protected.

They stopped a foot or so from the water. From the hidden house next door a procession of excited young children carried boxes on to a small cruiser which was swaying gently at anchor in the lapping water. The children called out to each other as they jostled for space on the narrow gangplank. A woman on board relieved them of their burdens and they scampered back out of sight. How the other half lived, Charles thought, morosely.

"Do you have a boat?" he asked a trifle sharply.

"No." Jane laughed. "It takes me all my time to cope with the house."

The boat's engine sputtered into life and the children ran back on deck with an assortment of fishing tackle and heavy anoraks. A man hauled in the short wooden board that separated the boat from its grassy dock. After they'd all donned life-jackets, the boat made its quiet way to the centre of the water and slowly disappeared from sight round the bend of the river leaving a wide "V" in its wake.

"Would you like to go back inside?" Jane suggested as she shivered slightly.

They retraced their steps and entered the warmth of the house.

"There's coffee in the den," Sasha said, coming to meet them.

The den was a cosy room, a fire burned cheerfully in its modern grate.

"Milk?" Sasha asked, a biro wobbling precariously behind one ear. Sasha loved her props.

"You're interested in the job then?" Sasha sensed Jane's nervousness and took matters into her own hands.

"Er, yes . . . yes." Charles was surprised by the bluntness of the question. Why was *she* the one asking, not Jane Anderson?

"We need someone tactful, someone at ease with people but also someone who can spot any . . . well fakes, really," Jane explained. She too was surprised by Sasha's brusqueness. As they sipped the coffee Jane outlined their plans and aims. ". . . and, as this is a dating agency, we have to be very careful to protect our clients."

"I understand completely," Charles assured them. "But I'm curious, how did you come to me?" He was *consumed* with curiosity.

"Do you remember Sally Munroe? You took her to dinner about ten days ago?" Jane looked faintly embarrassed.

"Yes, now that you mention it, I do."

"She offered to find someone for us. We didn't

really want to poach someone from another agency . . ."

"We tried that and didn't like them," Sasha interrupted to Jane's further discomfort. Jane wished Sasha would shut up. If she'd been beside her, she'd have dug her in the ribs.

"Well, Lucy – Sally – came up with the idea of hiring someone from an escort agency. Someone who spends a good deal of time with people should be a fair judge, she reckoned. She's used your agency several times for out-of-town clients – you came highly recommended. She made her booking under a false name and the rest you know."

Charles remembered the smart young woman. They'd spent an extremely agreeable evening together. He'd been surprised that an unattached woman with a large circle of friends would seek the services of an a escort just to go out for a meal. She was the type of woman who wouldn't hesitate to eat alone in a restaurant.

"Did I pass the test?" he grinned.

He's quite gorgeous, Sasha decided as she watched the mischievous glint in his eyes.

"You did," she said, earning a glare from Jane.

"We thought you'd be qualified for this sort of thing. It would slot in nicely with your job. Most of your work is at night, isn't it? That would leave you free at lunch-time to do interviews for us," suggested Jane.

Jane wasn't as sure as Sasha that he was the right person. But then she wasn't usually as impulsive as Sasha was either.

"I'm certainly willing to give it a go. A couple of questions. What about my fees? And would you need me here at weekends?"

Jane paused before answering. "Perhaps . . . a commission for each client who signs with us? I hadn't given any thought to the weekends. It might be a good idea at first."

"A great idea." Sasha smiled encouragingly.

"We do have another tiny bedroom on the third floor. It really *is* tiny. We've moved up there too so as to leave the bigger rooms free for clients," Jane apologised.

"That's OK, I'm adaptable." Very adaptable, he thought bitterly, remembering his opulent Belgrave Square home.

"Stay and have dinner with us?" Sasha invited. "You can get a late train back to town."

Jane nodded her agreement.

"I'd like that. Thank you." Charles awarded Sasha one of his well-practised smiles.

Jane glanced towards Sasha, was that a purr she heard?

While Sasha prepared the meal, Jane gave Charles a tour of the house.

"It's ideal," he said as they returned to the kitchen. "You've done a wonderful job. But I think what you propose to charge for a weekend is far too little. You're aiming at big earners, aren't you? This is all very luxurious and you're offering meals, drinks, de-luxe rooms and entertainment."

"*I* told you that," Sasha snorted derisively.

They ate in the kitchen, the dining-room was much too formal for just the three of them.

"If this is what you can do, then I say, go for it. Increase your prices. This meal is terrific, Sasha." Charles touched her arm.

Sasha beamed with delight. She was a dab hand at cooking and amazed even herself at times. Jane wasn't bad either. Both girls had just enrolled in a short hostess course to gain more experience.

They listened to what he had to say without interruption. Jane was afraid that Sasha's enthusiasm for this oracle would cloud her judgement. She'd jettisoned the suit before she started making dinner, the glasses had disappeared and her silky black hair had been freed from its torturous pins. Dressed in jeans and a pale blue blouse she looked pretty – and normal.

As they ate the chocolate roulade, Jane asked Charles what he thought about the idea of a drama weekend.

"It could work well," he said. "You certainly shouldn't have too many awkward silences."

Jane relaxed. If this urbane man was impressed, then others would be too. Susie and Matt's lack of enthusiasm had seriously dented her confidence but now, with both Sasha and Charles's approval, she began to believe again.

"If it isn't an impertinent question, what's the set-up between you both?" Charles asked.

"Sasha's my right hand," Jane answered, smiling now.

"And her clumsy left one too," Sasha added. Jane's discomfort hadn't been lost on her. Sasha still wasn't used to Jane's soft Irish ways and at times she was impatient with her. Maybe she could learn to curb that, but she doubted it.

"When do you intend to start advertising?" Charles asked, helping himself to a third slice of the creamy cake. His day had been interesting. He liked the two women, one quirky, sharp and kind, the other – softer, astute, and . . . vulnerable? This job could fit in very nicely with his own work and would earn him a good bit of extra cash too. It wouldn't be too much of a hardship to spend weekends here either.

"We thought we'd advertise at the end of the month," Jane said firmly. She could sense Sasha's stare as she made the hasty decision. "We've booked ourselves into a hostess course for two weeks, we'll be ready after that."

"Sounds good," Charles approved. "I'm sure it would take another three or four weeks after that before we've vetted people, that should give you plenty of time to tie up the loose ends."

"If you're happy, there's no reason why we shouldn't shake hands on it."

"Fine by me," Charles smiled, stretching an arm across the table. "I think we'll get on famously, I'm looking forward to the challenge."

Chapter Eight

Jane waited nervously for Sasha to make her appearance. She was looking forward to the course.

"Ready," Sasha called from the top of the stairs. Jane breathed a sigh of relief. Sasha looked quite normal – if you didn't count the Doc Martens and stripey football socks.

The atmosphere in the big lecture room was informal. Coffee and tea were arranged on a table in the centre of the room. A hand-scripted notice invited, *Help Yourself.*

Slowly people drifted into the room. The ones in pairs smiled their greetings, the solo students were a little more reserved and diffident. All were equipped with pens, aprons and sharp knives as advised. Conversation was stilted, even Sasha's effervescence was muted.

"Good morning, everybody." Two smartly dressed men joined the group.

"They've already boned up on etiquette," Sasha whispered.

"Good morning," they all chorused.

"Mmm, coffee," one of the two men approved. "A refill anyone?"

There were no takers.

"Anybody know anything about this course?" the taller of the two asked.

"Nope, but we soon will I'm sure," Sasha replied cheerfully, happy to speak in normal tones again.

A formidable woman with blue-rinsed hair entered the room. Some form of tutor to judge from her authoritative air.

"Good morning ladies and gentlemen, I am Mrs Grundy – Penelope Grundy. I wonder if I could have a volunteer to move this table and then bring that one forward." She inclined her head gracefully towards a flower-laden work-table in the corner.

A dozen people rushed forward to help.

"We will start with flower-arranging this morning. There are fact sheets available detailing everything we learn here, but please feel free to take notes and ask questions whenever you want."

"If you dare," Jane giggled nervously.

Mrs Grundy crossed the floor on her neat, sensible low-heeled shoes and extracted a large pile of plastic folders from a cupboard. "Please, pass these around, they'll come in handy for your note-taking."

Deftly cutting twigs into their correct lengths, she talked as she worked, explaining the principles of height and width. "Those of you who have gardens will look at your available material with a fresh eye now," she said, cutting an exquisite amaryllis lily to size with a cruel snip.

"That didn't come from any garden, probably

from one of London's top florists," one of the two men whispered loudly.

His remark earned him a cold stare.

"You can use any flowers you like," she continued, "whatever comes to hand."

After five minutes the arrangement was complete. She turned it slowly on its revolving base. Polite sounds of, "lovely, most attractive," brought a smug smile to her hard face. A vacuous-looking girl beside Jane stood up and said, "Good morning," then left the room. No one spoke.

Mrs Grundy ignored the incident and completed three more striking pieces. By eleven o'clock they were back in a group drinking coffee.

"Yours are as good as hers," Sasha told Jane. One or two people smiled.

"I'm picturing how my scabrous Michaelmas daisies would look in that." An exasperated woman laughed and pointed to the jardiniere overflowing with expensive blooms.

"Exactly. Our garden would serve as an escaped prisoner's delight," said the man beside Jane. "By the way my name's Justin, this is William."

"I'm Sasha and this is Jane. And I agree. These must have cost a bit. Garden flowers – ha!"

"Do you mind me asking, but why did you decide to take this course?" Jane had noticed the slender young girl scribbling feverishly throughout the demonstration and wondered what she was missing.

"We're opening a new business which will involve entertaining," Jane replied.

"A *residential* dating agency." Sasha grabbed the opportunity to pop in a free plug.

"Sounds interesting, tell me about it."

Briefly they explained, Jane with far more confidence than she'd previously felt.

"Why are you taking so many notes?" questioned Sasha.

"Can you keep a secret?" the girl asked glancing around furtively.

They nodded.

"I'm covering this for *Tomorrow.* Have you heard of our magazine?"

"No, I haven't. Have you, Sasha?"

"Never."

"We're fairly new to the market, the *up-market* if you like." She waggled her fingers to denote quote marks.

"They don't know you're a journalist?" Jane was surprised.

"No, it's better that way since I'm doing an investigative piece. Your idea could appeal to our readers, maybe when you're launched . . . Do you have a business card?"

"Not yet, "Jane said quickly.

"Not at all," Sasha added. Jane nudged her. Really, Sasha's honesty was too much at times.

"Let me write down the address for you." Jane fumbled red-faced in her pocket for her pen.

"*Personal Agenda*? I like the name. I'll be in touch. In the meantime, mum's the word."

"This blasted twig has a mind of its own," Sasha grumbled as the wayward branch stubbornly twisted in the wrong direction.

"May I suggest that you use one that curves to

the right," Mrs Grundy said as she passed quietly along the line.

May I suggest you stick it where the sun don't shine, Sasha raged inside with frustration. "What a good idea, Mrs Grundy," she said in a prissy tone which made Jane give her a sideways look. Jane could just imagine what Sasha really wanted to say.

"I've had it," Justin moaned, "I think I'll stick to cookery."

"Come now, we don't want to permit a silly flower to defeat us, do we?" Mrs Grundy encouraged.

"We couldn't care less what the flower's aims are, we're going to have a cup of coffee." Justin viciously snapped the stem of the flower, threw it on the table and sauntered over to the coffee pot. William was faring better – let *him* do this end of it, his own patience was exhausted. Sasha winked at Justin conspiratorially and gave him a thumbs-up.

By the end of the day, they were all drained.

"Another day of that blue-coiffed woman and I'm packing this in," Sasha announced as she lit a rare cigarette after dinner.

"She wasn't so bad," Jane consoled.

"She was a snob, and a sarcastic one at that."

"Never mind, tomorrow's the first of the cookery sessions, you'll enjoy that."

"Not if she's the cook," said Sasha.

Jane's heart sank. She hoped that Sasha wasn't going to be difficult.

They met in the same room the following morning. Justin had recovered his good humour and the greetings amongst the aspiring hosts and hostesses were slightly less frozen. A diminutive young woman introduced herself as Caroline, the cookery instructor. She gave them a humorous breakdown of the schedule. "Three days of fallen soufflés, burnt roasts and lopsided cakes, then we'll have you all competing for Chef of the Year," she promised. "See you in five minutes in the kitchen – don't even think of escaping." News of the previous day's defector had obviously spread.

"I'm sure she's grown in the last few minutes," Sasha murmured.

"I have. I'm standing on a box." Caroline fixed her eyes on Sasha.

"That explains it," replied Sasha unabashed at being overheard.

"I'll demonstrate this morning, you can take over in the afternoon. Please stop me if there's anything you don't understand."

Jane didn't hear a single complaint from Sasha all day. She was totally engrossed. Those not in a tearing hurry to leave, crowded round Sasha.

"A miracle," Justin said, as he examined Sasha's evenly baked cake.

Sasha's face dimpled with pleasure.

"It's sickeningly perfect," William agreed. "Well done."

"I don't know about any of you, but I could murder a drink. If you girls aren't in a rush, join us?" Justin invited.

"I'd love to, my nerves are frayed," Jane said with a glance at her cake which had cracked alarmingly in the middle.

The evening was warm and they took their

drinks outside the crowded pub to a little table on the pavement. The two men were amusing, easy company. They made no secret of the fact that they lived together in a Chelsea flat which cost them an arm and a leg. They ran three successful shops which specialised in second-hand books. William explained that they also kept the latest published titles in stock. But he concentrated on rare books.

"William has a knack of picking up valuable first editions for buttons," Justin said proudly.

They were thinking of buying a small house, of moving out of town, somewhere within commuting distance.

"What about that derelict cottage on the other side of Dornley?" Sasha piped up. "The village is about an hour from London, an hour and a bit if the traffic is bad."

"The cottage would probably need to be demolished. It's a total ruin but it does have a lovely old tangled garden," Jane said.

"That wouldn't matter if the price was right," Justin interrupted. "We're paying a fortune in rent. We wouldn't mind starting from scratch."

"Let me find out for you," Jane suggested, "it won't be until Saturday though."

By the end of the first week of the course Jane was moderately satisfied with her progress. They'd learnt the correct way to set up a table, how to decorate it by utilising everyday objects, how to give their flowers an original and artistic appearance. Their recipe sheets were building up into quite a bundle. Jane had mastered the art of whipping egg whites to a point where they didn't lose their elasticity, her sandwiches were almost as dainty as Caroline's and her head was full of ideas for the menu they were to produce for next Monday's practical. The four of them sat together during the classes. Justin's *sotto voce* remarks gave them many a giggle during the lulls.

"Why not invite them down for the day tomorrow?" Sasha asked during the Friday lunch break. "We could take them to the cottage, at least they'd have a chance to see what we're talking about."

"Sure, why not?" Jane agreed. Her spontaneous acceptance of Sasha's suggestion made them both laugh.

"And you didn't need an hour to make the decision!"

Both men were delighted with the invitation and accepted eagerly. Jane arranged to meet them at Dornley station at eleven-thirty.

"This is divine," Justin sighed as they rounded the pond and headed for the parking space behind the Drake's Inn.

Neither of them seemed particularly disappointed when they saw the condition of the cottage. They walked about it calmly and then saw what they could of the garden. William carefully noted the phone number of the London agent handling the property. Jane didn't press them for an opinion.

"Well, what do you think?" Sasha demanded when they'd settled in the cool interior of the Drake's Inn.

"More or less what I expected," Justin said, "what about you, Will?"

William scratched his forehead. "Same as you. The village is absolutely picturesque, I must admit, and sorely tempting. The air is so fresh you can actually take a breath without coughing."

The friendly landlord welcomed them. They ordered ploughman's lunches; great hunks of warm, crisp, fresh bread, wedges of cheese and wonderfully tangy, homemade pickled onions. The men ordered pints of beer, Jane opted for a small shandy and Sasha had a glass of cider.

"I could definitely get used to this." Justin wiped his mouth on the napkin and scratched his stomach like a contented cat.

"It's the best pub lunch I've had for years," William said draining his glass.

"I'll take you on a tour of the area, give you an idea of what Dornley's like," Jane volunteered.

It was almost three-thirty before they reached home. As they turned into the drive the sun came out from behind the clouds. Jane was proud of her lovely garden although she knew she couldn't take any credit for it. The golden interior of the hall made a visible impact on the two men. This Jane *could* take credit for.

They sat lazily on the patio while Sasha busied herself in the kitchen. The dining-room was to have its christening meal later.

"When do you plan to have your first weekend?" Justin asked, mesmerised by the swaying branches of the willow.

"In about five or six weeks from now."

"I know it will be incredibly successful," William said kindly to Jane. "Who wouldn't be bowled over by all this." His glance encompassed the river, the garden and their surroundings.

William thought Jane and Sasha made a remarkable contrast. He suspected there was more to Jane than met the eye, whereas Sasha was totally up-front and open.

"We're going to have a house-warming party, two weeks from tonight," Jane said dreamily. She was completely relaxed. "I hope you'll be able to come."

"Try and stop us," Justin replied. "Besides we want to test your skills as fully-fledged graduates of Mrs Grudging's Academy." He'd renamed Mrs Grundy after the first day but thankfully none of them had clapped eyes on her for more than a minute since.

"Have you chosen your menus yet for Monday?" Jane asked.

"More or less," Justin answered for them both. "I've still got a couple more ingredients to buy, but I'll do that in the morning. There are plenty of shops open on Sundays now. William's all organised."

Justin recited their menus and Jane was fascinated by their adventurous ideas, particularly Justin's. She tried to imagine the two of them preparing a meal for their guests and wondered what their flat was like. Did they really get on so well all the time? They were so unalike.

William always dressed formally, it suited his personality. This afternoon he'd made a concession and removed his tie. He snored gently on the sun-lounger while Jane and Justin chatted.

Jane found herself talking about her childhood, her parents and her miserable marriage. Justin listened quietly. From time to time he nodded his fair head, his round, soft amber eyes full of compassion.

". . . I suppose I didn't fit in with Hugh's image and his yuppie friends – all Armani, Versace, Gucci loafers and Filofaxes. Not one of his self-respecting men friends would be caught without his car phone. The women he mixed with had their affectations too. Designer clothes, mineral water during the day – champagne at night. Those women couldn't put their lipstick on, let alone make an appointment, without consulting the Filofax. I sneaked a look in one once, when the owner went to the ladies' room – how she found her way there without it I don't know. It was full of business appointments, birthdays and whinging about broken dates. None of that appealed to me. Hugh and his friends thought I was a drag, a no-hoper, couldn't-stay-the-course party-pooper. But I couldn't dance all night and work all day. Didn't want to either. After dinner, I'd leave Hugh and his night owls to it and go home. Eventually I dropped out of the scene altogether. So you see, it was all a bit of a mess." Jane stared down at the childhood scar on her knee.

"If you ask me, and even if you don't, I think you've come up trumps. He sounds as if he was a selfish bastard with lots of energy and very little sense. Frankly you're better off without him – if you'll forgive me saying so. If it wasn't for Milord there," Justin indicated the sleeping figure beside them, "I'd snaffle you up myself."

Jane smiled her sweet smile. What a sympathetic man he was.

"Do you know there's enough room for a tennis-court in that veggie patch over there?" said Justin.

"Funny, I was thinking that the other day. But I've spent up to and beyond my limit for the moment. If we make oodles of dough, I'll certainly think about it."

Sasha announced that dinner would be served in exactly ten minutes and disappeared again. It was still light outside but she'd drawn the long royal blue velvet curtains and lit the candles on the table. A beautiful Victorian arrangement of fruits, nuts and wild flowers stood at the centre of the table. The mellow room was lit by candles and a sparkling glass chandelier. The girls had removed the two centre sections of the table reducing it to an intimate table for four.

The door opened with a crash. "Oops! Sorry," said a voice.

The two men stared at Sasha as she made her way to the serving table. Jane bit down hard on her lip.

"Bravo!" William clapped his hands with delight.

"Thank you, Sir." Sasha bobbed demurely as her long black skirt swished behind her. Her hair was hidden under a white starched cap. Her face was bare of make-up except for a dusting of ghostly white powder. She wore a pleated white collar at the neck of her plain black dress, and over it a delicate apron which positively crackled with starch. It was the enormous wayward bustle, which swayed alarmingly under her long skirt when she turned her back, that made them laugh.

Sasha took her place at the table and insisted they start eating before it all got cold. The fingers of puff pastry were crisp and light and the filling of mushroom and foie gras exploded with flavour in their mouths.

"This is fantastic." William ate with enthusiasm. "You should do this for your menu on Monday."

"Don't worry, I will." Sasha wrinkled her nose. "You don't think you're here because we like you, do you? You're my guinea pigs."

"In that case can we criticise?" Justin wanted to know.

"Don't you dare!"

The ducks were gloriously brown. Sasha quickly carved the breasts from the carcasses and returned the leg portions to the oven to keep warm. She spooned black cherry and apple sauces on to the heated plates. Kicking aside her skirt with a dramatic swish, she placed little plates of steaming snow peas, tiny French beans and professionally piped duchesse potatoes beside each of them.

"Wrap your chops around that lot," she said.

"What a little charmer." Justin grinned protecting his plate with both hands as Sasha made a grab to remove it. "So much for elegance!"

"Are you going to serve these meals all the time?" William asked. "It'll be quite a task."

"We'll experiment. We decided the first night of each weekend should be formal. Then Saturday nights, buffet style. Lunches will be informal of course. We might be able to use the patio now that summer's finally arrived," Jane answered munching a crispy leg bone.

William was unusually silent.

"What's with you?" Justin demanded leaning back expansively on his chair.

"I'm working out the whys and wherefores of the cottage, if you must know. All this has got to me – the country life. No noisy traffic, no fumes, no grime, no Saturday afternoon excursions down the King's Road."

"But can you live without Harrods, I ask myself? And one of us will have to learn to drive," Justin retorted, pleased that William was seriously considering the move.

There'd been no further talk about the cottage. The sophisticated little village, the tranquillity, the lazy afternoon spent basking in the sunshine appealed enormously to Justin too. He was hooked. He could take to this kind of life.

Sasha sang a fanfare slightly off-key and carried a hot golden-crusted soufflé to the table. It disappeared like magic.

"How am I supposed to follow that in class?" Justin wailed.

"Or me," Jane groaned as she poured pungent Turkish coffee into tiny cups.

"I couldn't eat another thing," said William as he helped himself to a bittermint.

"So I see," Justin parried.

"I suppose we'd better call a taxi soon." William ignored Justin's comment.

"You're right," Justin said, looking at his watch. "We don't want to miss the train and end up camping on your doorstep."

Jane and Sasha glanced at each other. As usual, Sasha interpreted Jane's thoughts.

"We've got used to having you around, stay overnight," Sasha suggested.

"Yes, we've plenty of bedrooms. You'd be more than welcome," Jane added.

William answered for both of them, "It sounds lovely, but we don't want to impose . . ."

"He means we'd love to." Justin smiled his crooked grin.

They sat at the table long after the candles had burnt down. Sasha told them about her life as the middle daughter of five. Much of it was news to Jane.

". . . sister versus sister it was. First grabbed, first served at mealtimes. Sometimes I was convinced that my father would give up and run away from home. Imagine, six females – all talking at once. My mum is wonderful and always joined in the fun. We used to put on plays to entertain Mum and Dad and sometimes cousins, uncles and aunts would appear – a captive audience. I suppose that's where it started for me, why I wanted to do it for real. Mum encouraged us all to do our own thing. There was never a doubt in my mind that the stage was for me. Dad didn't like the idea and held firm to the old cliché of *getting a real job.* But nothing could stop me and so here I am, a million miles from Broadway, London's Shaftesbury Avenue theatres or even the local rep."

"What about your sisters?" William asked.

"Oh, they got *real jobs.*" Sasha popped a mint into her mouth. "And yes, before you ask, Dad is still at home – enjoying the peace and quiet."

♥ ♥ ♥

Jane made her way downstairs quietly so as not to wake the others. As she opened the kitchen door an aroma of freshly brewed coffee assailed her nostrils. Justin and William were sitting at the table reading the Sunday papers.

"Good heavens, I didn't know you were up, *and* you've bought the papers."

"And some lovely rolls. We walked to the village. Imagine, a village shop with fresh bread on a Sunday, I'm impressed." Justin pulled out a chair for her. "When you've opened your eyes properly you'll see it's a lovely day. We thought we could have breakfast outside."

Sasha appeared five minutes later wearing dark glasses, a multi-coloured bandanna, gauzy lounging pyjamas and a long, jewelled cigarette holder minus the cigarette.

"Come on Mata Hari, breakfast on the patio," Justin teased.

She flicked her non-existent ash at him and sashayed outside.

The jasmine on the wooden slats above their heads shaded them from the sun. They could hear the sound of a ball being thwacked on a tennis-court in the distance. The sweet voices of children rang out in the clear air, a small boat chugged on the calm river. The men served breakfast. Afterwards they all leafed through the papers, exchanging idle remarks about items of interest.

Jane felt a pang of regret, why couldn't she and Hugh have enjoyed this peace? Would living here have made a difference to their marriage? She closed her eyes and let her mind drift back to those unhappy days. No matter how hard she tried to convince herself that she'd been a victim, she still worried about the failure of their marriage.

"Are you asleep Jane?" William asked in a quiet voice.

"No, just daydreaming."

"Justin and I have a suggestion."

"Yes?"

"You have so much space here, why not take advantage of it? Have your residential weekends, of course. But perhaps, every six weeks or so, have a big party. Lots of people. It'll give your clients a chance to meet each other and be a terrific advert for you. No matter how well you describe the weekends in your brochure, it couldn't compare with the real thing. From your point of view it would be much more profitable. Just think, maybe a hundred people, each paying twenty or twenty-five pounds a head."

Jane was jolted from her unhappy reminiscences. William's idea wasn't what she'd had in mind when she planned *Personal Agenda.* Charles had made the same observation. She knew that other dating agencies offered parties and get-togethers for crowds of singles. But she wanted to make it more personal, more intimate. She'd hated hectic parties. Half-heard, disjointed, meaningless conversations. How could people get to know each other in that environment? Yet what William said made sense. They could do it, she supposed. After all, William did know how to run a profitable business. *Personal Agenda* would be her only income, sometimes she lost sight of that.

"It's an idea," Jane agreed, "I need to give it some thought."

To Jane's surprise, Sasha nodded wisely and

for once refrained from making any snap judgement. Justin said nothing either.

"We're going to give the barbecue a trial run at lunchtime," Jane informed them. "The weather forecast for today was good. I took steaks and sausages out of the freezer last night."

Justin leapt to his feet. "Lead me to it, believe it or not I've never been to a barbecue." He helped her wheel one of the two new gas barbecues from the thatched rustic shed to a shady corner near the patio.

Apart from the odd charred sausage or two, the meal was scrumptious. The afternoon melted away in a haze of laziness.

"And this time we *do* have to leave," William grumbled as he pulled his tie from his pocket.

Jane drove them to the station and Sasha went with her for company.

"It's been wonderful." Justin kissed both girls warmly on the cheek.

"An oasis." William hugged them self-consciously. "I can't remember when I've had such a relaxed couple of days."

"See you tomorrow," Justin shouted and waved as the train pulled out of sight.

Chapter Nine

They all survived the Monday cooking practical. Sasha amused everyone by changing into professional chef's garb: blue striped trousers and a high-collared white shirt with her name neatly printed in black ink on the pocket. She knotted a white kerchief around her neck and the spotless white sheet she wore reached almost to her ankles.

William didn't have lunch with them – pleading urgent business. When he rejoined them he was quietly jubilant.

"Where've you been?" Justin demanded as William took his place in the kitchen.

"Tell you later," he shushed as Caroline began her lecture.

Some of the students hadn't returned for the second week. Jane noticed that the reporter from *Tomorrow* was one of the absentees.

"Will you join us for a drink?" William asked when they finished for the day. The girls needed no urging. They made for the pub they'd visited the previous week.

"I'd kill for a Scotch," Justin said as they pushed their way into the bar packed with briefcased business men and women.

"I'll get the drinks," William said. "You grab a table if you can find one."

He came back a few minutes later carrying a bottle of champagne and four flutes. Justin looked as puzzled as the two girls.

"What's the big deal?" Sasha demanded.

"Yes, what *is* the big deal?" Justin echoed. William smiled but said nothing as he poured the fizzing liquid. He looked uncharacteristically smug. "A toast to the new owners of Oak Cottage." He waited for the impact of his words to sink in.

"I don't believe it." Justin choked as the champagne caught his throat. "So *that's* where you disappeared to at lunch-time. You crafty old sod. Tell me everything."

"I phoned Brookes and Tyson early this morning to find out what they were asking for the cottage. They gave me the impression that they'd take a reasonable drop in the asking price. So I took a chance and made a take-it-or-leave-it offer. The morning dragged by, I can tell you." William paused to take a sip of his drink. "I arranged to phone them back at lunch-time. By then their client had accepted my price, so I hopped into a taxi and scorched round there. Drink to your new neighbours." He held out his glass towards them, grinning proudly.

Justin was lost for words, his mouth open in amazement. None of them could imagine William's dignified figure *scorching* anywhere. The two women wished them luck. It would be fun to live near Justin and William. Jane suddenly realised how much this new friendship meant to her.

"We must have a proper celebration," Justin said, "Thursday night for dinner at the flat, OK?"

"Terrific," Jane beamed as she pushed back her chair. "Thanks for the drinks. See you in the morning."

"T'riffic by two," Sasha said as she hoisted her heavy bag on to her shoulder.

♥ ♥ ♥

"Serve to the left, clear to the right." Justin mimicked Mrs Grundy's modulated tones to perfection. "No! no! one doesn't use the tablecloth to wipe one's sticky mouth."

They laughed as he clumsily stretched across Jane to retrieve Sasha's plate with a deliberately shaky hand. "Has one finished?" he asked obsequiously.

"One has, and it was delicious," Sasha inclined her head in gracious consent.

"How did one organise such a lovely meal when two were out all day?" Jane demanded, impressed by their culinary skill.

"Harrods Food Hall and controlled genius," said William.

The flat was small and attractively decorated in pastel colours. Pinks, blues and yellows blended harmoniously with the beige, hand-tufted rugs spread across hardwood floors.

"We spent months rummaging through Portobello market searching for prints and tables that wouldn't dwarf these small rooms," Justin admitted.

The four were happily squashed at a table on the first floor balcony. Around them patches of muted light glowed softly as darkness fell. From terraces and balconies sounds of laughter and music floated melodiously on the air.

"Won't you miss all this?" Jane asked remembering her own tiny balcony in their Fulham house.

"Not a bit." Justin was definite. "I can't wait to get cracking on the patio at the cottage. At least there we'll be able to turn round without lacerating an elbow or skinning an ankle. And we'll have a garden that we can control, not like that messy one down there."

They'd already worked out a plan of action for the cottage. "We'd like to have a builder lined up as soon as we get possession," William said. "Would you recommend your man?"

"No problem, I'll give you his number right now." Jane searched in her bag for her address book. "Don't forget the party next weekend, will you? Maybe you could come down earlier that day and meet him."

The last day of the course was devoted to revision, questions, and a visiting chef who taught them how to make ice-sculptures. Only ten *students of entertaining*, as Mrs Grundy called them, completed the fortnight. Promising to keep in close touch with Justin and William, Jane and Sasha climbed into the car and joined the stream of commuters heading home.

Chapter Ten

Charles Graham drove slowly through the gates of The Willows. The house's nameplate was a new addition since his last visit. Sasha rushed to open the door for him. How pretty she looked in trousers and a matching oatmeal linen top covered by a flimsy coral overblouse.

"Hi! stranger," she greeted him.

"Hi! yourself," he grinned. "How are things shaping?"

"Ready for the fray. Jane's in the office, come through."

The office was a converted scullery behind the kitchen. Jane had dithered for days as to whether to knock the cold room and scullery into one but at the eleventh hour she decided that the marble shelf-lined storeroom might prove to be more useful for the purpose it was intended for.

Charles was surprised when he saw how bright and well equipped the little office was. On the pale ash desk stood a computer, printer and telephone with a built-in answering machine, and a fax machine. Two chintz-covered chairs filled quite a bit of the precious space on the red flagstone floor which had been varnished to a rich glow. He cocked his head sideways to look at a rug which at first glance appeared to be strewn with hieroglyphics.

"My friendship rug." Jane bent her own head at an angle. "I started it when I was twelve. My friends signed the canvas and then I hooked their signatures into it with rug wool. When it was full, and it took years, I filled in the bare canvas. It'll probably never wear out I'm glad to say."

"Amazing." Charles continued to twist his head this way and that. "Sasha says you're all set?"

"Yes, I have the advertisements here." She pulled a rueful face.

"What's wrong?"

"Cold feet I suppose."

"Rubbish. These are great," he soothed, glancing at the neatly typed pages. "Your phone will never stop ringing."

"That's what I'm afraid of," she laughed. "We'd better get started, I need your advice about so many things. First of all, the questionnaire for the brochure – I've printed a copy for each of us."

Charles read the list carefully and suggested a couple of additional questions.

"At this rate we'll have asked everything about their lives with the exception of what they had for breakfast," Jane said, wincing.

"I forgot that. Add it on," Charles teased. Then his face became serious. "Remember, it's our responsibility to know as much as possible about our clients."

Jane found the words *ours* and *we* comforting. They made the amendments, then checked everything carefully.

"OK, what's next?" Charles asked slipping the paper into a folder.

They worked steadily until Sasha popped her head round the door to tell them lunch was ready.

As they ate Charles asked about their course.

"You mean, Mrs Grudging's Academy for Wayward Peasants?" Sasha pushed up the end of her nose with her finger.

Taking it in turns they gave him a blow-by-blow description of the two weeks, their meeting with Justin and William, the weekend spent together – the cottage.

"Don't forget the reporter from *Tomorrow*," Sasha reminded her.

"Oh yes. She seemed keen to do an article about *Personal Agenda* when we're established."

"Sounds as though you had quite a time," Charles laughed, a little envious of their obvious enjoyment.

"We did. But back to work." Jane carried a pile of dishes to the sink.

"Leave them, I'll see to those and join you in a few minutes," Sasha ordered. Paperwork, she maintained, was not her thing. She avoided the computer like the plague.

"I'm a fully paid-up, card-carrying coward," she refused firmly when Jane offered to teach her how to use it.

Sasha joined them in the crowded office space and lolled in a relaxed manner on the flowery chair. Through half-closed eyes she studied Charles's handsome, serious face. God he's divine, she groaned inwardly. I wish he'd get rid of all those stupid papers and pay me a bit of attention.

"Most professional." Charles tapped the papers

into a neat stack and added them to the folder. Jane seemed to have thought of everything. He would drop the folder off at the printers tomorrow and, with a bit of luck, the proofs should be ready by the time he returned on Saturday for the housewarming.

Chapter Eleven

Jane and Sasha set aside three days to shop and cook the food for the party. They worked steadily stopping only to have a sandwich or a makeshift dinner.

"That's it, all done – *à la Grundy*," Jane said as she finally closed the door of the cold room. It was past midnight before they stumbled to their rooms exhausted but content.

Jane slept fitfully. There were strangers all over the house clamouring to be fed. It wasn't like her to entertain so many people without being prepared. Her fingers refused to move as she tried to peel the potatoes with a fork. Bread sticks cooled on a baking sheet on the counter.

"They smell good," said a man she didn't recognise.

"I hope they're crisp," Jane fretted.

One by one he snapped them in half. "They'll do beautifully," he approved.

She attacked the loaves of sliced bread which needed buttering. The butter was hard and tore gaping holes in each slice. At least the beef was ready. She floated slowly towards the fridge and removed a huge platter. All that remained was a rib bone. "Oh no! I forgot. Sasha used it for a snack last night."

People crowded into the kitchen. One girl in a swimsuit grabbed the beef bone and sat on the floor in a corner gnawing it.

"I need that!" Jane screamed at her.

The girl took no notice. Jane began to cry, her tears cold as they ran down her cheeks. She would never manage it all.

She could hear Sasha's voice but couldn't see her. "Jane! Jane, wake up."

Jane struggled to open her eyes.

"You've been dreaming, you were shouting in your sleep."

"Oh Sasha, what a nightmare I had."

"I gather from the racket you were making you weren't exactly enjoying yourself."

Jane slipped out of bed and threw on a robe. She glanced at the clock on her bedside table; it was almost seven a.m. "Let's go down and have a cup of tea, I'll tell you about it."

In the quiet kitchen Jane relived the anguish of her dream.

"Sounds awful," Sasha said thinking of all the food on the marble shelves in the cold room.

Jane was glad to be awake, her nightmare was still vivid in her mind.

"Throw me that list, I need reassuring that we really have done everything." Jane poured fresh tea into their cups.

Sasha handed her the list and tried to catch the roller that had loosened itself from her hair. "Ooh! An ant," she squealed and squashed it with her slippered foot.

"Where? I hate them," Jane shuddered. She looked around and found the tiny moving creature. "It's OK, I see it."

"Surely I killed it?"

"Sasha, look! There are four of them."

They watched as the little black dots scurried out of sight under the cold room door. Both girls leapt to their feet. Jane's chair fell backwards with a crash as they dived for the marble-shelved larder.

Sasha's scream echoed round the kitchen. Jane's throat closed over, no sound came out.

Over every platter and tray and in every bowl the ant-army swarmed. Jane and Sasha watched helplessly. The insects carried three or four times their weight in food. What they couldn't carry they pulled and tugged then pushed it through a small crack in the floor.

This was worse than her nightmare. This time she was awake.

"What are we going to do?" Sasha wailed.

"Cancel the party. What else can we do? We can't use any of this." Jane's face was ashen.

"All that work. All that food. How *can* we cancel it now? We mightn't be able to contact everyone."

"My dream," Jane said, "It's come true."

"Jane, forget the dream. Think practical. I'll go and get the insect spray, at least we'll get rid of the bleeding things."

Jane stared vacantly at the lines of black ants – how organised they were. Viciously she stamped on the ones nearest her feet. She could hear the telephone ringing in her office. The door of the cold room rocked on its hinges as she slammed it shut.

"Jane?"

"Hello, Justin." Her voice was flat.

"Just rang to see if you needed anything, we're leaving shortly."

"That's very kind of you but we're beyond that."

"What does that mean? Jane, what's wrong? You sound peculiar."

"We've had a disaster, just like my dream."

"What are you talking about? I don't understand."

In a choked voice, Jane explained.

"That's terrible," Justin said. He called William to the phone.

"Jane, I'm so upset for you, what can we do to help?"

"I don't think there's anything anyone can do. Unless . . ." Jane's mind suddenly meshed into gear.

"Unless what?"

Jane could hear Justin in the background. "Jane, how many people have you invited?"

"Sixty." It sounded more when she said it aloud.

"OK. We'll ring off, then you make a list of everything you need. Ring when you're ready and we'll scout around and find the nearest to it that we can. Will you contact the builder and make a later appointment for us?"

Jane nodded, as if he could see her. She'd hesitated to ask for their help, but they'd forestalled her.

"You're wonderful, Justin. Maybe it'll work. I'll ring the builder straight away then phone you back in a few minutes with the list."

The builder was shirty at first. "I don't need to work on Saturday," he growled. He knew these smart London types; their cottage in the country, arty ideas, cancelled appointments. But Jane had been easy to work with, quite a doll. He'd change the time for her sake.

"It's not their fault, Jimmy, it's mine. We're having a party tonight . . ."

"I'll hop over and see what I can do," he offered when she finished her tale of woe.

"There, that'll keep them in," Jimmy Green coughed as he threw the big roll of masking tape on the table. "With the amount of spray you've used they'll all be dead within half an hour anyway. Me too, probably."

He felt sorry for them standing there forlornly in their dressing-gowns. All that gorgeous spoiled food, he could go for those peanutty chicken things on sticks. "First thing on Monday I'll come back and seal every inch of floor for you," he promised.

"First thing on Monday you can rip everything out, *then* seal the floors. I'm going to order two chiller cabinets. I can't afford to take a risk like that again." Jane had recovered a little of her colour.

"Sensible idea," Jimmy said. "See you later."

A smart black van with *Wordsworth Bookshops* painted on the side in gold pulled up at the front door. A moment later it was joined by a taxi.

"Success!" Justin called out when he saw Sasha and Jane waiting anxiously at the door.

The kitchen counters and table were chock-a-block with tinfoil containers. As they opened the covers Jane's glance strayed to the cold room door; nothing had escaped through the wide bands of tape.

"You're absolutely wonderful." Jane hugged the two men, gratefully. "Without you, we were kaput."

"What are friends for?" William's face was pink with colour, he wasn't used to such affection.

Sammy, the driver of the van, had worked for years as a chef at a Thai restaurant which Justin and William frequented. Their first call had been to him. Within a couple of hours he'd been able to fill most of their order leaving them free to organise the rest.

"That looks scrumptious." Sasha sniffed a plate of chicken satay. She lifted the cover from a big bowl of Thai red curry. A spicy fragrance filled the kitchen.

"Look at this," Jane said delightedly staring at a professionally dressed cooked turkey.

"Harrods' best," Justin explained, "and see this." He uncovered a tray of perfectly sliced rare beef.

"Right, we'd better get started on the salads," he brushed off the women's thanks.

By five o'clock everything was ready. The desserts were still safe in the fridge, at least they'd been saved from the miniature marauders.

Jane insisted on driving Justin and William over to the cottage. Jimmy Green took a note of their instructions and added his own advice. The two men were precise and definite. He had no problem with that.

"The minute we have possession, we'll contact you," Justin assured him.

♥ ♥ ♥

There were dozens of people in the house. At least this time they were all friends, or most of them were. Jane had invited her single friends to bring a partner. The lights cast a magical glow over the gardens and the river. The moon shone as if to order. Extravagant compliments flowed non-stop; *the house, the rooms, the gardens – what a find, such a tranquil setting.*

Susie and Matt had visited Jane several times but even they were bowled over tonight as they sat and enjoyed their drink on the sweet-scented patio.

"I have to admit it," Matt told Jane, "you were right. This is going to be a great venture for you. Who could help falling in love here?"

Susie threw her eyes up to heaven. "Just listen to him. How the stubborn have fallen."

"Jane, sorry I'm late," Charles Graham apologised.

"My fault, I'm afraid." The girl at his side was slightly plump and stared myopically at Jane through lightly tinted glasses. Her dress looked expensive but frumpy, much too old for her.

"Amanda Brown, Jane Anderson." Charles introduced them.

"Nice to meet you," Jane said politely. "You're very welcome."

Matt rose from his chair as Jane introduced the two couples.

"Would you mind if I left you for a moment?" Charles asked Amanda. "I have some papers here I'd like to discuss with Jane."

Matt gallantly insisted that she should sit with them and rushed off to find another chair.

They spread the proofs of the brochures on Jane's desk.

"They look terrific," Jane said as if seeing them for the first time. "So . . . official."

"Are you pleased?" he asked. She looked lovely tonight. The blue of the soft silk dress accentuated her eyes. As he bent over the desk he could smell the sweet perfume of her shining hair. Suddenly he wanted to kiss away the frown which creased her worried brow.

"I'll go over them tomorrow when I can think straight. We've had the most traumatic day," she said, looking up.

Their faces were not more than an inch apart. Forget it, he told himself sternly as temptation grew.

"What happened?" He struggled to concentrate on what she was saying.

"We were having breakfast . . ." As she relived the horrors of the day, tears sprang to her eyes.

Without thinking, Charles pulled her to her feet and wrapped her in his arms.

She was soft and yielding as he kissed her silky head, then her lips.

How good it was to feel the warmth of another human being again. Jane revelled in the comfort of his strength.

They jumped apart as the door shut with a crash. They'd been unaware that anyone had entered the room. Footsteps echoed across the kitchen floor.

"I'd better get back," Jane sighed reluctantly.

"And I'd better see how Amanda is getting on. By the way, she'll be a perfect candidate for *Personal Agenda*."

"You mean she's not your girlfriend?" Jane felt her heart jump. What am I thinking of? He felt sorry for me for a minute and now I'm making a big deal out of it.

"Good God, no! She's really one of *my* clients. But I like her, she's bright, good fun – in spite of her appearance."

"Charles, isn't that a conflict of interest for you?"

"Not at all. I'd love her to meet someone. Someone of her own who'd care for her. When I come down tomorrow, I'll explain."

All conversation stopped in the big dining-room when Sasha appeared. Some of Jane's friends had heard about her eccentric companion, but they were unprepared for the sight of Cleopatra – dressed in pleated, shimmering gold lamé. Sasha's eyes were heavily kohled and on her head she wore a jewelled headdress. The snake, coiled round her slender body, looked remarkably real.

"Shouldn't we start serving?" she asked Jane.

"Yes, I suppose so."

Unasked, Justin and William acted as helpers. They dashed about the buffet table filling plates, refilling glasses and generally making themselves indispensable. They cleared away empty platters and replaced them with fresh ones from the kitchen, then explained to the guests what some of the unusual dishes contained. They took it all in their stride as if to the manner born. How she and Sasha would have managed without them,

Jane shuddered to think. Now she came to think of it, apart from her flamboyant costume, Sasha was quite subdued. Jane looked down the length of the table but couldn't catch Sasha's eye.

A girl was sitting snuggled up to Justin on one of the sofas. Much good it may do her, Jane laughed to herself. William stood on the fringe of a small group of people and glared at him. Jane went out to the patio to collect used glasses but came back empty-handed. She didn't want to disturb the couple in the shadows, locked in each other's arms. Her thoughts turned to Charles and that snatched moment of tenderness. She was becoming as fanciful as Sasha.

She could hear music from the den, someone had put a disc in the CD player. When she opened the door and peeped in the furniture had been pushed back against the walls and several couples were dancing.

There was no doubt in her mind now, she had definitely made the right decision. *Personal Agenda* would be a winner.

Chapter Twelve

Amanda Brown looked up from her work. The two girls smiled at her as they dropped their expense sheets on her desk. They were obviously on their way to lunch. She envied their sleek looks and their dress sense.

"Be a pet, Amanda, try and rush this through for me, I've overspent wildly this month."

"I'll do my best," Amanda promised. She didn't pass any expense claims without examining them thoroughly. That's what she was paid to do.

"Me too?" The other girl pleaded.

Amanda nodded. She felt plain and dull beside them. And she was fed up having lunch at her desk. Maybe she'd go out today, there was no need for her to punch a clock.

Not another tweed skirt, she warned herself as she rooted half-heartedly along the rails of the shop.

"Have you something a bit more . . . trendy?" she asked hesitantly.

"We have these minis, they have very nice matching jackets or trouser suits, they're popular." The shop's owner liked Amanda. The girl usually came in, bought something quickly without any fuss, then signed the bill and left. If only they were all like her, she sighed shifting uncomfortably on her tired feet.

Amanda tried on a miniskirt. It didn't flatter her plump knees. The trouser suit made her bottom stick out. Resigned, she chose a grey checked skirt and a sweater which, she knew in her heart, did nothing for her. It would be fine for the office.

"What about a dress?" she asked.

She'd been in the shop for over an hour. She should get back to the office and have her sandwich, but to hell with it, she'd hop round the corner and have lunch in that new restaurant, Hors d'Oeuvres. She couldn't remember the last time she'd allowed herself an extra five minutes at lunch-time.

Amanda selected her lunch from the vast array of cold dishes on the circular table and settled herself in a corner. She pulled a book from her bag and lost herself in the story.

The expense sheets were almost finished. She'd queried several items. Thank goodness it wasn't her job to question the girls. Her boss, Martin Howard, did that, he was far tougher than she was. The phone on her desk bleeped.

"It's Charles Graham, Amanda."

"Hello Charles, how are you?"

"I'm fine, how are *you*?"

"No complaints."

"Do you fancy a theatre tomorrow? We can eat afterwards."

"I'd love it. Anything special in mind?"

"The ballet?"

"I can't resist an offer like that," she laughed.

"I'll pick you up around six-thirty, we can have a drink first."

"Lovely, I'll look forward to it."

Amanda replaced the receiver. It's time to stop this charade, she decided. She felt sorry for Charles. Not once had he let slip that her mother was paying him to take her out. Not once had she hinted that she was aware her mother arranged their outings. She enjoyed his company and had been happy to keep up the pretence. But it must be difficult for him. Whenever there was a long gap between their meetings he usually muttered something about being away on business, but never said what it was. One night, in a mischievous mood, she'd tried to press him into telling her how he'd met her mother. He looked so uncomfortable that she felt guilty and immediately changed the subject.

Amanda knew her mother meant well. But tomorrow night she would clear the air. She'd rather have it that way.

♥ ♥ ♥

"A G & T, please." Amanda needed a bit of Dutch courage.

"Scotch for me," Charles said.

"I need to tell you something." She cleared her throat nervously. "I know my mother is paying you to take me out." Amanda held up her hand to silence him. "No, please, let me have my say. This must be very awkward for you. I enjoy these nights out but it's not much fun for you, I'm sure. No doubt you have loads of friends you'd prefer to be with. So if you want to pack this in I'll understand, really I will."

Charles looked at the girl facing him. What a dreadful admission for her to have to make.

"Obviously there's no point in denying it." His steady gaze met hers. "But regardless of your mother, I enjoy your company. There's no reason why we shouldn't spend a pleasant evening together, that is unless *you're* unhappy with the situation."

"It makes no difference to me, I've known about this arrangement for a while. But there's something you can tell me now – what do you do?"

"I work for an escort agency. Didn't you know that?"

"Oh! So that's it. No, I didn't know."

"You thought I was an acquaintance of your mother's?"

"Yes, I did at first. One evening when she was out I was rummaging through her desk in search of a stamp, and there was a cheque made out to you in the drawer. That's when I put two and two together."

"I'm sorry you found out that way, Amanda. But at the risk of repeating myself, I do look forward to our outings. If I didn't, I wouldn't be here." Charles desperately sought for words to diffuse the embarrassing situation.

"That's true, I suppose. In fact, it makes me feel better. At least this way I know I'm not spoiling your social life."

"Far from it. I must admit, I feel relieved now. This way we can start again – friends?"

"Friends." Amanda smiled one of her rare smiles.

"Now that we've cleared the air, will you tell me more about yourself?" she asked.

Charles hesitated – in a funny way they were similar. Neither of them spoke much about their personal lives. They usually stuck to generalities; their likes and dislikes, the papers they read, books they enjoyed, which television programmes amused them. It was a long time since anyone had shown any interest in his life.

"I'm half Scottish, half Irish – on my mother's side," he said. "I grew up in Scotland mostly. My father was the first cousin of an earl. You know, the branch of the family who gets nothing," Charles said wryly. "His cousin never married and when he died in a shooting accident, my father inherited the title. By this time he and my mother had very little in common, gardening was her life. She flatly refused to give up her home and the marvellous garden it had taken her years to create. Dad didn't put up much of an argument. Mother stayed put when he moved into the family castle. My brother and I were shunted backwards and forwards between them, there were just the two of us. I was sent to the same boarding school as my brother – he loved it and I hated it."

Amanda would liked to have touched his nervous, twisting hands reassuringly, but she was too shy.

"I preferred to live with my mother but Ian enjoyed being at the castle. Eventually he moved there permanently. In those days Ian was more like Dad. They liked the country but not as much as they enjoyed the London social scene. When I was fifteen, Dad met a so-called

Italian *Contessa* with a big gambling habit. He was besotted with her, so my mother said. He followed her to all the gambling clubs, then to the casinos in Europe. She lost vast amounts of money and he paid her debts. In a short time he too caught the gambling bug. But he had no luck and, worse still, was utterly reckless. Everything of value in the castle was sold. Then the castle itself."

"That's dreadful," Amanda sympathised.

"It was. After that they lived in just two rooms in his Belgrave Square house, using the money from the sales of its furniture and paintings. I stayed there a couple of times in the earlier years. It was a magnificent house. Finally he was forced to sell that too. The *Contessa* left him. In the space of three years, he'd lost everything. There was nothing left except my mother's house.

"Somehow Mother found the funds to keep me at school for my last year. I would have been quite happy to leave – but she insisted." Charles suddenly stopped speaking to call a waiter.

"Another drink?" he asked Amanda.

"Thank you, but go on."

"Where was I?"

"You finished your last year at school."

"Yes. By then, Dad had nowhere to go, and hadn't a bean to his name. He came back to Scotland full of remorse and begged Mother to take him back."

"Did she take him back?" Amanda asked as the waiter left the table.

"Yes, she did. I couldn't understand why. She told me at the time, that it would be clear when I was older. Now that I *am* older, I *still* don't understand. Three months later he died of a heart attack."

"And what about your brother? What happened to him?"

"When the *Contessa* appeared on the scene, Ian was at college learning estate management. Ironic isn't it? By the time he'd graduated there was no estate to manage. He's running some pop star's estate now. He doesn't use the title. Ian maintains it brought nothing but unhappiness. He's married now and, Mother says, has two lovely kiddies. I rarely see him anymore – nothing in common."

"What about you? What did you do?"

"In spite of hating school so much, I'd love to have gone to university, but it wasn't possible. Mother needed financial support so I took a job with a friend of hers who owned a market garden. It was quite enjoyable but seasonal. I needed more permanent employment. Then I tried farming, but soon discovered that I wasn't cut out for the hard life. In my wisdom I decided to go to London where I was sure I'd find something less demanding. Mother gave me the address of some friends to contact and also some of her hard-saved money to get me started.

"I didn't phone the people she suggested. Instead I roomed with a school friend at first. But frankly I couldn't afford the rent. It was difficult to find work, I'd had no formal training. I ran out of money pretty quickly and was glad to get a job in a smart Knightsbridge restaurant, waiting on tables. The pay was poor but the tips were good. Nigel, my school friend, wangled invitations for me to a load of debs' parties. That took care of my nights off. Frankly the parties were boring, but we ate free."

Amanda could picture the two men – ignoring the girls but giving the food their full attention.

"Eventually I managed to find a room of my own and just about kept my head above water. The customers appeared to like me and I was promoted when the head waiter left to open his own restaurant. Things were easier. I was able to send Mother a decent sum each week and I quite enjoyed the job." Charles looked at his watch. "I've been rabbiting on for so long, we're going to be late. We'll probably miss the first act now, I'm sorry."

"Are you mad keen to go?" Amanda asked tentatively.

"I don't mind, it's up to you," he said tactfully.

"Let's go and eat instead." She wanted to hear more.

Charles hailed a taxi and instructed the driver to stop off at the theatre. The heavy evening traffic delayed their progress through the narrow streets. When they finally reached the theatre, a small knot of disappointed people were beginning to straggle away from the ticket desk.

"Which ones?" Charles asked as he opened the door of the cab.

Amanda pointed at a young couple who were walking slowly, their arms entwined lovingly round each other.

Charles nodded his approval and approached them. The girl's face broke into a beautiful smile as Charles handed them the tickets. Her companion offered to pay, momentarily suspicious of Charles's kindness.

Amanda ordered her meal without much interest. "Please finish your story."

"I will, but then you'll have to tell me about yourself."

Amanda nodded, reconciled to stirring old memories.

"I stayed with the job for a few years," Charles continued. "A couple who ate with us regularly were joined one night by their daughter. She'd been studying abroad and lost contact with her friends. Her father caught me off guard at my desk. 'I was wondering,' he asked awkwardly, 'If you have a free evening, would you take my daughter to wherever it is that young people go? I'll foot the bill of course and pay for your time.' I readily agreed, the poor man looked so embarrassed. It worked out well. She was good company and we had a fun night. The following week he phoned me. We went out again. She went back to France to continue her studies and her father sent me a generous cheque. I forgot all about her until a friend of hers came to have a meal at the restaurant. She introduced herself, and diffidently, she asked me if I would take *her* to a disco or club and for something to eat. She knew few people in London and was a bit lonely. She was cute, and very French." Charles laughed. "I certainly didn't expect the generosity of the envelope that she slipped into my pocket after dinner. It gave me food for thought!"

Amanda itched to tell the waiter to go away. She said yes to his first suggestion – chocolate marquise. Not since her schooldays had anyone's life touched hers so closely. She was captivated by Charles's story.

"People did this for a living, I knew. It would be a lot easier than being run off my feet in a crowded restaurant. I phoned an escort agency on my next afternoon off – just for the hell of it. They said they would see me – they were always in the market for suitable people. I didn't like the owner, a shrewd, hard-faced woman who made it quite clear that my services would include sleeping with any client who asked me.

"'You're not what I'm looking for,' I said rudely." Charles smiled at the memory. "I was a bit put off by her but decided to try another agency and then another. I'd become quite choosy! Finally I came across the one I'm with now. It may not be the ideal way to earn a crust but it's lucrative and often interesting. I've enjoyed it but, I must confess, it's not something I want to do for the rest of my life. Now you know it all."

"I do, don't I? Except, you didn't tell me how you met my mother?"

"That in itself was unusual. Carol, the receptionist at the agency, phoned to ask if I'd go to your mother's office for an interview. I suppose I was peeved that I needed to be vetted so I told her I wouldn't. Carol talked me round . . ."

Amanda could visualise her mother, not a hair out of place, sitting behind her semi-circular desk. She smiled inwardly. He wouldn't have stood a chance. The wily woman with her public relations empire had intimidated better men than Charles.

"She was charming." He grinned. "Professionally charming!"

"That says it all," Amanda laughed.

"But her daughter means a lot to her," he added hastily, regretting his previous remark.

"I'm sure I do, guilty conscience no doubt."

"Why do you say that?"

"It's a long story." Amanda etched half-moon patterns on the white cloth with a spoon.

"Tell me?" Charles had a sudden urge to know what made Amanda tick.

He felt better than he had for ages, more light-hearted. A little of the bitterness he felt towards his father had evaporated. Judging from the pained look on Amanda's face it might do her good to unburden herself.

Chapter Thirteen

Jane was overwhelmed by the response to her advertisement. For two days she ate her lunch by the phone. At first she was concerned that she'd over-ordered the brochures and leaflets. And then there was the problem of where to stack the endless boxes of stationery. But her worries proved groundless; after four days she'd practically used them all. Charles was delighted when she phoned excitedly to ask him to place a re-order.

"That's terrific." He was genuinely pleased for her.

"Any chance you can come down at the weekend?"

"No problem, I'd be delighted. I said I'd take Amanda somewhere on Saturday, would you mind if she came with me?"

"Not at all. After all, she is our first client."

It had been remarkably easy to persuade Amanda to join *Personal Agenda*. Charles had expected her to refuse and had a dozen different arguments ready as to why she should.

"I'd like to try it," she said. She'd loved the atmosphere of the big house, the air of informality at the party. Jane was friendly, unthreatening. Besides, what did she have to lose? On the way home from the party she'd made up her mind to apply.

♥ ♥ ♥

Jane examined the sheet of paper critically. Her computer print-out looked almost as professional as the printer's leaflets. It was Sasha's idea to include a list of suggestions as to what type of activity people would enjoy most. They'd sat long into the night swapping ideas, agreeing on some, rejecting others.

"It doesn't matter what we think," Sasha argued. "Write them all down and let people decide for themselves what they like and don't like."

"Far better to be selective," Jane insisted. "The number of questions they need to answer is already daunting."

Sasha shrugged. Maybe Jane was right. It's a wonder she hadn't asked Charles to make these decisions. Everything lately was *Charles said this* or *Charles thought that.*

"Anything else you can think of?" Jane queried. Maybe she was overtired but she detected an air of irritability, bad temper even, on Sasha's part. The strain of the housewarming must have thrown Sasha – it had been traumatic. Once they'd returned to normal after the party Sasha had spent most of her time looking over her costumes in readiness for the drama weekend.

Jane rarely left her little office in the next week. She was anxious to set up a computer data-base in readiness for what she hoped would be an onslaught of clients.

Jane checked the list of options on the typed sheet. There were a dozen items which she hoped would capture people's interest. An enterprising firm of colour consultants had responded to her advert and offered their professional services. Jane thought it was an excellent idea. It pleased her to think that *Personal Agenda* could offer not only entertainment but useful lectures and demonstrations too. Jane contacted Caroline, the cookery instructor from the hostess course. Within minutes she was avidly enthusiastic about Jane's plans. Her weekends were free and she offered to teach "Gourmet Cookery on a Time Budget," in return for a weekend's stay. It was something she'd done once before, ideal for busy people. Her marriage had broken up recently, she confided in Jane, this could be just the shot in the arm she needed. Caroline suggested several other aspects which could be stimulating.

"How about Power Eating – which restaurants to frequent, how to get the right table, how to impress clients . . ."

Jane laughingly stopped her. "Let's deal with basics first," she cautioned. "The amount of paperwork that prospective clients have to deal with is enough to occupy them for a full day."

They arranged to speak in a week or so. Again Jane's thoughts were in overdrive. There were some excellent restaurants nearby for those who might want them, she was sure she could make block-bookings. The local riding school might be attractive to some people and then there was the golf course, that could be a draw.

In the end she limited the selection to twelve

and left an empty space at the bottom of the page for suggestions. "Who knows what they'll come up with," she observed.

♥ ♥ ♥

Charles and Amanda arrived early on Saturday morning. She and Sasha pottered about, then went outside to sit in the sunshine.

Jane and Charles upturned the box onto the kitchen table. Red-edged envelopes slipped and slithered from a mountainous pile.

"I am truly awed." Charles stared in disbelief. "You weren't kidding when you said there was a huge response."

"Frightening, isn't it?" Jane's voice faltered.

"Come on, this is the whole point of the exercise. You're not going to back out now, are you?"

"No, of course not. They're not all going to descend on us at once, are they?" she asked plaintively.

Charles didn't answer her question, his attention was focused on the pile of envelopes which were still sealed. "You haven't opened them?"

"I thought that we could do them together."

"Fine, let's make a start." How strong was Jane's will, he wondered?

They separated the contents into two piles, one which contained cheques and the other, application forms.

"Let's tackle these first," suggested Charles stapling the cheques to their respective forms. "This one seems OK. Listen." Charles read the accompanying letter. The writer was single, thirty-three years of age, loved company but was completely absorbed in her job as private assistant to a well known business tycoon. Her social life at present was nil. Her covering letter stated that she adored the idea of the drama weekend and wanted to be included. She'd enclosed a cheque to join *Personal Agenda* and another to cover the cost of her stay for the first weekend.

"Did she add anything to *Any Other Suggestions*?" Jane asked as she started yet another stack of responses – these were the definites for Charles to meet and vet.

"Yes, she'd like to learn how to compose really impressive business letters."

"Bit late in the day for a PA, isn't it?" Would something like that have an appeal? Jane noted the name and address of the sender.

"Here's another possibility. Cheque enclosed, doesn't fancy the drama weekend, loves the idea of colour consultancy. Male, by the way."

"Let's stop and have a cup of coffee." Jane stretched her back and walked stiffly to fill the kettle. "They must be parched out there in the garden."

"How's it going?" Amanda wanted to know.

"Not bad at all." Charles smiled at Sasha and Amanda. Sasha was not her usual chirpy self today. She'd greeted them with quite a frosty nod when they'd arrived. Maybe it was because she didn't know Amanda very well.

Amanda had been relieved to hear Jane's cheery voice calling them. Sasha seemed so preoccupied with her sewing she'd left Amanda to do most of the talking. That didn't come easily to the quiet girl. Funny, when they'd first met, Amanda judged Sasha to be a real extrovert. Shows how you can misjudge people, she concluded.

Jane stood in the doorway watching until the car was out of sight, then returned to her computer and the task of logging in the names that they'd agreed. She'd been acutely aware of Sasha's manner towards Charles today. There'd been no sign of her usual teasing humour.

"If we were meant to read computer screens we'd have been born with square eyes," Sasha snapped at him when he asked if she'd changed her mind about using the machine.

"Does that mean you should have been born on a stage if you want to act?" His sarcastic retort betrayed his annoyance.

His rebuke caused tears to sting Sasha's eyes and she left the room abruptly. She would be out of sight before the inevitable rivulets of black smudges ran down her cheeks.

Jane agonised about whether to tackle Sasha and find out what was wrong or just leave her alone. Everyone was entitled to their moods.

"Do you fancy a film and a Chinese meal later?" Jane kept her tone light.

"I have far too much to do – and then there are these costumes." Sasha's head was bent over her sewing.

"What's wrong, Sasha?" The words slipped out before Jane could check herself.

"There's nothing wrong. Why should there be anything wrong? You sit all day playing with that stupid machine and don't realise how much else there is to be done."

"Like what? I don't *play* with the machine, I work on it. And if there are things to be seen to, I attend to them and you know it." Jane's outburst caught them both by surprise. "Please tell me why you're so angry, maybe we can discuss it."

"There's nothing to discuss, now please excuse me, as I said, I have work to do."

Jane wandered aimlessly about the garden but for once it gave her little pleasure. They'd always got on so well together, she and Sasha. Since the night of the party Sasha had been exceptionally short-tempered. Even her dressing up had gone by the board. Each day she wore a plain black dress and no make-up. She slicked her hair flat and caught it behind her ears in two big, ugly grips. If Sasha didn't want to talk then she wouldn't press her. Jane picked up her bag and her keys and went to the cinema alone.

The film was mildly amusing and Jane enjoyed her meal. She was in a much happier frame of mind when she quietly let herself into the house. She fumbled in the dark for the light switch, Sasha must have turned off the hall light by mistake. Jane made her way upstairs and jumped slightly when one of the branches of a tree tapped against the picture window. She must have that laburnum trimmed, it would be quite eerie in winter. No light showed under Sasha's door, she was asleep early tonight.

Jane dithered. Could she be bothered to get out of bed and go downstairs for a glass of milk? She'd eaten a big meal but was still faintly hungry. I might be glad of a drink later, she decided. She threw on her robe and tiptoed quietly past Sasha's door.

There was a note propped up against the bowl of colourful garden flowers on the kitchen table.

Sasha had packed up and gone.

The costumes, Sasha had written, *are ready for use and I'll send for them after the drama weekend.*

Jane was stunned. Uncomprehending. Why had Sasha run off without a word, was someone ill? Jane lowered herself on to a chair and stared at the note, her eyes transfixed by the open, looped script. Suddenly she realised that she had no idea how to contact Sasha or her family, she didn't even know where they lived. Desperately she searched her mind and tried to remember if Sasha had mentioned the name of the town. But she drew a blank. That night when Justin and William were here, had she said anything then? Maybe there was something in her room, a letter from home, a postmark? Pale and upset she re-read the note then dashed up the stairs and flung open the door of Sasha's room.

The costumes hung in neat rows on the dress rail; women's clothes at the front, men's to the back. They were labelled according to size. Cardboard boxes were lined in rows by the side of the bed, brown impersonal containers. Jane lifted the lids of the cartons nearest to her. They contained hair switches, full wigs, beards and moustaches. In a daze she opened box after box. Her gaze fell on hats and head-dresses, tubes and pots of stage make-up, soft padding in every shape and size, but there were no letters. There was the Victorian bustle that had so amused them the first time Sasha cooked dinner for Justin and William. The last of the boxes held a collection of masks, eyeless and mocking. There was even a small cardboard shaker labelled "Dandruff."

For a wild moment Jane wondered if Sasha had been kidnapped. Sasha's wardrobe was empty and so were the big trunks that she must have dragged down from the tiny attic. She was being ridiculous, kidnappers would hardly concern themselves with their victim's fashion statement.

♥ ♥ ♥

Jane was waiting for him at the front door, exactly where he'd left her the previous day. She looked worried. Charles groaned inwardly, he hoped she wasn't having more doubts. At this stage she really had to settle down and get on with it. *He* was sure it was going to work, how often did she need to be reassured?

"What's up?" he called more cheerfully than he felt.

"It's Sasha, she's disappeared." Jane hadn't meant to greet him like this but she was perilously close to tears.

Charles locked the door of the hire car and joined her. "How do you mean, disappeared?"

"Just that, disappeared."

"Come inside and tell me what happened."

"There's nothing more to tell. She's vanished – without leaving as much a phone number or an address. I tried to talk to her yesterday, to ask why she's been so out of sorts lately, but she nearly bit my head off. Then I suggested that we go to the pictures, have a meal. She refused. I went alone and when I got home she'd . . . gone." Jane passed him the note to read.

"She certainly wasn't her cheeky self yesterday. Amanda found it difficult to talk to her too. Odd, isn't it?"

They sat on the patio trying to make some sense of the whole thing. "I think it would be as well to find someone else to help you, Jane, you don't have much time."

"I suppose so," Jane replied, her tone reluctant. "Do you think she'll at least phone and let me know what happened?"

Charles scratched his chin. "You know Sasha better than I do. I'm so taken aback that I must admit, I don't know what to think."

Charles reached his flat just before seven o'clock. Normally he would have stayed on at The Willows and had a bite to eat, but Jane was so disturbed by Sasha's disappearance that she obviously hadn't thought to invite him. It was better all round to leave her to sort out the problem. Besides, there were lots of calls he must make, arrangements to meet the prospective clients on his list.

"Not bad." Charles ticked off the names of the people he'd been able to reach. "Ten appointments in eight days, that should keep me busy." He was tempted to ring Jane but thought better of it, there was nothing more he could say. Possibly Sasha would phone her tomorrow. But somehow he doubted it.

Chapter Fourteen

Ray Parker cleared his desk top and unlocked the bottom drawer. The glossy red and white folder caught the glint of the afternoon sun. He glanced briefly at the loose pages and discarded them in favour of the fourteen page questionnaire. He clacked his pen irritably between his teeth, *Personal Agenda* left nothing to chance. The obvious questions came thick and fast on page one: name, address, age, telephone number, all pretty straightforward and expected.

"Ah! Page two, the nitty-gritty. Single, separated, divorced or widowed?" he read aloud. "Appearance? Healthy or otherwise?"

"Physically healthy, yes, if you don't count stress and hassle," he grumbled to himself. "Now what? Qualifications? Two here, university degree and technical qualification, might as well make the most of it." His pen left deep indents on the page. "Drink? Moderately. Smoke? No. Which of these descriptions apply to you?" Ray scanned the list. "The one that describes me best is missing, *pissed-off with life*. I can't write that down. Gregarious, shy, reserved or extrovert? Somewhere in between, I think. Affectionate, dependable, considerate. Who'd admit they weren't? How many people tell the truth about themselves anyway?" He pushed the booklet away and swivelled his chair towards the window. From where he sat, only the tops of the trees in the commercial park were visible.

Why couldn't he get it right? He'd put his heart and soul into this computer company, worked sixteen, sometimes eighteen, hours a day. He accepted that there were dozens of software companies out there but there were also thousands and thousands of users, so many of them needing specialist packages.

His hopes had run high the day he'd clutched that official licence, his degree. It took barely a month to launch himself on a computer-hungry world. Then he'd been salesman, advertising agent, publicity hound and programmer all rolled into one. It was exciting. Each day brought new challenges. He invested every penny he had in a new computer. He hired the answering machine and mobile phone. They helped enormously, he was always contactable. The answering machine picked up the calls from the fifth floor attic he'd regarded as his office.

Ray always met customers on site. He was a little ashamed of the shabby building which displayed his logo – CCC Inc. CCC had no meaning but the symmetry of the letters doodled on a pad appealed to his eye. He had a good rapport with clients, an easy charm. He never promised them anything he felt he couldn't carry out and never sold them software they didn't need.

Within six months he'd added a brilliant young programmer to his "staff." He laughed as he remembered his own pretentiousness in referring to *one of our associates at CCC. Our staff.* CCC was a two-man band.

Donahue Reilly was undoubtedly a whiz, a virtuoso of the computer. He lived, ate and breathed computers. His grasp of a problem was a joy to behold. Ray grinned ruefully as he remembered the day Donahue joined CCC. Donahue's appearance left a lot to be desired. His hair was long and often greasy, his beard untrimmed for weeks on end. He wore the same sweater and jeans to work every day for a year. Washing was not one of his more immediate priorities and Ray had been torn between saying something about soap and deodorant or being tactful in order to keep him. It occurred to Ray that opening the skylight would help, the other window in the stuffy room was purely an ornate, circular decoration. With a considerable amount of hacking and banging the paint-bound window finally sprang open. The cracked glass would do for a couple of days, the draught barely discernible if the Sellotape held firm.

Luck was with them. The equally squalid room next door became available. The private detective – *Specialist in Domestic Matters* – who worked there was obviously a little too private. She was so well hidden from public demand that her phone never rang nor did any mysteriously veiled wife or irate husband tread a path to her door. Ray and Donahue spent an entire weekend painting the cracked, bulging ceiling and the peeling wallpaper with a dozen coats of white emulsion. They scratched the previous owner's name from the buckled door and added their own shaky logo to the opaque, bubbled glass. The room was clean and bright but basic. Donahue was assigned the "studio."

"You'll be able to work here undisturbed," Ray said, relieved, now that he could remove those discreet little plugs of cotton wool from his nose.

In those days he seemed to be everywhere at once. Within months he'd lost contact with almost all his friends. He saw his family at Christmas and then only on the day itself. He doubted that Donahue took his eyes from the screen even then. But maybe he was wrong, Donahue had changed his sweater. Donahue only came alive when he was faced with a challenge. Ray knew nothing more about him now than he did the day they met.

A smile crossed his face, what would Donahue make of the abandoned questionnaire lying there on the desk? He'd probably ignore the context but find a more efficient way of presenting it. CCC's present suite of offices was a far cry from those stuffy little attics. The division of space was perfect for their use, three fairly spacious private offices and one large open bright room shared by the programmers. Theirs was the only first floor unit with a separate entrance. Donahue still roomed alone.

Ray swivelled back to the desk and focused his mind on the booklet. No one had forced him to send for it, his resentment was ridiculous.

"Hobbies." The subjects were laid out in a long column. "Precious few lately. Certainly nothing athletic, unless you count watching sport on television." He ticked the ones he liked.

"Entertainment. Cinema, theatre, dining out, dinner parties? I'd like to go to dinner parties but no one asks me. How could they?" All his acquaintances were wine bar and pub oriented these days. It was this boring routine that nudged him into applying for the brochure in the first place. He was fed up with the smell of stale beer, the occasional relationships with pass-in-the-night women. More and more people knew someone affected by AIDS and he dreaded becoming one of those sufferers.

"Religion." He ticked the box which stated no religious conviction. That had fallen by the wayside long ago. "There, all finished." He'd probably spent more time thinking about himself in the last half-hour than he had for years.

Linda Lou Green knocked perfunctorily at Ray's door and bounced towards his desk. She was quite attractive in a brassy way, not his type.

"These are ready for signing," she instructed.

Ray barely read the letters that she handed him. She removed each one after he added his signature. Vindaloo, as he privately called her, was bossy, manipulative and brilliant at her job. She could juggle customers and keep them at bay for days on end. At the moment she was earning more than he was, at least she was getting paid. When a payment cheque was received, her wages were immediately paid into her bank account. Clever girl, she took no chances. Then she attended to Donahue's salary. He doubted if Donahue would even notice if he was paid or not. As long as he had money for diskettes and toner cartridges all was well in his square-screened, flickering world.

It had been a blow to Ray's ego when he was forced to let three of his programmers go, but there wasn't enough work for them.

If there was no upsurge in business soon the rest of his staff would be redundant too. Other firms were thriving, why was CCC barely limping along? He was glad it was Friday. He'd go home first, have a shower, grab a bite to eat and go to that new wine bar round the corner. New faces might cheer him up.

They waved goodbye from the door. Through the haze of smoke Ray watched them laughing and playfully edging each other towards the anonymity of the dark street.

"What a waste of space *they* were," he said to himself draining his third glass of wine. He spent more time talking to himself than other people these days. He'd post that brochure to *Personal Agenda* first thing in the morning.

He settled himself on the settee and pointed the remote control at the television. He watched as it flicked through the channels; the usual late-night horror movie line-up interspersed with music videos. He switched off and picked up a book. It failed to hold his attention and he flung it on the floor in disgust. The worries of CCC crept back into his mind. What could he do to get out of this mess? Whatever the solution, it had to be soon or the whole thing would come crashing down around him.

The rent was paid for the remainder of the year, that was a plus. The computers, twelve of the latest and most sophisticated models, were paid for too. His insurance was up to date. And? There were no other ands. Only the downside. Apart from a couple of minor contracts and a small outstanding payment from Boothby's, that was it, the well had dried up. His own savings had dwindled alarmingly. Donahue, Linda Lou and the rest of the programmers had to be paid. And then there was the office suppliers, their non-too-subtle hints suggested – no payments, no further supplies. But it was the phone bill that had shaken him rigid. A final notice. Without a phone the life-line of CCC would be severed. The furniture was another worry, the instalments on that were three months behind. The suite of offices were comfortably furnished but could hardly be described as opulent.

Ray heaved his tall frame from the chair and pensively walked the few steps towards the kitchen. A cup of milky cocoa might lull him to sleep. The out-of-date carton of milk was sour and curdled. Angrily he threw it into the sink. The contents splashed on to the counter and the window. The smell turned his stomach. He glanced at the date on his watch, it wasn't the thirteenth. It might as well be, he thought, wiping the window with a smeared cloth.

"Now I've made it worse. I shouldn't have to do this. I need someone to look after these domestic details. A woman could manage all this, they're more geared for it."

The sun shone brightly through the thin curtains. Although it had taken him hours to fall asleep, he woke early. He'd go to the newsagent and collect his papers, then go to the grocers on the corner and stock up with milk, eggs and the few bits he needed. Maybe he'd cook at home this weekend. Perhaps a film tonight? He didn't relish going alone. He'd phone Trudy, she loved the cinema. Their casual relationship suited them both. They were more than acquaintances, less than friends – two lives barely touching in a large, lonely city. Satisfied with his plans, he showered and dressed in a casual shirt and a pair of well-worn jeans.

Trudy's voice was sleepy. "What day is it?"

"Saturday, sleepy-head."

"Oh goodee! No work today. What time is it?"

"Ten-thirty."

"Ray! You lunatic, why are you phoning me at this ungodly hour?"

"I wanted to take you to a film tonight."

"Tonight? Tonight, what's happening tonight? Oh, I can't, Ray, I'm sorry, I'm invited to a party. How about tomorrow?"

"Yes, OK, why not?"

"Good. Phone me tomorrow and we'll arrange a time. Not too early though."

"Midday?"

"Or later."

"Right, I'll call about one o'clock. Even you'll be awake by then."

"Don't bet on it," she yawned into the receiver.

The pile of empty chocolate wrappers and crisp packets formed a circle round his feet. He had eaten a normal week's ration by lunch-time. He heated a pizza but left most of it. He finished the papers, there was no good news there either. Maybe he'd go for a stroll, work off some of the rubbish he'd scoffed.

Wherever he looked there were people in pairs. Young couples, mothers pushing their babies in strollers, families. Was he the only one alone? This was depressing. The video shop was just round the corner, that would pass a few hours tonight. They sold snacks too, he would replenish his stock.

There was no reply from Trudy's phone – just a request to leave a message, she'd return the call as soon as possible. At three o'clock he tried again. The response was the same. He didn't bother to leave his name. The videos were due to be returned, he'd hire another couple. If she did phone back he'd claim to be busy. That envelope for *Personal Agenda* was still beside his bed.

There were fewer people about today. He found that even more depressing. The newsagent sold stamps. With his Sunday papers clutched tightly under his arm he walked along to the nearest post box. He spat on the envelope for luck and fed it into the impersonal open mouth of the red cylinder. There, perhaps that would be his introduction to a whole new existence.

The afternoon sun made the room hot and airless. He wished he could create a cross-draught but he couldn't. His doorbell rang. It made him jump. Trudy? Had she decided to call round?

"Mrs Delaney! What a surprise. And to what do I owe this honour?"

"Just thought I'd pop in on my way upstairs to remind you that the rent for your flat was due last week. It's not like you to miss." A smile hovered on her thin lips but her eyes were cold. "I'm just doing my job," she'd told him last year when the man on the opposite landing was given a week to pay his arrears or remove himself. For whatever reason, the man chose to ignore her warning. On that occasion she'd brought two of her sons with her. Ray remembered thinking at the time, no man in his right mind would take on those two bruisers. There had barely been a word exchanged. Only the noise of suitcases banging rhythmically on each of the stairs announced his neighbour's departure.

"My goodness," Ray said feigning amazement. "I'll write you a cheque immediately. I'm so sorry. I can usually rely on my secretary to remind me, she must have forgotten, pressure of business, you know?"

Mrs Delaney neither knew nor cared. Pay up or get out was her motto, but she feigned understanding nevertheless.

"Thank you, Mr Parker. *Usual* time next month?" It was more an ultimatum than a question.

Ray smiled charmingly, he could cheerfully have wrapped the cheque round her wattled neck and choked her.

He watched the seconds tick by on his watch. Despite his resolve he tried Trudy's number again.

". . . and I'll get back to you as soon as I feel like it," he mocked her lilting voice.

The pub was quiet, he didn't recognise anyone he knew and wasn't in the mood to chat to the barman. Ray sat and nursed his drink, the usual parade of problems followed each other in an orderly fashion through his mind.

"Evenin'," a voice piped from the next table.

"Good evening," Ray responded automatically.

"Quiet tonight."

"Yes."

"Meant to meet someone here half an hour ago, he didn't show."

"Maybe he's delayed," Ray didn't know why he was making excuses for someone he'd never met.

"Maybe, maybe not. We were supposed to do business." The man tapped the blue holdall by his feet. "Need any office equipment?" he asked.

"Not really." He needed to get rid of it, never mind buy more.

"Great line here." The man unzipped his canvas bag and produced a desk-set still in its wrapping, a heavy paperweight and a marble ashtray the size of a small table. "Fell off the back of a quarry," he sniggered at his own joke.

"No thanks. I'm not in the mood to buy anything," Ray said firmly.

"Things bad?"

"Not good."

"Anything to sell?"

"No. Look, I don't mean to be rude but I just want to finish my drink."

"Things are bad then. Know the signs. More than one way to skin a cat . . . you know."

"What does that mean?"

"Well, sometimes you can raise a bit of dosh . . . other ways, if you get my drift."

"No, I don't."

"There are ways. You know . . . ?"

"Look, either explain what you mean or leave me to my beer. I'm not in the mood for games."

"Accidental damage to goods . . . fire . . . you

know?" The man looked around satisfying himself that they couldn't be overheard. "Insurance . . . insurance claims . . . you know?"

"You mean set the place on fire and claim the insurance? That's a mug's game." He wished the man would stop saying "you know." It was getting on his nerves.

"There's other things. You get my meaning?"

"No thanks, I'll do it the hard way."

"That *is* a mug's game."

"I don't fancy doing time for fraud, thanks anyway." Ray vowed he'd pour his drink over the infuriating fellow if he nudged his elbow again.

"Well, if you change your mind, I'm your man. Here's my number, you never know." The man dug into a side pocket of the bag and brought out a tattered pad and a bitten pencil. He scribbled down a number and handed it to Ray.

"What's your name?" Ray asked strictly from boredom.

"No name, just a phone number. Fax too, same number, you know?" Ray watched as he packed away the desk set and ashtray.

At least he's innovative, Ray reflected, crime by fax.

"Cheers. Don't forget, we can solve most problems." With a shuffling gait and listing slightly to one side, he reached the door and left.

♥ ♥ ♥

In spite of all his problems Ray was glad it was Monday. It would be good to be back in the office. At least he could relate to the people there. The weekend had dragged, lonely and boring. For a fleeting moment he wondered how Linda Lou had filled in her time. Loads of boyfriends to take her out, no doubt. They never discussed their personal lives.

"Mornin' Ray," she shouted cheerfully through his open door.

"Hello . . . Vin . . . Linda Lou." Someday he was going to make that fatal mistake and use her nickname.

"Post's in. You'd better shift that furniture payment or we'll be sitting on the floor, or, at least *you* will."

Ray looked up, she wasn't in his line of vision so he gave her the finger. "Hard little bitch," he muttered.

"What did you say?"

"Nothing for your delicate ears."

"Better not be."

♥ ♥ ♥

"Ray Parker?" A polite voice enquired.

"Yes. Who's calling?"

"My name is Charles, *Personal Agenda.*"

"Oh! Yes."

"We received your application at the beginning of the week and I wondered if we might meet. It's our policy to have a chat with prospective clients if we can, just to clarify their likes and dislikes."

Ray's instinct was to tell him that he'd answered enough questions but he thought better of it. No point in antagonising the fellow. "That would be fine, when do you suggest?"

"How about next Wednesday, lunch-time?"

"Let me check." Ray held the receiver over the computer keyboard and tapped a few keys. He paused for a moment then said that would suit him, he was clear until three o'clock. He didn't bother to add, three o'clock next month.

"Where would you like to meet?" Charles asked.

"How about a sandwich at Fortnums?" Ray wasn't sure who was paying for lunch.

"One o'clock?"

"Perfect."

As he rang off he realised he had forgotten to ask Charles's second name.

Ray recognised the red and white folder on the table nearest the door.

"Charles?"

A pleasant-looking man about his own age rose to his feet and shook Ray's outstretched hand.

"Ray? Nice to meet you. I'm Charles Graham."

They settled themselves at the table, complained about the wet weather and ordered lunch.

"As you've no doubt gathered, this is your folder." Charles tapped the glossy cover. "We feel it's advantageous for us to meet and have a chat. We've done most of the questioning so far, is there anything *you'd* like to know?"

Nothing sprang immediately to Ray's mind. The leaflets had been comprehensive and explicit. "Not really. I gather it's a new venture?"

"Yes. In my opinion a terrific way to get to know people properly."

"What's the place like? *Personal Agenda* I mean."

"Beautiful. It's a big house with a lovely garden, by the river at Dornley. Not too far from Bray-on-Thames," Charles added.

"I know the area roughly. What about this drama weekend?" Ray asked. "Not that I consider myself an actor, my acting career consisted of a minor role in the school play, an angel with bent wings. But I gather from the blurb that there'll be a place for scenery painters etc?"

Charles nodded and laughed. "Your experience was like my own. I fought for the part of Jack, in *Jack and the Beanstalk*, our school Christmas pantomime. The other boy up for the part was equally keen and we argued endlessly who was best. In the end we fought it out in the playground."

"Who won?"

"Neither of us. The drama teacher was so furious we were relegated to playing the cow. When she'd gone we fought again – this time to decide which of us played the front half and who was landed with the rear! Naturally we both wanted to be the head. I won. I can remember dragging the poor unfortunate child all over the stage. We got hopelessly entangled in the beanstalk and proceeded to dislodge most of the beans. They were taped to the 'beanstalk' which was a prize climber belonging to one of the parents. Loaned under duress, I think, in return for a part for their daughter."

"How easy life was then."

Charles nodded and said, "I see you suggest

company management as a topic on your form."

"Yes, I thought it might be interesting." Ray didn't bother to add – desperately needed.

"We'll certainly give it some thought, obviously we're open to ideas. But it will take some time before we can collate everything."

"You've had a good response to your advertisement?"

"Excellent. People seem very taken with the idea. You were one of the first to reply."

"So I'm in at the off?"

"I don't see why not."

"Good. I can do with a break . . . pressure of work and all that. How is the divide – male, female, I mean?"

"Definitely half and half."

They checked through the booklet. Ray found himself emerging as a much more interesting character than he'd imagined himself to be. Skilful chap, he thought, as Charles drew him out. Finally Charles closed the glossy folder. "We'll be in touch in the next week or so. Pencil-book the twentieth to twenty-second, we'll confirm it as soon as possible."

Charles called for the bill. "I'm heading for Piccadilly Circus, is that in your direction?"

"No, I'm going the opposite way, Knightsbridge."

They shook hands.

Charles strolled along the busy street, his mind occupied with the interview. Parker appeared to be an amiable guy, very presentable, just the sort of client that *Personal Agenda* was geared towards. Charles could detect no problems here. He'd phone Jane when he got home to change for the theatre. He wasn't particularly looking forward to spending the evening with a Japanese couple who spoke very little English. Carol had booked for the latest musical. A play would be impossible for them. Never mind, he consoled himself, tomorrow he was booked to eat at Gavroche with a divorcée from Washington who was reluctant to venture into such a famous restaurant alone.

His next appointment wasn't until four o'clock so he stopped in at Hatchards, the elegant bookshop. It would be a real bonus to have some extra cash from *Personal Agenda*. Then he could buy some hardback books, perhaps pop into Simpsons and size up the clothes, stroll through the Burlington Arcade and price the cashmere sweaters he admired so much. Jane sometimes wore cashmere. She couldn't be too hard up. Her secretarial bureau must have netted her a few bob. Secretarial bureau! Now there was an opportunity to find clients. Had that dawned on Jane? She hadn't mentioned her former clients, perhaps it wasn't ethical to approach them now that she'd sold out. He must suggest it to her nevertheless.

The girl with short, curly, blonde hair apologised as she bumped his arm with her bag. He glanced at her briefly, there was something familiar about her face.

"Good God! Sasha!" he yelled. Two people standing beside him edged away. But it was too late, she'd been swallowed up by the crowd surging round the busy corner. It was the short blonde hair that had thrown him. Had she recognised him? Charles quickened his stride hoping to find her but there was no sign of the curly-haired girl.

♥ ♥ ♥

". . . and that's all for now. I'll phone you again tomorrow."

"Thanks Charles," Jane said. "I'm delighted we did so well, or at least, you did. It's a good idea to contact some of the girls from the secretarial agency. I have a couple in mind already."

Charles decided not to tell Jane that he'd bumped into Sasha or, to be exact, that she'd bumped into him. It would serve no purpose, probably upset her even more. He was relieved to hear that Justin had found a theatrical friend who'd be willing to advise Jane how to run the drama weekend. A professional director who adored his craft and was glad to help out, he'd enthusiastically volunteered to produce a play he'd written himself.

"A two act comedy that's light and fun," Mark Dunlop, the director, told Jane when they spoke. "At least you'll know in advance what you need in the way of costumes and props."

Charles was pleased that she'd found an alternative to the ebullient Sasha, and a pro at that. He suspected Jane still clung to the hope that she'd just reappear. He wished Jane would find someone else to live at the house, he didn't like to think of her there alone.

Charles bundled his washing into the laundry bag and put on his jacket. The car from the escort agency would be here in ten minutes.

♥ ♥ ♥

The Japanese couple were courtly but quiet. Communicating with them was difficult. The man spoke a little English but his wife just smiled benignly and inclined her head at regular intervals. Over dinner in the dimly-lit restaurant Charles tried to mark places of interest on their tourist map. He understood that they'd like to spend the following day with him, but he declined and suggested they contacted their embassy to find a guide who could speak Japanese. The man's face lightened, he bowed his understanding, thought that an excellent idea.

Charles's attention strayed from the couple, he was planning a different day for himself tomorrow. He'd made one appointment at lunch-time, another at five-thirty. But it was the hours in between that interested him most. Where else would Sasha be if not at the theatre? That's why she was in the area this afternoon. He doubted if she could have found a job so quickly, more likely she would be attending auditions. He almost whooped aloud when the thought struck him. Charles knew most of the cashiers in the theatres, he'd phone them or call in person and find out who was casting. Sasha was bound to have left her name and number.

Chapter Fifteen

Jane looked with dismay at the pastry cases cooling on the wire rack. *She* could do better than this, a lot better. Madge was thumping around the big living-room. Jane cringed as she heard the tinkle of breaking glass.

"Sorry Jane, I've broken this ornament. Still, not to worry, eh? It looked a bit tatty."

Jane eyed the precious crackle-glass vase that had been in her parents' home for as long as she could remember.

"Old doesn't mean tatty, Madge. It means memories, valuable, precious, irreplaceable memories." Jane pushed an escaped wisp of hair back into its wave. The action hid her anger.

Madge shrugged. To her it looked battered, she wouldn't give it house room.

Jane left the kitchen and went to her room. Madge was impossible. She had already broken the vacuum cleaner this week. That, she said, was due for an overhaul anyway. She claimed to be an expert cook but so far, everything was either overcooked or undercooked.

Why had Sasha run off like that? She could almost see the word in her head. *Why? Why? Why?*

"Stop it," she shouted at herself as she viciously tugged the sheet into place. She punched the duvet until it stood up in uneven lumps, then threw it on the bed. But no matter what, Madge must go. They had agreed she would work for a week and that ended today. She'd have to cope alone for now but it would be preferable.

She could hear the faint sound of the telephone. The answer machine would take up the call. She picked up Madge's wages and took a deep breath. "Better get it over with," she determined.

"Suit yourself." Madge shrugged. She threw her duster on the table half-covering the burnt pastry cases, collected her bag, and waving a cheery farewell, left Jane to the silence of the house.

"I'll place another advert in the newsagents and try again. In fact I'll do it now."

♥ ♥ ♥

The pond with its lapping water and quacking inhabitants soothed her mood. She smiled as the feathered flotilla glided towards her seeking their daily ration of bread. But today she'd forgotten their bread. Disdainfully they turned tail and gracefully swam away. I'm truly chastised, she smiled to herself again.

Mrs Reid was in her usual place behind the counter. Her son was stocking the shelves with the latest magazines.

"Good morning, my dear," she greeted Jane. "Oh my goodness, it's really afternoon, isn't it?"

Jane liked the friendly woman's air of confusion. Although Jane had never seen her leave her place at the till, Mrs Reid always seemed a little breathless, as if she'd been rushing.

"Hello, Mrs Reid. The day flies doesn't it?"

"I was just saying the same thing to my sister. She phoned a few minutes ago. Hasn't been too well, you know, she thinks she might be suffering from her *prostrate*."

Jane hid her amusement. Mrs Reid's malapropisms were legendary, now her biology had gone to hell too. The morning Justin and William visited the shop, Mrs Reid informed them that her niece had enrolled in *Condom Bleu* classes.

"I'll bet her cooking's a bit rubbery," Justin observed.

"I hope you get better news from your sister next time," Jane said politely. "I'd like to place another advertisement in your window if that's all right."

"Of course it is, dear. Madge didn't work out then?"

Jane was sure Mrs Reid knew all about her and everyone else in the small village. Jane placed her advertisement and a bar of chocolate on the counter. "That's it for now, thank you."

"Bye, bye dear. Better luck this time." Mrs Reid crossed two of her plump little fingers and gave Jane a dazzling smile.

Chapter Sixteen

The smell of fish and chips clung to everything. It oozed through the floorboards and seeped through the ill-fitting wardrobe doors. In an invisible trail, it skilfully avoided the wads of newspaper which protected the drawers and nested there defiantly. Sasha shut the window with a bang as the vent beneath it spewed oily particles into the airless night. She'd lingered in a cool bath for over an hour until her skin was pruney and wrinkled, but still the stale odour prevailed.

"Go away," she screamed at the top of her voice. "Get out, damn smell."

The misquote which would normally have amused her brought no more than a grimace to her lips. "Serves me right for bolting like that."

Sasha regretted her hasty flight, her idiotic reaction to the sight of Jane and Charles wrapped in each other's arms oblivious to all around them.

"But Jane knew how much I admired – no, that was too weak a word – loved Charles. She didn't even fancy him. The last thing in her mind, or so she led me to believe." She glared at her reflection in the mirror. The pitted glass remained impassive.

Sasha pulled a blouse from the jumble of clothes piled on the chair. She examined the collar and discarded the soiled garment in favour of a damp one she'd washed the night before. Holding it to her nose she could detect the inevitable odour. She had to find somewhere else to live, but first she must find work. Why had she squandered her money on those wigs? It hadn't cost her a thought at the time.

She tidied the bed with its worn blankets and shabby linen – a million miles from her cosy little room at The Willows with its downy duvet and thick padded curtains to match. Admittedly, there wasn't a lot of walking around space in the room compared to the larger bedrooms on the first floor, but it had everything she needed. For a moment she could almost smell the perfume of the pot pourri in its bowl on the painted chest of drawers, the crackle of dried petals which she stirred each morning with a delicate finger. She recollected the sweetness of the air whenever she opened her window, the scent of old roses which wafted from the garden and gently lingered on the flower-patterned bed. Sasha breathed in greedily. But there was nothing of her fantasy in the acrid fumes from the chip shop below.

♥ ♥ ♥

"Sorry, nothing for you."

"Nothing. Try late autumn. We'll be casting for 'Particles'."

Sasha was tired of hearing the word, no, tired of trailing from theatre to theatre. With a dejected air she looked around her, she was quite light-headed with hunger. She certainly couldn't afford West End prices, was there a McDonald's in the area or maybe a Burger King? She hoisted her bag high on her shoulder and bumped someone's arm.

"Sorry," she began to apologise as she came face to face with Charles. In blind panic she darted into the crowd and through the first open doorway she could find. Of all the people in the world she least wanted to meet, Charles headed the list. Had he recognised her? Possibly the blonde curly wig had thrown him. In the din of the traffic she thought she heard him calling her name. From her vantage point in the shadow of the window she watched him stop, search the street with a worried look, then shrug. Sasha released the air from her lungs as if holding her breath made her invisible.

She wandered blindly through the unfamiliar side streets until the smell of food halted her. The façade of the restaurant was narrow, its windows of black smoked-glass neatly lettered with the name "Damoni." She opened the door tentatively and looked for some clue as to whether or not it was too pricey. Maybe she could order just a pasta dish.

"Ah! Signorina, you've come about the job, no?"

"I came . . . about the job . . . yes, the job." Sasha's nimble brain sprang to her aid. What could it entail? Washing-up, waiting on tables?

"You can start immediately?"

"I haven't had lunch yet, but then I could start."

The man pursed his lips, then shook his head

and informed her she was much too thin. "But that is no problem here, we have the finest Italian food outside of Italy."

She took no offence at his criticism.

"Come, come, sit here." He pulled a chair from the table and flicked it with a cursory swipe of his white cloth.

There was nothing sleazy about him or the gleaming tablecloth on the neatly set table.

"What would you like to eat? Some pasta? Veal? Leave it to me, you sit."

Sasha sank gratefully on to the chair. What if Charles followed her? He couldn't have, he must be long gone. What would she have said to him? "I left because I was jealous, because you kissed Jane instead of me, because I loved you – she didn't." Sasha's cheeks flushed with colour at her own stupidity. God, it sounded pathetic. And Jane, how was she coping? She thought of her often and of how she'd left her to face the coming weeks alone. Her colour deepened even more. How was it possible to be so furious with someone and yet so concerned?

"These girls." The woman sighed, peeping at Sasha's forlorn figure through the louvres of the door which separated the kitchen from the dining area. "They come to London with such high hopes and end up here waiting on tables. And then they go. But all are too thin, too desperate."

Her husband nodded in silent agreement as he scooped a portion of spaghetti from the huge pan. He added two generous ladles of his renowned meat sauce to the wide soup dish, wiped away a slight smear from its rim and pushed through the door with his elbow.

Carefully he placed the steaming dish on the table and flipped open the lid of a bowl of finely grated parmesan cheese. "Eat, child, we'll talk in a minute."

Sasha wolfed down the delicious pasta. It seemed like forever since she'd had a decent meal.

"Buono?" He smiled at her tomato-stained chin.

"Molto buono," Sasha replied and hoped that was the correct way to say it.

"So tell me, what brings you to London and to us?"

Sasha was nonplussed for a moment. How was she supposed to have known about the job and, worse still, what would happen if the real applicant showed up?

"Wait," Signor Damoni said, "Let me get you the rest of your meal."

Thankful for the delay, Sasha searched for an answer to his question.

"Okay-dokey, here we are. My famous veal."

Sasha smiled her thanks and cut the paper-thin escalope. "No wonder you're famous," she flattered. "This is the best Milanese I've ever tasted."

"Not me, I'm not famous." Signor Damoni beamed nonetheless. Sasha poured another glass of sparkling water and slowed her eating pace.

"Well, you should be," she insisted.

He clicked his tongue and thanked her. "So, now you've seen the restaurant? You like it? There is a waiter, Gio, and there are eleven tables to look after. If you are not busy, you help each other. No union here, just me and my wife, we are the union." He chuckled at his own joke.

"What are the hours?" Sasha asked as she savoured the last piece of sautéed potato.

"Eleven o'clock until . . . about three, then five-thirty till midnight. Earlier if we are not busy, a little later perhaps if we are." He paused to allow her to consider the times.

"Do you live near here? Will you be OK to get home at night?" He frowned.

"I'm not too far away. I'll be fine at night, don't worry."

"We pay at the end of the week. So if you leave during the week without warning, no pay I'm afraid, you understand?" Signor Damoni looked faintly embarrassed. But the pay was good and there were tips too, he explained. They would be shared between Gio and herself.

"That's fair," Sasha said.

"You can eat here every day if you like, no charge of course."

Giuseppe Damoni stole a glance at the girl. She was fresh-faced, clean and tidy and, despite her bony appearance, probably energetic and tough. The skinny ones usually were. He and his wife Maria had no children. A quirk of nature. She used to cry about her barren state. But her life was busy and the crying bouts were rare, especially now that she was getting on a bit. The restaurant and its clients were their children. Damoni's attracted its share of tourists but their customers were mainly regulars, returning again and again for a pasta-fix or a top-up of their favourite dishes. He too regretted they hadn't been blessed with a family but accepted their fate philosophically.

Sasha gathered up her plates and followed Giuseppe Damoni to the kitchen to meet his wife. Maria was as pleasant as her husband. She asked solicitously if Sasha had enjoyed her meal.

"I adored it," Sasha said fervently.

Between them the couple talked her through the restaurant's routine.

"I'll have no difficulty with that," she assured them.

There was little for her to do before the evening meal, the tables were ready. She promised to return at five sharp. "I'll let myself out. Thank you for the lovely lunch. See you later."

She stopped a couple of times on her way to the door to familiarise herself with the layout of the room and examine the contents of the two serving tables. As she opened the door she almost collided with a girl clutching a piece of paper. Sasha looked around to make sure they couldn't be seen and closed the door behind her. "Can I help you?" she asked in a businesslike manner.

"I'm late, I'm afraid. The job, is it still vacant?"

"Oh dear," Sasha frowned. "I'm sorry, we've hired someone else. We thought you'd changed your mind."

The girl's face didn't change, no crumpled features, no tears.

"I'm sorry to disappoint you." Sasha wished she would leave the doorway.

"It's OK," she shrugged. "Plenty more waitressing jobs around. See you."

Chapter Seventeen

Kim Barrett woke with a start. The little quartz timepiece beside her bed was silent, the noise she could hear was the sound of her biological clock ticking away. She had plenty of time to get ready for the flight, it was only six-thirty. She could allow herself another ten minutes before she got out of bed. Kim glanced at the navy uniform with its brass buttons hanging on the wardrobe door. She liked the new wide-brimmed hat and the brightly patterned red, navy and white blouse.

Kim switched on the light in the kitchen. She preferred summer mornings when, even at this hour, sun streamed through the window. Kim pulled a face, the grapefruit was sour today. She sat at the little table with its gaily coloured cloth and forced herself to eat the bitter fruit, then she picked up her coffee and took it with her into the bathroom. Almost without thinking, she began her daily routine. Her make-up and creams were neatly laid out on the dressing-table beside the big magnifying mirror. She cleansed her skin then applied a massage cream.

". . . eighteen . . . nineteen . . . twenty. There, that's done thank goodness."

She examined her skin in the light over the mirror. Nothing disastrous had happened in the night, no wrinkles had appeared, no sagging chin.

"Another day's grace," she thought with satisfaction.

Wrapped in a big towel, she blow-dried her black, silky hair. She was pleased with the cut this time. Samantha liked it so much she'd made an appointment for the following week to have her own curls cut. Kim smiled with affection as she thought of her friend. Samantha copied most things she did.

"How come you don't look like a rag-bag at the end of the day," Samantha often grumbled.

"What are you talking about, Sam? You always look terrific," Kim assured her.

"Not like you," Samantha sighed. "And that fabulous skin! Have you changed your make-up?" she demanded.

"No, it's still the same old stuff." They'd had this conversation many times.

As far as looks were concerned they were chalk and cheese, Samantha petite and blonde, herself tall and dark. Her eyes were almost black-brown, Samantha's, a golden amber. Even their complexions were totally different, Sam was always lightly tanned, while her own skin remained creamy white.

Kim dried the long, straight strands and they fell into a curve on her neck. Yes, she liked this bob, longer on one side than the other. It made her face look a little fuller too. She hooked the last hank of hair over the brush and gave it a short blast with the drier. The wave fell into place.

She glanced at her watch, still plenty of time. She'd change at Heathrow today. Kim opened her wardrobe and selected a pair of scarlet leggings and a long, black sweater. She'd be embarrassed if anyone looked in this cupboard. Clothes were her weakness, so too were the accessories that went with them. From the time she was a teenager she knew exactly what suited her and she'd become an expert shopper. All her friends said she had terrific flair. She was convinced that this was a hang-up from her schooldays when her classmates were nasty about the skirts she wore – they were usually far too short for her growing schoolgirl figure. They sneered because her cardigans had darns in the sleeves. But her mother had done her best, better than her best. Kim was only a baby when her mother was left to cope alone. They muddled along from month to month, year to year. She'd been a happy little girl and adored her harassed mother. The only thing she hated were the men who came to visit her mother and to take her out. They didn't seem to make her mother happy either. One of them even hit her. Kim was hysterical with fright and ran out of the house to call a neighbour. By the time she'd sobbed out her story and she'd dragged their neighbour back to the house the man had gone. Her poor mother, she always seemed to choose the wrong person – until Bill came into their lives. Kim liked him from the start. He was kind and funny, always bringing chocolates or a posy of flowers for her mother. There were presents for her too. She still had the beautiful scarf he'd given her on her fourteenth birthday.

"How would you like to go to a wedding?" Bill asked her one day.

Kim looked at their smiling faces. Without being told, she knew whose wedding it would be.

As she stood holding her mother's bouquet, she silently thanked God for bringing Bill into their lives. Kim vowed that, unless she found someone just like him, she would *never* get married. No man would ever push her around or make her unhappy. Her husband would be perfect.

But Kim hadn't found the perfect man. She'd thought a lot about marriage and children lately. She was thirty-five now, but there was still time.

Kim blotted her lipstick and checked to see that she hadn't smeared it on her teeth. She was always threatening to have that eye-tooth straightened.

She threw a long black jacket over her sweater and gave herself a final inspection in the mirror. "Definitely today's woman. Thank heavens that grunge look is dead," she reflected.

♥ ♥ ♥

Today's passenger list had its usual smattering of celebrities. Quickly she scanned it for familiar names.

"One royalty, one pop star, one ambassador," Samantha read aloud.

"Who's the royal?" Kim asked.

"Princess Amine."

"She must have absconded from the health farm again."

The princess was a plump, pretty young girl who seemed to divide her time between English health farms, New York and her home. She looked older than her seventeen years and always travelled with a bodyguard. His eyes rarely left her and sometimes the flight attendants found his vigilance unnerving.

"I quite fancy Phil Bolger." Samantha scanned the list again. Phil Bolger was a regular passenger, good humoured and fun. Samantha usually found someone to bat her eyelashes at on the flight. She claimed it focused her mind.

The briefing drew to a close and the cabin crew gathered their bags before making their way to the aircraft.

The pencil-slim white aeroplane perched on the runway was fuelled and ready for its crew and passengers. Kim loved working on Concorde. The journeys were so much shorter and passengers were rarely troublesome. Sometimes they objected a little if the meal they'd requested wasn't available, but more often than not this was merely a nervous reaction. In Kim's experience there were very few complaints. They'd been trained to deal with any problems courteously and efficiently.

While the passengers sat in the opulent Concorde lounge and enjoyed their canapés and champagne, the cabin crew stowed the travellers' coats and hand baggage in the wardrobes on the aircraft. Princess Amine didn't believe in travelling light, her dress bags with their royal crests always weighed a ton. "Goodness knows what her suitcases must be like," Samantha groaned.

Kim and Samantha were working in the front

cabin today with the service director. They checked the drinks, uncorked the vintage wines and filled the ice buckets. Samantha passed the menus to Kim. "Ready to check the meals?" she asked.

"Canapés, appetisers." Kim counted the number of portions.

"Mains?"

"OK."

"Vegetarian?"

"Yes, all there."

"Cheeses?"

"Yep,"

"And desserts? What's on today?" Samantha's slim figure belied her love of everything sweet.

"Citrus Mousse with yoghurt and a lemon balm syrup." Kim closed the menu.

"That's definitely for me. No special meals?"

"No, none."

The flight wasn't full, just sixty-three of the available hundred seats were booked. It was strange how many people asked if there was a difference between the two cabins. But apart from the division of seating – forty in the front, sixty in the rear – they were both the same.

"Where's His Excellency sitting?" Samantha asked.

"The ambassador?"

"No," Samantha laughed. "Paul Dean."

The pop star with his rat-tailed, gelled hair was a familiar sight on television these days. He was a threatening figure with his malevolent scowls, aggressive movements and off-beat music.

"Let's hope he behaves better here than he does on telly. Each time I've seen him he looks so spaced-out you'd wonder why he needs a plane to fly him anywhere." Kim frowned.

"Maybe he hopes to link up with the mother-ship!" Samantha spread her arms wide and swayed along the narrow aisle to the cockpit as if she was flying.

Derek Martin and his flight crew were settling into the cockpit.

"I'll pop along and see if they want anything," Samantha said.

Kim finished her chores and used the few spare minutes to brush her hair and freshen her make-up. The black-brown eyes in her compact mirror were bright. "I wonder if I should change the colour of my mascara? Maybe brown instead of black?" she wondered. Her ruminations came to a halt as the first of the passengers entered the pale grey interior of the aircraft.

"Good morning, sir. Good morning, madam. Welcome aboard, Your Highness," she greeted them, smiling.

A tall, lean figure paused for a moment in the doorway as if deciding whether or not to turn tail and run.

"Good morning, sir, welcome on board." Kim recognised his face but couldn't put a name to it.

She watched as the man settled himself in his seat then glanced at the seating list. "Good Lord! It's Paul Dean," she said under her breath. The frightened blue eyes sought her own. Kim made her way to his seat and asked if he was comfortable.

"It's the first time I've ever flown – I'm a bit nervous I suppose."

Kim made soothing noises. She was astonished

at the difference between the man and the performer. His shoulder-length brown hair was neatly combed and shone healthily. His clothes were plain but expensive, a total contrast to the stereotype pop star image he'd created for himself. The voice didn't roar from his chest as it did on his videos, but was low and melodious.

"I'll be back a bit later to see how you're doing. Sit back and relax, there's nothing to be scared of. Just wait until you see the colour of the sky when we've reached our altitude. I bet you'll want to write a song about it."

"Thank you, I'll try," he said pathetically.

The cabin crew buckled themselves into their seats for take-off. The sleek, white dart, with its lowered nose, raced along the runway and soared effortlessly into the air. They wouldn't reach supersonic speed until they were out over the sea. Passengers were frequently amazed that this beautiful, two-hundred-and-four-foot streamlined aircraft, due to the heating of its air frame, stretched a further ten feet during supersonic flight. They loved to watch the Mach counter on the bulkhead reeling its way through the numbers until the big *2* was visible.

"What did you do at the weekend?" Samantha asked Kim, as the plane continued to climb.

"Tidied the flat mostly, sorted through a load of papers. I've been threatening to do that for ages. I hadn't read half the magazines I've hoarded so I finished those and was glad to get rid of the clutter. The flat looks positively respectable again." Kim took great pride in her compact flat. For years she'd been frugal in her spending, except of course for her clothes. Those long-haul flights, the overnight stays abroad, helped her to cut down on her expenses. It shouldn't be too long now before she could afford the deposit for a flat of her own.

Kim uncovered the appetisers – paupiette of smoked Scottish salmon filled with crab and avocado – and placed them on the linen-covered trays. They worked quickly. Kim wheeled the neat trolley down the narrow aisle and handed each passenger a tray. Samantha followed with the drinks. Paul Dean waved his food away but Kim coaxed him. "At least pick at it, it'll pass the time."

When she removed his plate later it was empty.

Today the rosettes of lamb with wild mushroom sauce were more popular than the grilled fish combination. Several passengers opted for the vegetarian meal. The crisp filo pastry roulade with celeriac and morel would be my choice, Kim thought. She'd see how she felt later.

Leaving Sam to fill the crystal glasses, Kim made her way to the cockpit with the meals for the flight crew. To avoid the danger of food poisoning, the captain and his first officer ordered different meals. The flight engineer could have his choice. Kim smiled as the captain good-naturedly tossed a coin. "Heads I get lamb, tails you get fish." She'd been through this routine before. "Tails it is. You get fish," he laughed.

"Hand over the lamb, Kim, he lost." Mike Shea jerked his thumb in the pilot's direction.

"Fish is better for you anyway." Derek Martin resignedly reached for the tray.

Kim stopped to have a word with Paul Dean. A couple of glasses of Krug champagne had relaxed him and now he appeared to be at ease and enjoying the flight.

"You were right about the sky. It's indigo – fantastic. I haven't found a song yet, but I'm working on it." He grinned engagingly.

"I'll listen out for it. See that line?" Kim bent down beside him and pointed through the tiny window. "We're flying at sixty thousand feet and what you can see is the curvature of the earth."

"How fast are we flying?"

"About thirteen hundred and fifty miles an hour. That's what the Mach Two counter means – twice the speed of sound. Outside, the skin of the aircraft will be quite hot."

"It's certainly a brilliant experience, mind you the champagne didn't hurt," he admitted.

"It's always a little scary at first, you don't know what to expect. But just think. When we land in New York, the jumbo that took off a couple of minutes before us will only be half-way across the Atlantic."

"How long is the flight?"

"Three hours and twenty-five minutes approximately. You'll arrive in New York at least an hour before you left!"

"May I give you this? I mean, if you'd like it," Paul said as he opened the small bag on the empty seat beside him.

Kim looked at the CD he'd handed her. On it he had written her name, his thanks and his autograph.

"I'm thrilled to have it. Thank you very much, I'll look forward to playing it when I get home." Kim meant it, his television image long faded from her mind.

On her way back along the aisle, a girl of about seventeen caught her sleeve. She lowered the sound on her inflight, state-of-the-art audio system. "Isn't that Paul Dean," she asked eagerly.

"Yes, that's right."

"Do you think he'd give me his autograph? Would you get it for me?" The girl eyed the CD in Kim's hand enviously.

"Hold this for me, I'll ask him."

Kim returned a minute later empty-handed. The girl's face fell.

"He'd be delighted to meet you. There's an empty seat beside him. Why don't you go back and he'll sign a CD for you too?"

Shyly the youngster made her way towards her idol and in a few minutes they were chatting like old friends.

Samantha was talking to the Princess and the service director was explaining US time zones to a woman who'd never left London before.

This was the quietest time on the flight for the cabin crew. Once they'd finished their meals the passengers usually settled down to read or talk to each other. There were days when Concorde was like a club. The two bars – one for cold drinks, the other for liquor and wines – either side of the aisle, were meeting places for those who wanted to stretch their legs. People who flew the route regularly became friendly. Movie stars discussed the film world and diplomats exchanged pleasantries. Today another one of those friendships were being forged. Paul Dean and the pretty teenager, their heads together, stared through the window talking nineteen to the dozen.

Kim stooped slightly as she walked through the short passage they called "the tunnel" towards the cockpit. "Get you anything else?" she asked as she gathered the crew's trays.

"I wouldn't mind another Coke," the pilot said.

"Mike?"

"Oh, go on then, I'll have a mineral water please."

"She really is a looker," Mike Shea said when Kim left the cabin.

"Yes," the pilot agreed. "But there's always a don't-touch air about her."

Derek Martin turned his attention back to his crossword while Mike Shea scanned the instruments.

Kim unwrapped her meal. She took a roll from the bread-warming cupboard, cut a small piece of cheese and poured herself some coffee. She slipped off her shoes and settled down to eat. As she chewed the roll she flicked through a magazine. The light above her head flashed several times. She popped her head round the galley and saw Samantha waving a napkin in her direction. Kim grabbed a handful of tissues and a cloth. She left the galley then turned back as she realised she had forgotten to put on her shoes.

"I've put the passenger in 5C," Samantha said as she mopped the coffee-spattered seat. The woman in seat 5D who'd spilt the coffee made vague noises of apology. They could see that her eyes were champagne-glazed. Samantha reassured her there was no damage done and Kim returned to finish her lunch.

Chapter Eighteen

"There's a snowstorm forecast for New York." Mike Shea grimaced as Kim brought their drinks. "We'll get in to Kennedy, OK, but I hope we get out on time tomorrow. I have a heavy date."

Their aircraft was the last to land before the airport shut down. The journey into Manhattan was treacherous and Kim was grateful to sink into a hot tub. She and Samantha spent their time playing Scrabble then watched television for a while. It was still snowing heavily as Kim closed the curtains to make the room cosier.

"What do you want to do about dinner," she asked.

"I'm lazy," Samantha said. "I think I'll stay put and order something here in the room, wallow in a weepy on the box. Join me?"

"I don't think so, I'll eat in one of the hotel restaurants tonight. I'm certainly not going out in this weather."

Kim took her time. She washed and dried her hair, applied some light make-up, then put on a red, fine-wool dress that she'd bought on her last visit to the States. She fastened a wide leather belt around her neat waist and threw a matching grey and red shawl over one shoulder.

"See you later," she said as she nimbly skipped aside to allow the room service waiter to deliver Samantha's meal.

"Hello!" the man at the next table said.

Kim gave him a frosty look.

"Kim, isn't it?"

Her hand instinctively reached for her name badge. It was still on her uniform jacket in the bedroom. Kim was used to strangers trying to strike up a conversation with her. But this man knew her name. Besides, he had a nice face and a ready smile.

"Alex Travis. Concorde, earlier?" The man looked uncomfortable, as though he regretted having spoken to her.

"Yes, that's right." Kim frowned trying to remember him.

"I was beside the woman who decorated her suit with coffee."

"Oh my goodness, of course! Forgive me. What a mess that was."

"She was so far gone by that stage she hardly noticed."

The woman had drunk at least six glasses of champagne. This was the passenger that Samantha had moved to a dry seat a couple of rows behind.

"Did you avoid the deluge?"

"Sure – an odd splash or two, nothing the dry-cleaners can't fix."

"You must let the airline know, they'll refund your cleaning bill."

Alex Travis dismissed her suggestion. "There's no need. I always end up crumpled after a flight anyway."

Kim looked at his immaculate jacket; she couldn't imagine anything he wore would look creased.

"May I join you, or are you fed up being pleasant to strangers? Say no if you're tired, I won't be offended. You're off-duty now."

"I don't mind, join me if you like. Judging by the weather report we're not going to get out of New York till lunch-time tomorrow at the earliest. I'll have plenty of time to rest."

Alex Travis moved easily for such a tall, broad-shouldered man. He stooped to put his book on the floor and returned his glasses to their case.

"I gather New York isn't your final destination?" Kim said.

"I'm supposed to be in Seattle tonight." He smiled. "But without skis it could be difficult. To be truthful, I'm delighted with the delay, it's been a bit hectic lately."

"It's nice to sneak a bit of hidden time here and there," Kim agreed.

"Do you always fly Concorde?" Alex concentrated on cutting his steak.

"Yes, now I do. I graduated from short-haul to the jumbo and then Concorde."

"It never ceases to amaze me, where do those extra supersonic hours we save go to? I can't work it out. But then I haven't come to terms with the radio yet." His green eyes twinkled with humour.

"I haven't worked that one out either."

"This wine isn't nearly as good as the one I had on the plane." Alex wrinkled his nose as the sharp liquid caught his throat.

"They are lovely wines, aren't they?" Kim wondered if she should tap him on his back.

Alex sipped a drop of water and his voice returned to normal. "I'm sorry now I refused more than one glass of wine on the flight."

"You might as well have, any open bottles of wine are emptied away. Customs regulations."

"You mean poured down the sink?"

"They used to be, but that caused a red streak along the underside of the aircraft so now we flush them down the toilets, they're sealed units." Kim laughed as he looked at her askance.

"What sacrilege, what a waste. I'll definitely increase my intake next time."

"I haven't seen you on a flight before. Do you travel a lot?"

"A fair bit recently. I'm on a lecture tour. I've taken a sabbatical for a year."

"That sounds exciting. What's your subject?"

"I'm an international investment consultant."

"Not one of my problems."

"Maybe I should give you my card, you never know!"

"When I reach that stage, I'll take it. You're lucky that your firm doesn't mind you taking time off to flit about the world like that."

"They probably do but they can't argue. I'm their boss. I promised myself I would do this globe-trotting bit *before* I reach the big 'four-o'."

"Pecan pie, please." Alex looked up with a guilty smile. "I shouldn't but I love it."

"Not for me." Kim shook her head.

"Coffee?" the waiter asked.

"Regular," Kim decided.

"Cappuccino for me." For a moment they sat in silence. She wondered if he was married and tried to imagine what his wife would be like.

"When would you normally leave New York – weather permitting?"

Kim gave him a rough idea of her schedule.

"I was surprised when I saw the interior of Concorde. It's smaller than I'd imagined," Alex mused.

"I suppose if you compare it to the wide-bodied jets, it is," Kim agreed as she thought of the cabin with its rows of grey leather and fabric seats divided by the narrow aisle. She knew that, in spite of the longer journey, some people preferred the roomier first-class seating on the jumbo. "They've made several changes to the aircraft recently. The seats for instance. The backs are taller, sculptured to give better back support, and the new head rests are more comfortable. There's extra space for carry-on baggage; brief cases and flight bags. The cabin crew haven't been forgotten either, we have new ovens and more space in the galleys."

"One of my business associates who uses Concorde frequently said that he wouldn't travel any other way."

"We do have a lot of regulars. One of our business passengers made the return journey at least sixty-eight times in one year."

"Do you *enjoy* flying?" Alex asked.

"Yes, I suppose I do." Kim frowned. "I enjoy the travelling and it's a wonderful opportunity to see so many places I'd never get to in the ordinary way."

"I'm sure it's exciting. I wish I had more time to spend in the places I visit. More often than not a car meets me and whisks me off to my lecture.

There's usually a lunch or dinner, a chat with the people involved and then back to the airport."

"You'll have to allow yourself an extra day for sightseeing, it's amazing how much you can see in a day."

"You're right and I suppose the business *can* survive without me, but I'm away so much . . ."

He must be married, Kim judged.

"But I really should take your advice, there's nothing to tie me."

Wrong, he's not married.

"Shall we have a look and see how the storm's doing?"

Kim placed her credit card on the table.

"Let me take the check," Alex said.

"No, thank you, really. We have an allowance."

They walked through the lobby to the front door.

"Do you feel like braving a quick trip outside?" Alex peered through the glass. "It's still snowing."

"A very quick trip," she agreed.

Kim wrapped her shawl around her. Alex pushed the revolving door gently. An icy wind cut through them like a knife. The snow huddled against the side of the building as if seeking protection from the cold. The street, dominated by skyscrapers, was almost deserted.

"Not quick enough," Kim laughed rubbing her arms as she rushed back inside.

"Dumb idea, I'm sorry."

"I'm a big girl, I could have said no!"

"Would you like a hot toddy at the bar?"

"If you don't mind, I think I'll call it a night. I hope you get to Seattle safely tomorrow."

"I've enjoyed meeting you. Thanks for making

what could have been a miserable evening so enjoyable."

"You were a long time." Samantha, surrounded by the debris of her meal, was munching a bar of chocolate.

Kim smiled at her friend, "Do you *ever* stop eating?"

"So why did it take you so long to stuff *your* face?"

"I met one of the passengers in the restaurant. Alex . . . Alex Travis, he was sitting beside that woman who spilt the coffee, you moved him to another seat."

"Oh yes, he was quite dishy."

"You think everyone's dishy."

"So then?"

"He was at the next table and he recognised me, remembered my name."

Samantha glanced at Kim's dress. She wasn't wearing her badge.

"Go on. This is like drawing teeth – tell me more."

"There's nothing to tell. I think I did most of the talking. He's an investment consultant, owns his own firm and has taken a year off to do a lecture tour."

"Married?" Samantha's eyes sparkled with mischief.

"Honestly, Sam! I didn't ask him and he didn't say."

"I can't send you anywhere, you're useless."

"And you, have you enjoyed your evening?"

"Not really. The adverts on television drive me mad. Come back BBC all is forgiven!"

"You should have come downstairs and eaten with me."

"And ruined your little romance?"

"You're impossible. Can't I have dinner with a man, a stranger, without you making a big deal of it?"

"Moi?"

"I'm going to get undressed, maybe by the time I get back you'll have unscrambled that brain of yours."

♥ ♥ ♥

When they woke next morning, Samantha switched on the television. It had snowed steadily through the night. "We won't be going anywhere this morning," Samantha moaned as she watched the weather forecaster imparting the bad news.

"Doesn't look too good, does it?"

"Let's get up anyway. I'll phone the airport."

The coffee shop was busy but they only had to wait for a few minutes to be seated.

"Orange juice. Waffles, bacon, two fried eggs – over easy and maple syrup please."

Kim grinned at her friend.

"What?" Sam asked.

"Nothing. I'll have orange juice, a poached egg and some wheat toast."

"Coffee?" The waitress tore the order off her pad, stuck her pencil behind her ear and the book in her pocket.

"Those people over there, they were on the flight yesterday." Sam craned her neck to look around the rest of the room. "And the people at that table too. I wonder where your boyfriend is?"

"He's *not* my boyfriend."

The waitress returned almost immediately and filled their mugs with steaming coffee.

"I love this custom, don't you? Often when I'm at home, I long for one of those gorgeous big mugs of coffee. It never tastes the same when I make it. That looks great." Sam smiled at the waitress as she eyed the overflowing plate.

"You snowed in for the day?" the waitress asked.

"Probably. Still, how bad?" Kim laughed.

"It's been a crummy winter so far, worst we've had for a long time. Can I get you anything more?"

"I might do this again," Sam said for Kim's benefit.

"You do and it's on the house," the waitress promised looking at Samantha's slim figure.

"She could," Kim assured her.

"I give up," Samantha gasped as she replaced her knife and fork on the empty plate.

"There's Alex Travis," Kim exclaimed. She wouldn't admit it but she'd been watching the door.

"He's *gorgeous.*" Samantha's eyes widened. "How did I allow him to escape?"

"Hardly gorgeous, quite handsome I suppose."

"Ask him to join us," Samantha suggested.

"Leave him alone, he may want to have breakfast in peace."

The manager led the tall American across the room towards the empty table beside them.

"Kim! Hi!" Alex seemed to tower over them. "Looks like we're stuck here for the duration."

"The forecast's not too hectic, is it? You remember Samantha?" Kim asked.

"Yes of course. Thanks for rescuing me yesterday."

"My pleasure. Are you having breakfast?" Sam asked.

"Yes."

"Why don't you join us? Kim has just ordered more coffee," Sam lied.

"I'd love to. Are you on rescue duty again?"

"Something like that."

Kim glared at her friend. Samantha smiled innocently in return.

"Thank heavens I remembered to pack the cards," Samantha said. "They're a must in winter."

"What do you play?" Alex asked.

"All the Ps, patience, pinochle and poker. Do you fancy a game?"

"Don't play poker with her," Kim warned. "She cheats."

"Kim! I don't."

"Yes you do. Especially if we play for chocolate bars."

"That's different!"

"I'm willing to pit my wits against all comers," Alex said wiping his mouth on his napkin.

"I'll hop upstairs and warm up the deck." Samantha rubbed her hands together. "I'm sure the room will have been cleaned by now."

"We can use my suite if you like. Not my idea – the suite – my hosts arranged it last night when they heard I was marooned." Alex's tone was apologetic.

"Fine by me. Kim?"

"Sure. What will we use as poker chips?"

"I'll buy some *M & M's* from the shop in the

lobby," Alex volunteered. "Never let it be said that I don't do things in style."

"Mine I think," Alex laid his cards down on the table and scooped the pile of sugar-coated sweets towards him.

"That's the last time I play poker with a pro," Samantha grumbled, making a grab for a handful of the coloured *M & M's* which she popped into her mouth.

"What games of patience do you play?" Alex asked slapping her hand playfully as she reached out for more.

Alex taught them a new and complicated game of solitaire. Despite their meal allowances, Alex insisted on buying lunch which they ate at the table in the window of the living-room.

"Just look at that snow. It's so pure, beautiful as it floats to the ground, then it becomes nothing more than a load of dirty tyre tracks and slushy grey ice." Kim shivered in the heat of the room.

"Do you ski?" Alex asked them.

"Not me," Kim replied.

"Nor me," Samantha shook her head.

"Skiing – the ultimate in snow." Alex's eyes had a faraway look. "Miles of unbroken white landscape, mountains of pure, shimmering crystals broken only by small craggy trees and the occasional treacherous rock, skies so incredibly blue they make your heart ache. I loved skiing. We rarely missed a year in Aspen."

"Don't you still ski?" Kim could picture his powerful figure speeding down the slopes, those green eyes hidden behind his dark snow-goggles.

"We gave it up when my wife became . . . sick."

The girls glanced at each other. Kim's ferocious stare silenced the question that sprang to Samantha's lips.

"I need to make a call to my mother," Samantha yawned. "I'll do it from the room. Thanks for a lovely day, Alex, even if you did bankrupt my blood sugar supplies."

Alex rose from his chair and looked out of the hotel window. "At the risk of losing your toes, do you feel brave enough to venture outside for some fresh air?" he asked Kim. He walked back to the coffee table in the middle of the room. Patiently he scooped the colourful poker chips back into their boxes. He handed them to Kim. "A peace offering for Samantha."

Luxurious though the room was, Alex's big frame appeared to dwarf the chairs and the three-seater sofa. Kim sensed his restlessness in this over-heated, silk-cushioned prison. Was his furniture at home larger than average, his bed longer, the ceilings higher?

The wind had dropped but it was still bitterly cold. The sidewalks were icy in patches. "Hang onto me," said Alex and tucked her hand through his arm.

They slipped and slithered for almost a block, their faces half-hidden behind thick woollen scarves. She could feel the warmth of his body as she huddled closer to him. Kim laughed as the large white flakes tickled her nose.

"I've never seen Manhattan streets so empty. It's like a ghost town." She shivered. Kim was no stranger to New York. She'd stayed in this city more times than she could count. She was familiar with every change of season, every type of weather. The towering buildings were awesome as their upper storeys reached for light in the gloom of the January afternoon. It was unusual to see them dark and unlit.

"Strange how the buildings affect our life. In winter they protect us from the air but in summer they deprive of us of it." Alex turned his eyes skywards.

"Where is home for you?" she asked.

"Washington, DC. But I'm often in New York, we have a branch here."

Kim tightened the belt of her warm coat and sank her face deeper into the scarf. Her eyes smarted from the cold. As they reached the corner, the snow whirled and danced around them in a gusting froth.

"You're trembling, let's turn back," Alex hugged her arm even more firmly against his body. "I forget not everyone's as impervious to the cold as I am."

The bar was almost empty. A couple with glum faces sat at a table nursing their drinks. Kim's face was glowing from the walk. Alex asked her what she'd like to drink and, when she hesitated, the barman suggested a hot whisky to ward off the cold. Kim wrapped her two hands around the napkin which protected them from the scalding hot toddy.

"This makes it all worth while," she said her teeth still chattering a little.

"I hope you haven't caught cold."

"I'll survive. I'm tougher than I look."

Alex blew on the hot liquid. How attractive Kim was – her cheeks rosy from the cold air, her eyes sparkling. What sort of life did she lead? He imagined her phone would always be busy although her unsociable working hours must be a problem at times. All those stories of mad romps with pilots didn't seem to fit her image. He could hardly ask if they were true.

"I didn't see any of the flight crew around the hotel," Alex probed.

"They stay at a different hotel."

"So those stories aren't true?"

"What stories?" Kim's tone was icy.

You clumsy fool, how could you? He was furious with himself. "I'm sorry, I can't believe I said that."

He looked so contrite that she hadn't the heart to make him suffer.

"I suppose I'd better go and see what Sam's up to."

"Don't go, it's early. At least let me make up for being such a jerk."

"Forget it. You're not the first to think we lead a steamy life and you won't be the last."

"I expect to be in London in about six weeks, can I call you?"

"I never know too far in advance what my plans will be."

"If I called a few days before I arrive. . ." His tone was almost pleading.

Kim wrote her number on the cocktail napkin. Alex folded it carefully and slipped it into his wallet.

"I must go now or Sam will be wondering what I'm up to. Actually, she'll already have made up her mind what I'm up to." The twinkle returned to Kim's eyes.

"Would you and Samantha have dinner with me tonight?"

"I'm sorry, we've arranged to eat with the rest of the cabin crew. We've hardly seen them since we arrived."

♥ ♥ ♥

The six members of the cabin crew waited in the lobby for the mini-bus that would take them to Kennedy Airport.

Kim looked about her and wondered if Alex had left the hotel. She'd found it difficult to concentrate at dinner last night, to give her full attention to what her friends were saying. Alex avoided their table and chose to sit across the room with his back to them. Her eyes strayed several times to his superbly-tailored broad shoulders, and the wavy reddish-brown head bent over his book as he ate. She blushed when Samantha knocked on the bathroom door earlier and shouted, "Lover boy for you!"

"I'm leaving shortly and just wanted to say goodbye," Alex said.

"Have a good trip." Kim waved Samantha away, but she stood her ground, eavesdropping unashamedly.

"I will. I'll call you before I get to London," he promised.

"He's smitten," Samantha pronounced.

"He's married," Kim retorted.

♥ ♥ ♥

The two girls worked on the same flight

whenever possible and enjoyed being together. Samantha would like to have shared a flat but Kim enjoyed her privacy.

She often teased Kim about being cool to the male passengers. It was true, Kim didn't encourage them. She didn't want to get involved. And Samantha, in spite of her bravado and flirtatious manner, was wary about men. More than once Kim had heard her bluntly ask a man if he was married.

Kim was content to go out with Hadley Talbot. When they first met she thought that they could be right for each other. But after a couple of unexciting days and nights in a small hotel in the Lake District, Kim knew that Hadley could never be more than a friend. If he was disappointed he'd hidden it well. They'd been seeing each other on and off for three years now. It was a comfortable arrangement – for her. Not exciting, not stimulating . . . companionable. Why she had given Alex Travis her phone number, she didn't know.

Chapter Nineteen

Jane Anderson manoeuvred the car through the traffic-congested streets and stopped at the entrance to the car park. There was only one car in front of her, she wouldn't have much of a wait.

She'd hesitated at first when Charles suggested that she join him for lunch.

"Come on," he urged. "It'll do you good to have a day in town, give you a chance to meet one of your future clients."

There was nothing urgent for Jane to do and it would make a welcome break from the solitude of The Willows. Justin and William would be at the cottage next weekend and they'd promised to stay overnight with her. The following week, just twelve days away, loomed the inaugural weekend of *Personal Agenda*.

Jane shook her head and wondered how she would cope with it all. As she tried to organise a plan of action in her mind she became aware of two children staring at her from the car in front. Through the back window two tow-headed youngsters aged about four and five were pulling grotesque faces at her. They twisted their eyes and pulled down the sides of their mouths with podgy fingers. For a moment the little boy disappeared from sight and then returned to his vantage point. The girl turned sharply towards him to see what he was chewing and accidentally banged his head with her elbow. A chocolatey dribble ran from his mouth as he howled his protest. Jane found herself laughing which brought a fresh onslaught from the two. She made sure that the driver was paying no attention to her and stuck a finger in each ear. With each turn of her hands she made her tongue appear and disappear. The children consulted each other then copied her.

"God help me, is this what I've come to?" she groaned, thankful to see the vacant sign light up at the top of the ramp.

Although all the tables in the attractive restaurant were occupied, sounds in the room were muted A fire burned brightly in the Victorian tiled fireplace and the tables with their floor length cloths were set well apart. Costume and hunting prints covered the walls and shining brass vases, filled with dried flowers and shapely twigs, lent a bye-gone atmosphere. Even the waitresses in their starched caps and aprons reminded Jane of the cafés of her youth, the days before self-service ruled supreme.

Charles kissed her chastely on the cheek. There had been no repetition of the embrace they'd shared in Jane's office.

"You look great," he lied. She's pale and washed-out, thinner too. She was obviously still upset about Sasha. So far she'd had no luck in finding a replacement.

"I'm fine." Jane avoided his eyes. Her mirror

wasn't as kind as Charles. The extra notch she'd added to her belt this morning was even more truthful. She leaned across the table and handed him his commission cheque. "Seventy-eight members. Can you believe it? All paid up."

"I can. I seem to have rushed from one meeting to another without ceasing," he laughed. "Mind you I'm not complaining."

The *Personal Agenda* brochure lay prominently on the table between them. As they finished their coffee a willowy girl with a mane of auburn hair approached them.

"You're from *Personal Agenda*?" she confirmed cheerfully as she pointed to the red and white brochure.

Charles jumped to his feet. "Yes. You must be Dale Trent?"

"Bull's-eye. May I sit?"

"Please do. I'm Jane Anderson and this is Charles Graham." Jane cleared the papers from the table and put her diary back in her bag while Charles tried to attract the waiter's attention.

"Hi, you two." She spoke with a soft American accent. "You want to know more about me, right?"

"We thought you might have some questions for us." This was Charles's stock phrase, his opening remark to every new client. It put people at their ease. "But first, will you have some coffee? A drink?"

"Coffee please, unleaded."

Charles presumed she meant decaffeinated.

"You obviously don't subscribe to the real thing?"

"Habit, to be truthful. At home everyone is

into health-food and diet drinks. Half of them drink Coke, the other half snort it! And then there's the hysteria about passive smoking, many of those people are quite happy to smoke a joint or are hell-bent on ruining their livers with alcohol. I can't tolerate the intolerant!"

"Do you smoke?" Charles asked.

"Sure. Don't mind, do you?"

Before either of them could assure her they didn't, she pulled a pack from her bag and lit her cigarette with a gold lighter.

"This agency of yours sounds great. Check this out, I don't think there were that many questions on my college exam papers." She grinned challengingly at them.

"It is a bit much." Jane couldn't argue with that. "But it's important that we do our best to encourage people who are . . . compatible."

"Hey, no sweat, that's cool with me."

The ashtray was almost full by the time she finished telling them about herself and her family. She'd packed a lot into her twenty-seven years. But in London, even with her gregarious manner, Dale had failed to find men fainting at her feet, or too many females with time to be chummy. Suddenly she felt the loss of that large crowd of friends who were three thousand miles away. "Frankly, I'm lonely a lot of the time."

"Well, we'll have to remedy that," Jane said. She'd enjoyed listening to Dale's fresh wit and admired her openness. There was something about her that reminded Jane of Sasha.

"I suppose I'm too late for your drama gig?"

"We've had a terrific response to that, I'm afraid."

Dale's face fell. "Oh well, whatever. Put me down for the first free date you have."

"Look I'll tell you what, we have one client who's due back from a business trip that Friday. There's a slight possibility her trip may be extended. If she phones to cancel I'll put you in her place. How would that be?"

"I hope she's extended!" Dale laughed and raised her eyebrows. "I'm only being truthful, a privilege of generation-X."

"She's certainly bright. She'd liven things up, I'll bet." Charles was quite taken with Dale.

"I'm sure she would," Jane said.

Charles wasn't quite sure whether Jane's tone implied agreement or disapproval.

"To change the subject for a moment," she continued. "About the play we're supposed to use. I . . . don't like it very much. It's meant to be a comedy but I read the copy Mark Dunlop sent me – Justin and William's friend, remember? To be brutally honest I hated it and didn't find it in the least bit amusing." Jane's brow was creased with worry.

"So what are you going to do about it?" asked Charles.

"I don't want to offend him or, more importantly, Justin and William. After all Mark is doing me a huge favour. I don't know what to do." Jane had been a people-pleaser all her life. She could probably count on one hand the number of times she'd lost her temper. But now she didn't know how to avoid the impending disaster without hurting Mark. Her gut feeling was that the play was weird and not at all suitable.

"Why not phone and tell him?"

"I couldn't!"

"Then tell him a half-truth – you can't see people appreciating his talent so you'd prefer to stick with something more pedestrian. Or, you think it's too sophisticated, or too clever."

"Too clever, that might work. It's so way-out, that would fit the bill. I think, after all, we should stick to something lighter, someone like Oscar Wilde, at least people will have heard of *Lady Windermere's Fan or The Importance of Being Ernest.* What do *you* think?"

"Good idea. But don't be nervous to talk to him. If you sense he's getting uppity about it, you'll find a way round him. Now, stop worrying. What are you going to do with the rest of the day?"

"I have some shopping to do. Susie and Matt have tickets for a theatre and I'm going to stay overnight night with them. I don't fancy driving back to Dornley in the dark."

"Forget about *Personal Agenda* till tomorrow, everything will work out in the end."

It will if I do something about it, Jane brooded. Easy for Charles to say *forget it,* all he has to do is to decide whether people will make suitable clients.

Chapter Twenty

Justin pushed the row of books to one side and pulled out the volume he was searching for. He checked the title then folded the letter and slipped it between the cover and the first page. There was just enough time to address the envelope before he left. He and William were meeting William's brother for dinner. Justin always felt a little uncomfortable in John's presence but for William's sake he agreed to go. William's family had found it difficult to accept his homosexuality but they were struggling to come to terms with it.

William and John were already seated when Justin arrived.

"That traffic is foul," Justin complained shaking John's hand.

"You didn't drive here did you?"

"No fear, I'm not that brave." Justin had been learning to drive and was due to take his test in a couple of days.

"We've only just arrived ourselves," William said as he handed Justin the menu. "What are you going to eat? I swore I wouldn't have pasta but it's always so good here, I'm weakening."

Justin smiled, William was as thin as a wafer

and could eat anyone under the table. Justin had a less fortunate metabolism and tended to add the odd pound here and there if he over-indulged – which he did frequently.

The waiter took their order and asked what they would have to drink. They left the choice to William. "I think we'll have a carafe of house Chianti." William closed the wine list and turned his attention to his brother.

"Have you had a successful day?"

"Not bad, I managed to pick up one or two pieces. But prices in London are prohibitive." John owned a small antiques shop in Chester. It had been hard hit by the recession but the beautiful town still attracted tourists. They were the ones who kept the business ticking over. "Strangely enough," John said with a puzzled frown, "the more expensive pieces are selling, not the bric-a-brac which was always the backbone of the shop."

"Surely that's more profitable?" Justin asked.

"It is and it isn't. I keep my mark-up lower on the big items, buying at London auctions makes it all so expensive. I don't buy everything here of course. I go to antique fairs in the north, locals bring in bits and pieces that they want to sell – they need to sell. There's a much larger profit margin on those once I can shift them."

"Gentlemen, your wine."

The carafe slipped from the girl's nerveless fingers as she stared at her customers.

"Bloody hell! Sasha!" Justin jumped from his seat in surprise. The rich red liquid spread across the table and dripped in a steady stream on to the grey carpet. They faced each other like ghosts, totally oblivious of the mess around them.

Without uttering a word Sasha turned and fled to the kitchen.

"Sasha, what's the matter?" Maria asked as the girl burst through the door. Sasha's face was rigid with shock. "Sasha, what's wrong?" she asked again. "Has there been an accident? Gio, go and see what's happened."

Gio could see the stained cloth and, on his way to the table, grabbed a handful of used napkins from under the serving station.

"Please gentlemen, let me move you to another table. Did the wine splash you?"

John shook his head. "I don't think so. William? Justin?"

"No, I think we avoided it," William answered.

Gio held their chairs as they reseated themselves at the fresh table.

"Let me get you another carafe of Chianti. Your meal is almost ready."

"Will you tell Sasha that we'd like to speak to her, please," Justin said quietly. They'd caused enough fuss already.

"Certainly. But I'm sure that it was an accident."

"I'm certain it was. It's nothing to do with that, I'd just like to talk to her."

"I'll tell her." Gio unfolded a napkin and handed it to John.

"Sasha, it's all right, they're not angry." He had mistaken the look on Sasha's chalky-white face as fear.

"I know, I know." The combination of the spilt wine and the shock of seeing Justin and William brought the tears coursing down her cheeks.

Gio wished Giuseppe Damoni was here, he'd

know what to do. But his boss was at home nursing a streaming cold, he felt his customers wouldn't thank him for spreading his germs.

"I'm sorry," sobbed Sasha. "It was a shock seeing them again."

"Quickly, Gio, take these plates to the table," Maria instructed. "Now, Sasha tell me why you're so upset."

"I . . . I don't want to see them. I don't want to talk to them."

"Have they done something to you? Have they hurt you?"

"No, they're friends, I mean . . . I don't know what I mean."

"Why are you so afraid then?" Maria couldn't make any sense of it. She kept her eyes on the bubbling pots and tried again.

"Sasha, I'd like to help if I can but I don't understand."

Sasha tore a piece of paper towel from the big roll and blew her nose. "It's difficult to explain," she sniffed. "Complicated."

"OK, but you will have to go to the dining-room, these plates are ready for table three."

"Oh please, can't Gio serve them?"

"He can't wait on all the tables at once." Maria was becoming impatient. She was coping well without her husband but Sasha must pull her weight. The girl said she wasn't in any danger and Maria didn't have time to try and work out what the problem was.

Sasha could feel three pairs of eyes on her as she studiously avoided their glances. Could she get through the evening and make her escape without causing a scene? Her work at Damoni's kept her off the streets while she waited for her big chance in the theatre and she didn't want to lose her job. The Damonis were nice people and Gio treated her like a sister. But in her heart she knew that before the night was over she'd have to face Justin and William.

"Miss!" Justin's voice carried across the room.

"I think that gentleman is calling you," the woman she was serving prompted.

"Can I help you, sir?" Sasha voice shook tremulously.

"Yes, Sasha, you can help me. We can talk here or I'll wait for you after work," Justin offered. "But I think you'll agree, we do need to talk."

"I'll meet you after work," Sasha's quick mind had found an escape. "There's a small hotel just round the corner, wait for me there."

"And wait, and wait!"

"No, I'll be there," she promised.

"I'll wait outside for you until you're ready. Or is there a back door here?"

"No, no back door."

"Right, see you outside later."

"There's no need. I'll be there, Justin, I give you my word."

"You might as well leave," Gio said to Sasha. "I'll see to the rest. Your heart's not in it tonight. You'll be safe with this man?"

"He's gay, Gio. It's nothing like that – just a friend. Someday I'll explain."

"See you tomorrow then."

♥ ♥ ♥

Justin wondered if he should contact Jane, ask her if she wanted him to tackle Sasha. During dinner he'd begun to get cold feet, to question if this was any of his business. He was interfering in Jane's affairs, did he have the right?

He and William agreed it would be easier for Sasha to speak to just one of them. Justin resigned himself to being the one to do it.

"Jane's our friend. She has no way of contacting Sasha and we do." William had doubts too at first but now he was positive. They explained the situation to John and he too felt they owed it to Jane. At least they'd find out why Sasha had run away.

"Hello Justin," Sasha said as she slipped into the chair opposite him.

"Thank you for coming. Please don't look so scared, I'm not going to attack you."

"But you're going to side with Jane."

"Come on, you're being unfair. Jane is upset, very upset. She thinks she must have done something very wrong but she doesn't know what. She didn't know your home address, didn't even know where to start looking for you."

"I don't want my family to know where I am." A look of alarm crossed her face. "I wouldn't like them to know I'm alone in London. They'd worry."

"That's OK, I'm not going to hunt them down and tell them."

Justin waited for her to say something but it was clear by her silence that he was going to have to take the initiative. How different from the old Sasha she was, her eyes dull, her spark missing. "Were you unhappy at The Willows?" he prodded gently.

Sasha shook her head.

"Did Jane say something terrible to make you abscond like that?"

"No, she was always very thoughtful."

Justin struggled to find the key that would unlock her tongue. "Was someone else nasty to you?" Desperately he wondered who. "Charles! Was Charles the reason?"

"Charles," she echoed the name.

Justin watched. Her eyes flashed for a second and then she looked down at her hands. Her fingers began to twist the piece of crumpled paper towelling she was holding.

"What about Charles? You're making this very difficult. Don't you trust me?"

"Yes, but . . ."

"But what?" Sasha was being very tedious and Justin could feel his patience ebbing away.

"It's so stupid, I've been a real idiot."

A breakthrough at last. "I'm sure you haven't. But if I don't know what he did, I can't judge."

"The night of the party, remember? I popped into the office before dinner to have a word with Jane. There they were, the two of them, kissing each other – X certificate kissing. Jane knew I was mad about him. She liked him, but she didn't fancy him. What chance did I have? I felt betrayed, jealous. From that night on it was nothing but Charles, Charles, Charles. His was the only opinion that counted – the great Oracular Cyberpunk."

"Pardon?" Justin jerked up his head in surprise.

Sasha lips trembled, her eyes brimming with tears, then suddenly she began to laugh.

"Sounds good, doesn't it?" she chuckled. "Charles was always nagging me to learn how to use the computer so I invented that name for him."

"Whatever you say." Justin smiled. "But is that it? That's why you left, on the strength of one kiss?"

"I was hurt. Jane didn't want him but she made sure I couldn't have him either."

"Sasha! You don't believe that. Jane doesn't have a mean bone in her body."

"See, I *knew* you'd defend her," she accused.

He'd have to tread warily here. "I do defend her as far as that's concerned. You must have been very upset to leave the way you did. But wouldn't it have been better to talk to her, discuss how you felt?"

"Of course it would, I *told* you I behaved stupidly."

"Don't be so hard on yourself." Justin agreed with her, she'd acted childishly, like a fool, but he wasn't going to get her back up by telling her that. "How do we go about healing the rift?"

"We don't do anything," Sasha replied stubbornly. "It's over and done with. A shame, but that's the way it is."

Justin refrained from saying that nothing was over till the fat lady sings. Instead he sat quietly for a moment while he planned his next verbal move.

♥ ♥ ♥

Justin slammed the door of the flat, flung his coat on the chair, poured himself a drink and rolled his eyes to heaven.

"Is she going back to Jane's?" William sat on the arm of the chair, astonished to learn the ludicrous reason for Sasha's departure.

"No she's not – not yet anyway." Justin repeated the conversation he'd had with Sasha.

"How petty," William snorted.

"She admits it."

"So now what happens?"

"I'll phone Jane in the morning and tell her the whole story. If she wants an intermediary that's fine, if not, I've done my best. My gut feeling tells me that, with a bit of careful egg-shell-walking, Sasha could be persuaded to go back to The Willows. But time's running out, Jane needs help now. Otherwise I'd have left it till the weekend when we could talk to her face to face."

"I'm sure it's a case of the sooner the better."

♥ ♥ ♥

Jane gave Mrs Jones a tour of the house.

"It's so lovely and bright," the woman said. "I'll enjoy working in such attractive rooms. It'll be dead handy for me, living so nearby."

Jane leant against the front door and sighed with relief. Mrs Jones didn't cook but otherwise she would do anything Jane wanted. She actually preferred to work at weekends when her husband could keep an eye on the little ones.

The phone rang and the doorbell sounded at

the same time. Quickly Jane opened the door. It was Jimmy Green, her builder, with some large sheets of plywood for scenery. "Hang on, I'll give you a hand in a minute – the phone's ringing."

Jimmy Green stood the sheets of wood against the garage wall and let himself back into the house. In the distance he could hear the sound of Jane's raised voice. He didn't think she had it in her to get annoyed like that. Might as well pop the kettle on now he was here, women always liked a cup of tea when they were angry.

Jane's cheeks were flamed with colour. "Sorry to delay you, Jimmy. Thanks for bringing the wood over."

"Pleasure. You sounded mad."

"I am."

"Anything I can do?"

"No thanks. I need to work this out for myself."

♥ ♥ ♥

"Well?" William looked at Justin expectantly.

"That was some tirade. I've never heard Jane so furious."

"What did she say?"

"She'd forgotten about the incident in the office. She was uptight, the trauma of the day caught up with her – the ants, remember? Charles comforted her. She remembered that someone came into the kitchen, but didn't see them. According to Jane there was nothing more to it than that. Sasha had no claim on Charles anyway. You heard me suggest that it was all a misunderstanding. They could apologise to each other and forget it ever happened. That's when she blew her top. She said she'd apologise when hell froze over. I could do with some of that ice for my poor ear!"

"So now what?"

"Now what, indeed? I don't know – try again or forget it."

"Seems a shame. Do you think it would help if they met?"

"How do we organise that? Kidnap Sasha and blindfold her? Drag Jane to London on some pretext and lock them in a room together?"

"That's not as far-fetched as you think. In fact, it might well be the answer. She owes us a favour, we could say we need advice about fabrics for the cottage and would she come to town and help us? It might work."

Justin pulled a face, he didn't think so. Jane wouldn't have any spare time this week. Any later and Sasha could have vanished again. "Let me think about it."

Justin left Domani's restaurant with a smug grin on his face. "I know I was brought up never to lie," he murmured to himself. "But there are times . . ."

♥ ♥ ♥

Jane heard the impatient hooting of a car horn and ran to the door. Today was Justin's debut as a licensed driver. She walked the few steps to the shining, red Honda with its L-plates still firmly intact.

"What do you think?" Justin stroked the bonnet lovingly. "I drove it here myself."

"And it's a wonder any of us are alive to tell the tale," William said sardonically.

Jane's mouth dropped open as the back door of the vehicle opened. "My room still vacant?" Sasha asked.

Chapter Twenty-One

Ray Parker drummed his fingers impatiently on the seat beside him. The taxi, stuck in traffic in a narrow side street, was costing him a packet. He didn't mind helping a new customer if they were in trouble, but Boothby's were getting more than their money's worth. All this at his own expense. Next time . . .

His mobile phone gave a couple of high-pitched bleeps.

"Ray, you plonker, where the hell have you been?"

"Good morning to you too, Linda Lou." If she wasn't so good with the customers . . . "Where's the fire?" He said calmly hiding his displeasure.

"Under you if you don't pull out your finger and get here right away. Where are you anyway?"

"Stuck in traffic. What's the problem?"

"Ray, get here – pronto."

". . . and then she said the timing was all important."

Ray Parker sat on Linda Lou's desk and listened incredulously. This was what he'd always dreamed about, longed for. A bigger contract than he'd ever dared hope for even in his wildest fantasies.

"How do you like them little apples?" Linda Lou finished triumphantly

He picked her up off her chair and whirled her around in the air.

"Incredible, unbelievable! We must be talking of a couple of million at least. Beamish and Chambers! I can't believe it. All those branches, all that work. No wonder you were so impatient." Ray's face burned with excited colour.

It was impossible to concentrate on anything for the rest of the morning. He paced the floor, shuffled papers and drank endless cups of coffee which jangled his nerves even more.

Ray Parker waited nervously in the reception area. He studied the walls with their photographs of Beamish and Chambers' branch offices – an architectural history of the firm since its inception. On a table beside his unyielding upright chair were the soap-giant's publicity leaflets which he tried to read. But nothing would register. He gathered the testimonial sheets together and pushed them furtively into his briefcase. Plenty of time to study them later.

Elizabeth Beamish, one of the two owners of the company, left her desk and met him half-way across the vast stretch of pale carpet. She was tall for a woman and slim. The severity of her pearl-grey suit was relieved by the soft folds of a snowy-white blouse. He doubted if her outfit had come from one of the usual high street stores.

"It's good of you to come at such short notice," she said as she led him to the group of chairs furthest from her desk.

The furniture here was more comfortable than

in his flat. And those lush green plants, there were so many of them they'd fill a florist's.

"Would you like some coffee or tea?" she smiled, pointing to the flasks on the table.

Ray shook his head. If he drank one more drop of the stuff today, they'd have to whip him into hospital with a caffeine-overdose.

She poured a cup of black coffee for herself and sat facing him. "I must be honest, this is not really my department, I deal more with sales but I like to be involved – maybe *some* day I'll understand the ins and outs of computers! Robert Hall from accounts will be along in a few minutes, he's the person you'll be working with. What I do understand is that, now we've expanded so much, our present system no longer meets our needs. Naturally we want to replace it as soon as possible." She leaned forward to pick a yellowing leaf from the plant on the table between them.

"We have an excellent team and I'm *sure* that we'll be able to supply exactly the system you need – speedily and efficiently," Ray said confidently. "Do you mind if I ask how you heard about CCC?"

"From Dicksons – they're friends of the family. They seem very pleased with the system you designed for them." Her voice was light and she had a lovely smile.

"Oh yes! Theirs was an extremely complicated system," Ray said. Actually it was a comparatively easy assignment but Ray maintained there was nothing like a bit of exaggeration to help things along.

"That will be Robert now. Come in," she called

in response to the knock at the door. "Let me introduce you, Robert Hall, head of our computing and accounts department. Ray Parker, Managing Director of CCC." The two men shook hands, each sizing the other up.

Ray prided himself as being a shrewd judge of character. Robert Hall had a pleasant demeanour but Ray guessed that under that polished exterior beat the heart of an exacting analyst. There'd be no friendly chats, no lingering over cups of tea, Hall wasn't the type who would accept delays or excuses.

Robert Hall recognised Ray Parker's ill-concealed excitement. In his opinion that was a good thing, the leaner and hungrier the man, the better the results. And Parker was both. He'd trip over himself to please Beamish and Chambers and that was what Robert Hall needed.

Elizabeth Beamish smoothed her short skirt and sat quietly as the two men talked. After ten minutes Ray had a fair idea of what was required.

"I'll take Ray down to accounts and we can begin to sort things out," Robert said.

Elizabeth Beamish rose to her feet and held out her hand. "It's been nice to meet you, Ray." Her grip was warm and firm. "I hope we'll be able to do business."

As she reached her desk she turned towards him. "If Robert isn't around and you have any questions, don't hesitate to contact *me*."

For a moment Ray wondered if that was a subtle invitation or was it wishful thinking on his part? Elizabeth Beamish was a very attractive woman.

It was five-fifteen before he returned to his

office, and Linda Lou had left for home. Donahue Reilly was still at his desk and greeted Ray with unusual eagerness.

"Can you spare the time to discuss this now?" Ray held out the thick pad in which he'd written copious notes.

"Let me make a phone call." Donahue frowned.

Ray was taken aback, it hadn't occurred to him that there could be anyone or anything outside Donahue Reilly's computer-controlled existence.

"I'm all yours for as long as it takes." Donahue pulled up a chair to the desk and sat back to listen.

♥ ♥ ♥

Alison Reilly went back to her easel and picked up her brush with a smile. Donahue's rushed phone call pleased her. For eighteen months she'd been begging him to look for another job, somewhere he could really use his talents. But Donahue was stubbornly loyal to the ailing firm that had given him his start. She doubted if Ray Parker even knew of her existence. She and Donahue had married quietly one bank holiday weekend. The following Tuesday he was back at his desk. That was Donahue's way of doing things.

They lived simply, earning enough to pay their bills and keep themselves supplied with materials for his computer and her art work. Donahue was on the verge of creating something big. He said it was such a simple system that, without a single lesson, anyone could use a computer. There wasn't the slightest doubt in her mind that sooner or later he would achieve his goal. She believed totally in her computer-mad husband and loved him to distraction.

♥ ♥ ♥

Ray stopped to draw breath. He'd been talking non-stop for over an hour. Donahue quietly took notes but didn't interrupt him.

"So basically, they need a larger version of the package we did for Farrells. Change a bit here or there," Donahue said.

Ray clapped his hand to his forehead. Donahue was right, in one fell swoop he'd wiped away the biggest of his worries; the time and expense of starting from scratch. Of course they'd have to add a considerable amount to the software, but so much of it was already done. It was a pity that Farrells were based in Scotland. But it would still be cheaper to fly Robert Hall – and Elizabeth Beamish, if necessary – to Glasgow in order to see the working prototype. What an analytic mind Donahue had, what an ability to cut through the chaff and get to the wheat. Ray looked at the man with new eyes. When had Donahue cut his hair, trimmed his beard? The open-necked shirt he wore was clean and pressed. Where was that sweater he always wore? For heaven's sake he saw the man every day, how could he have been so unobservant?

Ray could hardly wait to get to work each day,

and each day he arrived at the office earlier and earlier.

"You might as well sleep here – why don't you?" Linda Lou suggested.

"Why not indeed?" Her acerbic remark failed to rile him. She'd leave sharp at five even if the building was on fire.

Ray checked his costings again. There was no escaping it, he would have to borrow from the bank. He didn't think that it would be a problem but, until they agreed the loan, he'd keep on worrying.

"I suppose I *could* go with you." Donahue clicked on the save button and gave Ray his undivided attention.

It was imperative that Donahue accompanied them on the excursion to Glasgow. Donahue would be able to explain the system and answer the questions far better than he could.

Elizabeth Beamish refused his invitation, she was happy to leave everything in Robert Hall's capable hands. Ray was torn between relief and disappointment. He would have enjoyed seeing her again but, on the other hand, it would save the cost of the air fare and a day's expenses.

Ray was nervous. Things were progressing almost too smoothly. He'd spent a nail-biting week until the overdraft was agreed at the bank. The vision of a burly bailiff with his re-possession crew faded rapidly from his mind. Donahue was about as enthusiastic as Donahue could be – the work was coming along nicely. The rest was just a matter of time.

Chapter Twenty-Two

Jane watched Sasha's neat figure climb the stairs; she had lost weight. It must have been awful for her working in that sleazy café. Thank heavens Justin succeeded in talking her round. Jane winced as she heard Justin grind the gears and rev the engine in his hurry to escape.

"Hello, Jane." Sasha stood in the kitchen doorway dressed in jeans and a T-shirt.

"Hello, Sasha."

"I suppose we'd better clear the air?" Sasha's blunt ways hadn't changed.

"Yes I suppose we should. You first."

"I'm sorry I misjudged your motives – about Charles, I mean. And I'm sorry that I left you on your own. Justin said you were having a terrible time, coping alone, couldn't manage without me. But don't worry, I'm back now."

"Justin said *what*?" Jane nearly exploded with rage. "How dare he say that I couldn't manage?"

"I don't know. That's what he said. I'm sure it was difficult."

"I managed very well thank you." She'd tackle Justin the minute he got back from the cottage. "And what about you, Sasha, you poor thing.

Fired from that terrible café and nowhere to live?"

"*Terrible café? Fired?* I didn't get *fired*. The "café" was an Italian restaurant in the West End, and a damned good one at that."

"So it's not true?"

"No it isn't, it's all lies . . ." Sasha's cheeks were as flushed as Jane's. "How could he imply . . . Why would Justin say such a . . ." Sasha clasped her hand to her mouth, her eyes wide. "He conned us! Justin's been winding us up." A burble of laughter caught Sasha's throat and erupted in choking laughter. "We've been had, Jane."

Jane stared at the shaking girl, then she too began to chuckle. They laughed hysterically as tears ran down their faces. "Oh, what idiots they must think we are," Jane said wiping her face with the back of her hand. It was so good to have Sasha back again.

"We *were* idiots," Sasha said.

"Speak for yourself!"

"Listen, Jane, are we going to let them get away with this?"

"No way. But what can we to do about it?"

Like an old married couple set in their ways, Sasha filled the kettle and the milk jug while Jane put the mugs on the table and rooted in the cupboard for the biscuit tin.

"Right, I've got it." Jane's eyes shone with mischief. "What were they trying to do when they lied to us like that?"

"Trying to get us together again?"

"Exactly. So here's what we do."

"I'm almost afraid to go in to the house," said Justin as he turned the car into The Willows.

"You tried your best." William's tone lacked confidence.

Justin manoeuvred the car as if he were driving an articulated lorry. As he juddered to a stop the front door of the house opened. With horror they watched Jane push Sasha into the driveway and throw her case after her. Sasha pounded on the door but it remained firmly closed. She turned helplessly. She saw the car and ran towards it.

"Take me away, please Justin, take me away," she sobbed.

Both men jumped out of the car. William was beside her in a couple of strides. Justin picked up her case.

"Your face, Sasha! What happened?"

"She hit me – with a . . . tray."

"Justin look, she's black and blue."

Sasha winced as he touched her arm. The big purple bruise on her arm stunned them. But when Justin turned Sasha's face towards the sunlight her eye, half-closed and discoloured, shocked them more.

"But Jane's so gentle." William shook his head in disbelief. "How did she do so much damage?"

Sasha hid her face in her hands, her shoulders heaved with fright. "Please let me get into the car. She'll come after me again, I'm frightened."

"She won't dare touch you while we're here." Justin led her to the car. The poor girl, she was shaking.

"Maybe we should have a word with Jane." William frowned deeply. This was totally uncharacteristic of Jane.

"No, no, please take me away, take me from here."

The two men looked at each other. Sasha was so distraught that Justin nodded to William to put her case in the boot while he started the car. It lurched a couple of times then stalled. He started it again then turned and aimed it towards the direction of the gate.

Sasha's sobs grew louder until they almost sounded almost like laughter.

"She's hysterical," William mouthed as Justin jammed on the brake and lurched the car to a halt again. He hadn't quite got the hang of stopping yet.

"You are laughing," Justin accused. "You're *laughing.*"

"Serves you right," Jane said sternly as they watched Sasha lick a tissue and rub it over her bruised arm. The purple patch spread towards her elbow.

"And that's the thanks we get for trying to help. Come on, William. Don't worry, we won't bother you again."

The two men turned on their heels and left the house.

"Now we've done it," Sasha groaned. "We've gone too far. They were just trying to patch things up. Quick, let's go after them. Perhaps we can apologise." They ran to the front door and bounded into the garden.

They took no more than a few steps before they screamed with fright as the two men sprang from their hiding place behind a bush, roaring like lions.

"My heart is still pounding," Sasha grumbled as she drained her glass.

"I really thought you'd gone," Jane admitted.

"We should have," Justin pouted. "Those bruises! I don't know about acting, Sasha, but you certainly have a talent for make-up. A cruel talent."

"Right," William said suddenly. "End of story, no more recriminations. Sasha is back where she is . . . needed . . . belongs. So I say, let's drink a toast. To friendship and its human face."

Chapter Twenty-Three

Charles could hear the sound of laughter as Jane shouted at the culprits to keep it down.

"Sorry Charles," she apologised. "I have some wonderful news, Sasha's back."

"That's marvellous, what happened?"

Jane spared him none of the details. He could imagine Sasha's bruises, hear the screams of the two of them when Justin and William pounced. In his mind's eye he could see them seated around the kitchen table with their glasses. Their laughter he could hear for himself.

"I'm really delighted," he said enthusiastically. He wouldn't allow the resentment he felt to creep into his voice. How many hours had he spent tramping from theatre to theatre looking for Sasha? Justin and William hadn't done that, they'd found her totally by accident. But they were the ones celebrating at The Willows, not him. He was cooped up in a stuffy flat on this beautiful summer's day. Alone.

". . . Will you, Charles?"

"Sorry, Jane, I didn't hear what you said, will I what?"

"Will you come and join us? That is, if you're not busy."

Why did Jane think she could invite him at the last moment like this?

But in all fairness, Sasha *had* just appeared out of the blue.

"I do have a loose arrangement. Let me check and I'll phone you back."

Charles waited ten minutes then tapped out Jane's number. "It's OK, I can see my friends another night when I'm free."

"Justin and William are staying until tomorrow so bring your night-shirt and your toothbrush, they'll give you a lift home tomorrow. There's a train in an hour, I'll meet you at the station. You *can* stay, can't you?"

"I think I can manage that, tomorrow's diary is clear." He knew he sounded ungracious and probably a little pompous.

"See you soon."

Jane seemed evasive when he asked her why Sasha had left. It might have been difficult for her to talk while they were all in the room. He didn't know why, but he felt a bit awkward about meeting her again.

"Here I am again, the proverbial bad penny," Sasha said brightly as she gave him a quick hug. "Sorry I caused such a ruckus, I feel a right Charley."

They all laughed a little too hard at her unintended pun.

Charles squeezed her hand and gave her a light kiss on her forehead.

"Come on, let's go and have lunch in the garden." Jane was relieved that the moment had passed so smoothly. "Everyone grab a dish on the way out."

The men went into the garden while Sasha and Jane waited for the garlic bread to heat. Impulsively Jane put her arms around Sasha and hugged her. "I'm so glad you're back – even though I *could* manage alone!"

"I'm glad to *be* back even though I *wasn't* fired." Sasha picked up the bread basket and smiled.

"Where did this come from?" Sasha demanded as she eyed the garden furniture. "Blimey, you don't do things by half."

Jane's face wore the look of a guilty child caught with her hand in the sweet jar. "I needed to buy a bigger table and this lot was in a sale, so I splurged."

Her original table was ideal for four people, but hopelessly inadequate for the barbecues and *al fresco* meals she intended having when *Personal Agenda* opened its doors. The rectangular table with its snazzy lemon and white striped canopy and matching chairs had been impossible to resist. "I suppose it was a bit extravagant," she confessed.

"Jane, you don't have to justify your actions. I think it's divine." Justin placed a protective arm round her shoulders. "I also think I'm going to expire in this heat. So get under cover, stick bums on chairs and let's eat."

Jane ladled the iced borscht into the soup cups and told them to help themselves to sour cream.

"I can't resist," William said passing his bowl for a second helping. "I must have the recipe."

♥ ♥ ♥

The weekend's sweltering heat made it a pleasure to stay indoors. She ventured out only to shop and even then she was back home before ten o'clock. Jane divided her time between the office and the kitchen, dressed in the flimsiest of cotton dresses. She sat with her feet in a basin of cold water and leafed through her recipe books. Finally she was satisfied with her choice of menu, a trial run for the following weekend.

The salmon was perfectly cooked, pink and moist. She added some ice cubes to her foot-bath and sat comfortably cutting cucumber slices. She glanced at the illustration, the cucumber on her salmon really did resemble fish scales. The huge mound of parsley for the tabbouleh salad was reduced in size as she chopped rhythmically. She washed the leaves for the green salad and spun them dry in a tea cloth – enjoying the cool spray of water on her bare arms. She popped the lettuce leaves into a plastic bag and put them in the cooler cabinet. Jane never went into that little cold-room without shuddering, but obviously the ants had got the message as they'd never re-appeared.

"Beat the cheese and the egg yolks," she read. Justin loved tiramasu, and she relished the aroma of the espresso coffee as it simmered gently on the stove. She removed it from the heat then added a generous measure of Tia Maria. While it cooled she washed the berries for the summer pudding. She daydreamed as the cold water played over her wrists.

"That's it." Jane consulted her list. Satisfied that she'd done everything she could, she returned to her soothing water-filled basin and read her paper.

♥ ♥ ♥

"That was delicious, I don't know how you did it." Charles sat back in his chair and lit a small cigar.

"I second that," William agreed.

"I'll third it. I can't wait for the cottage to be ready, then I'll come for lunch every week." Justin laughed as he peeled a peach.

Jane couldn't resist a bitchy smirk in Sasha's direction.

"It was perfect, Jane." Sasha's praise robbed her of her sweet revenge.

"When are we going to see the cottage?" Jane asked.

"Very soon," William promised. "But not until there's some real progress. We're lucky that the owners gave us the key before the final contracts were exchanged. Our solicitor thinks they're mad. Mind you, any work we do there must be an improvement."

"How long do you think the work will take?" It would be totally impractical for him, but Charles would have loved the cottage for himself.

"How long is a piece of string?" Justin replied. "We'll probably be reasonably respectable in a month. Everything the builder ordered is in storage – bathroom fittings and kitchen units – all that kind of thing."

"The furniture is almost ready and the curtains are being made," William added. "The carpets are due next week. We hope to sign the final contracts next Friday."

"Let's put it this way, if we were chucked out of our flat next week we could just about sleep on the cottage floor. There's water and electricity, but that's all," Justin explained. "No beds of course, no carpeting."

"If you do get slung out of your flat I have loads of carpet in the attic," Jane said. "I couldn't bear to throw it away."

"Don't tempt me," Justin replied. "The heat in London this week was major-hell."

"It's a pity we have a full house next weekend. You could always sleep here – in the attic," Jane laughed.

"Hey, talking of next weekend, what's happening about the play?" Sasha asked.

Jane had completely forgotten about *Personal Agenda*, forgotten about Mark Dunlop, the director, and Mrs Jones who would be here later on.

"Let me get the coffee and I'll fill you in. Charles, would you mind giving me a hand to carry these plates?" Jane said lightly.

"Let me," said Sasha rising from her chair.

"You've had a hard morning, stay there and recover from your injuries!"

Jane pushed her gently back in the chair.

Justin was about to offer his help but Jane obviously needed to talk to Charles.

"Give Sasha credit for some sense," Charles said as he made a half-hearted attempt to load the dishwasher. "She couldn't expect you to sit around waiting for her."

"But what am I going to tell Mark? Now that

Sasha's back we don't even have a room for him. He sounded quite put out when I told him that I didn't think we should use the play. Now I'll have to phone again. What do I say – thanks but no thanks? And Mrs Jones, what am I going to tell her? She's really glad to have the work."

Justin clattered tactfully into the kitchen. "I won't interrupt you, I've brought the rest of the plates. By the way, Jane, now that Sasha's back I thought you might feel diffident about giving Mark the boot. Don't worry, I had a word with him this morning and explained the situation. He'll understand if you don't need him and wished you lots of luck." Mark had actually been quite narky and accused Jane of not recognising talent when she saw it. He was quite happy to back out.

"Thank heavens for that." Jane's face brightened. "I'll phone tomorrow and apologise for messing him about." That solved one problem.

Mrs Jones was delighted to hear that Jane's friend had returned and even more pleased to learn that Jane still needed her.

♥ ♥ ♥

"Oscar Wilde? Good choice," Sasha approved. "*The Importance of Being Earnest* is fun, I have a copy upstairs. Easy as far as scenery is concerned too, we can use the living-room. And I've plenty of costumes that will be suitable."

Jane didn't mention the pots of paint and the sheets of plywood stacked up in the garage. But there was a garden scene, they could use them for that.

Sasha said reflectively, "The more I think about it, the more sense it makes. By the time dinner is finished on Friday no one will feel like sitting down to write a play. Instead we can decide who's going to do what and give them a copy of their part. We'll also need a dresser, a prompter, someone to act as scene shifter – there'll be a bit of scenery to be painted." She'd suddenly remembered the garden scene.

"It all sounds very simple," William said. "I'm sure we can find some battered copies of the play lying around in the shops . . ."

They all jumped as Sasha shrieked. "An audience, we have no audience. We've forgotten the most important thing of all."

"Sasha, do you mind!" Justin said tapping his hand against his chest. "I'd like to live a little longer."

"We *must* have an audience," she insisted.

William thumped Charles on the back. "Where do we find one?" Charles asked in a strained voice when he finished choking.

"Do I have to think of everything?" Sasha replied tartly.

"She's right, where do we find one?" Jane wrinkled her brow.

William rubbed his hand over his chin. "This may not be the time to bring it up, but did you give any thought to my idea? Inviting more people?"

"In all due respect, William, we have enough problems at the . . . Oh my! I see what you're getting at." Jane's face broke into a smile.

"Exactly."

"But it's such short notice. How many people would we need, what do we do about food?"

Jane knew she was beginning to panic. She was glad she'd decided to keep Mrs Jones on, there'd be plenty of work for all of them.

"What do you think Sasha? About twenty or so?" Charles made his voice sound matter-of-fact. He was used to Jane's panic-attacks.

"Twenty would be loads."

"We could manage twenty, or thirty perhaps. They couldn't stay overnight of course." Jane's breathing steadied.

"There's no need," William soothed. "No one stayed the night of the housewarming party."

"I could invite Susie and Matt," Jane thought aloud. "I'll go through the list later, there were loads of people who wanted to come down next weekend. That American girl, Dale – she was very eager."

"Dale! I forgot – I was going to tell you about her," Charles said.

"What about Dale?" Jane asked.

"Do you want to discuss it now?"

"Go ahead, it's all right." Charles was quite right not to divulge agency business but Justin and William were almost as much a part of it as Charles, Sasha and herself.

A smile twitched at Charles's lips. "You remember Jill Lennon, the woman Dale hoped would be away on an extended business trip?"

Jane nodded.

"I had a phone call from her *husband* last night demanding to know what *Personal Agenda* was all about! He'd discovered the papers stuffed at the back of a drawer. He was spitting mad. It turns out that *he* was the one who was supposed to be away next weekend, not her. She thought she'd treat herself to a nice "singles" weekend on the q.t."

"Does that mean Jill won't be coming?" Justin laughed.

"By the sound of his temper she'll probably be here in a month or so – legitimately. I wouldn't like to have been in her shoes when she got home." Charles shuddered. "And before you say it, Jane, no, she can't have her fee back. That was total misrepresentation on her part."

"It sounds more like suicide," William said. "How do you protect yourself from someone like that?"

Charles shrugged his shoulders. "You're asking the wrong person. I contacted her at home as I do with everyone. Twice in fact. And I met her. Short of camping on someone's doorstep for a week to check who goes in and out, there's little more you can do."

"Have you had problems with other people?" Justin wanted to know.

"Not really, not like that. There were people who weren't suitable."

"Like how, not suitable?" Sasha asked.

"One man I met was a perfect candidate. Good-looking, nicely mannered, charming talker. But in the half hour we spent together he drank *six* double whiskies. And then there was the girl who worked as a model – a real cracker. She had all the attributes and just before we said goodbye she asked if it was all right if she brought her lion cub with her – part of her image! Shall I go on?" Charles grinned.

"Tell them about the company director from High Wycombe," Jane prompted.

"He was a powerhouse of a man – tall, tanned, the athletic type. We'd gone through the usual rigamarole when I noticed that he kept twisting the fourth finger of his left hand, if you count his thumb. By the time our meeting came to an end he'd rubbed away all the make-up he'd used to disguise the perfect white circle made by his wedding ring."

"You should have introduced him to Jill Lennon," declared Justin .

"Not all of them are funny," Charles frowned. "Sometimes it can be very touching. Remember, Jane, the rape victim? She wanted protection, someone to guard her door at night. A guarantee that no one would attempt to touch her. And then there was the application from the thirty-eight-year-old who was nearer to fifty-eight. I met her yesterday, she was pathetic, so lonely. Her hair was bleached to a frizz – fifties style. Her stringy little body was almost emaciated from dieting and she wore a miniskirt that was so short it would have made a docker blush. But that wasn't the worst part, she spoke in a baby voice and acted so coyly it was embarrassing."

"What did you say to her?" Justin's eyes were full of compassion.

"I told her that our lists were full at the moment but, as soon as we had a vacancy, we'd be honoured to have someone as attractive as herself on our books. She was disappointed but I think she accepted my excuse. At least I hope she did."

Charles sighed contentedly. Could there be a better way to spend a summer's afternoon – lying here in the drowsy heat surrounded by people he liked? The Willows always had such a soothing effect on him, a magic all of its own. Lazily, he looked about him. Sasha and Jane were sunbathing, their eyes closed. Justin, barefoot, stood at the end of the garden watching Jane's neighbour as he worked on his boat. William had removed his tie *and* his shirt, and was checking prices on the long list of items that the builder had given him. What more could anyone ask, Charles thought, as he drifted off to sleep.

Chapter Twenty-Four

Amanda Brown stared in dismay at the pile of discarded clothes on her bed. She'd rejected them all, every skirt and sweater, every pair of trousers and her dresses. "Nothing's right," she moaned. "I'll be the only one at *Personal Agenda* dressed in just a blouse and knickers. What am I going to do?"

She sat on the floor and tried think of a way to salvage the situation. "I'll take the afternoon off on Friday and buy a couple of new outfits for the weekend. Maybe I could ask one of the girls in account handling to go with me, they're always so stylishly turned out. Mother? No, she's always busy. Uninterested. Lois Hayes, she's the friendliest."

Amanda began to gather up her clothes and hang them back in the wardrobe. If her father had been here she knew she could have turned to him just as she always used to do when things went wrong. Anger welled in her throat and tears pricked her eyes. "Why did you leave me? What did I do wrong?" she'd asked the question of herself a thousand times since that awful day. A day that would be etched on her memory forever. Amanda walked to her window and stared out.

She could still see the waiting taxi, see her father's sad eyes as he watched her beating her little fists helplessly on the pane of glass. For a moment he'd hesitated but then climbed into the black car, closed the door and was gone. The pain had diminished a little over the years, but although his letters and phone calls constantly assured her of his love, he had left her. He wouldn't have done that if he loved her.

At first her mother tried to explain to Amanda that it wasn't her fault, it was something that happened when parents no longer loved each other. But Amanda stuck fast to her argument, it was her fault. Then she tried to blame her mother. But it always came back to being *her fault*, something *she'd* done to upset him. For months her school work suffered along with her appetite, then finally her health. Her mother was at her wits' end with her rebellious daughter. Suddenly Amanda knew how to right the wrong. She'd work like a demon in school, get brilliant marks and when her father heard how clever she was, he'd come back.

Amanda smiled at her reflection in the window. How foolish she'd been, but she'd certainly stuck to her plan. By the time she was ten she had passed every exam with flying colours and every girl in her class. That hadn't helped her popularity. How she'd worked, cutting herself off from everyone except her teachers. She still had those term reports, carefully pasted into a scrapbook in her drawer. The thought of the past made her long to talk to her father. Ignoring the messy pile of clothes around her, she went to make her call.

"May I speak to my father, please," Amanda's tone was cold, she hated that woman who'd taken him away.

"Amanda, darling? How are you?" She loved the warmth in her father's voice.

"Hello, Dad. I'm fine, just thought I'd ring to say hello."

"How's work?"

"Fine."

"What's new?" David Brown knew that sometimes Amanda found it difficult to get to the point. It was unusual for her to phone twice in one week.

"Oh, nothing really. I'm going to a dating agency thing at the weekend."

"That should be fun. I'm sure you'll have a great time."

"Perhaps. Maybe if I had the right clothes to wear, I would."

So that was the problem. "Are you short of cash? Can I help?"

"No, thanks. The only thing I'm short of is taste and judgement."

"Nonsense. You mustn't put yourself down like that. I told Lisette how well you looked when I came back from London last time."

"*Lisette* was thrilled no doubt." Amanda's tone was laced with sarcasm.

After all these years Amanda still hated his wife. When would she accept the fact that Lisette hadn't been the cause of the break-up? His marriage to her mother had been rocky for years before Lisette came on the scene. "Believe it or not, Lisette is extremely fond of you." He'd like to have added, "I don't know why."

"I'd better ring off now." Amanda was furious with herself. She hadn't meant to sound so sour, it always seemed to happen whenever Lisette's name came into the conversation.

"Goodbye sweetheart. Phone when you get back and tell me all about the weekend."

"I will. 'Bye."

Amanda stood waiting for her boss, Martin Howard's, attention. She rarely went to those meetings but she needed to have a word with Martin and with Lois Hayes. It would take a bit of courage to ask the glamorous woman for help.

Amanda had only been there for a few minutes but if the clients were as impressed with the storyline as she was, the account would be theirs, she was certain of it.

"Thank you, Bob. Let's break for coffee and then we'll discuss this fully," Martin Howard said.

"Yes, Amanda, what can I do for you?" he smiled at the serious-faced girl at his arm.

"I'd like to take the afternoon off tomorrow, I don't have a lot to do."

"No problem," he assured her. Amanda was the most conscientious person he'd ever met.

Now for Lois Hayes. "Excuse me, Lois, could I have a word?"

Lois's face clouded for a moment. Amanda Brown looked worried. Had she overspent on her expense account again?

"Sure. What's up?"

"Are you busy tomorrow afternoon?" Amanda asked.

"Not especially."

"I . . .. I need some help. I have to buy some

clothes and wondered if you could advise me?" There, she'd said it.

"Well . . . yes, of course, if I can. What did you have in mind?"

Awkwardly Amanda explained she was going away for the weekend and that her wardrobe was sadly lacking. "Totally wrong . . . hopeless actually," she admitted. "The thing is I seem to buy, keep buying, the same type of clothes and I know they don't suit me. You're always so glamorous I thought . . ."

"I'd be delighted to help. Flattered." Amanda could be a great ally to have. The poor girl was so dowdy, so matronly, it would be fun to play Professor Higgins for an afternoon.

Fridays at Coogan, Howard and Green, were casual. Amanda studiously ignored the inter-office memo which gave permission for the "suits" to adopt the new dress code. She understood this had become the norm in a lot of large firms – a copy-cat idea from the States. Each Friday now, unless there were meetings with clients, formal business suits were replaced by open-necked shirts and casual trousers. Both sexes wore jeans, although some of the women preferred denim skirts or loose cotton trousers. But Amanda stuck firmly to her tweed skirts and good-quality, shapeless sweaters. In this warm weather she usually exchanged her woolly tops for plain, manly cotton shirts.

Half an hour into their expedition Amanda was ready to give up and go home. They trailed from store to store, shop to shop. It took almost two hours before she made her first purchase, but Lois was relentless. Then suddenly they were surrounded by shopping bags.

"Four o'clock, time for a cup of tea. We've earned it," Lois said firmly.

"How do you spend your weekends?" Amanda ventured pouring the milk into the cups.

"Oh, you know – the usual thing. Nothing special. I read, watch telly, sometimes one of the girls comes over for a bite and we go to a film . . ."

That was the last thing Amanda expected to hear. She'd imagined Lois surrounded by admirers, dashing about with barely enough time to change her clothes, turning down invitations by the score.

"You must be looking forward to your weekend. Do you often visit these friends of yours?" Lois asked.

Amanda had been too embarrassed to tell her the truth about *Personal Agenda.* She wasn't used to confiding in anyone. Charles was her only real friend. "To be honest, they're not my friends," Amanda heard herself say.

Lois put her cup on the saucer and listened avidly as Amanda explained.

". . . I suppose you think what I'm doing is awful?"

"Far from it. I think it's a super idea, a brilliant way to really get to know people. I'd love to try it myself. Will you tell me all about it next week? Can we have lunch together one day?"

Amanda was flattered. Lois was so attractive, so poised. And she was asking her if they could have lunch together.

"I'd be delighted," Amanda said shyly. "Wednesday perhaps?" She didn't want to appear too eager.

"Wednesday's fine, I think." Lois consulted her diary. "By the way you don't need to worry, I won't mention this to anyone, it's your affair. Or, come to think of it, maybe it'll be your *affaire*," she laughed.

Amanda felt quite excited as she packed her new clothes into the case. The gaily-coloured blouses were ideal for her new jeans. It had taken Lois a lot of bullying to persuade Amanda that she could wear jeans. She insisted that Amanda try the dressy black silk trousers and red silk jacket trimmed with touches of black, and again she'd been proved right. Very up-to-the-minute and feminine, Amanda decided as she carefully refolded them in their tissue. The chunky earrings and the pearl choker were the finishing touches. "You should wear trousers more often," Lois advised. "They look terrific on you."

♥ ♥ ♥

Charles smiled as he sat beside Amanda. She was a careful driver and, as she wove her way in and out of the traffic, she chattered happily about her outing with Lois. Her face was unusually animated, her eyes bright.

"I think this weekend is going to be exciting. . ." her voice faded as she became aware of her garrulousness.

Charles gently squeezed her arm gently. "I know it is," he said.

Chapter Twenty-Five

Alex Travis phoned Kim in February, as he said he would, three days before he arrived in London. Kim refused his first invitation. She'd thought long and hard about the charming American. She was convinced that if she did meet him again, she'd become involved in a relationship that could never amount to anything. Alex Travis had a wife. She refused again when he "rang on the off chance . . ." The day after that Kim relented.

The Houses of Parliament, Buckingham Palace, the Tower of London . . . Alex's list of places he wanted to visit was endless.

"You're the best guide there is," Alex said as she struggled to keep up with his long strides.

"Slow down," Kim begged, "I'm not as tall as you."

"Sorry, shorty," he apologised and tried to match his pace to hers.

That night they ate at her favourite restaurant, a tiny French bistro in the heart of Belgravia. She was so exhausted from the unaccustomed walking that she sat back in her seat and asked him to order for her.

"I've hired a car for tomorrow, I thought we could go to Windsor," he said smoothly.

"That's a lovely idea." Kim was enthusiastic. She'd always wanted to tour the Castle and see the Dolls' House.

She exclaimed with delight at the miniature fittings and furniture, the minute books, the tiny porcelain ornaments. To make viewing easier, many of the objects had been removed from the Dolls' House itself and were displayed just inside the glass case which protected it. She was captivated by the size and beauty of it all.

"Alex, look at these wonderful tiny prints." Kim tugged at his sleeve. "The books are real, specially printed."

But Alex's attention was focused on her. "I'd rather look at you," he said.

To her discomfort a couple behind them smiled knowingly.

"Please don't," she begged, flustered.

It had been an exhilarating day, even the cold weather and persistent drizzle failed to dampen their spirits. This time Kim chose a Chinese restaurant, and they gorged on Peking duck, chilli and ginger beef and feather-light, battered lemon chicken washed down with pots of fragrant jasmine tea.

"I can't remember two more marvellous days," he said as he handed her a cigarette packet.

Kim frowned, Alex knew she didn't smoke.

"Open it," he instructed.

Kim lifted the flap and peeped inside. Pink tissue paper shrouded its contents.

Gently she removed the paper, hidden in its

folds was a tiny gold key. "It's beautiful," she exclaimed. "Thank you, but why?"

"Because you hold the key to . . . to London," he stammered.

Kim guessed that wasn't what he'd intended to say and suddenly felt inexplicably tongue-tied.

They strolled leisurely back to her flat. She made coffee while he poured the drinks. They compared the differences between London and New York, spoke about everything and anything the way polite strangers do. There were stilted silences and difficult lulls.

"Kim, can we have dinner in New York on your next trip?"

"It's very kind of you. But, Alex, is there really any point? You are married, aren't you?"

"Yes, I am. But in name only."

Kim's heart sank. She didn't want to hear that type of excuse, it was insulting. They'd spent a pleasant couple of days together but it must end, right here and now.

"It's been a lovely couple of days, but . . ."

"Before you refuse, at least let me explain," Alex interrupted. "My wife has suffered for the last five years from a severe mental illness. It started when our daughter died. Cassie – my wife – never recovered from the shock." His eyes, normally bright and alert, were clouded. "Louise was a beautiful little girl with blonde curly hair and the sweetest smile you've ever seen. One day when they were out walking, she pulled free of my wife's hand and darted into the street after a puppy . . ."

"Don't upset yourself," Kim pleaded as Alex's voice faltered.

"It's OK." He swirled the liquid in his glass. "After Louise . . . died, Cassie tried to commit suicide – a couple of times. I thought it might help if we had another child. The doctors agreed, but she wouldn't hear of it. She even moved out of our bedroom to make sure it couldn't happen. She's been in and out of therapy, in and out of hospitals, ever since. Now she needs constant supervision. She doesn't talk to me, doesn't communicate at all. Sometimes I feel that she's punishing me for what happened.

"I've tried everything in my power to help her, but nothing worked. At times she's totally irrational. If I talk to her she doesn't answer or doesn't hear me, I don't know which. Now we live in the same house but that's about the sum total of it. So that's what I mean by – in name only."

Kim stared into her empty glass. Poor man, what a terrible tragedy. What a miserable life he must lead. Lonely and empty. Not only had he lost his daughter, but his wife too. Kim broke the silence. "I'm truly sorry, Alex. You must have suffered so much."

"You learn to cope, work helps. Somehow God gives you the strength to carry on, at least He helped me. Cassie wasn't so lucky. Anyway, enough of this depressing talk. Now you know the score."

Kim nodded but didn't speak.

"Can I get you another drink?" Alex asked.

Kim shook her head. "But help yourself."

"Not for me. So, will I see you next time you're in New York?"

"Yes," she replied quietly.

"Will you call me a couple of days in advance? I'll give you my office numbers in New York and Washington and my home number too."

He wrote the numbers on the scratch-pad beside her phone then stood up and stretched. "I'd better be off, you've got an early start tomorrow."

Kim rose to her feet, Alex hesitated for a moment then reached out and pulled her into his arms and kissed her. A long lingering kiss which left her breathless.

♥ ♥ ♥

Kim was almost late for the briefing.

"What kept you?" Samantha said.

"Late night," Kim replied. She hadn't told Samantha that Alex was in London.

"Oh? With Hadley, I suppose." Secretly she had little time for Kim's boyfriend, Hadley Talbot. Samantha had met him once. In her opinion he was stolid, unemotional and about as exciting as yesterday's news.

Kim was grateful for the routine which prevented Samantha from asking any more questions. Apart from one special meal which hadn't been delivered to the plane, everything in the galley was in order. Sam went to the flight director to report the missing meal while Kim began decanting the wines.

She stood inside the entrance to the aircraft greeting passengers.

"Good morning, sir, welcome on . . . *Alex*! You didn't tell me you were flying back today." Kim was totally taken by surprise.

Alex smiled. "The guide who volunteered to show me around London for the past couple of days absconded! Suddenly it was lonely."

He liked the way the colour crept into her high cheekbones, the way that wave fell across her high forehead.

"I'll speak to you later!" she threatened.

"Can't wait."

The flight was fully booked, apart from an empty seat or two. There was the almost obligatory smattering of movie stars, business people and diplomats on board. Tandy Lord was queening it up and causing quite a stir. She always did.

"I've never known anyone make such a fuss," Samantha grumbled as she re-mixed Tandy Lord's cocktail. "I've a good mind to take this one back to her."

"It's not worth it. She's notoriously temperamental," Kim said. "Let her have her moment of glory, poor old thing."

Tandy Lord had been one of the biggest name in films in her heyday. She was still a beautiful woman but, apart from a cameo role here and there, she worked very little now. In her own mind she was still a great star, charming, vivacious and every bit as important as the top box-office actresses of today. She crossed and re-crossed the Atlantic constantly in search of a new career. But as far as the viewing public knew, she remained a has-been in Hollywood's eyes.

"Your steak Dumas, Sir." Kim smiled at Alex as she served his meal.

"Would you mind cutting it for me?" he asked shaking a limp wrist.

"Oh you poor man, I'll do it for you," the woman beside him immediately offered. "Have you hurt your hand?"

Kim tried not to giggle. "Serves you right," she whispered as the woman struggled to unfasten her seat belt and prepared selflessly to help her neighbour. Alex looked mortified. Shaking with suppressed laughter, Kim left them and returned to the galley.

♥ ♥ ♥

New York pulsed with a vigour no other city possessed and the Chinese restaurant was throbbing with life.

"How is your wrist? Would me like you to cut your chicken," Kim asked with a cheeky grin.

"No thank you," Alex said, "I'm cured."

"Does this beat your restaurant in London?" he asked later.

"I must admit, the food *is* great here." Kim chased a piece of water chestnut round the plate with her chopsticks. Everyone used chopsticks here, there wasn't a knife or a fork to be seen.

"Who were those men sitting behind me on the plane?" Alex wanted to know.

"I'm not sure, a bit creepy weren't they?"

"They looked like they'd stepped out of a gangster movie, all dark shirts and light ties. You must run into some oddballs in your job."

"We do." Kim regaled him with stories about some of the people she'd met. "But also I've made some really good friends over the years. I still keep in touch with some of them."

Alex called for the check and they walked

back to her hotel. The streets were teeming with people, the traffic still bumper to bumper. Everyone seemed to be in a hurry even at this late hour. For Kim, this was part of the vibrancy of New York, a never-ending, never-slowing cavalcade of movement.

"When will I see you again?" Alex asked as they strolled. "I have to be in Toronto next week, I'm addressing a group of students at the University of Toronto. It should be fun. I haven't visited Toronto for years."

"Was that your alma mater?"

"No, Harvard. I graduated from the Business School. After Toronto, Harvard is next on my whistle-stop tour. But we're digressing, when *will* I see you?"

"It'll be a while before I'm back in the States. I have a break coming up, I'm going to take a couple of weeks holiday."

"What are you planning to do with your vacation?"

"I haven't made any plans. Probably catch up on some films, spring-clean the flat, maybe start looking for another one – I want to buy a flat instead of renting one."

Kim lengthened her stride, Alex had started walking quickly again.

"This will probably sound crazy, why don't you spend part of your vacation with me? No strings, separate rooms of course. Do you know Toronto? . . . I . . ." Alex's voice trailed away.

"I couldn't," Kim replied instinctively.

"I didn't mean to sound pushy. It was just a thought – two people who enjoy each other's company, a few days exploring together. Besides,

I've sort of got used to having you around."

Kim's thoughts were in turmoil. She really liked this big man with his unassuming manner and gentle ways. He made her laugh, made her come alive. But to spend time with him in the same hotel? That was asking for trouble. What had he said – no strings? She didn't doubt that it would be enjoyable, different. She'd heard a lot about Toronto and would like to see it for herself. How would she spend her time at home – cleaning, an odd film or two, dinner with Hadley?

"Separate rooms?" she asked.

"Absolutely."

"No strings?"

"No strings," Alex repeated.

"When are you due to be there?"

"Next Tuesday, a week from today."

"What about your schedule?"

"I'll only be busy part of the day. You'd probably find it boring but if you'd like to come with me to the lectures . . . I mean, you'd be welcome."

"Let me phone you tomorrow night with my answer, OK?"

"Sure. I'll be waiting."

♥ ♥ ♥

She watched the passing scenery through the window of the cab.

"That's Lake Ontario," the driver explained as they drove along the vast stretch of still water. "Fabulous in the summer."

"What's that tall building over there?" Kim asked.

"It's the CN Tower, it really dominates the skyline doesn't it? You see it almost everywhere you go in *Tronna*. You must see the city from the top. It's the tallest free-standing building in the world," he explained proudly.

Kim walked around the suite. Alex had really pushed the boat out. Two bathrooms, no less! There was a beautiful arrangement of flowers on the table in the small sitting-room and a dish piled high with fruit. She kicked off her shoes and opened the note.

Welcome to Toronto.
Back at 6 p.m.
My room number is 403,
call me when you're ready.
Alex.

She peered at her watch in the dim light from the windows, it was six-thirty. She'd dozed for almost two hours. Even though she'd flown on Concorde, and been lucky enough to catch an excellent connecting flight, she must have been more tired than she realised.

"Hello, Kim," Alex's deep voice answered.

"Sorry I didn't ring you earlier, I fell asleep," she confessed.

"It's hard work flying! How long will it take you to get ready? Let's have an early dinner then we can talk about how we spend the rest of our time. It's my turn now to act as guide."

♥ ♥ ♥

Kim wandered around the smart, indoor shopping mall at Hazelton Lanes. It was fun to spend the morning browsing. Alex would be back in time for lunch and they planned to visit the Royal Ontario Museum in the afternoon. She meandered in and out of the attractive shops. As she passed the tobacconist's her attention was attracted by the sight of the assistant expertly lopping the top off a cigar, then lighting it. Great curls of blue smoke formed a halo round the smoker's head; it was the first time Kim had seen a woman smoking a full-sized cigar. The aroma of freshly brewing coffee drew her into a shop which sold dozens of varieties of beans. She walked slowly along the row of glass coffee jugs which steamed temptingly. Spoilt for choice she selected a mocha flavoured one and took it outside to the communal area shared by several of the cafés and restaurants. She returned her cup to the shop and bought two packets of the mocha-flavoured beans, one for Samantha, the other for herself. In the window of the jewellery store she saw a pair of earrings she liked. Half an hour later she left the shop with attractive cuff-links for Alex instead. She noticed that he usually wore them. She smiled mischievously and thought of ways she could package them.

Alex dashed through the lobby of the hotel and into the bar. "I hope you haven't been waiting too long," he said.

"Hours and hours."

"That's cool then," he laughed as he reached into the dish for a handful of nuts. "Don't keep me hanging about, girl, I'm starving."

"How was the lecture?" Kim asked trying to find the best way to get her mouth around her enormous sandwich.

"It was fine – at least from my point of view. No one fell asleep as far as I could tell."

"Do you give the same lecture each day?"

Alex briefly explained what his lectures were about and how he prepared and presented them to the students. "One day they could be employed by my firm. They probably already know far more about international investments than I did at their stage."

Kim listened to his beautifully modulated voice and admired his humility. "Do think I could go along with you tomorrow morning?"

"I'd be delighted," he beamed. He resisted the urge to take her hand in his own and raise it to his mouth. It had been an exhilarating morning. The students were intelligent and alert, their questions challenging. The time had flown but, best of all, when he'd returned to the hotel Kim was waiting. "Come on lazy-bones, let's go to the ROM."

They spent an absorbing afternoon. Kim was fascinated by the antiquities and Alex loved the natural history floor. He had a hard job convincing her that the stick insects which clung to the small twigs were indeed alive. She squealed with fright when the tarantula in the glass case suddenly moved. They sat on a wooden bench surrounded by giggling schoolchildren. Alex ate a candy bar while they watched a film about making porcelain.

They visited the museum's shop. Kim was disappointed not to find anything more innovative than gift-wrap with which to parcel Alex's cuff-links.

They strolled along the street arm-in-arm.

"Guess what? I'm hungry again!" Alex said eyeing the hot dog stand.

"Let me buy you a chilli dog," Kim offered.

"I won't argue with that," he agreed.

"You wait here, I'll get it."

Kim handed him the hot dog wrapped in a paper napkin. "Let's walk along Bloor Street," she suggested.

"Oh for heaven's sake! There's something in this. There's metal in the darn thing."

"Metal? Can't be," Kim said. "Open the roll and take a look."

Alex wrinkled his nose as he picked out some white tissue spattered with mustard and ketchup. He pulled the paper apart and discovered the links. "How did they get there? They're beautiful – I think!" The ketchup had seeped through the paper, hiding the beauty of the gift. "Did you. . . ?" he asked.

"I put them there," Kim said quickly, fearful he'd think they got there by accident.

Alex kissed the top of her head. He was touched by her thoughtful present, amused by her ingenuity.

"Didn't you want one of these delightful gourmet snacks?" Alex asked, biting a chunk of the soft roll. Metal or no metal, it didn't put him off his hot dog.

"No thanks, I have a sweet tooth. I'll save my appetite for later."

"In that case I know just the place."

♥ ♥ ♥

Kim sat at the back of the hall and listened to Alex.

This was a side of him she hadn't seen before; serious, commanding and totally in charge. The students hung on his every word. The only sound in the room was that of his voice. She smiled reassuringly as he looked her way, not that he needed her approval. It was a masterful performance.

In the last couple of days she'd tried not to analyse her feelings. There was something vital about Alex, sophisticated yet unaffected. When she was with him she forgot about time. As she sat in the shadows, Kim finally came face to face with reality, she had fallen in love with Alex Travis.

The students crowded around him and plied him with questions. Kim was sure her face revealed her thoughts and she avoided his gaze whenever he looked her way. Finally they made their escape.

He held her hand and led her to the waiting car.

"That was terrific," she said. "You could have heard a pin drop."

"These aren't like college lectures, they don't *have* to listen to my ramblings. So, what have you planned for me today?"

"Let's go back to the hotel, put on our 'working clothes' and take a tour of the city before lunch."

♥ ♥ ♥

As the bus wound its way through the city streets, Kim could feel the warmth of Alex's body beside her. One more day together, then what? Would their relationship die a natural death, or would it become a series of one-night meetings – dinners, snatched moments when they were both in New York? Or would Alex settle down in Washington once his sabbatical ended, leaving her to go back to the steady, dependable friendship of Hadley Talbot? A wave of depression gripped her. Her instincts had warned her to avoid just this sort of situation and now she'd landed herself right in it.

The sound of Alex's laughter jolted her back to reality. "That's unusual."

"What is?"

"The bank – their windows."

"Sorry," she apologised. "I wasn't listening."

"Two thousand five hundred ounces of gold are built into the windows of that bank. Look – there." He pointed over his shoulder to a building they'd passed. "It's real gold. They used it to tint the windows in order to reduce the glare."

Normally Kim would have taken an interest in everything around her but she was totally submerged in misery.

Alex glanced at Kim's reflection in the window of the bus. She was subdued today. He didn't think she was bored, the tour had been her idea. Her face was serene, her eyes half-hidden by her wavy hair.

The bus driver pointed out places of interest along their route. "We'll stop here for a short break," he informed them as he drew alongside the other vehicles in the park.

The sun shone through the bare branches of the trees streaking the grass with golden, wintry rays. From the platform overlooking the gardens they watched a bridal party picking its way across the green slope. A photographer, his breath white in the wintry air, blew on his hands as he waited for the couple.

"Brave young things," Alex remarked to the driver who stood beside them smoking a cigarette.

The man looked at him quizzically, brave to get married or brave weather-wise? He chose to play dumb. "Yes, it's not the best time of year. In summer you can't move here for the stretch limos. You can get up to twenty or thirty wedding parties a day. They come here after the church and before the reception. So many people live in apartments now, they really like the idea of an 'outdoors' album."

Kim watched the young bride, her dress scooped up into her arms in a puff of lace and satin. She looked into the face of her groom. He laughed at something she said and hugged her – almost knocking the flowing veil from her head.

They stopped while one of her attendants repaired the damage then walked across the green and gold path towards the waiting photographer.

Kim glanced at Alex but his face was impassive. Would she ever walk across a garden or stand outside a church, veil streaming in the wind like this youngster?

"They're hardly out of their teens," Alex broke the silence.

"I was thinking the same thing," Kim replied in a flat voice. "Let's go and have a cup of coffee." The whole episode was having a strange effect on her. Suddenly she wished she was alone. She needed the luxury of a good cry.

As they left the park and drove through the

outskirts the driver continued to fill their heads with statistics and points of interest. ". . . This is the Italian area . . . round here it's mainly Chinese . . . named Cabbagetown when the Irish settled here after the famine. Instead of planting flowers they grew cabbages . . ."

Kim thought the tour would never end.

♥ ♥ ♥

They walked around the Eaton Centre restaurant hall with its central seating space. At least the lunch-time crush was over. Kim bypassed the delicatessen with its endless array of salads, showed little interest in the freshly made tempura at the Japanese section. She rejected the juicy burgers from the restaurant beside the Chinese counter with its dishes of finely diced vegetables and stir-fry ingredients. Even the tempting aroma from the bakery section did nothing to whet her appetite.

"What do you fancy?" Alex asked patiently as they completed the circuit.

Kim made an effort to pull herself together. Alex, she'd discovered, was always hungry.

"A sandwich. I think." She couldn't muster up enthusiasm for anything more. Kim loved these North American food halls and often chose a starter from one, main course from another and ended with what she called a light, no-conscience, whipped yoghurt cone.

"You grab a table," Alex said, "I'll get the food. What do you want in your sandwich?"

"I don't mind, choose for me."

"What will you drink, coffee?"

"Yes, please."

She helped Alex to remove the food from the tray. While he ate his double burger and fries she picked at the sandwich on her plate. For the first time since she'd arrived in Canada they sat in silence, each lost in their own thoughts.

"It's probably not the time to ask, but what would you like to do tonight? A movie perhaps, or the theatre?"

Kim wondered how she would make it through the evening – facing Alex across a restaurant table would be torture.

"The opera would be nice." Kim wasn't crazy about opera but it was the first thing that came to mind.

"I think it's *La Bohème* tonight." Alex frowned. "I seem to remember seeing it advertised somewhere. What's on the agenda for this afternoon? Would you fancy climbing the seventeen hundred and sixty steps of the CN Tower or would you prefer to chicken out and take the elevator?"

She knew Alex was trying to cheer her up, chivvy her back to her usual good humour – but her mood refused to lift. "Would you mind if I skipped it?" she asked.

He looked at her pale face. "No problem. A lot of people don't like heights."

"It's not that, I have . . . a bit of a headache." She hated lying but it would give her the time she needed to pull herself together. "Why don't *you* go? It's not too far from here. You could visit the Sky-Dome after that." She knew Alex was eager to see the huge sports arena with its retractable roof. "I'll take the subway back to the hotel and see you there later."

The subway, affectionately known locally as "the rocket," was an excellent system of transport. But Alex stubbornly refused to allow her to use it. "At least take a cab," he insisted.

For the sake of peace she gave in and offered to book the seats for the opera when she got back to the hotel.

♥ ♥ ♥

Alex sat in the bar and waited for Kim. He was hopelessly in love with her and troubled by her distant manner. Last night he'd planned to try and persuade her to stay on and travel to Boston with him. Now he was certain she'd refuse. He was so mad about her but it was painfully clear that Kim didn't feel the same way about him. Kim, with her lovely face and laughing eyes, so quiet and withdrawn today.

Since they'd met on that snowy night in New York, he'd shed twenty years. He'd laughed, teased, been more light-hearted, happier in these last few weeks than he'd been for years. His investment consultancy business had given him little time for socialising or making close personal friends. Cassie had never minded. She'd been quite content, flattered, that they mixed in such exalted political and money oriented circles. She had regarded congressmen, senators and their partners, as her friends. But Alex knew she was deluding herself, they were merely business acquaintances with a thick veneer of charm.

Kim stood in the doorway and her heart skipped a beat when she saw him. He looked so distinguished sitting there, lost in concentration.

"Hi," she said softly.

Alex jumped to his feet and smiled. Kim hoped he wouldn't notice the extra make-up she'd had to use on her eyes. By the end of the afternoon she'd cried so much she hardly recognised her own face in the mirror. Room service brought some ice with the tea she'd ordered, the only thing she could think of to remove the puffiness from under her eyes.

"What will you drink?" he asked.

"A glass of white wine. How was the Tower?" She was determined not to ruin their last night together.

"Fantastic. There were two circular viewing platforms which jutted out from the Tower. One above the other. The lower one was glassed in and, at every window, there was a map of the area seen from that particular viewpoint. In an extended section of the platform, the floor was made of glass. When you looked down you could see everything beneath you. Not for the faint hearted or those who suffer from vertigo!"

"Did *you* walk on it?" Kim could feel her stomach wiggle.

"I put one foot on it and then chickened out. I didn't care how strong it was. But lots of people tested it out. Some lay on it, others jumped on it and one young man even practised his somersaults. I left them to it and went up to the higher floor. That was open to the air but strongly protected by metal mesh. I had a quick look around but was quite happy to get back on firm ground." He pushed the bowl of olives across the table. Poor Kim, that headache must have been bad, her eyes looked sore. "How's the head?"

"Much better – thank you. What else did you do?"

"I went to the Sky-Dome but unfortunately the roof was closed. There was no game today. Then I browsed round 'World's Biggest Bookstore' – that's what it's called. I found a couple of books I wanted to read."

"Is it the world's biggest bookstore?" Kim asked.

"I don't know. It certainly is enormous. Twenty-seven kilometres of shelves, according to the bookmark they put in the bag. I could have spent a whole day there, or even a week."

♥ ♥ ♥

The music did nothing to distract her thoughts. Kim closed her eyes and let it wash over her. She didn't want to think about the sad story unfolding on the stage, she had enough problems of her own. The opera seemed endless and she practically leapt from her seat when the final curtain came down. There was still dinner to get through.

"I hope you don't mind, I've ordered a meal to be sent up to the suite," Alex said. "I reckoned it would be late by the time we left the theatre."

"That sounds lovely." Kim forced herself to sound cheerful.

They sat apart in the darkness of the cab. If only Alex wasn't married, if only they didn't have to be separated by time and tide, if only . . . if only. Thoughts spun round her head in ever decreasing circles until she felt it was being gripped in a vice of negativity. Their situation was hopeless, it had no future. Alex was the perfect man for her if only he wasn't – slightly married.

They talked about their childhood, their parents and families. Alex's parents were dead, Kim's mother and stepfather very much alive and living in the English Midlands. "One day I'll bore you with college photographs," Alex teased.

Kim's spirit lifted a little, would there be a *one day?*

"I'd like that. You'll be there in a couple of days, won't you? Are you looking forward to being at Harvard again?"

"Very much. Kim, would you . . ."

The intermittent buzz of the phone jarred the quiet of the room.

Chapter Twenty-Six

"Who can that be? Nobody would phone me in Toronto," Kim said as the telephone twittered.

"I'll get it." Alex walked the couple of steps to the shrilling instrument.

"Hello? Speaking. Yes, . . . yes. I see. I'll take the first flight I can . . . That's all right, you're only doing your job. See you tomorrow, goodbye."

Alex's face was grim. "I'm sorry, I'm afraid I'll have to leave Toronto on the first available flight. There's no need for you to cut short your stay."

"What's happened?" Kim felt excluded.

"It's my wife," he said tersely. "She slipped out of the house while her nurse was having dinner. Unfortunately she took my car and in the space of five minutes she side-swiped half a dozen others. She ended up hitting a fire hydrant. Her shoulder is slightly damaged and she has a fractured wrist. Cassie shouldn't have taken the car . . . the medication . . . she's forbidden to drive." Alex's face was dark with anger and shock. "She could have killed herself, or someone else."

"I'm so sorry, Alex. That's frightening. Please don't worry about me. I'll organise something in the morning."

"When will I see you again, Kim?"

"I don't know."

"I'll call you when you get back to London." Alex looked at Kim's strained face.

"Suit yourself." Kim shrugged resignedly and made no move to rise from her chair. "But you'll probably be busy coping with things at home."

Alex bent awkwardly to kiss her upturned face. In a couple of strides he crossed the room and was gone.

"You idiot," she railed. She wanted Alex to take her in his arms, to kiss her, to make love to her. Instead she'd sounded like a cold, uncaring bitch. The whole thing was such a mess. And there would always be his wife.

Kim dozed, tossed and turned, then finally fell into a deep sleep. When she woke the hotel message-light was flashing on the phone beside her bed. Alex had left. He'd been able to get an early morning flight and didn't want to call her room and disturb her.

The return flight to London was long and tedious. A child cried incessantly. Kim's nerves crawled with frustration and uncertainty. She vowed that from now on she'd ignore Alex's calls, wouldn't see him again. She just wanted to forget him.

♥ ♥ ♥

For two months she succeeded in avoiding him. But he didn't give up. If she was at home she let the answering machine take her calls. Alex's plaintive voice in the quiet room shattered her peace of mind. She gnawed on her knuckles to stop herself from picking up the phone. He would stop calling eventually. And then, to her dismay, he did. For three weeks she heard nothing. That was what she wanted, wasn't it?

♥ ♥ ♥

Kim saw him before he saw her. He was standing at the barrier in the arrivals hall at Kennedy Airport. She slipped behind Samantha and tugged at her sleeve like a child. "Look, it's Alex. I don't want to see him. Tell him I'm not on the flight. Tell him anything, I don't want to talk to him."

"What makes you think he's waiting for you? He might be meeting someone from another flight," Samantha asked sharply.

"You're right, I suppose. But I don't want to see him."

"Kim, wouldn't it be easier if you just faced Alex and told him that it's over, finished?"

"Maybe . . . no . . . yes, I don't know. How *did* he know I was on this flight?"

"Search me, perhaps he meets all the flights." Samantha averted her gaze. If Kim suspected that she was the one who'd given Alex the information, she would probably never speak to her again. But Alex had made it so difficult for her. His voice was pleading, so woebegone that she'd weakened. He promised never to tell Kim that he'd enlisted her help.

"You didn't tell him, did you?" Kim demanded accusingly.

"How could I? I don't have his phone number." At least that much was true. But Alex did have hers, Kim had given it to Alex herself when her answering machine wasn't working.

"Listen, Kim, have a coffee with him here at the airport. I'll wait for you. Tell him it's finished – or not. But don't hide, that's stupid."

"All right," Kim agreed sullenly. "But you *will* wait?"

"I'll wait."

Her resolve melted as she looked at his face. He was a little thinner than she remembered, sadder. The teasing humour was missing from his voice.

"Why wouldn't you answer my calls?" he asked as soon as they were seated.

"I don't know. I didn't . . ."

"You didn't what?" he demanded angrily.

"I didn't think there was any point. It won't work, Alex."

"I've missed you so much, Kim."

"And I've missed . . ." That was not what she intended to say.

"This is all such a mess. I'm on my way back to Washington, we don't even have time to talk properly. When will you be in New York again? When will you have some free time?"

Kim shrugged. "I'll be in New York on Friday, but as far as free time goes, I don't really know. Probably not for a couple of months."

"Will you let me know as soon as you find out? It doesn't matter when it is, I'll make sure I'm free at the same time. We can be together – talk. Please Kim, promise me you will."

"I promise."

"Will you be home in London tomorrow night? I'll call you there."

"OK. Have a good flight."

"Oh, Kim, you're driving me crazy."

"I must be crazy myself." Kim laughed for the first time in ages.

♥ ♥ ♥

Kim sat in her flat watched the clock anxiously and grabbed for the phone at the first ring.

"Did you miss me?" Alex's voice was soft.

"Yes, I really did," Kim admitted. "I forgot to ask you yesterday, was your wife all right after her car accident?"

"As right as she'll ever be. But physically, yes."

They talked for almost an hour until Kim reminded him that it wasn't a local call.

"It's worth every cent just to hear your voice. I'll call you tomorrow, same time?"

"I'll be waiting. Goodnight, Alex."

♥ ♥ ♥

New York was at its worst; overcrowded and unseasonably hot. Even at night it was airless and the humidity was draining. Kim walked slowly and longed for even a slight breeze. It was only a couple of blocks to the restaurant and already her St Laurent blouse was clinging to her like a second skin. The restaurant was noisy and Alex was late. An argument had erupted between two couples waiting for a table, each claimed they were first. Tempers always seemed to flare more rapidly in the heat. The men began to push one another and one of the women yelled obscenities at the other. Within minutes, both couples were escorted unceremoniously from the building.

Kim touched the box with her foot and smiled. Alex would find it difficult to guess what was inside it.

"I'm so sorry, Kim." Alex rushed to the table mopping his forehead. "It's hotter than hell out there and every cab in the city has vanished."

He didn't tell her that his flight was late or that he'd flown in specially to be with her. He couldn't face another week without seeing her lovely face or hearing her laugh.

"I've had three showers already today." She grimaced pulling the collar of her blouse away from her neck. Kim waited as he slid into the seat beside her. "Have you had a busy day?"

"Kind of, yes. How did you spend your afternoon?"

Before she could reply a waiter appeared at their side with the menus.

Kim wasn't hungry and decided to have a salad. Alex chose his favourite meal of steak, French fries and salad.

"Help yourselves from the salad bar, I'll have your steak in a few minutes." The waiter gathered the menus and dashed to the next table.

The salad bar was the focal point in the centre of the room; two bath tubs side by side, filled to the brim with ice. Kim loved the crispy lettuce nesting in the big glass dish on the bed of ice. Such imaginative use of vegetables, fruit, pasta and shrimp.

"American restaurants do this so well. The salad is a meal in itself," she said as she peered at the bewildering variety of dressings.

"For you maybe! I like rabbit food but give me

a good healthy dollop of starch any day." Alex was amazingly trim for a man who ate so much.

"I have to go to Harvard at the beginning of May. Remember the lecture I was supposed to give after Toronto?" Alex mumbled as he concentrated on his steak. "We . . . I . . . have a beach house at Cape Cod."

Kim was ahead of him; whenever Alex had something difficult to say, he refused to meet her eyes. One of his French fries skidded on to the cloth. He prodded it nervously with his fork and returned it to the side of his plate. "Will you spend some time there with me?"

This was what she'd longed for, yearned for, been frightened of – the turning point in their relationship. She still had time to get out, to say no.

"Yes," she answered simply.

The rest of their meal was forgotten. Alex's smile lit up his face. Gently she released her hand and bent to retrieve the big box from its hiding place under the table, now was a good time to give it to him.

He tore the wrapping away and opened the flaps of the box. The cloth it was loosely wrapped in fell away revealing the crude figure of a woman sculpted in modelling clay. The misshapen figure brought an even broader grin to his face. "OK, what's this?"

"A model of myself," she teased.

"You've changed," he parried.

"Use your knife, that way you can alter the bits you don't like."

Alex began to pare away the coloured modelling-clay. "Will the knife do any damage?" he asked.

"Keep going," Kim said complacently.

The couple at the next table stopped talking and openly watched Alex perform the delicate operation.

"Come on fella, we gotta go soon," the man said impatiently.

Alex smiled at him good-naturedly, nothing anyone said could perturb him tonight.

The pile of discarded clay grew as Alex carefully sliced it away from the sculpture.

"Wan' any help? I think you've been had," the man chipped in again.

"He's doing fine," Kim replied. "This is good therapy for him."

The instant she'd said it, she could have cut her own throat with the blunt knife. Poor Alex – he didn't need to be reminded of his wife, he was here to forget his problems not add to them. As colour raced up her neck and into her cheeks, she stole a glance at him. Either he'd chosen to ignore her remark or hadn't heard it, his attention was wholly on what he was doing. He was getting close to the base of the disfigured sculpture.

"I think you should peel the rest off by hand now," she advised.

Slowly a glass rim appeared, then a central column.

"Oh Kim, it's a beauty!" He leaned across and kissed her cheek. "Thank you."

"What the hell is it?" The man had left his seat and was standing at Alex's side.

"It's a candle-holder, and a rare one at that."

Alex smiled at Kim as he pulled away the last pieces of clay.

Alex once mentioned his collection of candlesticks. Singles, pairs, it made no difference. She gathered that as long as they were attractive he was happy. Seemingly he had dozens of them now. Kim had spent two Saturdays wandering around Portobello market in search of an unusual pair of candlesticks for him. She fell for the one she'd bought even though its partner was missing.

Triumphantly Alex held the saucer-shape holder up to the light. The tiny rods of colour embedded in the glass delighted him. "It's fabulous, I've never seen one like this before."

The man patted Alex on the shoulder. "Enjoy," he said with a puzzled frown. All that fuss about a crummy candlestick.

♥ ♥ ♥

They talked every night. Long, frustrating conversations that separated lovers hate, yet welcome. Cold, impersonal telephones linked the divided miles, a poor substitute for the warmth and love of human contact.

Kim was surprised by Alex's early phone call from Washington one evening.

"I thought you were in London, I've been calling for ages. When there was no reply, I was sure you'd been mugged or worse," he said.

"So how did you find out I was here in New York?" she asked.

"I phoned Ros, at the airline. She must have thought I was crazy. But she set me straight. I don't know how I got the days mixed up."

"Only five more," Kim said soothingly.

"More like five lifetimes."

Chapter Twenty-Seven

Alex dumped his bags inside the door and looked around in amazement. His long-range refurbishing scheme had paid off. The beach house was unrecognisable. Sunlight flooded the open-plan room with its white oak floors. The gauzy drapes were open and, from where he stood, the beach was clearly visible. The serviceable beige-coloured sofas and chairs had gone and, in their place, a couch-potato's dream – bed-size settees and vibrantly coloured armchairs. Rugs, woven to match, added subtle splashes of colour to the bleached wooden floor. The niche at the side of the fireplace was piled high with logs. He would light the fire later, even in May the nights could be quite chilly. Alex walked over to the windows which ran the full length of the back wall and wondered how the house stayed up – all that glass, it didn't seem possible. Still, he reckoned that Granolli, his decorator, knew what she was doing. He slid back the huge glass door and stepped onto the veranda; the air from the ocean had a salty tang.

Granolli had knocked two bedrooms into one. "Shades of cream – soft and restful. A perfect room for sleep," she described soothingly over the phone. But sleep wasn't what he had in mind. The enormous bed, custom-made, was almost lost in the big room. He pressed one of the buttons on the generous sized bed-table and the drapes swished silently to a close, diffusing the bright light to a soft shadow. They were fun, all these switches. He pressed one marked radio, then another for the television which was hidden behind a glass panel in the wall. When he pressed the third button, he was bombarded with Latin-American music from the CD player. He switched again and the tempo instantly changed to a soft soothing melody. A seduction-chamber if ever there was one. He smiled. His smile broadened as he closed the bathroom door.

Alex reversed the car onto the quiet street and drove to the nearest shopping mall. He had no intention of eating out this week, he was sick of restaurants. It was years since he'd cooked and he hoped he still remembered how. There used to be an excellent deli in the mall, he could stock up there, then go to the supermarket.

♥ ♥ ♥

"We're here ma'am." The cab driver's voice reached her through a fog of sleep. Kim was expert at cat-napping and the drive from Boston to Cape Cod was a lengthy one.

Alex rushed outside as the cab turned into the driveway. Without any self-consciousness he swept Kim into his arms in a bear hug which left her breathless.

"I thought you'd *never* get here." He laughed at his own impatience. "What do I owe you?" Alex's eyes didn't leave Kim's face as he handed the cab driver a pile of notes. "Keep the change," he said.

"Have a good trip," the driver said to Kim.

Alex circled her slender shoulders with his big arm. He picked up her case and stood beside Kim as she looked around her. The beach house was set in a large garden surrounded by a white picket fence. Apart from the lawn, there were a few spiky shrubs and one wind-blown tree. She glanced at the houses either side, they too were built of clapboard, little grey wooden tiles whose colours had faded and softened with age.

Kim gasped with delight, the room was beautiful. For a moment she thought of her own flat, so tiny compared to this. It was sensibly furnished in dark colours – right for the English climate. Even though it was night-time, she could imagine that this softly-lit, almost too-delicate-to-live-in room would be heavenly in daylight too. White floors!

"It's absolutely gorgeous, Alex," she said as she turned in a circle.

"Let me pour you a drink, dinner will be ready soon."

"You can cook?" Kim asked.

"Sort of!" He laughed. "I'm good at following directions on the packets!"

Kim lay on the sofa in front of the fire and let her mind drift and her eyes wander. On the fireplace wall there was a bookcase crammed full of books. Attractive modern art almost filled the other large wall. How could Alex bear to spend time away from this haven? He'd said he hadn't been here for years.

Kim's last few days in London had been hectic. After a mad shopping-spree her case was full of new clothes. It had been impossible to resist those trendy T-shirts with their matching wrap-around skirts. She'd fallen in love with a deliciously feminine chiffon dress with narrow, jewelled straps. It was so short that at first she'd mistaken it for a top. And all those lightweight, gauzy trousers with their bare-midriff tops, they would be perfect here. The lacy underwear had cost her a fortune. That would be perfect anywhere.

"Chef Travis would like to present his *plat du jour.*" A delicious odour of herbs filled the room as Alex pushed the swing door open with his shoulder. Kim's stomach rumbled its approval. "Don't get up," he instructed. "We can eat here at the coffee table."

"I must wash my hands. Which one is the bathroom?"

"Would you mind using the kitchen? The bathroom is a bit messy, I'll fix it up when we've eaten."

The pasta with its pesto sauce lived up to its promise, the salad was crisp and fresh.

"You're a *terrific* cook, this salad dressing is brilliant," Kim said appreciatively as she mopped up the sauce with a crusty piece of bread. "I didn't realise how hungry I was."

"The dressing is good, isn't it?" Alex asked with a grin. "I bought it with my own fair hands."

Alex left half his meal, for once his appetite had forsaken him. He refused to let her help with the coffee. In a couple of minutes he returned with a cafètiere, two brandy balloons and a gaily wrapped package festooned with ribbons. He handed Kim the little parcel and busied himself pouring the coffee and brandy while she opened it. She smiled as she saw the battered cardboard container, a display box for fibre-tipped pens. Alex was getting his own back for the hot dog and the candlestick. As she wound the ribbon over her fingers she wondered where he kept his collection. Obviously not here. They were probably in his Washington home, and she'd never see that, she thought sadly.

"Aren't you going to open the box?" Alex frowned.

"I think I'll leave it till later," Kim teased, spinning it out. Alex looked a little disappointed.

"Oh all right, I'll open it now." She pulled what looked like a black handkerchief from the box. The fabric sprang apart in her fingers. It was the sheerest nightdress she'd ever seen. "It's gorgeous! So delicate, it's as light as air." Kim could have kicked herself, she was blushing like a virgin schoolgirl.

"Would you like to unpack? I'll show you where to hang your clothes. While you're doing that, I'll tidy the bathroom."

The colour rose in Kim's face as Alex led the way through the spacious bedroom. No separate rooms this time.

"Here we are," Alex said opening a door which revealed a walk-in closet. "I've left this side for you." The rail was bare except for a soft, satin-edged, pink bath-robe. The pocket was embroidered with her name.

"Thank you, Alex, that's . . . very thoughtful."

She appreciated his tactfulness. Had he brought other women here? She felt a momentary twinge of jealousy, Alex was a most attractive man.

"I'd love to take a shower," Kim said as Alex came back to see how she was getting on.

"The bathroom awaits . . ." Alex's voice broke off.

A dreadful feeling of *déjà vu* crept over her as the telephone rang. "Not Cassie again, please not again," she prayed as Alex picked it up.

"Hello," he answered quietly. "Hello . . . hello."

"Must be a wrong number," he said, smiling with relief. "As I was saying, your bath awaits."

The bathroom was stunning. A large square room lit entirely by candles, dozens and dozens of pale pink, perfumed candles. In the centre of the room, sunken into the floor, was the most enormous, rose-pink marble bath she'd ever seen. "It's like a miniature swimming-pool," she gasped.

The carpet was warm under her bare feet. It must be a foot thick, she thought. As her eyes grew accustomed to the light she saw that the candles on the wide rim of the bath were set into an extraordinary collection of candlesticks. Next to the twisted brass guide rails, beside the steps, was the holder she'd brought Alex from London.

"It's incredible. I've never seen anything like it."

"I must admit I'm astonished myself," Alex confessed. "I took a real chance when I hired someone I hadn't met to carry out the work, but she was highly recommended. I'll leave you to it or the water will get cold. Press that switch there if you want bubbles."

At least no one else had dipped their dainty

little toes into this rose-pink extravaganza, Kim thought. She walked down the couple of marble steps, then giggling, swam two strokes until she reached the side.

Kim rested her head on the waterproof pillow. She held on to two of the handles under the rim so that her body floated weightlessly in the perfumed water. The walls of the room were marble too. A smoked glass door led to what she supposed was the rest of the bathroom. The bath was the only object in the room apart from an ornate, brass what-not stacked high with luxurious fluffy towels. Samantha would adore this. All these candles and the beautiful glass bottles filled with perfumed oils. If she clapped her hands, would a handmaiden appear carrying fruit or whatever it was handmaidens carried? She tried it out and almost drowned with fright as music filled the room. She'd seen a lamp that lit up when you clapped your hands, a key ring that bleeped, but this was taking technology a bit too far for her liking. Tomorrow's world, today.

The bubbles were wonderfully soothing and she was practically asleep when Alex tapped at the door.

"Come in," she called.

"I thought you might have fallen asleep." He wore a white terry robe and carried a bottle of champagne and two flutes.

She'd settle for a manservant instead!

She lay in the water and sipped her drink. Alex sat on the pink marble rim behind her. Her body tensed as he trailed his fingers across the back of her neck and then slowly began to massage her taut muscles. The aching tension faded from her body as he moved his fingers up and down her neck. She closed her eyes as his gentle hands moved over her shoulders to her breasts. Slowly he caressed them. Her breathing quickened. There was nothing else now, no existence outside this water filled paradise. Alex slipped off his robe and slid into the water beside her. Instinctively she turned to him and they drifted towards one another like magnets.

"If you knew how I longed for this," she whispered, afraid that her voice would break the spell. The music playing softly in the background was hypnotic. She relaxed under his gentle touch.

He kissed her face, her eyes, her lips. His hands explored her body, sensitively at first then urgently. "You are so beautiful," he said in a rough voice. When he entered her it seemed the most natural thing in the world. All the waiting, the frustration floated away with the rhythmic movement of their bodies. He moved slowly inside her and her control slipped away as her excitement mounted. She shouted his name as together they quivered to a climax. He held her tightly, his face buried in her damp, sweet, perfumed hair. "My wonderful Kim, how I love you. I've thought of nothing else but being here together."

"I'd begun to believe it wasn't meant to be." She snuggled into his lean body and shivered slightly in the cool water.

"You're cold," he said. He wrapped her in a big fluffy towel and carried her back to the bedroom. Gently he dried her and again she felt the thrill of his touch.

It was almost dawn before they fell asleep in

each other's arms, content, fulfilled and exhausted.

The smell of coffee woke her. Alex was singing in the kitchen. Kim stretched and smiled, his voice was strong but not very melodious.

"Good morning," she called.

"Good afternoon," Alex replied. He carried a tray piled high with waffles, pancakes, maple syrup and coffee into the bedroom.

Shyly Kim smiled at him. He set the tray down and took her in his arms.

"Did you sleep well?" he asked kissing her tousled hair.

"When you let me," she laughed.

"Just listen to you! Who woke me up out of a deep sleep at four-thirty?"

"The tooth fairy!"

Their teasing soon stopped and the coffee went cold as once again they made love, slowly and sensuously this time, each aware of the other's needs.

"I'll make more coffee," Kim said throwing on a robe.

Alex watched her cross the room, her bare feet making no sound on the thick carpet. She was a delight, serious and funny, compassionate yet sensible. He luxuriated in the comfort of the downy cushions, a whole week stretched before them. When Kim came back with the coffee, he was fast asleep.

She kissed him awake and in his drowsy state he began to make love to her again.

"Oh no! Two wasted pots of coffee are enough." She laughed and pulled away from him.

"Heartless creature," he grumbled.

There was a slight breeze as they walked hand in hand along the water's edge. "It's still quiet here at this time of the year," he explained. "Some people live here of course but most of them come for the summer, or Christmas, or both. My parents bought the house when my sister and I were still small kids."

Kim was surprised, this was the first time Alex had mentioned a sister.

"The minute school was out, we'd pack up and move here. It was a wonderful way to spend a vacation. There were always loads of kids our age. Dad commuted at the weekends. That was the *best* time. He was crazy about boats, mad about fishing. He'd take two or three of us out for the day and teach us all he knew about sailing and marine life. All we wanted to do was catch great big fish to prove how smart we were! Whenever I think of those trips it reminds me of an old ditty we used to sing – *Cape Cod girls they have no combs, they comb their hair with codfish bones.*

"Sometimes we'd get together with the other families and have huge barbecues. If we did strike lucky and catch fish, our parents would make a great fuss of us, and the slippery fish would then be treated to a special place on the hot coals." Kim held his hand a little tighter. At least his childhood memories were happy.

In the distance she could see rocks rising from the water like bizarre sculptures pummelled by the lashing waves. They watched a bird rise into the air and drop a shell on to the rocks. It swooped, collected the shell, then repeated the exercise several times. The shell finally cracked and opened. Crowing noisily, the bird retrieved its prize, flew a circle of honour, then flapped off triumphantly down the sands.

They ate that night by the fire, happy in each other's company. Kim insisted it was her turn to cook dinner. She walked barefoot about the bright kitchen. It was fun to use strange ingredients, fun to cook for someone besides herself. Happiness was a wonderful state. All her senses were heightened, even the classical music which played in the background was more poignant, pulsating. She laughed as she found herself conducting the invisible orchestra, she'd become a regular Simon Rattle of the spatula.

"More wine?" Alex asked lazily.

"I'm almost asleep, I'd better not. It's too lovely a night to be missed."

Alex opened the big glass doors and they could hear the gentle lapping of the waves as they broke on the shore. "Come and look," he said. Beyond the peace and stillness of the beach, the full moon wove a shimmering silvery path which stretched towards the horizon.

She leant back against Alex, his arms around her, and they watched the gentle motion of the inky sea.

"Doesn't it make you long to walk across that path of moonbeams?" Kim reflected. "On and on till you reach the land beyond."

"I hate to tread on your dreams but, after the meal I've just eaten, I'd sink after the first step."

"You're all heart," Kim accused.

Kim told him about her mother, her much loved step-father, about her aspirations and disappointments. ". . . I'd love to have been a pilot," she admitted.

Alex's eyebrows rose in surprise, she was the least predictable woman he'd ever met. Flying lessons would make an unusual Christmas gift for Kim. He wondered how he would wrap a present like that. Christmas – it was a long way off. When would they have another opportunity to spend such perfect time together? With a supreme effort Alex forced himself to concentrate on what she was saying. They still had another five days – four, his lecture at the university would take up most of their last precious morning.

♥ ♥ ♥

Kim walked along the beach. The sea was an angry green. She turned back into the wind, and in the distance she could see Alex moving about the veranda. He'd been working on his lecture for the following day. Her heart filled with dread at the thought of parting. She'd never been so happy. She would always remember their walks along this magical sandy bay, their words of love shared only by the wind and the sea. Alex was wonderful. And the sex was wonderful too. "You've become a positive sex-fiend," Alex had laughed this morning.

"Any complaints?" she asked.

"Absolutely not," he assured her as he grabbed her and pulled her down on to the bed beside him.

They rarely left the house except to go to the

nearby shopping mall, walk along the sands or explore the unpopulated streets. Kim was fascinated by the uniformity of building materials, the colourless little tiles were everywhere.

"Construction laws are quite strict and that also applies to colour," Alex explained. "But apart from their outside appearance, some of the homes are quite magnificent inside." The clapboard houses changed only in shape or size, many with their green and red Christmas wreaths still attached to the front doors.

"In the summer the wreaths are exchanged for straw-coloured boaters. As well as ribbons, the brims are decorated with colourful dried flowers. When we were kids that's how we knew when our holiday friends had arrived."

If they saw anyone coming along the beach towards them, they lowered their heads to avoid eye contact. Alex felt guilty that Kim had come all this way and seen nothing of her surroundings.

"This is all I want, all I need," she insisted vehemently, and he didn't object.

Stretched out on one of the deep sofas, Kim discovered the delight of Anthony Trollope's novels. She learnt how to complete the *New York Times* crossword with Alex's help. They argued laughingly about which videos to watch – weepies or westerns – and settled for thrillers. They watched the movies curled up together on the huge bed, separated only by a gargantuan bowl of popcorn.

♥ ♥ ♥

The wind whipped her hair over her face.

Tonight would be their last night together, how would she exist without him? How long until they were together again? Or would it be back to the same routine – a few snatched hours in New York during a stopover? It was too painful to contemplate. A couple of drops of rain splashed onto her cheeks. She quickened her steps as the shower turned into a downpour.

Alex looked anxiously into the sheeting rain, Kim couldn't be too far away. Her bedraggled figure came into sight as he waited inside the open doorway of the veranda with a towel.

"Where did that downpour spring from?" she asked shaking herself on the wooden slats like a rain-soaked dog.

He wrapped the big soft towel around her and hugged her to him. They didn't speak, aware of the precious moment of closeness ticking away.

Their lovemaking that night was bittersweet. She clung to him tightly, her heart heavy. She hadn't felt so miserable since their last day in Toronto. His breath was warm on her forehead and she stirred in his arms, ashamed of the tears that flowed down her face.

"Don't cry, darling." He hated to see her unhappy like this. "We'll work something out," he promised.

"What?" she sobbed. "More frustrating dinners in New York? More long-distance phone calls? Oh Alex, I feel so sad."

He stroked Kim's hair and rocked her like a baby until she fell into an uneasy sleep. He lay quietly at her side and listened to her even breathing, his mind despairingly searching for a solution.

Chapter Twenty-Eight

Kim eyes filled with tears as she folded the filmy nightdress and placed it in her case. There was still over an hour left before Alex was due back from his lecture. He wanted to drive her to the airport himself. She wandered restlessly on to the sun-deck and stared moodily at the sea, it was rough today. Large waves lashed the beach, receded, then attacked again leaving a mass of broken shells and shingle in their wake. She hurried back inside and shut out the sound of the ocean. Even in her misery the colourful room cheered her. She looked around deliberately, photographing every detail in her mind.

A car horn sounded outside. Alex was back early, he must have raced along the roads like a madman. She must not let him see her dejection, there'd been enough tears last night. He deserved better than that. Kim ran to the door and opened it with a smile.

"Hello, I'm Cassie Travis, you are . . . Kim?"

Kim stared stupidly at the woman.

"You don't mind if I come in, do you?" Her voice was light but firm.

Kim stepped back as Cassie Travis passed her in a haze of expensive perfume. "My, my, the decorator has done a good job," she said running a light finger over the fabric on one of the chairs.

Kim stood, transfixed.

"Is Alex here?" Cassie Travis asked as she picked up a small sculpture from the top of the bookcase. She searched in her pocket, brought out a dainty lace handkerchief which she used to dust the figure.

Kim shook her head dumbly. Was this Alex's *irrational, suicidal* wife, this elegant, beautifully-groomed woman?

Cassie was taller than Kim, slimmer, with beautifully sun-streaked blonde hair. Her make-up was so artfully applied that her skin looked totally natural. Her mint-green and white striped suit shrieked quality.

"Why don't you come and sit down here? I'm sure this must be a shock for you. It always is," she sighed, crossing her long legs.

Imagine wearing tights in this heat, Kim thought hysterically.

"Have you had a wonderful visit with my husband?" Cassie's green eyes held no malice.

Kim's face was deathly white.

"Oh dear, I can see this *has* hit you hard. Alex is wicked. You see most of his . . . ladies, shall we say, know the score. I feel so sad for you, Kim."

"What do you mean – *most of his ladies?*" The voice that spoke was rasping and harsh, it didn't sound like hers.

"You reckoned you were the first? The only one? Oh Lordie, what line did he spin you? The sick wife? Or, my wife's a basket case? That's what he told the last one. But I'm sure he has a different tale for each of you. You look like a nice person, not the usual tramp . . ." Cassie gave her an apologetic look.

Kim winced at her words. She had believed Alex, trusted him completely. This woman sitting calmly on the settee was as sane as she was. Saner perhaps. How could she have been so gullible?

"When will Alex be back?"

"In an hour or so," Kim replied, lifelessly. "How many others were there?"

"Seven, eight, I've lost count now." Cassie's face was sympathetic.

Kim's heart raced alarmingly, her head was muzzy. I mustn't faint, not now. She balled her hands into fists and fought desperately not to black out.

"If I were you, I'd get out of here now while you can. Sometimes it can get very messy," Cassie advised the shaking Kim. "One thing's for sure, you won't win. Alex always walks away smiling – to the next one."

Kim could feel the bile rising to her throat. She felt used, cheap.

"I must call a cab." She couldn't bear to spend another moment in this house.

"No need, I told *my* cab to wait. I felt it might be needed."

Kim fled into the bedroom. There, on top of her clothes in the case, was the beautiful nightdress. She hurled it as hard as she could across the room but it was so light it just floated to her feet. How many of these had he bought, perhaps he had a standing order at the lingerie shop? And the bathrobe, did he order those by the dozen – initials to be added at a later date? How did he dispose of them? How could Cassie Travis accept her husband's infidelity with such complacency, as a matter of routine? How did she know who I am, where we were? Had there really been a child or was that another of his lies? If he'd made that up it would be the worst lie of all, the most depraved.

Questions tumbled round in her mind like clothes in a spin dryer. Was anything he'd said true?

The little wheels rumbled noisily as she dragged the case over the wooden floor. She had to know about the child.

"Do you have . . . a family?" Even in her turmoil, she worded the question tactfully in case the story of their dead daughter was true. Why the hell was she protecting Cassie Travis?

"I'm afraid not. Unfortunately this is part of Alex's problem. You see we . . . *he*, couldn't have children. We went through the usual barrage of tests of course. When we finally got the results, learnt the bad news . . . poor Alex, he was devastated. He wouldn't hear of adoption, something to do with his macho image I guess. He refused to discuss it. But we're still young enough to adopt, he may change his mind. This is why I indulge him in these little . . . indiscretions. Turn a blind eye."

"I don't believe you, I don't believe any of it." Kim blurted out.

Cassie shrugged her elegant shoulders. "Then

why not come and sit down. Wait for Alex, watch him try to wriggle off the hook." Cassie laughed throatily. "It should be amusing to hear his explanation as to why he left your name and address in such an obvious place, the time of *your* arrival at Boston and his own flight times. Come now, Kim, nobody can be that careless. And why do you think he found it necessary to make a note of the beach house address? He's been coming here since he was a kid. I'll *tell* you why. When he's bored and can't find a way out of these . . . tawdry little affairs, he leaves clues around the house so that I'll find them. Rescue him, do his dirty work for him . . ."

Kim didn't want to hear any more. She felt physically sick, shaken to the core. She remembered that endless parade of men who had hurt her mother, who'd used her, then cast her aside. She wasn't going to allow Alex to humiliate her any more, she wouldn't give him the satisfaction. Her head felt as if it would burst.

"Sorry it had to be this way." Cassie smiled coldly as Kim opened the front door and left without a backward glance.

♥ ♥ ♥

Samantha replaced the receiver helplessly. She was utterly stunned. Poor Kim, if only she could be with her. But Kim was three thousand miles away in Boston, distraught and alone. Samantha sat on the edge of the table and tried to make sense of Kim's call. She knew that Alex had a wife, but the woman Kim described definitely sounded quite normal and, as Kim said, as if she'd stepped from the pages of *Vogue*.

Samantha considered herself as cynical as most, but Alex . . . sincere, charming Alex . . . playing rich men's games? He certainly hadn't struck her as the manipulative type. If only she wasn't on a break this weekend. She'd promised to spend the few days with friends in their new Palm Springs home, it had been arranged months ago. She'd offered to cancel her trip but, even in her distracted state, Kim wouldn't hear of it.

"Promise me, Sam," she'd sobbed. "If Alex rings you, you won't talk to him, slam the phone down. If you really care about our friendship you'll do that. Promise me!" Kim sounded hysterical.

"I promise. Oh Kim, I wish I was there with you. I'll phone you tomorrow. Take care of yourself."

The phone rang again. Samantha grabbed the receiver, "Kim?"

"Samantha?" She recognised Alex's voice.

"Samantha, is that you?"

"I have nothing to say to you, Alex, please don't phone again . . ."

"You must listen, Samantha, please. . ."

She pressed the button which cut off the phone, then left the receiver purring quietly on the table. Alex sounded strained. "Tough!" she said to the poor inoffensive instrument. No doubt he was ringing her with another pack of lies. Imagine inventing a story about a dead child, how low could he sink? There'd be no more help for Alex Travis from her. Now she thought about it, she regretted having helped him last time.

♥ ♥ ♥

"No, I don't mind a smoking seat," Kim said. She moved into the 747's first class cabin, grateful for the luxury of the empty seat beside her. Her head ached and her eyes stung with tears behind her dark glasses. Cassie Travis's words rang in her head. Alex's accomplished lies. How credible he was, how concerned, how loving. How insulting, she raged. A fresh stream of tears flowed down her cheeks.

"You OK, Kim?" She and Angie had worked together often in the past and had been quite friendly.

Kim nodded, she didn't trust herself to speak. Angie gave her an anxious look. "Give me a shout if you need me."

Kim tried to smile her thanks but failed, and nodded instead.

♥ ♥ ♥

The flat seemed dark and unwelcoming. Even the flowers in their glass vase drooped sadly, the water a murky brown. Kim could see the answering machine was flashing furiously. She counted six calls from Alex and was grateful for the anger that gripped her. How dare he phone me. Even if he swore on a stack of bibles that today was Tuesday, I wouldn't believe him.

"I love you with all my heart, Kim . . . we'll be together . . . the happiest week of my life."

His words echoed mockingly. There must be hundreds of women who'd be happy to spend a week with such a handsome man. Why had he chosen *her*? Why couldn't he have picked on someone nearer, easier, someone who didn't mind having a bit of fun – *no strings attached.*

"I hate you!" Kim screamed at the top of her voice. "I *hate* you, you liar. Why me? I loved you, why me?"

♥ ♥ ♥

Her throat ached, and her tongue was dry. Kim dragged herself from the couch where she'd sagged in despair. Nothing could help but perhaps a cup of tea would relieve the tightness in her throat. She filled a kettle and took a carton of milk from the fridge. It smelt all right. She opened the box of tea bags, it was empty. Feverishly she scrabbled through the cupboard, she had coffee, she *knew* she did.

She spooned some of the granules into a mug, her fingers shaking so much that most of it spilt on the counter. She tried another spoonful, poured the boiling water on it and, sobbing quietly, added the milk. Through her haze of tears she watched the milk separate. Uneven, curdled, blobs of white chased each other round the top of the liquid. Kim threw the mug on the counter and didn't care when it broke into dozens of pieces. She dashed her sleeve across her blurred eyes then took a few deep breaths before she telephoned the airline and reported in sick. Without bothering to open her case or even get undressed, Kim climbed into her cold bed. She pulled the duvet over her head and wept until she could cry no more, then finally sank into a merciful, exhausted sleep.

Chapter Twenty-Nine

"Who's ringing at this hour?" Kim grumbled as she dragged herself out of bed. The bright summer sun shone through her closed curtains. She thought she could hear the birds chirping.

"Hi, Kim, it's Sam."

"What's wrong?"

"Nothing. We arranged to have lunch, remember?"

"What time is it?"

"Ten-thirty. Did I wake you?"

"I thought it was still the middle of the night."

"How about lunch?"

"Would you mind if we skipped it?"

"I *do* mind – for your sake. Come on Kim, you can't stay brooding forever. Why don't I pick something up at the local shop and we can eat at your place. OK?"

"I suppose so."

"See you soon." Samantha was determined to rouse Kim from her self-pitying state. She had moped around for long enough.

Samantha tried to hide her surprise when she saw Kim's kitchen. There were dishes and cartons strewn everywhere. Judging by the food-encrusted plates they must have been there since before Kim's last trip.

"Sorry. I'm afraid it's a bit of a mess, I meant to tidy up later."

Kim's flat was always immaculate, this was so unlike her.

"Don't give it a thought," Samantha breezed. "I'm permanently counter-space-challenged. My kitchen would catch tin-foil-pneumonia if I moved all the stuff on my sink and tops."

♥ ♥ ♥

"Did you have a chance to look at the brochure I gave you from *Personal Agenda*?" Samantha dried the last mug.

"Just a brief glance. But I'm really not interested."

"It could be fun. New people, a nice weekend away from routine, I think you might enjoy it."

"You're very kind, Sam, and I do appreciate what you're trying to do. But it won't work. As I've said before, there'll never be another Alex. I don't even *want* another Alex. One experience like that is enough."

"But there wouldn't be another . . . encounter with anyone who's married. *Personal Agenda* is for single people."

"I have Hadley, he's single."

"Oh Kim! Get a life. He's not for you. Going out with him is like going out with your brother."

"He's very nice, very kind and at least he's truthful."

"Yeah, yeah. And so is Mother Teresa."

The ghost of a smile appeared on Kim's lips. "You're impossible. You'll make someone a wonderful, nagging wife one day."

"Proper order! Where's that brochure?"

Kim sorted through the mess of papers on the coffee table. "Here we are, let's take a look."

"I thought you sent for two copies," said Kim.

"Mine must have got lost in the post."

"Liar."

"Stop changing the subject. Anyway what's a little fib between friends? Sit down here and listen. Here goes – are you single, married, separated or divorced?"

"Married," Kim retorted. "I just forgot to mention it."

Samantha threw her a scathing look. "Single. How would you describe yourself . . . ?"

By the time they reached the end of the booklet Kim had cheered up considerably. It was very difficult to resist Samantha's happy-go-lucky nature.

"That wasn't too painful was it?"

"I'm not sending it. I only let you fill it in to keep you quiet."

"Right, message received." Samantha grinned as she pushed the completed brochure into her own bag. "Come on, let's go for a walk and stretch those sexy legs of yours. You need to keep in trim to wow all those gorgeous guys at *Personal Agenda.*"

Chapter Thirty

Jane took a deep breath, the first of the weekenders had arrived.

"Break a leg," Sasha shouted as she disappeared towards the kitchen.

"Welcome officially to *Personal Agenda.*" Jane smiled as Amanda handed her a pretty bouquet of perfumed yellow roses.

"These are to wish you luck," she said awkwardly. It was the first time Amanda had bought flowers for anyone except herself.

"How lovely." Jane sniffed them appreciatively. "I have just the place for them."

"Charles is with me, he's parking the car round the side of the house to leave room for the others."

Within the space of an hour all but one of the ten guests had arrived. It was Mrs Jones who'd solved the problem of where Justin and William could stay. Justin had been positively peevish about missing out on the opening weekend, he'd even suggested that they sleep in their windowless cottage. But Mrs Jones's neighbour had plenty of space and Justin's equilibrium was restored.

In each of the bedrooms was a bowl of freshly picked flowers, a little box of chocolates and a very short list of rules and regulations. Jane, Charles and Sasha had agonised over the do's and don'ts. *No drugs of any kind* – Jane had had enough of that with Hugh's friends. *No visiting other bedrooms, uninvited.* Sasha felt strongly that everyone was adult enough to make their own decisions. Charles agreed. Jane had doubts. Visions of a stage farce; bedroom doors quietly opening and closing, people creeping around in the middle of the night, crossed her mind.

"*You* won't be any the wiser if there are any shenanigans, we couldn't hear anything from our floor anyway," Sasha pointed out.

Jane compromised and added the word *uninvited.*

Inform someone of your absence if you leave the house at night. Even in this rural setting burglaries were not unheard of.

♥ ♥ ♥

Amanda replaced the short list of rules on the dresser. She was her own sternest critic but she had to admit that the black silky trousers did made her look a lot slimmer. The pearl earrings and necklace definitely added a bit of glamour to the outfit. She would always wear earrings in future. She took one last look at herself in the mirror, pulled in her stomach and went downstairs to join the others for a drink before dinner.

Jane was looking forward to talking to Kevin O'Hanlon. Charles had already filled her in on his background and she felt an instant sympathy for the tall, slim, separated young Irishman.

"Please help yourselves to a drink." She smiled

at the small group that she'd manoeuvred together. She looked attractive in her miniskirted blue suit, her skin golden from the summer sun.

Dale Trent made her way over to Charles. "Hi, again. I'm so thrilled your other client cancelled out. I love this gorgeous house."

"We're delighted you're here. Our *other client* is no more. We discovered that she was hell bent on taking a weekend break from her marriage!" Charles had no hesitation in spreading the word.

"Cool chick! Still as my Daddy always says, there's no harm in trying."

"Not as long as she tries it somewhere else. Let me introduce you to Ray Parker, he's in computers."

". . . Kevin O'Hanlon – Amanda Brown. Amanda is an accountant with Coogan, Howard and Green Advertising. Kevin has been with Derby's for the last six months." Charles was certain that, apart from their common interest in advertising, Kevin would be a good choice of person to put Amanda at ease. He had true Irish charm, easy to get along with. Amanda had made a real effort to look glamorous tonight and Charles was determined to do everything in his power to see that she enjoyed her weekend.

Kevin O'Hanlon's ears pricked up, Coogan, Howard and Green were chasing the Stourley account too. It could be useful to learn what they were up to. Very useful.

"Have you been with CHG for long?" he asked.

"Almost four years now. Do you enjoy working at Derby's?"

"I do. Of course I'm still very much the new boy."

"Where were you before that?"

"A firm called Dooley and O'Brien, in Dublin."

"I thought I could detect an accent. How did you get into advertising?"

"Thanks to a virus!" he laughed. "I was doing business studies in college and, during my final year, I picked up a bug which clung on for dear life. It refused to react to the tablets – probably hadn't read the instructions on the bottle. It was frustrating to lie in bed for weeks. One day when I was bored stupid, I entered a caption competition in the local paper. The prize was a weekend for two in Paris. Instead of submitting one slogan, I sent ten. I didn't win the prize. Then, out of the blue, I had a letter from Dooley and O'Brien asking me to come and see them. They were always interested in . . . new, young people." Kevin didn't add the bit in the letter which stated, *talented and bright young people such as yourself.* "You don't need a map to imagine the rest."

"I think that's marvellous. Why did . . ." Amanda stopped as a burst of applause and surprised laughter greeted Sasha's appearance. Dressed in her Victorian maid's outfit, complete with bustle, she announced in a dramatic voice, "Dinner is being served in the dining-room."

Amanda smiled at the bemused look on Kevin's face.

"Sasha is really an actress," she explained. "She likes to dress the part."

They followed Sasha's gliding figure towards the dining-room. She threw open the double doors melodramatically and stepped aside.

Charles led the way into the room. Jane had finally chosen a grey, silver and white theme for her floral decorations. "I think it looks effective against the rich, royal-blue of the room, don't you?" She sought Sasha's approval.

The arrangement of white roses and delicate, trailing grey leaves on the table would have delighted even Mrs Grundy. Jane had bound tall white tapers with narrow silver ribbon and they stood either side of the flowers – like sentries. She'd found time to write the menus and place-cards in silver ink. Jane has a real eye for detail, Charles thought as he counted four more beautifully filled vases.

A tall, carelessly elegant figure dressed in red paused for a moment in the doorway. Charles went forward to greet her. "Let me introduce you to everyone, Kim."

Jane had placed her beside Charles at the table. Kim had arrived earlier than they'd expected and, after a quick sherry, she'd rushed upstairs to change. As she dashed around getting dressed, Kim cursed herself and then Samantha. Why had she allowed herself to get talked into this?

Kim smiled at Jonathan Campbell-Smith as he held her chair for her.

Ray Parker was sitting between Jane's friend Laura, and Dale Trent. After ten minutes at The Willows he decided it was like his birthday and Christmas all rolled into one. At last he'd been invited to a dinner party. A quick glance round the table convinced him this was the most exciting social event he'd attended since his christening.

Amanda was delighted to find herself next to Kevin O'Hanlon. She liked his sense of humour.

Jane was the last to be seated at the table. The two brothers either side of her, Ian and Tony Ainsley, jumped up politely.

"Nerds or gentlemen?" she wondered unkindly.

All was calm in the kitchen. Sasha had shooed Jane out from under their feet. Sasha and Mrs Jones were an unflappable team.

Charles poured the wine while Sasha served the first course. She had decorated each plate of smoked trout mousse with a white flower and some of the grey leaves.

Charles passed the silver basket of melba toast to Kim.

"This is cool," Dale said as she buttered the delicate toast. Cool was her favourite expression at the moment.

By the time the chilled apple and curry soup arrived everyone was chatting happily. The Ainsley brothers were extremely open and friendly and Jane was sorry that she'd been so unfair in her judgement. They worked as reps in their father's business, they explained, and spent all their time travelling – at home and overseas.

"You must have covered a fair few miles," Ian Ainsley said to Kim.

"I tried to work it out once," Kim admitted. "I can't remember the total."

"Shame *you* don't get free air miles," Dale declared.

"I do. Not actually air miles, but free travel."

"Good for you," Dale approved.

Kim smiled at Jonathan. She thought that his

light-framed glasses suited him. He wasn't conventionally handsome but his wavy, corn-coloured hair and his narrow, aristocratic nose gave his face a studious air.

As she cleared the plates Sasha whispered to Jane, "How's it going?"

"Great as far as I can tell. The soup was terrific," she confirmed.

"You tried enough of it before dinner!" Sasha grinned.

The poussins with honey-rice stuffing were delicious. Jane wondered how she could have possibly coped alone. She certainly wouldn't have been sitting here enjoying herself. At the end of the table Dale's neighbours were laughing heartily as she described some of the jobs she'd been fired from.

". . . the last straw as far Dad was concerned."

"I missed that," Jane said although Dale had told her and Charles a lot about herself at their first meeting.

"You mean my grave-digging career or the shortest career in history at a food-chain?"

"Either – both."

"OK, the fast-food restaurant was hot and hellish. One *woman*, and I stress, *woman*, changed her order about ten times. 'If you don't make your mind up soon, lady,' I said, 'your hair will revert to its natural colour.' The manager unfortunately overheard my remark! I still don't know if he fired me for being sassy or for being politically incorrect. *Lady* is no longer acceptable, unless of course it's a real title. As for the grave-digging bit, quite simply, I kept falling in. The director reluctantly parted with my services. He said he couldn't afford to hire a sitter to keep an eye on me! But that was cool." Dale, with her attractive Bostonian accent, was in full flow and they egged her to go on.

"What can I tell you?" she asked without pausing for breath. "I was born in Boston and, when they cut the cord, I'm sure they re-attached it to my father. I was his princess, his cutie. I could do no wrong and played him up for all he was worth. My mom had a more jaundiced view of her little darling. If I got myself in trouble in school, Dad was there – cheque book in hand. To him that cured all ills. It took two years and a lot of heartache to discover that the other kids didn't worship at my altar the way he did. They soon set the record straight and me with it. Once I'd entered the land of 'get-real', I changed – fast. I aped the other kids. Their dress, their speech, even their lunch pails. From then on, if there was a hassle Dad was the last to hear about it. When I graduated I turned down the new car he bought for me. I wanted a banged-up jalopy just like my friends drove. He almost freaked out when I said I wanted to work in the vacation. That's when the fast-food-digging-career flopped.

"Then I became a plastic-princess, a credit-card-kid. But I just wanted to be a regular college girl. I hid the card, it wasn't cool. Broke was good! At the end of our last semester, before we started college, a whole bunch of us piled into cars and headed for the Cape.

"Check this out, I got fired there too – hate to spoil a good record."

As Dale talked about Cape Cod, Kim felt the blood drain from her face. But nobody noticed. They were all too engrossed in what Dale was saying.

"At the inn where I worked, the manager kept a huge dog. One of my jobs was to feed it. That was until the day I added certain cans of ground dog's-meat to the big pot of chilli . . . get the picture? The manager was fired too. The next place was a bummer. I conned my way into a job at a pool – as a life-guard. Problem was I couldn't swim. When an emergency did arise luckily there were people in the pool, they did the life-saving bit. I guess I was lucky I wasn't sued. I headed back to Boston double quick. Then came a stint as a maid in one of the smart downtown hotels. Even I could clean rooms without getting into too much trouble. One of the guests set out to prove that he liked the look of me – a lot. I was cleaning the bathroom at the time and a bar of wet soap in his eyes convinced him that the attraction wasn't mutual."

They were still laughing when Sasha carried in the desserts. She placed platters of cut fruit on the table and an enormous chocolate-covered meringue in front of Jane. "I'll hop up and change now. Take your time. I'll call you when coffee is ready."

"What happened to your career after that? What brought you to England?" It was the first time Evie, the girl with the red hair, had spoken.

"There was no way Daddy's little girl was going to school out of state. Luckily I'd been accepted by Vassar. I fought like a tiger to live like the other students – away from home. It took me a long time to realise the sacrifice Dad made when he finally caved in and agreed. But there was no living on campus, that was out. It had to be an apartment, a designer-dorm, or nothing. My two friends were to room with me, expenses free. Dad arrived with Miss Colour-Swatch and her team of fabric-groupies. One, two, three – and there it was, 1735, Luxury-Pad West. I have to admit it was cool. Loads of space. We threw wild parties, experimented with drinks and drugs – nothing heavy – we weren't into that. We discovered the joys of trying to remove Coke stains from a white carpet. The drink I mean – not the drug. Dad found out. He gave us a long lecture about the evils of partying and a dark-coloured rug. Mom gave up.

"I majored in economics and felt quite sad as the end of my college years loomed. I was also quite scared. I'd became the owner of a personal stalker. The phone in the apartment rang first thing in the morning, last thing at night. When we picked it up no one spoke. Then he began to show up everywhere I went. He never approached me and, the one time I made up my mind to challenge him, he turned and ran. I was scared shitless . . . Excuse me! Scared stupid." Dale looked round at the grinning faces, no one at the table had fainted. "Then came graduation. For Dad there was only one graduee or graduess

– whatever. His archangel, Dale. Dad sat in the front row and beamed at me, proudly. He beamed at my teachers, my mother, my friends, he even beamed at the man with the sprinkler. The poor gardener was so unused to this attention he almost soaked Dad with his high-powered spray. The greatest gift I ever gave Dad was my graduation-scroll. I'm sure if he could have bronzed it he would have done. Instead it's framed and hangs on the wall above his office desk.

"Then came work proper. I moved back home. My stalker stopped calling but still hung around. I thought of going to the cops but they'd be sure to call at the house and then Dad would probably have put a contract out on him – Al Capone style." Dale peppered the occupants of the table with an imaginary gun. "I was amazed Dad agreed to let me take up a profession which wouldn't tie in with his work. Even *he* accepted there was no need for an economist in a plant which manufactured plastic joints for piping. I'm sure he called in every favour he could to secure a prestigious position for his little genius. I found work in a branch of the bank where – guess what – Dad had his accounts. But that was cool. I worked hard and learnt fast. Then I learnt something else, this time from my mother. The stalker, my shadow, had been hired by Dad to keep an eye on me. I went ballistic, threw a full-volume fit." Dale's face was serious despite her bantering tone.

"'That's it,' I yelled at Dad. 'I've had it with

you, you're nothing more than a control freak. I'm old enough to stand on my own two flat feet and that's what I'm going to do.'

"I could hear my folks arguing for the rest of the night. The following morning I had a long talk with Mom for the first time in my adult life. She *wasn't* the bad guy. She was the anchor that kept our family steady. Away from the rocks.

"I called the airlines and booked a ticket to London. I was outta there. There *were* times during the next few months I wished I'd stayed put. It was lonely, real lonely. After a while I found a job, a good one too, but most of my co-workers are either married or involved. Then came the advert for *Personal Agenda.* That's the answer I thought, and, this is where I'm at." Dale flopped back against her chair, exhausted.

They all began talking at once even though Dale's rapid-fire delivery had left them almost breathless.

"She must be a first cousin to a machine gun," Ray Parker said quietly to Laura.

Amanda was fascinated that anyone could speak so openly, so flippantly about their life – their family. *She'd* curl up and die.

"I suggest we move back into the other room for coffee." Jane rose from the table. "Sasha has a copy of the play for each of you and she'll fill you in on the details."

Tony, the darker of the two brothers, tapped lightly on a plate with his spoon. "I'm sure we'd all like to propose a vote of thanks for that superb meal?"

They all clapped loudly. Jane, embarrassed, escaped as fast as she could to the kitchen.

As Jane carried in the tray of coffee, Justin and William arrived. They helped her to serve it and Jane seized the opportunity to introduce the two newcomers to her guests.

Sasha waved copies of the play in the air. "Help yourselves, folks," she invited. She'd changed her costume and looked positively pretty in simple, tailored trousers and a multi-coloured silk blouse. Only the mass of chains and clanking bracelets gave a hint of her eccentric ways.

She waited until everyone had helped themselves to a copy of the play. "Park your bods and I'll tell you all about the play we've chosen. *The Importance of Being Earnest*, it's by Oscar Wilde. Purely for our convenience, you understand, he chose this month, July, and a morning-room, not too unlike this, as the setting for his first act. The second act takes place in a garden, which we'll create with the magic of plywood and paint. And finally, act three, a drawing-room – even more like this. There are nine characters in the play, the plum role is that of Lady Bracknell. You may remember her famous raised-eyebrow question – *a hand-bag?*"

There was a chorus of, *oh yes!* and *I remember now.*

"We did The IOBE – as we called it, in school," Justin said.

"Me too," Laura, Jane's friend, admitted.

"What part did you play?" Justin asked.

"Miss Prism, the governess."

"I was Lady Bracknell! Fourteen years old and fifteen stone."

"Were you *that* weight?" William looked astonished.

"Oh yes! Not slim and beautiful like I am now." Justin stood tall and waggled his ample hips.

Sasha's lips twitched, Justin would make a marvellous Lady Bracknell. His slightly plump frame could be padded. He would give the role all he'd got, she was positive. In her mischievous mind, that was one part settled. "Briefly, the play opens with Algernon Moncrieff stuffing himself with cucumber sandwiches made especially for his aunt, Lady B's, visit. Enter John Worthing, a friend, known also as Earnest. They squabble amiably until the arrival of Lady B and her daughter Gwendoline, by which time Algernon has eaten all the sandwiches. Earnest and Gwendoline fancy each other something rotten. But Milady isn't having any. Mr Worthing, *a foundling*, is not suitable as a husband for her daughter."

As Sasha told them the story, Jane reluctantly tore herself away and went to help Mrs Jones clear up the kitchen.

"It seems to be going smoothly." Jane sounded surprised. "Everyone enjoyed the meal and they all appear to be getting on well together."

"Don't you fret, dear, it will run as smooth as silk, you'll see." She was a kindly woman fascinated by the whole idea of a dating agency. Even in her day, and that wasn't so long ago, you went to the local dance, met someone and got married. But working with Jane had injected a much-needed breath of fresh air into her mundane existence.

Chapter Thirty-One

By ten o'clock next morning everyone was in the garden either learning their lines or painting scenery. The temperature had already climbed higher than forecast and there wasn't a cloud in the sky. Jane watched idly through the kitchen window as she put the finishing touches to lunch. It was still difficult to accept that her dream had become a reality. But she was calm today, the worm of worry banished for the moment. Laura seemed to be enjoying herself enormously. She'd always been one of Jane's favourites when she ran the secretarial bureau, and Jane was delighted to see her again. As soon as she had a free minute she must catch up with Laura's news. Dale, as Jane expected, was funny, warm and entertaining. Ian and Tony were easy-going and polite, and her matchmaking instincts turned towards Laura. Either of them would be ideal for her. Amanda and Kevin seemed to have hit it off, but then they did have a fair bit in common. Kim Barrett was friendly but reserved, cool, as Dale would say, but it was early days yet.

Jonathan Campbell-Smith was anxious to have a complete break from medical talk. Once people discovered his profession, a plastic and cosmetic surgeon, they plagued him with questions about their ears or their nose. Liposuction was a favourite topic. He'd had more than one party ruined by drooping eyelids, heavy hips and cellulite.

Ray Parker was pathetically happy. He'd complimented Jane on everything from her choice of guest to the weather. The only question mark in her mind was Evie Gilbert. She was very reserved. Perhaps she needed a little time to warm to people. Jane had noticed that last night too and, when she'd mentioned it to Charles, he promised to keep an eye on her.

"Any help needed?" William asked through the open window. "It's hot out here and I'm out of a job for the moment."

Jane smiled at his grave face. "Come in, I'll always find something for you to do."

"Lunch everyone," William called.

They straggled towards the patio, quoting lines and arguing about how best to paint stone steps.

"Self-service today, please help yourselves," he announced.

Jane's expense-account-conscience was clear as she watched them sitting under the protection of the striped awning at the new table. Her extravagance had paid for itself, the heat was oppressive and they were all happy to dive under cover. The table could seat twelve comfortably, more at a pinch. Lunch was a repeat of the previous weekend but, with Sasha's help, had taken far less time to prepare.

Charles had taken Evie Gilbert under his wing and was doing his best to keep her talking. Jane did have misgivings about Evie, she'd been divorced less than three months. Too short a time perhaps for her to have recovered? But Charles was convinced that *Personal Agenda* was what she needed and Jane had to be guided by him.

♥ ♥ ♥

"Jane, come and see this," Sasha called from the garden.

They all crowded round the large plywood panels which formed the backdrop for the garden scene.

"They're wonderful! Who painted them?" asked Jane.

"Evie, mostly." Charles smiled paternally at the paint-spattered girl.

"Nonsense, I only drew the outlines, everyone did their share," she objected. "Amanda is the one with a flair for colour."

The three panels were a mass of flowers, they looked just like the real thing. There were roses, carnations, petunias and geraniums. Honeysuckle coiled its tendrils around the fat, fake, stone banisters that bordered the steps. Jane bent to examine the *trompe l'œil* of flowering weeds which flourished in the cracks of the steps.

"Even the weeds look genuine." Charles took the words out of Jane's mouth.

Evie's smile broadened. She had always liked painting and drawing but hadn't developed her talent. Brian considered anything like that a waste of time. He considered most things she'd wanted to do, a waste of time. Marriage had tin-lidded most of her ambitions and her self-worth had dwindled like a spent match. He'd Svengali'd her. She blushed to think how spineless she'd been. Although she'd rushed to Brian's defence at the time, her best friend's comment, that *Brian* was happily married, subsequently rang true.

Never had she feared anyone as much as she did him when she was told him she was pregnant.

"You can't be! It's not mine, you've been sleeping around, you slut." His roars, she imagined, could be heard by everyone this side of the Channel. "Get rid of it," he demanded. "Get an abortion." He'd slammed out of their flat and hadn't returned for two days. It was then that Evie did something she vowed she'd never do. She went home to Mum. And Dad. And her family of sisters and brothers. People who loved and cared about her. They'd enveloped her, fretted over her, protected her from Brian and from herself. He'd bombarded her with phone calls – too cowardly to call and see her personally. That was sensible on his part because her brothers threatened to flatten him if he dared show his face.

The baby was loved and fussed over, just as she was herself. Evie smiled as she pictured her son's little, round face, golden from the summer days spent in the garden, spoilt by her family, happy and content. Her father had noticed the *Personal Agenda* advertisement in the paper. He was the one who'd sent for the brochure.

Evie turned back to the flower-strewn panels, her heart suddenly lighter. As soon as she got home she'd apply to join art classes.

Jane left them to fasten the wooden stanchions to the back of the panels. Sasha had called a dress rehearsal for three o'clock. How she managed to stay cool in those thick jodhpurs and leather jacket was beyond Jane. She'd even made herself a megaphone from a stiff piece of cardboard.

Roars of laughter halted Jane. Justin, padded and gowned, swanned into view delicately waving a lace fan.

"Enough of that, you peasants," he insisted in a voice two octaves higher than normal. "My husband, Lord Bracknell, y'know, would not take kindly to your levity."

"Justin couldn't be happier if he'd found a signed copy of the ten commandments," Sasha told William. William smiled indulgently. He envied Justin's ability to adapt to any situation, his gregarious nature. His capacity for fun was one of the things that William liked most about Justin.

"He's terrific." Sasha was thrilled with Justin's appearance, all pouter-pigeon bosom and trailing skirts. "Kevin, you're next."

Kevin rolled his eyes and obediently followed Sasha to the dress rail on the patio. He'd been dragooned into playing the part of Lane, the manservant and Merriman, the butler. His appearance a few minutes later clad in a tail-coat and black trousers – several inches too short – brought further gales of laughter.

♥ ♥ ♥

If the noise from the garden was anything to judge by, the rehearsal was proceeding happily. William, the prompter, was doing more work than the actors. They were laughing so much they hardly remembered a line between them. Wisely, Sasha took no notice of their fluffed lines and hilarity. After all, it was only for fun. She placed prompt cards on all the props, William could do the rest.

Jane scooped the last of the ice cream into the cones, put them into a pretty flower-decorated basket, and took them out to the garden. The afternoon heat soared towards the high eighties. Everyone flopped wherever they were, grateful for the cold cornets. The Victorian costumes made them look like children who'd slightly outgrown their clothes.

Dale played her part as Miss Prism, the governess, with enthusiasm. Jane wondered what poor Oscar Wilde would have thought of his Miss Prism in her beautiful silken gown – topped by a baseball cap which read *Having a Bad Hair Day.*

Justin and Amanda dabbled their feet in the river while Justin tried to remember his lines. ". . . *I had some crumpets with Lady Harbury* . . ." he recited.

"I bear her hair has turned quite gold with grief." Amanda filled in for Algernon. Nothing would induce her to take part, she was a backdrop-girl she insisted. They splashed their toes lazily as they read.

"The audience will be arriving soon," Justin yawned.

"Wouldn't you love to slide into the water," Amanda replied as the sunlight on its surface rippled with each movement of their feet.

"I'd adore to. But can you imagine Sasha's face? Her costume . . . her wig. I think I'll content myself with a shower, it's safer than risking her ire."

♥ ♥ ♥

Charles introduced Jane to the new arrivals. She'd invited only four of her personal friends to be part of the audience, the others were clients anxious to find out what *Personal Agenda* was all about. They'd sent invitations to thirty people, twenty-six of whom accepted.

People gathered cheerfully in groups around the garden. William was right, this was an excellent way to include more of their clients. Jane watched to make sure no one was left on their own.

The "morning-room" was ready for act one and the actors disappeared to their rooms to prepare for the performance.

Kim sat on the edge of her bed and towel-dried her hair. She winced as her finger caught the edge of the binding. Jonathan Campbell-Smith had been fast off the mark when she'd yelped as she caught her finger on one of the panels. Gently he eased the splinter out, then disinfected the cut. He bandaged it with the skill of an expert. It was quite fun playing Gwendoline to his Earnest. In fact, the whole day had been fun. It was so relaxed here, no pressure, just a small group of people out to enjoy themselves – the purpose of *Personal Agenda* almost forgotten. Neither Jane nor Charles made any move to push people together. They did nothing more than make everyone feel welcome in the free-and-easy atmosphere. Maybe Samantha was right, this was what she needed.

Kevin O'Hanlon slowly buttoned the skimpy shirt. It was a long time since he'd had such fun. Work didn't really count, his acquaintances there were solely business associates thrown together by circumstance. His mood of elation dipped as he thought of Derby's and that precious Stourley contract. Come to think of it, he'd spent very little time with Amanda today, somehow there hadn't been much opportunity. Jane Anderson certainly created a friendly relaxed atmosphere here. It was easy to forget that *Personal Agenda* was a dating agency, not a private house-party. He'd put himself on the waiting list for the weekend after next. He'd be happy to come here every week. With a last glance at his script he adjusted his tie, picked up both jackets and went to find Sasha.

♥ ♥ ♥

Susie and Matt arrived early. She smiled encouragingly at Jane. "There's a great buzz, Jane. Don't look so worried."

"I'm not really, there seems to be such a crowd."

"Only as many as there were at the housewarming. I'm dying to hear everything – ring me and we'll have a good natter on Monday night."

The big room had been divided in half. One area for the stage, the other for the audience. People settled happily on the floor, on chairs, even on the arms of the comfortable sofas. A couple of screens, which Sasha discovered in the attic, acted as a curtain.

Jane stood at the back of the room and watched Kevin O'Hanlon's entrance. Laughter greeted him as it had earlier. At least now the long black socks hid his ankles even if the trousers didn't. He busied himself arranging afternoon tea on a little table. The sound of a piano could be heard. Charles had been coerced by Sasha to play the part of Algernon Moncrieff and he was clapped enthusiastically as he sauntered into view. He must have slathered at least two ounces of gel on his hair. She laughed as she watched Charles squinting at his cue cards. In fact there was barely a surface that didn't sport prompt cards. The play went smoothly, nonetheless, with Charles and Jonathan giving remarkably polished performances as Algernon and Ernest. Everyone laughed and clapped as Justin's padded figure waddled majestically into view. He faced the audience and fluttered his false eyelashes. He tapped his fan on his hand, then on his stage daughter, Kim's, shoulder and turned an aristocratic face towards his nephew Algernon. Poor Kim, she was being totally upstaged by Justin.

Jane insisted that Mrs Jones must stay and watch for a while. "You'll enjoy it," she said. "I'll go and switch on the ovens."

It had taken them a lot of searching through the cookery books before she and Sasha decided on the best meal for tonight.

"Not salads again?" Jane frowned.

"No, I agree."

"How about curry?" Jane asked.

"That's a good idea," Sasha said. "We can make it during the week and freeze it."

In the end they'd settled for chicken curry with rice and all the trimmings, and a spicy dish of Moroccan lamb cooked with sesame seeds. Jane remembered a cous-cous dish that she'd bought but never used. Cous-cous would be perfect with the lamb.

Jane could hear the applause, the play must be over. Amanda dashed in to tell her to come and listen to Sasha's speech.

A pink-cheeked and triumphant Sasha thanked everyone. William presented her with a bunch of flowers that had wilted slightly in the boot of the car – the only place that Sasha wasn't likely to discover it. A bouquet of exotic orchids couldn't have been more graciously received.

"Could you do this again, please?" The fairer of two sisters waylaid Jane on her way to the kitchen. "It must have been great fun getting it all together."

"It was," Sasha answered for her. "When are you booked in?"

"About five weeks from now, end of August I think. We don't mind sharing a room by the way."

'I'll take a look at the programme," Sasha promised. "I'm going to have a quick shower, Jane, join you in a few minutes."

"It was terrific, what I saw of it," Jane called above the din to Sasha's retreating figure.

"Naturally! We had the best actors this side of Broadway," she yelled back. "Or do I mean Broadmoor?"

"It's such a lovely night, how about taking the food outside?" Mrs Jones suggested.

"We could . . . but the table isn't big enough."

"It wouldn't take the men a few seconds to move the dining-table on to the patio, it comes apart, doesn't it? We can set it up again in no time."

"I'll go and find Charles and ask him."

"I love that bit where Lady Bracknell asks – *'Do you smoke?'* When he says yes, she replies, *'I am glad to hear it. A man should always have an occupation of some kind.'"* Dale could have gone on quoting lines from the play all night.

"Excuse me, Dale. Charles, could I have a word?"

"Sure, Jane. What's up?" He smiled at Dale and took Jane's arm.

"Mrs Jones suggested that we eat outside tonight as it's a warm night." Jane's frown had reappeared.

"And?" Charles waited. He knew Jane wanted a yea or a nay from him, but she must make her own decision. Why was she faltering now?

"And what do you think?" she asked.

"What do you think?" He put the ball back in her court.

"I think it's a good idea if the men would move the table for me. There's plenty of light on the patio and in the garden."

"That's it then, decision made. That didn't hurt too much did it?"

Jane was stung by his sarcastic response. Was Charles trying to make her independent? He was probably right, she admitted grudgingly, she must decide things for herself. From now on she would.

♥ ♥ ♥

"Goodbye, and thank you. See you in two weeks."

"Cheers, super night! I can't wait for next weekend."

Jane was overwhelmed by their demands, their questions and the flattery. Even she knew that the weekend had been a great success so far. But the amount of requests for a place was frightening. There were a hundred and twenty-two members now. It would take at least twelve weeks to fit them all in. They'd have to open a waiting list. She must ask Charles . . . No, she wouldn't ask him anything. For a moment her anger flared. From now on Charles could conduct the interviews, vet the clients, but nothing more. She could talk to Sasha if she needed a mental-splint for her doubts, or Justin and William, they were more than helpful and only a phone call away. To hell with Charles Graham, if he wanted to be treated as a business associate from now on that's how it would be.

Chapter Thirty-Two

Charles Graham sat quietly in the moonlight. The lights from the patio cast an ethereal glow over the garden. Not a branch of the magnificent willow swayed, not a ripple disturbed the river. The clients of *Personal Agenda* relaxed in the scent-filled garden. They were worn out by the heat and the exhilaration of the day. He'd found an ideal mixture of people for Jane. Just look at them now. Dale was chatting with Evie, Tony and Ian. Kim and Jonathan were sitting apart from the others enjoying a nightcap. Amanda and Kevin were deep in conversation and, in the shadows, he could see Laura and Ray Parker lying on the grass oblivious to the others. He had done his bit, the rest was up to chemistry and themselves.

Jane had seemed a little cool tonight. When he offered to stay and lock up, she'd shrugged her shoulders and said it wasn't necessary – "The last one to leave the garden can do it." She barely said goodnight to him, but was sweet and charming to Justin and William. Surely she wasn't offended because he'd tried to make her stand on her own feet? He'd be extra nice to her tomorrow, he certainly didn't want to antagonise her.

Sasha sat in front of her mirror and removed her make-up. Justin had been a riot tonight, over-acting for all he was worth. If ever there was a lull in the second-hand book business he could definitely switch to acting. It was difficult to pretend that Charles was just part of the scenery, but she must. It was painfully obvious that he wasn't interested in her. Now that she came to think about it, he took no special notice of Jane either.

Sasha pulled the brush through her hair. She must make notes about the play – things that worked well, others that could be improved. But that could wait until later in the week.

She was asleep as her head reached the pillow.

"All this acting has tired me out," Jonathan laughed.

"I think I'll turn in soon too," Kim yawned.

"See you in the morning." Jonathan helped her to her feet.

Kim wandered towards the lapping river, reluctant to leave the heady perfume of the peaceful garden. If she ever had a garden of her own she would fill it with night-scented stock, jasmine and honeysuckle, maybe some roses – perfumed flowers only. She loved the way the river curled in that lazy sweep. She sat on the bank, slipped off her sandals, and paddled her toes in the water. It was difficult not to compare Jonathan to Alex. They were totally different; Jonathan serious and intense, Alex light-hearted and amusing. Jonathan was a listener, Alex a talker. But Jonathan could sit calmly, Alex was a pacer, rarely still.

Kim splashed her feet angrily, disturbing the calm surface of the water. As the circles spread to the opposite side of the bank she kicked even harder.

♥ ♥ ♥

Jane Anderson glanced through her bedroom window; she could see Kim's hunched figure sitting alone on the river bank. There was something about Kim that reminded her a little of herself. A certain way of closing people out – friendly but firm, a don't-overstep-the-mark kind of message. Jane wondered if she should go and see if Kim was all right, but it was late and she was tired. Maybe Kim needed to be on her own. Yawning widely, Jane closed her curtains and sank into bed.

Chapter Thirty-Three

Kevin O'Hanlon stirred in his sleep. The *tap, tap, tap* at his door was irritating. He jolted up in bed and called, "Come in."

But the noise continued. *"Come in,"* he shouted, a little louder this time. The sound wasn't coming from his door, it was outside his window.

He stumbled out of bed and opened the curtains. Two black, spatula-shaped tails were beating a tattoo on the metal gutter. He smiled as he watched the magpies, squabbling and squawking like a pair of old women as they searched for grubs. It was going to be another magnificent summer's day.

Jane and Sasha were already in the kitchen preparing breakfast when Kevin stuck his head round the door.

"Hi! Kevin, what got you up so early?" Sasha asked.

"Two magpies having an argument." Where did Sasha *find* these get-ups, he wondered. She was dressed in a skimpy black dress, sheer, black-seamed tights, five inch stilettos and a lacy cap and apron. She wouldn't have looked out of place in a French farce – and at this hour of the day too!

"Would you like breakfast now, here in the kitchen? Or would you prefer to wait for the others and have some juice or a cup of tea?" Jane turned her head to avoid laughing at Kevin's look of wonderment.

"Here, please. I miss the atmosphere of a real kitchen. Mine is two cupboards long, and very narrow. So narrow that, if I put on an ounce, I'd get stuck in the doorway."

"You lot are early risers, I thought everyone would still be asleep," Amanda said cheerfully as she bounced into the kitchen.

"Hello, Amanda," Jane said. She was pleased to see that Amanda had come out of her shell a little, positively outgoing compared to the shy, quiet girl of a couple of weeks ago. "Are you going to have breakfast with Kevin?"

"You bet, I'm starving," she laughed.

"I was just talking about my palatial kitchen," Kevin said dryly.

"You should have seen *my* last excuse for a kitchen," Sasha groaned. "One hot-plate balanced on top of a rickety cupboard. Lethal!"

"What about you, Amanda, what's your kitchen like?" Kevin asked, as he buttered a piece of toast.

Amanda looked thoughtful for a moment. "It's . . . fairly big. Not like this, purely a working space. You can't eat there. If I'm on my own I take a tray up to my room, if Mother is at home we eat in the dining-room. To be honest, I don't cook very much, the housekeeper does it all."

"Sounds great," Kevin said. Amanda sounded apologetic, a bit embarrassed, he thought.

Amanda and Kevin sat and ate while Jane and Sasha dashed backwards and forwards to the dining-room. The windows were wide open and the morning heat was already streaming into the kitchen.

"Do you fancy going for a walk?" Kevin asked.

"Yes, why not." The only exercise she ever had was hopping in and out of her car.

They walked along the leafy avenue, lush with summer foliage. Kevin pulled an overhanging branch from a tree and stripped its leaves, just as he had when he was a child. He ran it along the hedges as they walked. The sound of a bicycle bell disturbed the quiet lane. A man on a large tricycle raised his cap politely and puffed on his way. Amanda contained herself until he was out of earshot. "He looked a real nerd," she giggled. "Do you ride a bike?"

"I used to. Couldn't live without one when I was a kid." Kevin could clearly remember the look of horror on his mother's face the day he sold his precious transport.

"What are you thinking about?" Amanda asked as Kevin drew the stick noisily along the metal struts of a gate.

"About the day I sold my bike. My mam was *furious* with me. Five pounds I got for it. 'They saw you coming, my bucko,' she said. 'Why didn't you give it to your brother?' I was moving to Dublin and I needed to get my hands on every penny I could. Looking back, I suppose she was right. I should have given it to Tommy, it was only a fiver."

"Was that when you went to work in Dublin?" Amanda gently probed.

"Yes, my first job. I studied in Cork and then, as you know, got a job in advertising. I thought I was the bee's knees," he laughed. "If you'd have seen the state of me – a suit which crackled when I walked and new shoes that squeaked every time I took a step. What I must have looked like! I carried an old brief-case with me wherever I went to add to my *advertising-man-of-the-year* image. All that was in it were my ham sandwiches and an apple."

"Why did you leave Dublin?"

"It's a long story." Kevin's face was wistful.

"We have plenty of time," Amanda urged.

"I suppose you could say it was a spur-of-the-moment decision. I really enjoyed living in Dublin, and I enjoyed my job. I shared a flat with Aidan – we'd grown up together – and another guy called Niall, who was also from our village. We all got on well apart from the odd barney or two. No *roommates from hell* stories in our flat. At night, we'd do the girls a favour, give them the benefit of our company, so we went to the clubs. They returned the favour by ignoring us. But we didn't care, we had great fun anyway. Then came *Le car* as we called it. A battered Mini Metro that was my pride and joy. You'd think I was driving a Roller. It was washed every two or three days, no one was allowed to smoke in it. For the first couple of weeks I covered it with a tarpaulin every night. What an idiot I was! We shared the petrol money, especially when we went home for the weekend. We'd sail along the Wexford road – that was the main road home – with all the other weekenders. The poor old banger was flat out at fifty, but it got us there. On Friday nights we'd hit the local dance like conquering heroes, but the girls took as little notice of us there as they did in

Dublin. If I was the blushing type, I'd be red in the face when I think of how we carried on. The only girl who was at all impressed was Mary O'Brien. Or *Meriel*, as she insisted on being called."

"I'm sure lots of people would like to change their names," Amanda said and then hoped that Kevin didn't notice the sarcasm in her voice.

"She was always eager to know about life in Dublin. Always wanted details of where I went, what I did at work. She lapped up my stories of the night life, though often she knew more about where to go than I did. Magazines were her bibles. Her mother swore that if she didn't shift them out of her room, the floor would cave in.

"Meriel was doing a secretarial course. She wanted to get a job in Dublin the minute she was finished. But her mother had other ideas. If I remember rightly, *over my dead body* was what her mother said.

"Meriel was hysterical. They argued and fought, rowed and screamed. She was a lovely looking girl with wild red hair and a temper to match. But she could melt anyone's heart with her big green eyes. Anyone but her mother's."

She sounds worse by the minute, a real spoilt brat, Amanda thought but said nothing.

"Her father died years ago when the children were small. I suppose that made her mother feel doubly responsible for her kids.

"I nearly always took Meriel out when I went home. Sometimes she'd let me kiss her but she'd slap my hands if they roamed. And, oh boy, did I try! I wanted to get to know what was under that blouse, she wanted to know about the latest

Leeson Street club. I wanted to unhook her bra, she wanted me to find her a job. And that's how we went on for months. She had me where she wanted me and took full advantage of it."

"I'll bet," Amanda thought to herself.

"Whenever we were together she pleaded and begged me to find work for her in Dublin. Her mother would allow her to go if she had a definite job, she was positive. I wasn't so sure. She worked in an insurance company, and did well for a nineteen-year-old. Six months later she got a promotion. But she still wasn't happy."

Amanda bent to pick up a beautiful pink flower that had fallen from the tree in the garden they were passing. Neither of them had a clue what it was.

"One day a client of ours was tearing his hair out looking for a secretary who could actually type and write a proper business letter.

"I told him I might have just the person he needed.

"Meriel was beside herself with excitement when I told her the news. At last, off came the blouse! The maddening thing was, I don't think she even noticed.

"She was round at our house next morning before eight o'clock. Her eyes were red and swollen, the tears still flowing. My mother gave me a look that sent the blood rushing to my toes. She asked me what I'd done – in front of Meriel.

"'Nothing,' I said. That was typical of my mam – her favourite sport, jumping to conclusions.

"Mam demanded to know why she was crying like that.

"Meriel explained that I'd found her a terrific

job, but her Mam wouldn't even listen, she had forbidden her to go to Dublin.

"You could see the relief cross my mother's face. She didn't know Meriel like I did!

"I walked her back to her house and she pleaded with me to talk to her mother.

"'What's the point?' I asked. Mrs O'Brien was the most intimidating woman I'd ever met.

"She convinced me that her mam would listen to me. '*She thinks you're* it,' Meriel assured me. That wasn't the impression Mrs O'Brien gave me. I thought she hated my guts.

"'I'll try,' I promised as she linked my arm close to her body. She really knew how to press my button. I was quaking in my trainers by the time we got to her door."

"You were brave!" Amanda said.

"Wait, you haven't heard the half of it. Meriel practically pushed me into the house.

"'*Meriel is not going to Dublin,*' Mrs O'Brien roared at me. Then she said when Meriel was twenty-one she could do what she liked, but she wasn't leaving the house till then. And nothing would make her change her mind. She asked me if I'd like her to put that in writing. Then accused me of a being a real trouble-maker, always filling Meriel's head with fancy ideas.

"The woman bellowed like a bull, she was so ill-mannered. I saw red. Then, before I could draw another breath, I heard this voice saying. 'Meriel *is* going to Dublin. We're getting married, she's going to Dublin as my wife.'"

Amanda looked at him in surprise. She hadn't pictured Kevin as the marrying type. "Did you mean it?" she asked.

"I didn't think about it, I just heard the words coming out of my mouth."

"What did Meriel say?"

"Not a whole lot! She flung herself into my arms and yelled *yes, yes, I do – I will*, or words to that effect."

"Then what?" Amanda prompted.

"Mrs O'Brien called me son, then shook my hand until it was loose in its socket. I can't remember what happened after that, I must have been in shock. By the end of the day, wedding plans were flying thick and fast. Mrs O'Brien still wouldn't agree to let Meriel go until she was married, and my ma and da supported her.

"We were married four weeks later. You can imagine the rumours that flew round the village. I was given just two things to do; find somewhere to live, and turn up on the day."

"That would help I suppose," Amanda laughed.

"My pals, Aidan and Niall, thought I was nuts. But when I got used to the idea, I was looking forward to getting married. And to the honeymoon.

"Meriel looked gorgeous as she floated down the aisle in a cloud of white. I know all brides are supposed to look beautiful, but she really did look fantastic. I was proud to call her my wife.

"Our honeymoon, two weeks in Corfu, was disastrous. The day after we got there, Meriel sat too long in the sun. She ended up stuck in the apartment for the two weeks with sunstroke. At one stage I was scared, I thought she was going to die. Doesn't that sound ridiculous?"

"No, I've heard sunstroke can be frightening," Amanda replied.

"Needless to say, she got better, and we had a half-a-day's holiday at the end of the fortnight.

"I had no trouble finding a home, there were plenty of one bedroom flats on the market. Meriel started her new job with O'Rourke Associates, and loved it. At first, we went out almost every night. She couldn't get enough of the clubs and the bars, the restaurants. It didn't matter how modest or expensive they were, she just wanted to go, and go, and go. I found it all a bit much. I longed for a night in front of the telly, a laugh with the boys, some sort of normal life. When I suggested that we stay in the odd night or two, she wheedled her way around me somehow, and off we went again. I suppose I was weak. But if she wasn't in a good mood she'd have a temper tantrum and I hated that. The apple and the tree – she was very like her mother."

"Typical redhead!" It was as much as Amanda dared say, but Kevin was so deeply immersed in his memories he just kept on talking.

"She dragged me to the shops every Saturday. She loved clothes, couldn't buy enough of them. I was so bored that, after a while, I refused to go with her. She locked me out of the bedroom. That lasted for two weeks. We struck a compromise, I'd go shopping with her every second Saturday providing we stayed in three nights a week. She wasn't too happy with the arrangement but she agreed.

"We were very busy at the agency, there was a big contract coming up. You'd understand the hours that go into that."

Amanda nodded, she had a feeling she knew what Kevin was going to say next.

"Meriel sulked like mad. She hated being on her own in the flat. By the time I got home at night I was wrecked, and then I had to cook dinner."

Amanda pursed her lips and shook her head. Imagine treating Kevin like that. She'd be delighted to cook for him.

"Do you really want to hear the rest?" Kevin asked.

"Of course," Amanda said, hanging on his every word.

"A couple of weeks later Meriel came home from work with shining eyes. She'd been offered a super new job, as a personal assistant to a company director. The money was terrific. She'd have to do a bit of travelling, not very much. She was almost jumping up and down with excitement.

"I was all for her bettering herself, but she gave her boss just one day's notice. I was furious, embarrassed too. John O'Rourke was a good client of ours and I was frightened that because of what Meriel had done we'd lose his account.

"She argued that if she didn't grab the chance there and then . . ."

Neither of them had noticed Justin's red car puttering sedately towards them until he honked the horn.

"What are you two doing here?" William asked as he wound down the window.

"We were just having a walk," Amanda said.

"Would you like a lift back to The Willows?"

Amanda wasn't used to the exercise and normally would have grabbed the chance of a lift.

But she was far more interested in hearing what happened with Meriel. "I'd prefer to walk back, what about you, Kevin?"

"I'm quite happy, either way."

"I think we'll pass, thanks anyway. See you back at The Willows."

William winced as Justin screeched the car into gear and shot off down the road in a cloud of dry dust.

"That car won't last too long," Kevin forecast.

"You were saying that Meriel got a new position as a PA," Amanda reminded him.

"I'm sure you don't want to spend a beautiful morning like this listening to my gripes and groans."

"Sometimes it's good to talk." Amanda couldn't think of a better way to spend her time. Poor Kevin, he was obviously such a softie.

Amanda struck Kevin as a sympathetic person. He'd never told anyone except Aidan about his marriage.

"After a few months, Meriel began to work longer hours than I did. She rarely got home before me. She was always so tired she wouldn't even eat a meal. And then there were the business trips. They'd take up a couple of days a week. She bought even more clothes, designer labels. Even I knew they cost the earth. She *needed* to be well dressed, she objected when I mentioned it. I didn't pass any remarks after that, it was her money and she was entitled to do what she wanted with it. Then she had her beautiful red hair cut short. That really upset me, although I had to admit that the new style was very flattering. Meriel was absolutely up-to-the minute with everything.

"And then tragedy struck. *Le car* died on the Wexford road it had travelled so often. It had been a great little car. Meriel was away on one of her business trips and I was on my own. She rarely went to Wexford at the weekends any more. I thumbed a lift and completed the journey in the heated luxury of a Saab.

"She was delighted that my poor old Mini had kicked its bucket seats.

"'About time you bought some decent transport,' she scoffed. *'That old thing was a disgrace. Why don't you buy a Toyota MR2?'*

"I was surprised that she knew such a car existed. She went on and on about how sporty it was, how safe, what kind of mileage it did. It was even more surprising considering she didn't know the registration number of *Le car*." Kevin's tone was scathing.

"My mam was puzzled by Meriel's behaviour. Her mother practically accused me of keeping her a prisoner in Dublin. Neglecting her. I tried to explain the pressures of her job. 'No one works at weekends,' Mrs O'Brien snorted. She said that Meriel was to ring her, she'd fix her.

"It was Mrs O'Brien's remark that set me thinking. Why *did* so many of these trips have to be at weekends? And why did her work take up so much of her time? Surely she was entitled to free time just like everyone else? When I suggested that to Meriel she looked at me as though I'd come from another planet. She called me a poor misguided fool, and asked if I thought it was possible in this day and age to get to the top of the tree by working from ten to four. Then she pointed out that sometimes, I'd had to work all God's given hours to finish a presentation. I should understand. I'd been brainwashed by her mother, she said. I felt ashamed because it was true."

"You were only trying to help." And I sound like a real creep, Amanda thought.

"She was away for her twenty-first birthday – an important business trip to France that she couldn't possibly get out of. I was disappointed that we couldn't celebrate it together. She arrived back two days later full of the joys of Paris, with a beautiful gold and sapphire ring that she'd bought. I took the little earrings I'd bought for her back to the shop. Suddenly they didn't seem grand enough for this elegant stranger.

"We were almost living separate lives by then. I spent quite a bit of my time with Aidan. He never mentioned Meriel. By then, Niall had emigrated to the States.

"It was getting close to Christmas and I really lost my rag when Meriel announced that she wouldn't be going to Wexford. *Everyone* went home for Christmas.

"'Why not?' I asked.

"She had to go away on Boxing Day. There was a conference starting the day after that, and it was important that they got to meet some of the people socially before it began, she explained.

"'That is ridiculous,' I ranted. 'You're never home. Even that greedy bastard Michael Coyne, must draw the line somewhere. I'll phone him myself. I'm not going to put up with this.'

"Meriel went white with anger. *'Pick up the phone and it'll be your ex-wife you're discussing. Dial his number – and I'm gone.'* I can remember those words as if it was yesterday," Kevin said bitterly.

"I didn't doubt for a second that she meant it. I spent the rest of the week trying to find some good excuse for her mother – and mine. I didn't want to go myself by then, there'd be too many questions, too many funny looks. In the end I rang and said we'd be abroad for Christmas but would be home for New Year instead. There was no mistaking the disappointment in my mother's voice. Dad was really looking forward to Christmas, they all were. *'Couldn't you come home, son, just like you always do, and then go away?'*

"I think at that moment, I changed. How dare Meriel ride roughshod over everyone's feelings? How dare she spoil everyone's happiness with her selfishness? This must stop, and stop now.

"'I'm going home for Christmas,' I announced firmly, 'And you are coming with me. If you don't, that's the end of us.'

"'Suit yourself,' she said, cool as you like.

"I was lost, didn't know what to say, so I said nothing.

"Neither of us mentioned Christmas for the next couple of weeks. I had no heart for shopping. I bribed one of the girls at the agency with a day off if she took my list. Meriel's name wasn't on it. I didn't know what would please her and, by then, I really didn't care."

"I don't blame you." Shut up you idiot, Amanda berated herself.

"Two weeks before Christmas I asked her what she'd decided.

"There was nothing *to* decide, she was off as

planned on Boxing Day. She was very tired and planned to spend Christmas Day quietly at the flat. She said my present was in the drawer in the living-room.

"'Stuff your present. Stuff you,' I yelled at her. 'Just make sure that by the time I get back tomorrow you're gone for good, and all your things with you. Anything that's left goes on the bonfire. And that's a promise.'

"How I was supposed to light a bonfire in a block of purpose-built flats was another day's work, but I don't think that struck either of us at the time.

"For once Meriel had no answer. I think she was stunned that I'd finally stood up to her. I was being ridiculous, she said, and came to sit beside me on the sofa. She wanted to know what had got into me. Then she said I'd always understood the pressures, been under pressure myself often enough. She promised that when she got back from her conference, we'd go to Wexford for four days to make up for Christmas. She cuddled up to me on the couch and was staring at me with those huge eyes of hers. We hadn't had that much contact for months. I could feel my resolve ebbing away. All the fascination I felt for her, flooded back.

"Then the doorbell rang. I was glad of the excuse to break free.

"A small child stood on the mat clutching a black sack. He wanted to speak to Meriel Hanlon. He was a cute little fellow.

"'You mean, Meriel O'Hanlon?' I asked.

"The child nodded. I called Meriel. She came to the door and smiled at the child.

"The child handed her a black bag. *'My mammy sent this,'* he said and fled down the hall.

"Her face drained as she looked inside the bag. 'What's wrong?' I asked. She didn't answer. I took the sack from her and looked inside. On top of some crumpled clothes was a note. *He's all yours, so is his washing.* It was signed, *Alicia Coyne.*

"All hell broke loose. Meriel protested that it was disgraceful, libellous, and that the neurotic woman was taking her frustration out on her.

"Meriel picked up her handbag, said she was going to settle that woman's hash, and, before I could stop her, she left the flat.

"I stared at the crumpled sack. No one would do this kind of thing without good reason. The Coynes' number was in the phone book.

"Alicia Coyne spelled out the situation for me in no uncertain terms; the dinners after work, the phoney business trips, bills from small country hotels, a receipt for a gold and sapphire ring from a Parisian jeweller. She'd found them all.

"Suddenly it was as plain as day. I'd been a first class fool, a right eejit."

"What did you do then?" Amanda slowed her pace, they were almost at the gates of The Willows.

"I was in a blind fury and stormed round the place like a headless chicken. Alicia Coyne wasn't the only one with a ruined marriage but, as far as I was concerned, Michael Coyne could have Meriel for keeps – I'd had enough. That was it. I got into the car – a Honda like Justin's by the way – and drove to Wexford. By the time I was half way there, my mind was made up. I would wash my hands of the whole thing, go to England and make a fresh start.

"It was too late at night to land in on my parents, so, full of righteous indignation, I slept in the car. We sat round the kitchen table the next morning and I told them the whole story.

"There'd be no separation in our family, my mother insisted – quietly for her. There never had been and, there never would be if she had her way. Then she said that if everyone gave up as easily as I had the whole country would be living apart. *Go home to your wife and forget all about it. Have a few kids and you'll have no more problems,* was her advice."

Amanda, single though she was, couldn't imagine a more ludicrous statement.

"I couldn't believe my ears. My da didn't speak. My brother didn't dare. My father was a quiet man, I don't think he ever raised his voice to us. He looked at me sadly but I knew he understood. My mother was a different kettle of fish. Women like her ruled their roosts according to what the neighbours might think. There were harsh words sometimes, maybe the occasional clip on the ear when we did something she didn't like. I suppose I should have known that she wouldn't understand, but I didn't expect her to be *so* unsympathetic, so adamant. She didn't say as much, but I felt sure that she blamed me. Talk about turning the other cheek! But I'd made up my mind, I was leaving Dublin and there was no going back. Meriel could tell *her* mother the news herself.

"I hardly saw Meriel for the next ten days. I didn't know where she was living and couldn't care less. I had no intention of getting into a hassle with Michael Coyne, his wife could fix *him* – or not. That was their problem.

"My boss tried to persuade me to stay, which was very flattering. God knows, I needed a bit of a boost, but then he didn't know the situation. The firm clubbed together and gave me a lovely suitcase and a great send-off. I went to say goodbye to my parents and Ma would hardly speak to me. Then I met Meriel in Bewley's in Grafton Street – that's a well-known cafe in Dublin – and gave her my keys. I wanted nothing from the flat except my clothes and my Walkman. I told her I'd be in touch, said goodbye, and that was it. The end of a marriage. My marriage. I think it was only then that she too realised I was definitely leaving.

"I *was* utterly miserable. Desolate. I had no wife, no home and no immediate prospects. But the worst part of all was when I went to the airport.

"Dublin Airport at Christmas is like no other airport in the world. It's one huge, happy welcome home party. You can't imagine the atmosphere.

"All along the grassy verges there are big Christmas trees, dozens and dozens of life-size snowmen, decorations and garlands of twinkling lights. Enormous banners wish everyone Happy Christmas and Welcome Home. People make special excursions just to see the decorations.

Planes arrive every few minutes and whole families gather excitedly in the arrivals hall, impatient to see their loved ones. There are choirs, dancers, entertainment. It's magical. I don't want to sound full of self-pity, but it was awful. The full force of what I'd done suddenly faced me. I was alone, so completely alone that it made me ache with longing for another chance. When I boarded my plane I didn't even know where I was going to stay."

Amanda touched his arm sympathetically. "It must have been dreadful."

"I was miserable for the first week or so. But I soon got over it. I found a flat and that gave me a sense of belonging. I was blessed that Derby's were looking for a copywriter. My reference must have impressed them, I began two weeks later and, fingers crossed, hope to stay there."

"It must have taken courage to pack up like that." Amanda was convinced she couldn't have done it. "What about Meriel? Did she end up with Michael Coyne?"

"I don't think so. Aidan said in a letter that he saw her one night at a club with a crowd of girls. She told him that she was working in a shop which sold cosmetics and perfumes. She asked him if he'd like to meet her one night for a drink. He didn't want anything to do with her. It was then that he told me he'd heard rumours about her and Michael Coyne, long before we broke up.

"I haven't bothered to contact her since I left. When, or if, the time comes, then I will. I don't think about her so much now and, I suppose to be fair, a lot of it was *my* fault. It was a stupid way to get into a marriage, but then not all of them are made in heaven. Sometimes people marry for the wrong reasons. Now my main concern is to stay in my job and make a new life for myself. Now you know why I'm here at *Personal Agenda*."

Chapter Thirty-Four

Amanda and Kevin walked through the quiet house and heard roars of laughter coming from the garden. Two rows of sunloungers faced each other and Dale, arms waving madly, stood between them.

"Come on," Dale prompted, "Think!"

"No talking allowed," Ian Ainsley warned.

"We're playing charades," Justin explained. "Come on, pick a side."

"Take that chair there beside Justin," Kevin said. "I'll sit beside Kim."

Amanda collapsed gratefully onto the comfortable sunbed; she'd been so engrossed in Kevin's story that she hadn't realised how hot it was.

Dale's team finally guessed the answer. "You made heavy weather of that," she accused.

"Kevin, you go next," William said.

Sasha handed him a folded slip of paper. It was a film – *Apocalypse Now.*

"How do I do that?" Kevin groaned.

"You'll find a way," Sasha assured him.

Kevin faced his team and turned his hand to show it was a film.

"Two words," Kim translated.

He'd better break this word up, Kevin thought and placed four fingers on his arm.

"First syllable," Jonathan explained to the rest of the team.

"A?" Laura asked.

Kevin nodded, then stuck his hand in his pocket.

"Pocket," Kim said.

Kevin drew his hands close together to show it was a shorter word. Then he stuck out his lips and made a kissing noise.

"Got it," Ray Parker yelled, "A pocket full of kisses."

"That's not a film," Kevin said.

"No talking," the other team objected.

"Time up," Justin banged a coin on the tin can he'd found. "Two to us, one for you. Our turn."

They continued to play until Jane appeared with big jugs of iced fruit punch.

"I think it's even hotter than yesterday." Evie passed the glasses.

"Throw me the *Sunday Telegraph*," Kevin said to Justin.

"Swap you for the *Observer*," Justin pointed to the paper behind Kevin's chair.

Amanda watched Kevin from behind her sunglasses. He hardly glanced at the headlines but turned straight to the Appointments section. Strange, she thought idly, he wasn't looking for a job. He said he was happy at Derby's.

♥ ♥ ♥

At two o'clock, Justin and Charles lit the barbecues. Sasha and Jane were grateful that lunch was an easy meal. The potatoes, wrapped in their tinfoil covers, were baking in the oven and the salads were ready to be dressed. Now that she'd got the hang of it, Mrs Jones was having a whale of a time in the kitchen, piping big swirls of cream on to the trifle.

Jane had bought some extra barbecue tongs and they all crowded around waiting for a chance to turn the steaks and poke the sausages and chicken pieces. The Ainsley brothers insisted that Jane and Sasha must eat with them. The men added another small table to the one under the awning.

Ray Parker stopped eating to watch a crowd of lazing people drift by on a boat. This must be what it's like on the continent, he thought; eating out of doors, the perfume of flowers, bottles of wine, wonderful steaks cooked over charcoal. That's where he'd go for a holiday as soon as the Beamish and Chambers contract was complete. But, for now, he was more than content with The Willows.

"Any more for any more?" Justin asked. He looked comical with Dale's baseball cap perched on his blond head. The sun shone mercilessly outside the protection of the awning. Evie had made a hat from newspapers for Charles to protect him from sunstroke.

"No takers?" Jane rose from the table and began to collect the plates.

"You should use paper plates and plastic knives and forks," Dale suggested. "Then we could throw them straight into trash sacks."

"And we could fold up the table until it was a

small square and throw that in too," Kevin added, he was a bit tiddly from the wine.

"We could collapse the chairs, roll them up, and that would fill another sack." Ray didn't want to miss out on the fun.

"Then the garden and lastly, the river. We could black-bag the lot." Kevin was used to thinking along crazy lines, it was part of his job. Lateral thinking, he called it.

"And the house," Dale added.

"And the house," Kevin agreed.

"And I thought *I* was mad," Justin sighed.

"You get used to mind games in advertising," Kevin said, feeling foolish.

"What about art?" Evie asked. "Salvador Dali's bent watches, for example? I think it's fun to let your imagination lead you."

Kevin threw her a grateful smile. Somehow she made it all seem sensible.

They sat at the table until after six o'clock, reluctant to pack and leave for home. Charles was staying on until the following day. He wouldn't be at The Willows next weekend, there was no room for him. Caroline, the instructor from the cookery course, would have *his* room. That was how he'd come to think of it. Amanda offered to drive Kevin back to London, and Jonathan was taking Kim to her flat.

"It was brilliant," Ian Ainsley said as he hugged Jane.

"The best," his brother agreed. "See you in three weeks."

"I've enjoyed every minute, Jane," Evie said.

♥ ♥ ♥

Jane went back to the garden, her head dizzy with pleasure. It had been a terrific weekend. Everyone seemed determined to enjoy themselves and made her life easier because of it.

"Well, Madame Anderson," Justin said, "you must be very proud of yourself."

"I'm thrilled that it all went so well," she admitted.

"And so you should be," William smiled. "You and Sasha did a hell of a job."

"I wish the cottage was finished." Justin yawned. "I hate the thought of going back to that stuffy flat. Can you imagine the heat in London?"

"You shouldn't complain, at least you'll be out of it soon." Charles's voice was harsh.

"You're welcome to stay at the cottage, any time." Justin refused to rise to the barb. Charles could be quite sharp when things didn't suit him. His comments sometimes had an acid ring to them. He hoped that Jane would learn to keep her own counsel. Suddenly, Charles Graham was not his favourite person.

"Thank you for all your help," Jane said as she hugged William. He'd become quite used to her affectionate gestures now. "And you too, Justin. As usual, I don't know what we'd have done without you."

"Very well, that's what. Mind you, Lady Bracknell mightn't have been as good!"

♥ ♥ ♥

When everyone had left, Jane, Sasha and Charles checked the list of clients for the following weekend. Ray Parker was the only client Jane had already met, he'd booked for the next two weekends.

"I can't believe that we had no problems," Jane said.

"Why should we?" Sasha asked. "We did everything *we* could, the rest was up to them."

"They were a good crowd of people," Charles reminded them.

"Dale was fun, wasn't she?" Sasha recognised a kindred spirit in the American girl.

"I liked Evie," Jane said, she could relate to the browbeaten mother.

"Kim was a cool customer." At first, Charles had fancied his chances with Kim, but it soon became plain that she wasn't interested in him.

"To change the subject for a moment, I've decided to double up two of the largest rooms." Jane shifted in her chair. "That way we can manage extra people each weekend."

"You didn't say anything about that before," Charles said sharply. "When did you decide that?"

"I decided last night. Sasha agrees with me. Several people said that they wouldn't mind sharing a room."

"Do you think that will work? Shouldn't we discuss it first?" Charles asked.

"There's nothing to discuss, I've made the decision."

Jane was obviously still in a snit. How long was she going to carry this on? All this revenge because he'd tried to boost her confidence. He wasn't pleased to be excluded next weekend.

But he'd better be careful, not allow his displeasure to show. He needed Jane more than she needed him now. There would still be people to interview of course, but the stream of applicants would slow down. It already had. He liked the added income, enjoyed treating The Willows as his country retreat and, more than anything, he liked the feeling that he belonged to a group of friends. "For what it's worth, I think it's an excellent idea. It will certainly make it easier to cope with the waiting list."

"I've thought about that too. We're going to invite an extra thirty people on the Saturday night of the next drama weekend." Jane twiddled a button on her skirt. She felt a bit ashamed of her prickly response, her dogmatic attitude. Enough was enough, she'd made her point. "It worked well last night, so it shouldn't be difficult to repeat it. Don't you agree?"

"Absolutely," Charles replied to the rhetorical question. This was the first time she'd consulted him about anything all day.

"Thank you for all *your* hard work, Charles," Jane said in a softer voice. "I'm going to make a cup of tea before I go to bed. Either of you fancy one?"

"I do," Sasha said.

"Not for me thanks, see you both in the morning." Charles was subdued.

Jane's attitude towards Charles surprised Sasha.

'Why so tetchy with Charles?" she asked as they sipped their tea.

Jane explained how uncooperative he'd been, ". . . almost patronising. Perhaps it was childish to ask his opinion about a simple thing like eating outside, but my question didn't deserve that kind of answer. We'll manage very well between us – won't we?" she asked dubiously

"Of course we will," Sasha replied. There were times when she felt as if *she* was thirty and Jane twenty-four.

♥ ♥ ♥

Amanda drove with all the windows open. "It was a terrific weekend, I really enjoyed it," she said.

"I hated to leave," Kevin confessed. "We have a busy week coming up at Derby's, we're doing a big presentation in a few weeks time." Maybe this was a good opportunity to do a little fishing. "Have you heard about the new hangover-free lager?"

Amanda's shook her head, her face didn't change. Either she knew nothing about Stourley's new product, or she was an accomplished actress.

"That sounds too good to be true," she laughed.

"Yes, I agree. I tried it, it's good lager. But I didn't drink enough of it to find out if it works!"

Amanda wrinkled her brow. Now that Kevin mentioned it, she *had* heard about the lager, it rang a vague bell. Maybe she'd read about it in the papers.

"Are *you* looking forward to getting back to work tomorrow?" Kevin asked.

"I suppose so. My job's not as exciting as yours, I'm in the financial department. Nothing to do with the advertising accounts."

"I must admit, I do find it exciting at times,

challenging. But nerve-racking too." Kevin's forehead was creased in a deep frown.

Amanda glanced at his worried face. "It's none of my business, I know, but this morning you went straight to the advertising section of the paper, are you going to change your job?"

"You're observant! I hope not, but there are rumblings at the office. I shouldn't say this to someone in a rival firm, but things are quiet and, because I'm last man in . . . I'm probably being pessimistic, paranoid. But still I like to keep an eye on the job front. For all the government claims that things are getting better, there's a lot of unemployment out there. I don't need to tell *you*, our business suffers like all the rest."

"I'm sure you're worrying unnecessarily and that you're very good at what you do," Amanda said soothingly.

"Amanda, you're a tonic. Where were you when I needed you?"

Kevin's tone was bantering but nonetheless her cheeks flushed with pleasure.

"Would you like to go to a film next weekend?" he asked as they drew up outside his flat.

"Yes, I'd love to," she smiled.

"I'll give you a ring on Thursday. You decide what you'd like to see. I'll phone you at the office, if that's OK?"

"That's fine. Just ask the girl on the switchboard for Amanda Brown's office, she'll put you through to my extension." She wanted to make sure that Kevin knew exactly how to contact her.

"I look forward to seeing you then, and thanks for listening to my woes this morning. You have a lovely nature." Kevin reached into the back seat for her case, then leaned across and kissed her cheek.

♥ ♥ ♥

Jonathan turned the car in a circle and pulled up at the entrance to Kim's flat. He switched off the engine but made no move to get out.

"Thank you for the lift," Kim said as she opened the door.

"Hang on a minute, I wanted to ask you something."

If he's going to invite me out, the answer is no, Kim determined.

"How's your hand?" Jonathan asked.

"It's fine, thanks. Not bothering me at all," she said and held up the blue-plastered finger. Sasha had rushed out to buy a box when Caroline told them that blue plasters were more practical in cooking than flesh-coloured ones, especially when mislaid in a pie.

Was that all Jonathan wanted to know?

"You probably noticed I didn't talk about my . . . occupation."

Now that he came to mention it . . . "That's true. Is it a deep, dark secret? Are you a spy, an undercover agent?" Kim teased.

"Nothing like that," he laughed. "I'm a doctor, a plastic surgeon."

"So that's why you did such a nifty job with that pin." Kim waggled her finger.

"Not my normal operating implement, I assure you."

"Why the cloak and dagger? Surely you're proud of what you do?"

"I am, but away from the hospital I hate medical talk. I work long hours, and need to relax. That's why I joined *Personal Agenda.*"

"What about all those devoted nurses?"

"What about all those handsome pilots?"

"Touché," Kim laughed.

"I find that as soon as I mention my profession, I'm inundated with questions. People, women mostly, want to know whether they should have a face lift, a tummy-tuck, a nose job. They ask if it's safe, what guarantees there are, how long it takes, how much it costs? Need I go on? I've spent more time at parties holding impromptu consultations than in a normal working day."

"I suppose all the media hype has made people aware of what can be done. Every time you switch on the television there's someone proudly boasting about the thousands they've spent improving their appearance. I'm sure no one is entirely happy with the way they look, and you're the man with the answers."

"That's true. But not all my work is cosmetic. There's reconstructive surgery too, that can be devastating at times. I have a gorgeous little girl in the unit at the moment suffering from a dreadful scald, a teenager whose face was lacerated beyond recognition in a car crash. They are the heartbreaks. But they can also be the joys, the most rewarding – when I'm able to repair the damage. However that's not what I wanted to talk to you about, I wanted to ask you if you'd like to come to the hospital ball with me?"

"When is it?" Kim had forgotten she was going to refuse any invitation. And she did have that gorgeous black dress with the jewelled straps. Damn Alex Travis.

"It's on Wednesday week."

"I'm not sure, I may be working."

"When will you know? Can I give you a ring?"

"Would Thursday be too late? I'll be away for the next few days."

"Thursday's fine."

Kim dithered, should she invite him in for a coffee or not? It was nice of him to give her a lift.

Jonathan solved the problem for her. "I'd better get moving, I want to pop into the hospital on the way home," he said.

"Thanks again for the lift."

Jonathan closed the boot and got back into the car. Kim stood for a moment and watched him drive away. As she turned to go inside, it struck her that she hadn't given him her phone number. And it wasn't in the book either. No doubt that was the last she'd hear from Doctor Jonathan Campbell-Smith.

♥ ♥ ♥

Amanda let herself into the house and stopped nervously on the stairs as she heard a noise coming from the kitchen. Mrs Judd, the housekeeper, didn't work on Sundays and her mother was staying with a prospective client for the weekend. She tiptoed silently to the front door.

"Who's there?' she called from the safety of the open doorway.

"Is that you, Amanda?" her mother's voice answered.

"You gave me a fright, I didn't expect you back till tomorrow," Amanda accused.

"I'm in the kitchen," Emma Brown said.

"That's a first," Amanda mumbled under her breath. "What are you doing home?

"The client was impossible. She was so entrenched in *her* way of doing things, *her* opinions, frankly it was a total waste of my time. I'm always prepared to listen but I refuse to be dictated to. What's the point of hiring a PR firm if you're going to do the work yourself?"

"That sounds reasonable to me," Amanda agreed.

"How did your weekend go? Wait! Before you tell me, why not come and have a cup of coffee with me in the study? Do you want a sandwich?"

"OK. Give me a couple of minutes while I dump my case."

Emma Brown glanced at her dishevelled daughter. She hadn't seen Amanda wearing jeans before. Actually the blue and white blouse was an improvement, usually she settled for such miserable colours – dull grey or muddy beige. She longed to advise her daughter but anything *she* suggested was always dismissed out of hand. She'd learnt to hold her tongue. There was so much Amanda could do to make herself more attractive, Emma Brown sighed.

Emma carried the tray into the study and set it on the coffee table. As she straightened up she caught a glance of her reflection in the mirror over the fireplace, she looked a lot younger than fifty-five. Years of rigid exercise and beauty treatments had stood her in good stead. Her size twelve figure hadn't changed since she was a teenager. That face-lift hadn't done her any harm, she decided, as she ran her finger along her cheek bone. Maybe next year she'd do something about her eyes, but for the moment they didn't look too bad either. She slipped the long cotton cardigan from her shoulders and draped it carefully over the back of a chair. She hitched up the knees of her trousers and settled herself elegantly on the attractively covered sofa.

"I like your blouse, Amanda, bright colours suit you."

"Thank you." A compliment from her mother? Another first.

"Tell me about the weekend," Emma said.

"It was great fun." Amanda's eyes suddenly sparked into life behind their lenses. "There were ten of us, evenly split. Charles Graham was there, of course." Amanda had tackled her mother about her dates with Charles and Emma had apologised profusely. "Apart from us there was Jane, she owns The Willows, Sasha her helper and two of Jane's friends. They've bought a cottage nearby, they're gay and wonderful company – I've met them before . . ."

How animated Amanda was for a change, Emma thought as she watched her daughter's face.

". . . and Justin was marvellous in the part." Amanda laughed. "This morning I went for a walk with one of the men, Kevin O'Hanlon, he's in advertising too, a copywriter with Derby's." Amanda didn't feel it necessary to mention that Kevin was separated from his wife. "When we got back everyone was in the garden. It was a glorious day. We read the papers and played a game of charades which was almost as funny as the play. We had a barbecue lunch. Everyone had a go at the cooking. When it came to six o'clock we were all still at the table, no one wanted to leave."

"It certainly sounds super," Emma said wistfully. What a shame there was nothing like that available when she split up with David. But then she wouldn't have had time, she had Amanda to look after. "Are you going to go again?"

"In two weeks' time."

"Will that be a theme weekend?"

"Yes. Jane's very keen that her guests are entertained."

"What's she planned for that week?"

"There'll be a colour consultant there. She's going to give a . . . talk," Amanda mumbled.

Emma's face didn't change. After Amanda qualified she'd suggested that her daughter should go to a consultancy session, a high-profile firm near her office. Amanda wouldn't hear of it and sulked for days. But then anything she suggested brought on a fit of the sulks. Nowadays she gave her daughter little or no advice, that way they avoided any conflict.

Emma chose her words carefully. "I'm sure in its own way, that will be just as much fun as this weekend was."

Amanda searched her mother's expression for a gleam of triumph. But she hadn't crowed or said, *"That's just what you need."* No doubt it was what she was thinking. Her mother said very little these days, obviously she was no longer interested. Perhaps it was better that way, at least there were fewer rows.

As the door of the study closed, Emma Brown relaxed in her chair. They'd been together for over two hours and there hadn't been a cross word between them. It would be wonderful if her daughter could accept her as a friend instead of her sworn enemy. Funny, just like Amanda, she'd never had a close friend, there'd never been enough time. Her public relations business mopped up every spare moment like a sponge. David hadn't shared her ambitions, and that was the trouble.

She was the one who'd chased clients relentlessly, she was the one who'd worked fifteen hours a day while he played with Amanda. She'd sacrificed her home life in favour of boring drinks parties, stifling dinners and stultifying business gatherings while he took Amanda to the pictures or the zoo. She'd stood till her feet ached and her smile locked. But it had paid dividends. She'd signed more clients at those get-togethers than she had by introductions or advertising.

She'd allowed herself just three days maternity leave when Amanda was born. In those three days, David managed to lose one client and a second threatened to take his business elsewhere. It was wrong, she admitted, to bawl him out in front of the staff. But it had taken months of hard slog to woo them both into Leland Brown. That was the straw that had almost broken her back, and Amanda's heart.

Even now she could barely bring herself to think of those awful months after David left with that little bimbo. Amanda made her life hell. She adored her father. Humble pie was not one of Emma's favourite dishes, but she swallowed it and asked David to take the child to live with him and that creature. But he had no job, no permanent home. He couldn't give Amanda the security she needed. So she soldiered on and did her best to ignore her daughter's tantrums, while she struggled to come to terms with the break-up. Emma was honest with herself, she'd suffered more from hurt pride than the loss of David. Imagine leaving *her* for that mousy Lisette, it was insulting.

The change in Amanda's behaviour was insidious. Her school reports were a mother's dream; nothing lower than an A. Amanda gave no explanation for the change, she became even more uncommunicative – locked up in her room and her head. But Emma was grateful for whatever it was that spurred Amanda's burst of academic talent. It lasted right throughout her schooldays and university. If only her daughter would join her in the business, what a team they would make.

Emma looked round her study. It was an elegant room with a lofty ceiling and coral silk-covered walls. She was at ease here surrounded by her precious belongings. The soft jade green of the curtains and carpet were restful and blended perfectly with the coral and jade chairs. The furniture and the lamps added warmth to the big room. The small collection of porcelain ornaments, in a dainty corner cabinet, were reminders of her success; the clown she'd bought after she secured a circus contract. The fine china waif on the bottom shelf which looked nothing like her client – the glamorous film star Nina

Parry. But most precious of all were a pair of Dresden figures, trophies from the fee she earned when she rescued a German electronics company from bankruptcy. It was then that she knew Leland's had arrived.

The first step Emma took after the divorce was to drop David's name from the company. Emma smiled as she looked at the little dog with its exquisitely painted face. She'd bought that on a whim when the number of staff at Leland's reached double figures. The most lucrative of all her deals paid for her precious rosewood desk. It was here at this desk that her ambitions became reality; contracts that she had believed were beyond her reach. It was this room that prevented her from selling the house which was far too large for the two of them.

Emma plumped up the cushion and smoothed the chair. She had an early appointment tomorrow – more talking, more scrambling for publicity that would enhance her client's image. For a moment she envied Amanda. She would have a life, friends, and with a bit of luck, a happy marriage. But this was no time to stand here regretting the past, she must do her exercises and choose what to wear tomorrow. And there was still her ultimate fantasy – she and her daughter, chairman and managing directors of Leland *PLC.*

♥ ♥ ♥

Ray Parker whistled as he emptied his case onto

the bed. How cramped his flat seemed after the spaciousness of The Willows. Never mind, he consoled himself, once that Beamish and Chambers' contract was in the bag, he'd consider moving. There was so much he would do. Funny, he'd hardly given the office a thought the whole weekend. He couldn't wait for next Friday. It was a pity that Evie wouldn't be there. She was very gentle, very talented. Maybe he'd ask Jane for her phone number if he didn't meet anyone he liked better next weekend. Jane Anderson was also very nice, very attractive. But he sensed that she wouldn't be interested in him. And then there was Dale Trent. She was a character. Yes, Dale would be fun to be with. It was all too much, such choices he'd have to make.

♥ ♥ ♥

Evie sat on the carpet with her little son gurgling on her lap.

"It was absolutely brilliant," she told her family. "I can't remember when I laughed so much. Everyone was there to enjoy themselves and they did . . ."

Evie's parents listened eagerly to all she had to say. It was marvellous to see their daughter happy and smiling again. They were even more thrilled that she had decided to go to art classes. She'd always been artistic but also had a practical streak. That was what decided her to earn her living as a receptionist rather than an artist.

"You *must* go again," her father insisted.

They'd find a way to pay for the weekend even though it would be a strain on their finances. Now that there were two more mouths to feed, they'd have to be careful. But Evie deserved a little happiness. Besides, her brother would be finished college this year and that would be quite a saving. Yes, they'd manage.

"You have to go again, Evie, it sounds so good I think I'll go with you." Her mother laughed and earned a hurt look from her husband.

Chapter Thirty-Five

"I can't get used to all this quiet." Sasha folded the last of the sheets for the ironing service.

"It's odd, isn't it," Jane agreed. "But don't fret, Friday will be round again soon enough."

"Charles was subdued this morning. He can be quite moody, can't he?" Jane nodded absent-mindedly, she was trying to work out how to double up the bedrooms without too much expense.

"What are you thinking about?" Sasha asked.

"About the bedrooms . . . Is that the phone?"

Jane's smile broadened. "I'd *love* that, Susie," she said. "A week tomorrow? It's ages since we've had a chance to spend time together. Give my love to Matt, see you next week."

"You look pleased with yourself," Sasha said as she carried the bag of linen to the back door ready for collection.

"I am. That was Susie. Matt's away for a couple of days next week and she's coming to stay with us."

"I'm delighted for you."

"It will be lovely to catch up on all the news, I miss her," Jane admitted as she helped Sasha to load the washing machine with towels.

"Mm . . . Tell you what, why don't I pop home to see the family while Susie is with you? You'll have loads to talk about and I won't worry about you being here alone."

"If you want to go and see your family, that's fine. But don't feel that you're intruding, because you're not. This is your home too."

"I know that. But it would be a nice opportunity to spend a couple of days with them. We can double up on some of the cooking this week and then it will leave you more free time to be with Susie."

"Good idea. Talking of which, we'd better decide what we're going to do this weekend. It'll be a bit intimidating to have a professional here." Jane liked Caroline but she was a terrific cook.

"Jane Anderson, you're a real coward. Our meals are brilliant, even if I say so myself. Do you need cookery medals hanging from your hair to convince yourself that you can *chefer* with the best of them?"

Jane laughed and held up her hands in submission. "I'm not copping out, I was just thinking."

"Don't," Sasha said sternly.

"I'm really upset, Jane. I wouldn't let you down for the . . ." Caroline's sentence ended in a bout of coughing.

"Don't try and talk. We'll arrange another date when you're better. Hang up the phone and go back to bed."

Sasha listened to Jane and watched her face, obviously Caroline wasn't well.

"She's flat on her back with a temperature of a hundred and three," Jane frowned.

Sasha's heart sank. Jane would panic now, they'd all be here in less than twenty-four hours. "Could we contact Nikki Gardiner? Maybe she'd change the colour consultancy to this week instead," Sasha suggested.

"That won't work, don't forget that people booked specially for that. No, we'll have to think of something else. A cup of tea, that's what we need to get the old brain cells working."

"Is this the same Jane Anderson I know and fear?" Sasha laughed.

"Belt up and put the kettle on," Jane instructed. She wouldn't admit it but, in a strange way, she was relieved that they wouldn't have to impress Caroline – for the moment.

"Problem solved," Sasha said triumphantly.

"Well done." Jane clapped. "I suppose we'd better contact everyone and tell them the programme's changed."

"Do we need to?"

"Just to be sure," Jane decided.

"To be sure, to be sure," Sasha mimicked Jane's soft Irish accent. It was always more prevalent when Jane was upset. But Jane handled the setback calmly, there was no sign of her *wet nelly* attitude.

"I'll go and make a start on the calls."

By seven o'clock Sasha and Jane were satisfied that everything was under control for the weekend. Their meals were organised and, with Sasha's encouragement, they'd done quite a bit of preparation for the following weekend too. The freezers were a real boon.

♥ ♥ ♥

Amanda glanced at the clock for the thousandth time. It was two minutes to five and Kevin O'Hanlon hadn't phoned. Perhaps he'd forgotten or was in a meeting, or more likely, had changed his mind. There was no point in staying late at the office, she didn't know how to operate the switchboard.

She picked up her bag and left the building. This would have been her first real date. What would she tell Lois Hayes? She'd casually mentioned Kevin's name to Lois at lunch yesterday. Then, even more casually, she told Lois that he'd invited her out. Lois listened to every word, eager for the smallest details about the weekend. "It sounds fantastic," Lois said.

"It was," Amanda assured her smugly.

Now her bubble of happiness had burst. In the privacy of her car, she allowed the tears of disappointment and rejection to flow freely down her cheeks. What a fool she felt, she could have sworn that Kevin was sincere.

Amanda trudged up to her room and lay on her bed. Through the open window she heard the front door close and the sound of their housekeeper Mrs Judd's heels tapping smartly along the path. Amanda switched on the radio and music filled the room; a sad, haunting ballad. She listened to the words and tears of self-pity trickled into her hair and tickled her ears. Her head was beginning to ache. She slid off the bed and slouched into the bathroom. With the bottle of tablets clutched in her hand she wondered what would happen if she swallowed them all? Would she die, or would she end up in casualty having her stomach pumped? With her luck it would be the hospital and the pump. When the phone rang she flew to answer it. Thank you, she prayed.

"Oh, Jane, it's you." Amanda said, obviously displeased.

"Don't sound so thrilled!" Jane laughed.

"Sorry, I was expecting a call from someone else."

"Kevin O'Hanlon for instance?" Jane teased.

It was no concern of Jane's, but she didn't want to be rude. "Yes, as a matter of fact, it was."

"Kevin is in Wexford. A family funeral – his aunt – I think he said. The line wasn't great. Anyway he wanted your home number and, as you know, we don't give out clients' numbers. He asked me to tell you to keep Saturday night free and would *you* phone *him* on Saturday morning? He'll be back about eleven o'clock."

Amanda's black mood vanished. "Hang on, I'll get a pen."

"Let me read that back to you," Amanda was taking no chances.

"That's it," Jane said. How Amanda's voice had changed. They would be good together, she and Kevin. They certainly hit it off at the weekend. "I'm looking forward to seeing you next week."

"Me too, I mean, I'm looking forward to being there." Amanda was so thrilled she didn't know what she meant.

♥ ♥ ♥

Kim flicked through the channels, each programme looked more boring than the last. Impatiently she switched off the set and threw aside the remote control in disgust. It was hot and her thin lawn nightdress stuck to her back. Maybe a cold glass of grapefruit juice would cool her down. As she passed the answering machine she glanced at the message light, but it glowed steadily without a flicker. "What did you expect, you silly cow?" she chided herself.

She toyed with the idea of ringing Samantha then changed her mind. It was too hot to go to the pictures, she wasn't hungry so there was no point in going out for a meal. Maybe she'd start that book she'd bought at the airport yesterday, there was nothing else to do.

Kim read the first two pages, then turned back and read them again. But the words refused to sink in. She couldn't remember the last book she'd enjoyed. After that bout of misery when she came back from Cape Cod she'd forced herself to push Alex from her mind. His face haunted her dreams, his eyes mocked her. And there was always the vision of Cassie Travis, cool and self-possessed, pitying. Her image refused to fade. There had been days when, if he'd walked through the door, she'd have rushed into his arms, taken him back. But those days were few, mostly bitter anger ruled her head. She'd have staked her life on Alex's love, but, as Cassie bluntly pointed out, so too would a lot of other women.

It had been a real body blow when Hadley Talbot met someone else. A blow to her pride mainly. She couldn't blame him, she'd hardly thrown herself at his feet. How had Samantha described him? Her *male comfort blanket.* She'd objected at the time, but Sam was right. And now, on her bedroom dresser, was an invitation to his wedding. Kim tried to picture herself in his fiancée's place, but she couldn't. Hadley was not for her, not after Alex.

"Alex," she said his name aloud. "How I loved you . . . how I hate you."

She jumped when the phone rang. What if it was Alex? Should she talk to him, listen to his excuses?

"Hello?"

"Kim, it's Jane Anderson."

"Jane, what can I do for you?" Kim didn't intend to sound so abrupt.

"I've had a call from Jonathan Campbell-Smith, he wanted your phone number. I explained that we don't give out our clients' numbers or addresses . . ."

"It's OK, he said he'd contact me."

"Well, he's given me *his* number to pass on to you. He'll be at the hospital until midnight, or you could phone tomorrow between eight o'clock and noon."

"He works long hours, doesn't he?"

"Certainly does," Jane agreed.

"The weekend was terrific, Jane. As soon as I have an idea of my schedule I'll phone you and book another one."

"I know it's difficult for you, but give us a fair bit of notice if you can, we're inundated. We've decided to double up a few of the rooms, some friends prefer to share, it makes it slightly cheaper for them. Would you be interested in sharing if necessary?"

"I must confess, I'd prefer to have my own room."

"No problem. We'll look forward to hearing from you. If you have a pen I'll give you Jonathan's number."

Chapter Thirty-Six

Amanda could hardly wait for the day to end. Tomorrow she planned to have her hair done and treat herself to a manicure. She'd already decided what to wear, now all she had to do was phone Kevin.

Emma Brown looked up from her desk. "I didn't hear you come in, Amanda," she said.

"It was so hot that I took off my shoes in the car."

"Mrs Judd left early, what time would you like to eat? It's all ready in the fridge."

"Any time, I don't mind," Amanda said lightly.

"Let me finish this and then I can relax. I'm not going out tonight."

"Would you fancy trying the new French place round the corner instead?" Amanda asked hesitantly.

Emma's head snapped up in amazement as she struggled to hide her surprise. Amanda, asking her to go and have a meal? She'd go to the end of the earth, never mind round the corner, for an invitation like that.

"I'd love to, what a splendid idea."

"I'll phone and book," Amanda said.

Amanda sat on the edge of the desk and

dialled the restaurant. Emma's concentration vanished, she could finish the rest of this paperwork tomorrow. She closed the folder in front of her. What had brought this on? She was delighted, but puzzled. Her offers to take Amanda out had always been met with a surly excuse or often a firm refusal. Emma had given up long ago.

"We can have a table about seven o'clock," Amanda mouthed.

"Perfect," Emma said. Midnight if necessary, she thought.

♥ ♥ ♥

"You order for me," Emma said.

Amanda wondered why her mother had left the decision to her. "How about a pâté to start with?" She asked nervously.

"Lovely, I'm a push-over for a good pâté." She'd have agreed with anything from whale blubber to octopus ink salad.

"Then . . . steak au poivre, maybe?"

"Perfect."

"Will you choose the wine?" Amanda's self-possession deserted her.

"I'm not sure what to pick, shall we ask the waiter?" Emma knew exactly which wine to order.

This is so enjoyable," Emma said scooping some pâté on to a piece of toast.

"It's good, isn't it?" Amanda sipped her wine.

"Actually, I meant being here together. Amanda, if you don't want to talk about it, I'll understand, but I've never really explained about the break-up with Daddy – or at least my side of it. I'd like to tell you." Emma held her breath, she'd probably ruined their night out.

Amanda shrugged her shoulders. "If you want to." But she wouldn't hear anything bad about her father.

"You know how we met?"

"At work?"

"Yes, we both worked for the same PR firm. We were terribly young and inexperienced. But we muddled along and eventually established ourselves. After three years, David decided that we could manage beautifully on our own. I wasn't so confident, but he could be very persuasive – that's why he was good at his job. I was crazy about him and, when he proposed, I accepted – gladly. He finally convinced me that we should start our own company. David would handle the clients, I could do the publicity and all the rest.

"We made the break. It worked well for about six months. But . . . for whatever reason, things began to fall off. We weren't attracting any new clients and we had to fight like mad to hold on to the ones we had. I offered to switch jobs with him, I'd search for clients and he could do my work. He wouldn't hear of it, accused me of having no confidence in him.

"Then quite by accident, I discovered that he wasn't even trying to make contacts. One afternoon I phoned home by mistake. David answered. I was worried, thought that he was ill, but he wasn't. He decided that the client he was due to meet wasn't worth following up, so he'd taken the day off to catch up with some reading instead. I was furious, that was the best opportunity to create new business that we'd had in months.

"By that time I was pregnant with you. Maybe my hormones were out of control but when I got home that night we had a ferocious row. It was then I found out that several of the leads I'd given him had been totally ignored. He was content to amble along with the accounts we had. Needless to say things don't work that way. Clients move on for many reasons. I was frightened. Where would we end up? How could we manage? He told me I was being foolish, but I watched our income drop alarmingly. We had a lot of rows, but that didn't get us anywhere. After a week of sleepless nights, I decided to take a gamble. I hired Lizzie and went after the accounts myself. I don't need to tell you how terrific she was."

Amanda nodded her head. Lizzie was still the mainstay of Leland's, Emma had often said she wouldn't be able to carry on without her.

"Whether it was my tummy-bump or my personality I didn't bother to ask, all I know is that slowly, but very surely, Leland's began to turn around. Things were humming again. We added four new clients in as many months. Nothing spectacular but we were on an upward curve." Emma paused and sipped her wine.

"What was Daddy doing?" Amanda asked.

"I don't want to sound horrible or to hurt you, but he spent his days playing golf. But in all fairness," Emma added quickly, "when he suggested that joining a club would be a good way to meet people, I agreed. Unfortunately the only people there during the week were either retired or the wives of businessmen. We certainly didn't make a single new contact."

Amanda didn't comment, she just avoided her mother's eyes and concentrated on her meal.

Nervously Emma continued, "When you were born I allowed myself three days off. I wasn't being a martyr, I just couldn't afford any more time. We hired a nanny and I went back to work full-time. I hated to come home at night and be told that I couldn't disturb you. When Nanny went to bed I used to sneak in to your room and have a cuddle. I got caught a couple of times! What a ticking off she gave me, but I didn't care, it was worth it and you always looked happy." Emma laughed. "One day she complained to David that I was interfering with her routine, I had no right to, she wouldn't tolerate it, so I fired her.

"In those days it was easy to find well-trained people and I chose a caring, young nanny who understood my frustration. You adored her, by the way. I was able to go back to work with an easy mind. I knew that you were in good hands. By then, David's handicap was down to three, he'd become a very good golfer. As you began to grow up you were very attached to him and he to you. I felt like a stranger, locked out. It was awful. But quite honestly, if I hadn't worked all those unsociable hours, I don't know what would have happened to us. I worried that we'd starve.

"David was a good father – an excellent father. At least when I sat at those ghastly dinners I knew he'd be there to read you a bedtime story, to take you for outings, and for that I was always grateful. Please Amanda, don't think it was all *his* fault, I made *my* mistakes too. The week you were born, we lost an account and damned near forfeited another. I bawled him out in front of Lizzie and the office junior. He was furious – quite rightly. I accused him of not caring about anything except you and his golf. I suppose I was jealous. Even when I was at home you ran to him for everything – if you fell or cut your finger, bruised a knee, anything.

"Leland Brown began to thrive . . ."

"Leland Brown? I've never heard Leland's called that before," Amanda interrupted.

"That was my revenge when your father left, I had his name removed from the company and he didn't object. I'd earned that luxury. But it was still Leland Brown up till then. We added two more people to the staff – including that snake, Lisette."

"I love her too," Amanda said sarcastically.

"David used to laugh and joke with her whenever he did manage to appear at the office. I was too busy to notice anything out of the ordinary. When I finally realised what was happening, I handled it badly. I yelled and screamed at him – but kept on working. I was *obsessed* with Leland's. It became the very core of my life. Then out of the blue, he decided to call it a day. Lisette went too. You probably remember that."

"Yes, I remember the day Daddy left." Amanda's voice was almost a whisper.

"Finished, Madam?" the waiter asked as he looked at Emma's half-eaten steak.

Emma nodded.

"Dessert?" he enquired hesitantly. "Perhaps you'd like to wait a while?"

Emma nodded again. Suddenly she felt better than she had for years even though Amanda's reaction was difficult to judge. Emma didn't know how much David had told Amanda, but she desperately wanted to clear the air with her daughter. There was just one more thing she wanted to say, and Emma agonised about whether she should or not. Here goes, she decided.

"I know you've always thought that I didn't care about you, but you are one hundred percent wrong. Perhaps I didn't know how to show my love, went about it the wrong way; buying toys, clothes, telling you to choose a car – any car. But one thing you may not know, I was prepared to let you go and live with your father. It was the last thing I wanted to do, believe me, but if it made you happy . . ."

"Why didn't he take me?" Amanda's eyes were suspiciously bright.

"He had no job, nowhere to live, no one to look after you."

For the second time in two days, tears streamed down Amanda's cheeks. Emma searched in her bag for a tissue, her head bowed to hide her own emotion. As Amanda reached for the tissue, their hands touched and she clung to her mother's fingers as they wept silently.

"What we must look like," Emma laughed through her tears.

"I don't care," Amanda sniffed.

"Me neither," Emma laughed. "I suppose it's selfish of me but I'm so relieved now that you know the story from my point of view."

"I'm glad you told me. Dad never did. I suppose I did take his side."

"Let's forget all about that, enjoy the rest of our meal. Suddenly I fancy a wicked dessert, how about you?"

Like greedy children they eyed their heaped plates and laughed.

"I have a date tomorrow night," Amanda said shyly.

"Wonderful! Would that be Kevin?"

"Yes. I have to phone him in the morning."

"Things have changed since I was a girl," Emma smiled.

"Oh no, it's not like that." Amanda blushed with confusion. "*Personal Agenda* don't give out phone numbers so he left his number with Jane."

"That's sensible. I'm new to this kind of thing but if there'd been something . . . Never mind, it's too late now."

"You mean if there'd been a dating agency when you split with Dad you might have joined it?"

"Absolutely. I think it's a wonderful way of meeting people." Emma was genuinely delighted that Amanda had made the effort to join the agency.

"Then join *Personal Agenda*." Amanda leaned forward in her chair. "They have weekends for over-forties."

"I couldn't, besides I'm over fifty, never mind forty."

"Mum, don't be so negative. That's what you always said to me! You'd love it. You don't have to go there to find a husband, just have a fun weekend. I'll get you the forms next weekend and you can have a look at them. Maybe Jane will give us a family rate."

Emma laughed. Imagine something like that at her age. "Where are you going on your date?" She was anxious to change the subject.

Amanda explained the complications about the date, even told Emma about Kevin's marriage. She found it strange sitting here with her mother. All her life, she'd thought of her as an ogre, an enemy.

"He sounds like a nice person." Emma frowned.

"But?" From habit Amanda waited for some adverse comment.

"No but. I was thinking how stupid his wife was. As a fully qualified, failed one, I should know."

"Don't say that," Amanda pleaded.

"That's kind of you. When your turn comes, Amanda, put your husband first, love him, do your best for him. Don't repeat my mistakes."

As she sat on her bed Amanda's head was reeling. Her mother *hadn't* put all the blame on her father as she'd expected. If what her mother said was true, then they were both at fault. Suddenly she felt angry, angry that she'd wasted years hating her mother. For she might as well admit it, she *did* hate her at times. Now she was confused. Almost as confused as the day her father left. Amanda walked to the window and looked into the darkness. Try as she might, she could no longer conjure up that familiar picture of her father as he opened the taxi door, climbed in and left them. Amanda drew the curtains and hoped with all her heart that she would never be asked to serve on a jury. She would be utterly useless at deciding between innocence and guilt.

Chapter Thirty-Seven

For once both trains were on time. Susie arrived less than ten minutes after Jane said goodbye to Sasha.

The two friends hugged each other. "What an age it's been since we've had a chance to be together like this," Jane said.

"I thought it would be nice if we dropped your case home then walked to the pub for lunch. How does that sound?"

"Wonderful, I'd love some good fresh country air."

Susie looked pale, Jane thought. Was it her imagination or did her friend seem a little out of sorts? She turned in the drive and cut the engine.

"People aren't over-friendly here, are they?" Susie observed as they seated themselves at a table near the open window.

"No, I suppose not." Jane frowned. She'd smiled at a couple she'd often met in the village but they barely nodded in return. "To heck with them, let's order lunch."

"Tell me about the weekend, was it disastrous or a roaring success?" Susie demanded.

"Somewhere in between," Jane said modestly.

"When Caroline phoned to cancel, I knew that Sasha expected me to get hysterical. So I bloody well didn't!"

Susie burst out laughing. "Good for you. What did you do? I was afraid to phone you."

"Thanks a lot. I tackled it the way I tackle everything nowadays, with a cup of tea. I sat at one side of the table and stared into my cup and Sasha sat opposite me staring into hers. And then Sasha yelled in her cardiac-arrest-provoking voice. '*Pottery*, that's what we'll do, *pottery*.'"

"Pottery?" Susie frowned.

"I thought she'd gone gaga too. Before I could ask any questions she was on the phone like a shot talking to some man about pottery."

"How did she know him?"

"One day when we were at the cottage with Justin and William, Sasha wandered off for a walk and discovered a man who taught pottery classes. Sasha being Sasha, she went to investigate. To cut a very long story short, he agreed to come to The Willows on Saturday and teach us how to make pots. Luckily he had a sense of humour. I must confess I was worried how people would take to the change of programme, but no one cared."

"I've never tried to do pottery but have often been tempted to have a go," Susie volunteered.

"Me too, and I still haven't. Unfortunately we were busy that day but we'll certainly ask him back later in the year. Marcus his name was, six foot seven and as skinny as be damned. He arrived on Friday and set up his wheels and kilns in the garage. Just as well we have electricity there.

"Early on Saturday he appeared with the clay,

the paints and all his bits and pieces and, most importantly, large aprons. I'd never have thought of that. He was brilliant. He told everyone that the plates and cups they made would be used for lunch on Sunday to save Sasha and myself the bother of washing up. I've never seen so many misshapen cups, bowls, saucers and plates – all signed no less. Such designs and colours! Because the plates were crooked the food fell off and some of the cups leaked. They thought this was hilarious. We also lost most of the milk from a jug, there was a hole in its side. The messier the table became, the more they enjoyed it. The irony of it was that we spent ages washing up after all, everyone wanted to take their work of art home with them."

"Sounds crazy," Susie said.

"It certainly was. Those Sunday barbecues have been a blessing. This weather has been a boon. Long may it continue," Jane raised her glass. "To sunny days and barbecues."

"How are William and Justin?" Susie asked.

"They're fine. I missed them last weekend, can you imagine Justin making pottery? He'd have thrown pots all right! I remember how impatient he was at the flower-arranging classes. They'll be staying at the cottage next weekend for the first time and eating at The Willows."

"You may have someone else eating at The Willows next weekend," Susie said.

"Oh? Who?"

"Me."

"Will Matt be away?"

"Matt may be away permanently. He wants a separation."

"What are you talking about? . . . Susie, you don't mean that." Jane's face drained. Matt, stolid, dependable Matt.

"I do. There's someone else." Susie's voice choked.

"I . . . I . . . It can't be, not Matt."

"The same."

"Oh my God, I don't believe it. I won't believe it," Jane stammered.

"Believe it."

"How, I mean, who?"

"I don't know her, she's a customer of his, recently divorced and obviously not prepared to let the grass grow under her feet," Susie said bitterly.

"How did you find out, did Matt tell you about her?"

"No, I had a sympathy phone call from Jill Metcalf. She wanted to commiserate with me."

"That bitch," Jane snorted. "She simpered around me too, remember?"

"I'd forgotten that."

"Sorry – I interrupted you."

"I couldn't wait to tackle Matt. He turned every colour under the sun and stood there saying nothing – like the dumb fool he is. Finally he admitted he'd been seeing this woman. For about three weeks now. He said she was the first woman in years who'd found him attractive, made him feel good. He offered to move out there and then. I could have the house and the car, all he wanted was his own car."

Jane stared at her friend. Matt was the last

person in the world she could think of who would have an affair. It was absurd, Susie must be making more of this than there was.

"*Did* he move out?" she asked.

"Yes and no. He's away this week, travelling. He's staying with his mother in Cambridge. He offered to tell me who the woman is, but honestly, I'd rather not know. I think all this has shocked him as much as it stunned me. That probably sounds ridiculous."

"No it doesn't. I can't take it in, Susie. Let's get the bill and walk back."

The ducks on the pond quacked noisily, but they failed to bring the usual smile to Jane's lips. She was trying to understand Matt's . . . indiscretion. She was positive that's all it was . . . an indiscretion. No matter what Susie said, Jane knew that Matt loved Susie. Matt had always loved Susie.

"So what's going to happen now?" Jane asked.

"He wants time to think, to make a decision. He'll be home on Friday and then I'll know. I told him not to phone. And there's something else I haven't told you – I'm pregnant."

"How wonderful! Oh, how awful. No, I'm . . . of course it's wonderful. When did you find out? Why didn't you tell me? Does Matt know?"

"I found out yesterday and Matt doesn't know yet. And I'm not going to use that to get him back, so don't even suggest it."

Jane wanted to reassure Susie, promise her everything would work out, get hold of Matt and shake some sense into him. How well she understood her friend's heartbreak, she'd suffered from it often enough. But she and Hugh were different, their marriage was hopeless, a mess. But Susie and Matt . . . Jane tucked her arm into Susie's to give her comfort.

"Hang in there, Susie. I *know* Matt will be back, and he'll be thrilled about the baby."

♥ ♥ ♥

Susie stood in the heavy shower gazing at the river. The raindrops mingled with her tears. What would she do without Matt? They'd been together ever since they were children. She couldn't imagine life without him. Maybe Jane was right, he'd come rushing home on Friday and beg her to forgive him. Matt, with those funny ears and soft, kind eyes. Was he attractive? She could only think of him as Matt, the man she loved. He was forever sticking his big feet in his mouth. She was constantly apologising for his tactlessness. Was that where she'd gone wrong? And what about the baby, could she bring up a child alone?

"Susie!" Jane called from the open kitchen window. "It's lashing, come inside."

Poor Jane, Susie thought as she trudged towards the house. What a miserable couple of days I've given her. I don't know how I could have got through this week without her. Strange how their roles had reversed. I'm sure I wasn't as supportive to her as she's been to me. If only it was Friday, she sighed.

Susie watched Jane stringing some French

beans. "Jane, you won't say anything to Sasha, will you?" she asked.

"As if I would," Jane replied in a hurt voice.

"I'm sorry, I shouldn't have said that."

"Come on, let's have a game of Scrabble, either I win, or you get no dinner," Jane threatened, but her comment didn't raise a smile on Susie's glum face.

Chapter Thirty-Eight

Kim examined herself critically in the mirror. Not bad, she assured herself. Her short black dress looked even better with the new higher heels. She'd never really liked flat shoes. She smoothed her sheer black tights and threw the red satin shawl over her shoulders with a flourish.

Jonathan introduced her to his colleagues at the table. She smiled at the notice pinned on an easel: All hospital talk suspended for the duration of the evening.

"I've never been to one of these dinner dances before," Jonathan admitted.

"I used to hate dances when I was a kid. You could spend hours gyrating madly and not exchange a single word with your partner."

"If you promise never to tell a soul, I'll let you in on a secret. At the age of thirteen I was so clumsy and uncoordinated that my parents sent me to dancing classes," Jonathan grinned.

"I won't mention a word to the heads of MI5 when I see them," Kim promised solemnly.

"That makes me feel a whole lot better. Come on, let's see if I learnt anything." Jonathan pulled Kim to her feet and they joined the dancers on the floor.

"That was money well spent," Kim said breathlessly as they returned to the table. "You're a very good dancer."

"You're no slouch yourself." Jonathan poured a glass of iced water from the jug.

"Excuse me please, aren't you Dr Campbell-Smith?" asked an attractive woman in her early thirties.

"Yes, that's me." Jonathan rose politely from his seat.

Without invitation the woman sat in the vacant chair. "I understand you're considered to be a gifted surgeon."

"I'm a surgeon, yes. Are you a journalist?"

"No, no. I'm a prospective patient. I wanted to meet you, perhaps ask you a couple of questions," she said in a matter of fact voice.

Kim glanced at the notice on the easel, then at Jonathan's angry face.

"I am Dr Campbell-Smith's secretary. The doctor is off-duty tonight so I suggest you telephone his consulting room at your convenience."

"Hmm! If you don't need patients then I'll find someone else." She strode away from the table bristling with rejection.

Kim waited for Jonathan to reproach her. She had no right to say what she'd said.

"Marry me!" Jonathan laughed, his momentary annoyance forgotten. "That was marvellous."

"I thought I'd overstepped the mark," Kim confessed.

"No way. Now you see what I mean. How did you come up with that answer so quickly?"

"'In my job you learn to think on your feet."

"If you won't marry me, how about coming to work for me – out of hours, be my social secretary."

"No, I think I'd prefer to marry you," Kim teased.

"I'll ask my secretary when I have a free day."

"I am your secretary!" Kim laughed.

"Are we on the same page?" Jonathan asked.

Kim wiped the make-up from her face. She was pleased she'd changed her mind about going to the dance. Jonathan was a thought-provoking man. There was a lot more to him than she'd first believed. She was glad she'd offered to go with him to see his patient. The little girl had held up her bandaged hands when she saw Jonathan enter the cheerfully decorated children's ward. He rested them gently between his own as he read the child's chart.

"I hear that you've been hurting my friend," he said sternly to the white gauze dressings. "I don't allow anyone to upset Judy."

The child nodded solemnly at her hands.

"Shall we give them another chance?" he asked.

"They hurted me," Judy objected.

"Let's ask Kim what she thinks," Jonathan smiled and nodded imperceptibly.

"Hello, Judy. I'm sorry that your hands hurt, but I think if you tell the bandages that you're very cross with them, they'll listen to you."

"They hurted me," the little girl insisted.

"Do you want to hear all about the dance?" Jonathan took a tiny plastic measure containing Judy's medicine from the nurse. "There was music, big, loud music. Do you like music?"

Judy shook her head. "I like likkle music."

"Now, if you take your medicine, I think Kim might have a surprise for you," Jonathan smiled.

Judy pulled a face but opened her mouth obediently.

"There we are, that will help you to get better. Do you have a surprise for Judy, Kim?"

Kim brought some balloons from behind her back and Judy's face lit up.

"Shall we tie them to the bed?" Kim asked. She tied them by their streamers and the brightly coloured, helium-filled balloons floated upwards.

A half-smile lit the child's face.

"What do you say to Kim?" Jonathan prompted.

"Do you like big music?"

Judy's eyes were already beginning to droop.

"I'll come and see you tomorrow, OK?" Jonathan released her hands and placed them carefully under the sheet.

"Kim come too," she said drowsily.

They tiptoed away from the sleeping child.

"Will she be all right?" Kim asked.

"I think so, in fact I'm sure she will, the skin grafts seem to be taking nicely." Jonathan didn't explain the reason for the operation, and Kim didn't like to ask.

She'd thought very little about Alex during the evening. Jonathan's colleagues were charming and easy-going. Kim noticed that there were a lot of very attractive girls there and felt flattered that Jonathan had invited her. Yes, Kim thought, I'm glad I said yes.

Chapter Thirty-Nine

Ray Parker pushed the tie out of sight into the drawer. "Come in," he called.

"Can I have a word?" Donahue Reilly's face was grim.

"Something wrong?"

"It's my blasted computer at home, it's acting up again," he complained.

"Your own machine?" Ray checked.

"Yes. If it's OK with you, I'd like to transfer my software onto a spare machine here at CCC. Mine needs to be repaired properly this time or I'm going to have a disaster."

"No problem. I think you're right, once faults start beginning to recur it usually spells trouble."

Donahue always had some project on hand. He'd made himself quite a bit of extra money over the years, and Ray had no objections as long as it didn't interfere with his work. In fact he welcomed it, that way he didn't have to worry about giving Donahue a rise. But he would increase Donahue's salary when the Beamish and Chambers' contract was complete.

Ray looked at his watch again, another couple of hours and he'd be on his way to *Personal Agenda.* Last weekend was almost as good as the first one. Jane told him who would be there. No doubt Dale would be in cracking form. That fellow Justin had a great sense of humour too. Amanda was pleasant enough, he could take or leave her, but Kevin was good fun. And of course there'd be other new people.

Ray opened the drawer and took out his tie. The bright colours would be his new colour image.

The night out with Serena Mayhew hadn't really worked. They'd got on well last weekend at The Willows but somehow, on their own, the evening spent together fell flat. The film wasn't good and the meal not much better. He'd been relieved when the time came to part. There was no chemistry between them.

"I'm off, Ray. Have a good weekend," Linda Lou called through the closed door.

"And you," he answered. If she knew where he was going, she'd probably make some smart remark and get right up his nose. No one knew what he did with his spare time, and he liked it that way.

"Hi! Ray, it's Trudy. Where've you been? If you fancy going to the flicks tomorrow give me a shout. If I'm out, leave a message on my machine, bye."

Ray pressed the rewind button and smiled smugly as he picked up his case. He hadn't spoken to her for weeks.

Half-way to the door, he stopped. Maybe he shouldn't be so smug, if he didn't meet anyone this weekend he might be glad of her company. *Personal Agenda* was booked out for weeks. His name was first on the waiting list for the middle of August, but his next confirmed booking wasn't until the bank holiday weekend.

"Speak after the tone and ye shall be heard – mess and you're dead." Trudy's voice announced.

"Trudy, it's Ray. The messages you leave on that machine! I'm away this weekend but I'll give you a buzz when I get back. *Ciao.*"

Trudy was something else, she'd scare a heavy breather.

Chapter Forty

Justin and William were first to arrive at The Willows. They'd taken a few days off so that they could organise the cottage.

"How civilised it is here," Justin groaned and threw himself into a comfortable chair. "Squatters would reject our place at the moment. Why do humans accumulate such a lot of possessions? Animals don't."

"When am I going to see this *squat*?" Jane asked.

"Monday? We're really skiving off this weekend," William admitted.

"There's the doorbell, help yourselves to a drink, you look as though you could do with one." Jane smiled at them warmly. How lucky she was to have found such good friends.

Nikki Gardiner, the colour consultant, walked confidently into the hall. "It's nice to meet you at last," she said. "I have another case in the car, will someone give me a hand? I can't carry everything."

"I will," Jane said.

"There we are, that's the lot." Nikki closed the boot with a loud bang.

"I wonder if you'd mind moving your car over

there, by the hedge. We'll have several more later," Jane asked.

Jane picked up Nikki's case, it was surprisingly light.

Nikki made a moue with her mouth. "It would be a lot handier to have a room on the first floor – these cases. One flight of stairs less."

"Don't worry, we'll help you." Jane tried to hide her instant dislike of Nikki Gardiner. "Now, I'll leave you to settle in. If you'll excuse me, I must see to dinner. Come downstairs when you're ready, two of my friends are in the living-room, they'll look after you."

"She's been thirty-six ever since she was forty-two," Jane bitched. "First floor room, indeed. She *offered* to come here and do the demonstration, she's the one that pushed and shoved. *Carry her case!* I could have carried them both with one hand."

"Calm down. Don't get your teddy in a twist," Sasha advised. "Anyway, lighten up, she can't be that bad. I'll take these hors d'oeuvres into the living-room in a few minutes and have a look for myself."

"Good God!" Nikki Gardiner exclaimed.

Sasha looked behind her to see what had startled the woman.

"What's wrong?" Sasha asked.

"Forgive me – your make-up, do you always wear foundation like that?"

On a whim, Sasha had whitened her face with a chalky powder, outlined her eyes with kohl and gashed her mouth with scarlet lipstick.

"Doesn't everyone?" Sasha retorted acidly.

"Sasha is an actress," Justin rushed to her defence.

"Oh! I see. Sasha, I need a model for my colour demonstration tomorrow, would you like to sit in the hot seat?"

"Sorry, I don't have time. We have a busy day."

"What a pity, I think under that . . . *make-up* you probably have a nice face." Nikki sat perfectly poised, one foot crossed neatly over the other. She wore her red suit and casually knotted scarf the way Sasha imagined it should be worn, casually and elegantly. She didn't care that she was staring rudely at the woman. Sasha counted four rings, two bracelets, a watch and large gilt earrings. Nikki's auburn hair was caught back in a gold clip and, in Sasha's opinion, she was far too heavily made up.

"I'll leave these hors d'oeuvres here, Justin. Look after Nikki." Sasha flounced out of the room, Justin knew that she was bristling with annoyance.

"The cheek of her! From now on I shall call her *The Destructor.*"

"Don't get your teddy in a twist," Jane mocked.

"She didn't insult *you,*" Sasha fumed.

"I know. But she's only here for a couple of days so let's make the best of it," Jane grimaced. "We don't need to invite her again, we can find someone else. So bite your tongue and ignore her remarks. I have a feeling we won't win. OK?"

"I suppose so. But any more attacks on my appearance and I'll let her have it right between her apricot-shadowed eyes."

Jane was happy with the buzz of conversation

around the table. Amanda confided in her that she and Kevin had had a good night out on Saturday. Jane was pleased for Amanda. Wouldn't it be marvellous if they were *Personal Agenda*'s first success story, she thought fancifully. Dale was running true to form, her neighbours were laughing as she repeated the exploits of an under-qualified plumber she'd hired. Nikki Gardiner was remarkably quiet considering her manipulative arrival. She picked nervously at the border of the linen table mat in front of her.

The pale cyclamen flowers and candles looked attractive on the polished table. Jane hadn't been sure whether the colours would look good against the deep background of the room, but they did. She liked the way the wax dripped down the candles forming designs of its own.

She thought about Susie and Matt. She didn't really expect to hear from Susie until tomorrow but worried about her nonetheless.

The few days they'd spent together had drained her, brought back so many of her own unhappy memories. But she was totally convinced that Susie and Matt's rift would heal, their marriage wouldn't crumble like hers had. She must pay attention to her guests and not let her mind wander like this.

"Do you find it awkward being identical twins?" Peter Connolly asked.

"Not really, it's quite funny at times," Lara said.

"Especially when we muddle people on purpose," Laura added.

"I'm sure your teachers must have had a job distinguishing between you," Peter persisted.

"Everyone did. One teacher got so frustrated she insisted that I wore a red ribbon on my school sweater and Laura wore a blue one. When we were in a mischievous mood we swopped them."

"We had great fun on dates too," Laura chipped in. "Our boyfriends never knew who they were going out with. They made a date with one of us and the other showed up."

♥ ♥ ♥

"Right guys, your turn," Sasha said when she came back to the kitchen.

Justin and William had refused to eat with the others. "Fifteen round the table is too many, it will make it a real squash," William insisted.

Sasha waited anxiously as they cut into the pastry.

"Smells delicious," Justin said taking his role as food critic seriously.

"What do you think?" Sasha asked as Justin chewed the first mouthful.

"What is it?" he asked. "It's so unusual."

"But do you like it?"

"I love it," Justin assured her.

Sasha relaxed. She shouldn't have risked something new without trying it first but the mangoes had been so tempting she couldn't resist them.

"Let me guess," William said. "Chicken, orange, mangoes?"

"Yes," Sasha smiled.

"How do you get the filo pastry so crisp?" Mrs Jones asked enviously.

"It just cooks that way." Now that they all approved, Sasha could enjoy her own meal.

"So how's it going in there?" Justin asked pouring a little more of the port and orange sauce on to his plate.

"*The Destroyer* is quiet, not making any trouble as far as I can see. Dale's in good form, she makes everyone laugh. The twins seem to fit in easily enough. They must have the most unimaginative parents in the world, fancy calling your children Lara and Laura! Ray Parker is chatting up Jennifer." Sasha had grown to like Ray, he was easy-going and quick to laugh. He was always so complimentary about her cooking too.

"What about Amanda and Kevin?" Justin wanted to know.

"They're nattering with Peter. That guy, Peter Connolly, he's fun, he and Dale make good sparring partners. Tarquin! He has about as much personality as a block of wood. Talk about names! *Tarquin Devereux de Longueville!* Can't you just picture it – the swashbuckling hero of a romantic novel!"

"He's a very handsome man," Justin objected.

"I don't think so," William said.

"You're just jealous," Justin accused.

"I'm not, I think he's . . . oily. I've never seen so much oil on anyone's hair."

"Gel, William. Get with it," Justin instructed.

"Don't split hairs," William said, then laughed at his own pun.

"Stop arguing you two," Sasha begged. "I have to serve dessert now, then I'll come back to fill you in with part two."

♥ ♥ ♥

The rainy days had given the garden a new lease of life. The flowers had perked up again and the willow's sweeping branches were springy and green with sap. Jane served coffee outside, the moonlight and the gently lapping river gave the mellow night an air of tranquillity. When she'd made sure that no one was left on their own, she went back into the house to help Sasha and Mrs Jones.

Out of the corner of her eye Amanda saw Nikki Gardiner making her way towards the group.

"Would you like to act as my make-up model tomorrow?" Nikki asked Amanda.

"No thank you," she replied tartly. She'd noticed Nikki staring at her across the table earlier and had shifted uncomfortably under her gaze.

"Go for it, Amanda, it's cool," Dale said.

"Then you do it," she retorted.

"Hey, I didn't mean to upset you."

"You didn't," Amanda snapped.

"You have such good colouring, such wonderful potential," Nikki said. If ever anyone needed a bit of help it was Amanda. Her hair was mousy, her make-up made her skin sallow. *I could do a really great make-over on her.* "You'd enjoy it."

Amanda was seething. If she refused it would be churlish, if she didn't, it would be humiliating. Why had Nikki picked on her? She hated this smug woman with her patronisingly false charm.

They were all looking at Amanda expectantly.

"Yes, I would enjoy it, why not?" Amanda thought she sounded convincing and hoped that no one could see the fiery colour of her cheeks.

♥ ♥ ♥

Dressed in a navy blue wool suit and a pale blue blouse, Nikki had made it obvious that she was not pleased to hold the demonstration in the garden. But Jane ignored Nikki Gardiner's displeasure, she too could be quite determined when she wanted. "I'm here to please my clients," she said. "They all prefer to be outside in this lovely weather. We can line up the chairs outside the patio. You can work inside, it's quite sheltered under the jasmine."

"Well I just hope my make-up samples don't melt in the heat," Nikki said petulantly.

Jane swallowed the retort that sprang to her lips. Nikki seemed constantly discontented, contrary. Nikki's own make-up was so heavily applied it would survive fire, wind and flood.

"If you like we can keep your cosmetics in the living-room until you're ready, it's cool there."

Amanda sidled self-consciously into the waiting chair.

"We'll begin by cleansing Amanda's face. Would you mind removing your glasses, Amanda. This is not just for you, ladies, men are equally affected by grime and dust," she pointed out as she worked. "Moisturising the skin is almost as important as cleaning it."

Sasha nudged Jane. "Poor Amanda, she looks as if she's been dipped in an oil-slick," she whispered.

"Shush," Jane said sternly. She was right, but Sasha's asides had earned her plenty of dirty looks during the entertainment course; besides she didn't want Amanda upset.

"We'll leave the moisturiser to soak in while we discuss colour. People fit into four categories, Spring, Summer, Autumn and Winter. Amanda is Summer. Each season has its own colours, but for now we'll deal with Summer. As you can see, Amanda doesn't have strong colouring so she wouldn't suit vivid make-up, she needs blended colours. The overall effect should be soft and subtle. The colours of the clothes you wear are very important. Sasha, would you mind bringing me the colour swatches."

"Yes, m'lady," Sasha muttered under her breath. She did a little curtsey and moved the small table nearer to Nikki. "I wonder what colour *please* is?" she said a little louder.

Jennifer Downs giggled and a couple of the others snickered. Jane glared at Sasha. If Nikki heard Sasha's remark she chose to ignore it. She tied a plain white cloth round Amanda's neck. "This will give us a background for the colours," she explained.

"May I put my glasses back on?" Amanda asked.

"We use two shades of each of the colours," Nikki said handing Amanda her glasses. "One either side of the face. That way we can decide which is best."

Nikki selected two pieces of pink fabric and draped them close to Amanda's neck. "You can see that the one on the right drains her skin, the other gives it a warmth."

"Do you think I could have a mirror, please?" Amanda asked

Nikki clicked her tongue with annoyance.

"I'll get one for you, Amanda, you must be able to see what's going on," Jane said.

"In the meantime we'll test the blues." Nikki picked up the next two pieces of material.

"Why not wait for a minute until Jane comes back with the mirror," Kevin interrupted. "Then Amanda will be able to see what you're talking about."

Amanda threw him a pathetic look of gratitude. She was decidedly uncomfortable, and felt like a prize guinea pig. This was a mistake. She hated the whole set-up, disliked Nikki Gardiner intensely.

"Nikki," Jane called from the living-room. "Can you take a look at this?"

Irritated by the delay, Nikki stepped inside the room. "What is it?" she asked sharply.

"Nikki, I'm very grateful to you for doing this demonstration, but frankly the atmosphere is . . . less than pleasant. Amanda is obviously uncomfortable, she didn't ask to do this and I won't have my clients upset by your attitude. This is supposed to be *fun.* If something has upset you, tell me what it is and I'll try and put it right. But I expect you to be more . . . agreeable, professional. You offered to come here, and we've tried to make your weekend a pleasant one. Please honour *your* commitment graciously. I suggest we take an early break. We'll have some coffee or a cold drink, and then start afresh."

Nikki Gardiner stared moodily at her feet. "OK," she agreed.

"We're going to take a coffee break while Nikki sorts out her creams, I'm afraid I knocked them flying when I went for the mirror," Jane apologised tactfully.

Amanda followed Jane into the house. "Jane, I don't want to do this." Her face was flushed.

"I understand, I don't blame you. I've had a word with Nikki – between you and I – read her the riot act. I don't think she'll give us any more hassle. If you really don't want to continue with this, I'll sit in for you or . . ."

"Or what?"

"Well, I really need to see to the lunch. Perhaps Dale or Jennifer would do it instead. Dale might be better, Jennifer is a bit shy."

"Look, it's awkward for you. But if as you say you've had a word with her, I'll go ahead with it. She's such a bossy cow."

"I agree with you," Jane said. "You're a good sport, Amanda."

Justin and William popped into the kitchen to say they'd arrived and to bring Jane some extra cream.

"What's happened?" William asked when he saw Jane's stern face.

"Nothing really, just Nikki being her charming self. Amanda's upset, quite rightly, and there's an atmosphere. I gave Nikki a real going-over then told her we'd take an early coffee break. She agreed reluctantly. I think it's the first thing she's agreed to since she got here."

"Don't worry, if you have any more trouble with her, I'll beat her up," Justin promised, his chubby fists flailing the air.

In spite of herself, Jane laughed. It took Justin all his courage to beat up an egg.

"Oh, Justin! You always see the funny side, don't you?" she said.

♥ ♥ ♥

Once again Nikki placed pieces of fabric either side of Amanda's shoulders, then eliminated the one which was least flattering.

". . . And that's how we decide. Even when a colour is good, there's always one shade which is marginally better than the other," Nikki said as she tested the last two colours. "Now we'll do Amanda's make-up."

It had taken all Nikki's will-power to continue with the demonstration. She'd been in a foul mood ever since she'd arrived. Her life was a mess. Any hope she'd had of meeting someone suitable was dashed when the men arrived, they were far younger than she'd expected. Anyway those twins had grabbed most of the attention, they were very attractive. And that American girl, Dale, she had a terrific personality. Even Jennifer, shy as she was, had Ray Parker running around her in circles. There was no one plainer than Amanda Brown but that young Irish fellow, Kevin, rarely left her side.

"I don't say you *must* use them, but brushes and sponges make the process a lot easier." Nikki held one up as an example. There was one for applying eyeshadow, another for the concealer, a lip brush, there seemed to be a brush for every part of the face. "We start by applying concealer. You gentlemen needn't be afraid to use it either.

It hides blemishes, dark shadows and broken veins. You'd be astonished how many men make use of this little secret," she confided. "Amanda has very red cheeks so I'll tone them down with a green concealer."

Amanda's colour deepened even more with the implied criticism.

"If you attend a business meeting for instance, you won't want any tell-tale discomfort or, worse still, anger, to show. This will completely camouflage the high colour. Now the foundation . . ." As Nikki shaded and shadowed one side of Amanda's face, it began to take on a new shape. Her cheekbone was highlighted, Amanda's right eye appeared to be larger, more open than her left, her narrow lips fuller. It was a subtle but definite transformation.

"This afternoon I'll show you how to improve your general appearance. You'll learn how to choose the right clothes, deal with hair styling and colour, wear the right glasses. This will interest the gentlemen as much as the ladies. Now if any of you would like to buy the brushes or make-up pads, I have some spares."

Amanda examined her face in the mirror. She turned her head from side to side, the difference between the two sides was amazing. She'd definitely try to make-up like this in future although it was difficult to remember exactly what Nikki had done to get this effect. The brushes would be useful, she'd buy those and the wedge-shaped sponges. Maybe Nikki would tell her what colours she'd used, but did she want to talk to the sour woman again?

Sasha stood beside the small table and gestured to Jane. "Look at this," she said quietly. "It's daylight robbery. These are ordinary brushes you can buy in any chemist but she's charging five times the price. I know what these things cost, I use them all the time for my stage make-up."

Jane picked up a large fluffy brush which was marked twenty-two pounds.

"Do you want to buy it?" Nikki asked moving towards them. "I'll let you have it for twenty."

"Nikki, put these away." Jane's expression was grim. "We both know these prices are extortionate, what are you trying to do?"

Sasha moved out of earshot, let Jane sort this one out.

"They're extremely good brushes," she protested.

"They're ordinary brushes. I bought one last week, it's almost identical to this," Jane said pointing to an eyeliner brush. "Eighteen pounds! I paid four."

"You seem to object to everything I do or say. Perhaps it would be better if I packed up and left," Nikki bristled.

"If you wish to leave *after* you've given your talk this afternoon, feel free. But you've undertaken to do it and I expect you to keep your word. I'm sure you wouldn't want me to report you to the Consumer Association, would you?" Jane never thought she'd resort to blackmail. But she was determined not to have any more problems with this woman. In future she'd make it her business to meet someone like Nikki before she agreed to let them give lectures or demonstrations.

To Jane's horror, Nikki began to cry.

"I'm sorry," Nikki sobbed. "Nothing ever seems to go right. I can't cope any more."

"I'm sure it's not that bad," Jane said sympathetically. She found it difficult to stay angry for long.

"Can I talk to you in private?" Nikki asked.

"Yes . . . but after we've served lunch. Come on, pack up your gear and cheer up. There's usually an answer."

♥ ♥ ♥

Jane and Nikki were the only two left in the dining-room. Everyone else had taken their plates and glasses into the garden, greedy for the beautiful sunshine.

"Now tell me what's wrong, maybe I can help," Jane said gently.

Nikki was quiet for a moment. "When I first spoke to you, I told you that my marriage had broken up. I have two children, and Phil, my husband, doesn't give me a penny for their upkeep.

"It was very difficult to keep an eye on the kids because I travelled around so much, I did a lot of corporate work. If I did evening consultations Mum looked after them. When Phil left, it cost me a fortune for child minders. Because of that I decided to set up on my own. I work mostly from home now. It wasn't too bad at the beginning, customers recommended me to their friends and I managed fairly well. I plagued the journalists I knew to write articles about me, but they refused – colour consultancy had been over-exposed in the press. My business dwindled to a trickle. I rang companies that I thought would have a big staff and offered my services. Most of them were already linked into other colour consultants.

"And then there was another problem. When I did manage to attract customers, I no longer had the products to sell; the make-up, the brushes, the books. They were a big part of my income when I worked for *Images in Colour*. I began to buy ordinary brands and add my own labels. In order to do this I had to buy inferior products, ones without names. Needless to say, the cosmetics weren't always the best. One woman complained bitterly that she'd broken out in a terrible rash from a blusher, she threatened to take me to court if I didn't give her back her money. I was glad to get off so lightly. Then it happened again – with eyeshadow this time. That customer arrived on my doorstep one night with her husband. Her eyes *were* in a dreadful mess, all puffy and cracked. He demanded to know what I was going to do about it? I didn't know what to say. They wouldn't return the eyeshadow. All I could think of was my label on the box. I could see myself being charged with fraud, my kids taken into care, I was terrified. In the end I gave them a hundred and fifty-four pounds which was all I had. Thank goodness they took the money. They gave me back the eyeshadow, and left.

"At that stage I didn't care how much I'd laid out for those inferior cosmetics, I took the lot and threw them in the dustbin. Then I borrowed a bit of money from Mum – I hated to ask her – and bought brands which I knew were good quality and safe to use."

"Do you label those?"

"No. I tell clients which colours and brands I use, it's up to them if they want to buy them or not. And another thing, at *Images in Colour*, when a client came for a consultation, she would be given a wallet containing small samples of the selected colours. I couldn't afford to do that, I couldn't make up a wallet for my customers. That's why I started concentrating on the brushes. I suppose it was stupid to try and make up the money that way. Most of the time people are so thrilled with their new appearance, they don't stop to question my prices. I am good at my job."

"I'm sure you are," Jane agreed.

"It's like a vicious circle, I don't have money to advertise, so I get very few customers. If I don't get new customers, there's no business – people rarely have a need to return. Now my bills are starting to pile up, I can't buy even the smallest treats for the kids. My car is in dreadful condition. I can't afford it, but can't afford to be without it." Nikki hung her head and dabbed at her eyes.

"I really sympathise, it must be dreadful for you. It's a stupid question I suppose, but can't you get *any* assistance from your husband? Surely there are ways to *make* him help you?"

"I don't even know where he is, which town he's living in. To tell you the truth, I don't want to see him ever again. He was vile and the kids were terrified of him."

"You mean he hit them?"

Nikki's eyes flickered nervously. "Yes, and me."

"I see . . . Obviously you've thought of going back to your original job?"

"They wouldn't take me back now."

"Have you asked them?"

"No, I haven't," Nikki admitted.

"Then why are you so sure, did you leave on bad terms?"

"Not at all. They were very understanding. But even if I did take up where I left off, there's still the problem of child minders. They're murderously expensive."

"What about your mother? Could she not help you?"

"Mum works part-time. She doesn't earn a lot but she needs that money."

"Does she earn as much as you pay a child minder?"

"Nowhere near that, she . . . Oh! Why didn't I think of that before? How blind I've been . . . Mum adores the kids. *I* could pay her. I'm sure she'd agree to look after them. Even if *Images* won't take me back, there are plenty of other firms I could try. I've been so caught up in my problems I wasn't thinking straight. Jane, thank you." Nikki put her own warm hand on Jane's arm. She cleared her throat and took a gulp of juice from her glass. "I thought if I came here to *Personal Agenda* I might meet someone, someone with some money, someone who'd whisk my problems away." She laughed wryly. "There's something else I'd like to get off my chest, I didn't tell the truth about my age, I'm not thirty-six."

Jane feigned surprise. "No one would guess," she lied. Nikki needed a bit of bolstering.

"I married late, and my children are young, that's how I get away with it."

Nikki twisted and turned the ring on her finger.

"I hate to break this up but I must go and get the desserts. You will let me know what happens?" Jane asked. She wanted to get off the subject of Nikki's age before her face gave her away.

"Of course I will."

"Do me a favour?" Jane asked.

"Name it," Nikki said.

"Take Amanda upstairs and show her exactly how you made up her face. It was difficult for her to see what you did. I have a magnifying mirror you can use."

"I'll go and find her. I haven't been very nice to her, have I?"

Jane looked at Nikki's perspiring face and evaded the question. "Do you have anything lighter that you can wear? Something less formal? You must be very hot in that suit."

"I felt it was more professional to wear this, it is a bit heavy I admit."

"Excuse me, Amanda, I wonder if you'd like to make up the other side of your face yourself? It must have been difficult for you to see what I was doing."

"It's all right, I won't bother, thanks," Amanda's tone was truculent.

"I think it's a killer idea," Dale said. "You look really neat on one side, cool."

"Why *not* have a bash?" Kevin encouraged.

Why don't they butt out? Amanda thought savagely. It's my face, not theirs.

"I would really like to show you how to do it. I owe it to you." Nikki said apologetically.

Amanda was taken aback by the plea in her voice. Did Nikki regret her nasty attitude?

"All right then," she said petulantly. She would like to learn how to do the make-up herself.

"You look pretty with your hair loose," Amanda said. Nikki had changed into a full skirted sun-dress and looked much less severe, younger.

"I usually tie it back while I'm working, I must admit I like to wear it like this. Let's put a towel round your shoulders and then we won't mess up your blouse."

Amanda settled herself in front of the magnifying mirror and pulled a face. "I hate these big mirrors, they show every splotch and blotch."

"In a minute there won't be any," Nikki smiled. "Do you remember where I started?"

"With the concealer?"

"Right. Put some on the brush and dab it gently, then blend it in with your fingers. That's good, don't forget the side of your nose." Nikki turned Amanda's face towards her and patted a bit she'd missed.

"It's difficult to see it properly without my glasses," Amanda complained.

"I know, but you'll get used to doing it. Now your foundation."

With Nikki's guidance Amanda completed her make-up. "It's not bad," she said. "Not as good as your side."

"It's exactly the same as my side. You've done very well, it will become second nature after a while."

"I wish my hair looked better."

"How, better?" Nikki asked.

"I dunno, better." Amanda shrugged.

"I know what I'd do if it was mine."

"What?"

"I'd wear it shorter, fuller . . ." Nikki was treading on eggshells. She knew she'd hurt Amanda's feelings earlier with her harshness.

"And? Go on, Nikki, tell me."

"I'd lighten it a little, add some golden highlights. Nothing harsh."

"Sort of . . . streaks?"

"Exactly. Look . . ." Nikki wrapped Amanda's hair round her fingers and held it away from Amanda's neck. "You see how it shows off your neck? It can be cut into shape and it would be no trouble to keep. It's naturally wavy?"

Amanda nodded. "I have it cut every six months and that's about all."

"I can't promise that it would last for six months, but it will suit you better."

"I'll make an appointment next week and have it done. Thanks, Nikki."

"My pleasure. We'd better get back to the others, Jane will be wondering where we are."

Nikki collected all her pots and brushes and put them into her make-up case.

"Nikki, if you need a model for this afternoon, I'll do it."

"Thanks Amanda. Would it upset you if I discussed your hair, and which would be the best clothes for you?"

"Not now. It would have done this morning," Amanda said honestly.

"Then I'd be delighted to accept your offer."

Amanda was pleased by the remarks her *new* face received.

"You look a right cracker," Justin teased.

"Wait till you see me next time I'm here," Amanda promised.

"If you don't mind sitting here, Amanda, then everyone else can stay where they are."

Nikki pulled the seat into the circle of chairs and stood behind Amanda.

"What is the first thing you notice about someone when they come into a room?" she asked.

"Their clothes," Jennifer said.

"More than that," Nikki prompted.

"Their appearance?" William asked.

"Exactly. You see a complete image; clothes, hair, shoes . . ." As Nikki explained the secret of dressing well on a tight budget, Jane admired her professionalism. There was no sign of the ill-temper she had shown earlier. She looked around her, they were all totally engrossed in what she was saying. Even Sasha was listening intently.

"Amanda has offered to be my model again. When we were upstairs we discussed her hair. We decided it would suit her better if it was shorter, like this." Again Nikki looped the hair away from Amanda's shoulders and held it either side of her ears. "You see what a lovely shape it gives her face? She has a slim neck but it's hidden by her hair."

"Don't forget the colour," Amanda prompted.

"The golden tints in her hair, they could be highlighted even more."

The *golden tints* were news to Amanda, she'd describe them as mouse-brown.

"A lot of people ask me about their glasses. Look at Amanda's – now watch what happens when I lift them slightly. Her eyebrows and her glasses are in a line, don't they look better now?"

They all agreed that they did.

"What about contact lenses?" Amanda asked.

"Better still if you can wear them, not everybody can. The best person to ask about that is your optician. Does anyone have any questions before I go on?"

Nobody did.

Nikki turned her attention specifically to the men. "If you go to an interview do you think you'd look better in a suit or a woollen sweater?"

"A suit," Ray Parker said.

"You've just excluded Richard Branson." Nikki laughed. "There are times when formality is best. But that doesn't mean you have to follow the fashions slavishly. It's good to have your own individual style. Men also look better in some colours than they do in others. Take Ray, for instance. He'd look good in most colours, although . . ."

"Go on, tell me," Ray urged.

"That shirt, I don't think it does . . . as much as it could for you. That sludgy green is difficult to wear. But a lot depends on how you feel."

"What about *my* shirt?" Justin asked.

"It's fine, blue suits you."

"Anyone else?" Nikki asked.

She went round the circle, approving their choices or suggesting alternatives.

"Does black suit me?" Sasha asked. She was wearing her Morticia dress, Long sleeved, figure-hugging and black, and she'd whitened her face again. Sasha liked the Addams family and copying the character had been no trouble to her.

Answering Sasha would be like crossing a mine-field. "Do you like it?" Nikki asked tactfully.

"Sort of. But do I suit black?"

Jane held her breath, Sasha's tone was belligerent. The bad atmosphere of the morning had vanished and she hoped Sasha wasn't going to make things unpleasant again.

"Do you want an honest answer?"

"Of course," Sasha said.

"I don't know what you look like under that make-up, what your skin is like. But I do know one thing, that make-up is very chalky, very drying. For your own sake I wouldn't wear it for too long. I think it's brilliantly applied, the whole effect is marvellous – you look exactly like the character on TV."

Jane let out her breath, Nikki had handled Sasha tactfully.

"I think Nikki has earned a round of applause and a cup of tea," she said.

They clapped Nikki loudly and when she sat down they crowded round her to ask her more questions. Now she didn't look much older than thirty-six, Jane decided.

♥ ♥ ♥

"Are we going for our Sunday walk?" Amanda asked.

"Yes, I suppose we could." Kevin said.

They walked in the opposite direction this time. Kevin searched for a suitable branch and, as he pulled it from the tree, a dog began to bark ferociously. They ran down the tree-shaded lane like a pair of children.

"I'm out of puff," Kevin said.

"My heart's hammering," Amanda admitted as they paused to catch their breath. "So how are things at Derby's?"

"Hectic. I'm still plodding along with that Stourley's ad. Not getting very far either."

"It'll come to you, the more you try to force things the further away they get."

"That's very profound for a Sunday morning," Kevin teased. "But kidding aside, you're probably right. How are things with you, at home? Are you still getting on well with your mother?"

Amanda had told Kevin all about herself after their visit to the cinema. She was mellow from the wine she'd drunk with her meal. She was so pleased to be reconciled with her mother. Kevin had listened, fascinated. He seemed genuinely pleased for Amanda, and said so.

"I've seen very little of her this week, she's been busy. But we have tickets for the ballet next week and we're going to have a meal afterwards."

They mooched along the lanes, peeking between the hedges as they tried to get a glimpse of the houses.

"Would you like to go out next weekend?" Kevin asked.

Amanda was beginning to think that she'd enjoyed her one and only date.

"I'd like that," she said. She'd have her hair done the way Nikki suggested and surprise him. Maybe she'd go to her optician too and hear what he had to say about contact lenses.

"I'll give you a buzz on Friday. Where would you like to go?"

"I don't mind. You decide." She couldn't care

less where they went so long as they were together.

"You two are devils for exercise," Justin said when they got back to The Willows.

"No charades this time?" Amanda asked.

"We were waiting for you," he smiled. Amanda was perspiring slightly but her make-up was exactly as Nikki had taught her to do it. There were signs of a swan in that duckling.

"What's this about charades?" Peter Connolly asked.

"A couple of weeks ago we had a crazy game of charades," Justin said.

"What are we waiting for?" Peter asked. "Let's play."

They divided into two teams, the men against the women. Tarquin fancied himself as an expert and offered to go first. *I Claudius* stumped his team.

Dale successfully solved Jennifer's *Bird Man of Alcatraz*, and Peter made short work of *Supercalifragilisticexpialidocious.*

"How did you work that out?" Kevin asked, disgusted that he'd been landed with what he considered an impossibly difficult title.

"How many one word song titles do you know that has fourteen syllables?" Peter replied.

"True for you," Kevin agreed.

Jane dialled Susie's number. As the phone rang she stared out of the window. Nikki was laughing heartily at Lara's contortions; if nothing else, Nikki had forgotten her worries for a day. Where was Susie? Why hadn't she phoned? If she hadn't heard by tomorrow morning she'd drive to London and find out what was going on. Jane was worried about her.

Just another few hours and they'd be finished for this week. Jane was emotionally wrung out. She'd better get on with it, it was time to light the barbecues.

Chapter Forty-One

The exterior of the cottage was all old world charm and inside, a miracle of modern technology.

"So what's the verdict?" William asked.

"I'm stunned with admiration," Jane said.

"You've done it beautifully," Sasha agreed.

"We've had a lot of help," Justin admitted.

They'd sloped the ceilings up to the eaves in order to create an illusion of height. In the main living area they'd used old beams which were suspended to disguise the generous fanlight windows.

Jane peeped under the dust sheet covering a lemon corduroy chair.

"I've never seen so many beautifully bound books," she said as she watched William dust them lovingly and place them in the bookcase.

"'If we didn't have them, who would?" William asked.

The smell of fresh paint sweetened the air.

"The pictures look so different here," Sasha said.

"At least you can see them now. It's marvellous to have the space to hang them properly." Justin straightened one that was hanging crookedly. "You know what I love best of all? The doors that lead to the garden. It's wonderful to be able to walk from the kitchen, the bedroom and this room, into the garden. It'll be murder to go back to the flat after this."

"You can say goodbye to it forever in another couple of weeks." Jane knew exactly how Justin felt.

"Come and have a look at the garden or what there is of it so far."

"Can you believe that's the same derelict place we took them to just a few months ago?" Sasha reflected. "What really grabbed me was the outside of the cottage, it looks as if it's been there since the flood. Weren't they clever to use that old granite? It will be even better when the roses climb the arches. I could retire there quite happily. I'd take an old rocking-chair into the garden and sit in the sun with my knitting and sewing. Then, with my cat on my knee, I'd have a bit of a doze."

"You're just the type!" Jane laughed. "You won't find any old rocking-chairs amongst their furniture. I've never seen anything as terrifying as those electrically operated, expanding chairs. But I must admit they did look very comfortable. And that kitchen! I thought ours had all the mod cons, I loved the rubbish compactor, boy could we do with that after a barbecue! And the tap for the boiling water, I didn't know anything like that existed. Imagine sticking your tea bag in a cup and shoving it under a tap. Talk about instant tea . . . ."

"Would you like that?

"Not really," Jane wrinkled her nose and turned into the drive. "I'm quite attached to our kettle."

Sasha switched off the alarms. "I'll go and put another load of towels into the washing-machine then switch on our *old-fashioned kettle*. Obviously I was put on this earth to suffer," she sighed exaggeratedly

"Suffer then, I'll have a coffee when you're ready."

The answering machine was blinking madly. Jane sat with her pen poised and pressed the button.

"Hello you two, it's Charles, where are you on a Monday afternoon? How did the weekend go? I'll be home until five-thirty if you want to give me a ring. If that's awkward I'll be here in the morning."

The call didn't sound urgent, she'd phone him tomorrow.

"Jane it's Susie. We're away for a couple of days. I think everything's going to be OK. Ring you when I get back."

Jane breathed a sigh of relief. Susie's voice wasn't exactly bubbling but at least she sounded calm. For a moment her relief turned to resentment, why had Susie left her to worry like that? Even a call to let her know where she was would have stopped her fretting. Those few days with Susie had upset her too. Still, she was delighted that they were together. Susie would no doubt give her chapter and verse when she phoned.

"We really enjoyed the weekend. Can you book us in again? Bye for now. Oh! I forgot, it's Laura and Lara."

That would wait until tomorrow too.

"Hello Jane, Kim Barrett. I'd like to book for the Hallowe'en Weekend. Can you pencil Jonathan in too? I'll phone again on Thursday."

Sounds like they got together after all, Jane smiled. The Hallowe'en weekend programme must have appealed to them.

"Evie Gilbert speaking. I'd love to spend another weekend at Personal Agenda. *Can you phone me and tell me when? Thank you."*

Jane was delighted to hear Evie's voice, she had taken a liking to her. Not for the first time, Jane regretted that there never seemed to be enough time to sit and talk to people, especially the shyer ones like Evie and Jennifer.

"Jane, it's Nikki, just to let you know that Mum thinks your idea is terrific. I haven't spoken to Images *yet, but I'll keep you up-to-date. Thanks again for everything. Bye for now."*

♥ ♥ ♥

Jane switched off her computer and stretched her hands above her head. Their new programme of events was ready to be printed out, but it could wait. She was going to fill a plate from the fridge and flop in front of the television.

"Sasha, are you ready to eat?"

"I'll be down in a minute," she called.

Jane settled into the chair and looked through the TV guide. She glanced up as Sasha came into the room. "You look *nice,*" Jane said.

"I decided to give Nikki's make-up technique a try. It's not bad is it?"

"It looks lovely, Sit down and relax. *Keeping up*

Appearances is on in a few minutes."

"Why is it that food always tastes so good on Monday?" Sasha asked as she crunched the apple and celery salad.

"Because you have time to enjoy it. This carrot and ginger is really delicious, we should certainly add it to our repertoire, it's so easy to make. And I love the spicy mackerel."

"It's my cousin's recipe," Sasha said. "She doesn't give it to too many people."

"I don't blame her."

Last week Sasha, her sisters and her mother had spent a fun evening digging up old recipes and inventing new ones. When her cousin popped in to say hello, she too was roped into the search for fresh ideas. When she came back from the family visit, Sasha had enjoyed being mysterious and made Jane wait to see what culinary delights she had up her sleeve. So far, with the exception of a chicory salad which they both decided was too bitter, everything had been delicious.

Apart from the incident with the ants, they'd had few disasters in the kitchen. They worked well together and luckily they had similar tastes in food. Jane smiled at Sasha affectionately; what would she do without her?

"Here comes Hyacinth," Sasha laughed as the programme credits began to roll.

Chapter Forty-Two

The crew made their way through customs into the arrivals hall at Kennedy Airport. Kim missed Sam's cheery company on the flight. She didn't see Alex until he stood directly in her path. "I'd like to talk to you, Kim," he said tersely.

Kim's heart turned somersaults and ended somewhere in her throat.

"I . . . I have nothing to say to you, Alex. *Please* get out of my way."

Mike Shea, nearest to her, heard the distress in her voice. "Is there a problem, Kim?"

"Yes, Mike, this man is bothering me." Her face was ashen except for two bright-red spots of colour on her cheeks.

Mike Shea's eyes scanned the vast hall but there were no officials to be seen. He cleared his throat. "You've got exactly one second to get lost or I'll call a security guard," he threatened. He hoped the athletically-built man would be suitably cowered and not take a swing at him.

"That isn't necessary," Alex said quietly. "I'm sorry that you won't give me the opportunity to explain, Kim."

"There's nothing to explain," she said and swept past him.

He watched her walk towards the exit surrounded by her protectors and shook his head. He understood that she was angry and hurt, but her cold, inflexible manner was almost frightening.

Alex stared moodily into his drink. Their meeting had upset him more than he imagined possible. He *did* appreciate how Kim must feel, he was sympathetic. But if they had just a few minutes alone, he was sure they could talk the whole episode through and then they'd be able to take up where they'd left off. After all, he reasoned, what harm would it have done to answer one of his calls? What harm would it have done just to listen? He was three thousand miles away and, even if she didn't want to talk to him, she could listen.

♥ ♥ ♥

He asked the hotel operator for Kim's room number.

"I'm sorry, sir, we are not permitted to give out that information," she said.

Alex didn't bother to say goodbye. He flirted with the idea of going to her hotel in person, but then changed his mind. Even for Kim he wasn't prepared to risk the indignity of being asked to leave or, worse still, be thrown out by the hotel security. Besides, he reasoned, she probably wouldn't be on her own anyway.

"This is impossible," he said to himself angrily. "I'm wasting precious time trying to communicate with someone who has a heart of stone."

But then he'd told himself that ever since the

day he'd last seen her. Was he becoming obsessive? In a few months time he'd be in London, perhaps by that time she'd have missed him enough to change her mind.

He'd go to her flat, and then they could sit down together and thrash it all out like two civilised adults.

Chapter Forty-Three

Ray Parker replaced his receiver with a frown. Robert Hall's queries were becoming increasingly frequent since Beamish and Chambers' last board meeting. Donahue had explained the whole system very clearly, Robert Hall even complimented him on the presentation. But now he was questioning the very things that he'd accepted from the beginning. Robert was fully aware that the system they'd designed for him was more or less a prototype. There *were* similarities to the one they'd supplied to their Scottish customer, but this system had been created specifically to fit the needs of Beamish and Chambers. Robert appeared to be concerned about the support CCC could offer.

". . . after all, CCC is a small firm," he pointed out. "What happens if . . . if you go down the tubes – to put it bluntly?"

Ray searched his desk for an antacid tablet, his stomach was churning uncomfortably. When Linda Lou put the Beamish and Chambers' call through to him, he was certain that this was the big moment. His hopes, his future were pinned on that contract. Now instead of opening a bottle of champagne all he wanted was soda water, anything to dispel this gnawing unease.

It was almost lunchtime, a stiff drink at his local might cure his apprehension, calm his anxiety.

Elizabeth Beamish had failed to return his calls this morning but, perhaps after lunch, when she was out of her meeting, she'd phone.

Ray ordered a second Scotch and tried to focus on his date with Evie. She'd appeared a little hesitant at first but, after some whispering in the background, she'd accepted his invitation to have dinner and see a show. If Beamish and Chambers turned this system down, he'd be lucky if he could afford breakfast let alone a night out in London.

"Stop being so pessimistic," he rebuked himself. "One glitch and you're like a bowl of jelly."

"I'm sorry Mr Parker," the receptionist said after a long delay. "Ms Beamish has left for the afternoon and is unavailable."

"Liar," Ray said under his breath. "Would you mind asking her to contact me in the morning please?"

"I'll make sure she gets your message."

Chapter Forty-Four

Amanda was a mass of nerves. Jane and Sasha never behaved like this, they were always calm when they entertained, or were they? Amanda checked the list Mrs Judd had pinned to the oven gloves near the cooker and went into the dining room. Everything was just as she'd left it ten minutes ago.

She paced up and down until the bell chimed, then ran to the door.

"Amanda! Is that really you?" Charles asked.

"Come in, Charles, take your coat off," Amanda said chirpily, then realised he wasn't wearing one. "Oh! What a fool I am. I'm sorry, I'm just nervous."

"Let me look at you." He ignored her mistake.

Amanda's hair was short and stylish and, since he'd last seen her, she'd changed dramatically. The make-up gave her face real shape and colour but most startling of all were her eyes, they were clear, deep hazel. He'd never seen her without her glasses before and presumed she must be wearing her new contacts.

"What a change!" he said and could have kicked himself. "I mean, what a difference."

"Don't worry," she said cheerfully. "I

understand. As I said to you on the phone, I'm thrilled with my contact lenses. They'll take a bit of getting used to, but I love them."

As Amanda poured him a drink, he gazed around the big study. It was an elegant room, a woman's room, full of dainty pieces of furniture and all the touches that only women seemed to possess. His eyes travelled upwards to the high ceiling. This is how the Belgrave Square house should have looked. That was even more beautifully proportioned, more imposing. He heard the muffled sound of a door closing.

Emma Brown had presence, he decided, as he rose to his feet and shook her hand.

"It's lovely to see you again Charles," she smiled. "Hello darling, do you need any help?"

"I think everything's under control," Amanda said with a worried frown.

"I'm sure it is. Do I have time for a quick shower? I've been stuck in traffic for the last hour and when I got out of the car I expected my blouse to stay glued to the seat."

"Kevin won't be here for another five minutes, take your time."

Charles added a drop more water to the generous drink and tapped the seat beside him. "Tell me all your news," he said to Amanda.

"Just let me take a quick peek in the oven."

Now that he'd seen Emma and Amanda together, Charles realised how unalike they were in looks. Although Amanda's appearance had improved enormously, she would never be a raving beauty. Emma was far more attractive than her daughter and a little warmer than he remembered. Amanda's last phone call to him had been full of surprises, the most astonishing of which was Emma's decision to join *Personal Agenda*. He wasn't looking forward to interviewing her later this evening; the memory of that day in her office still lingered in his mind.

Amanda was delighted by the new relationship with her mother. He'd been pleased for her at first but then a twinge of jealousy crept in. He'd been her only friend up till now, she'd depended on him. And then there was Kevin O'Hanlon, his name seemed to crop up in every second sentence. And that woman – Lois, she too exerted quite an influence over Amanda. Charles was pleased that he was going to The Willows next weekend, he'd begun to feel left out. His mind wandered to Jane's garden, the soothing sound of the lapping river, the gently swaying willow and the heady perfume of the flowers. It was strange, he always associated his visits there with the garden.

"That must be Kevin." Amanda interrupted his reverie. She smoothed her hair and licked her lips nervously.

How nice to have that kind of effect on someone, Charles thought.

Emma sized up the young Irishman, he was quieter than she'd imagined from Amanda's description, but she liked what she saw. Amanda obviously liked him a lot too. If Amanda was fussed or nervous it certainly didn't show on her happy face. She listened to them chatting about *Personal Agenda*. The more she heard about it the more appealing it became.

" . . . have *you* seen it, Emma?" Charles asked.

"Sorry, Charles, my mind strayed," Emma apologised.

Charles enthused about the latest musical. "I've no doubt that won't be my last visit either," he laughed. "In the course of a month I saw *Les Miserables* four times, *Phantom* . . . ."

Kevin listened to Charles with half an ear. The meeting this afternoon had depressed him. The rumours floating around the office for the last few weeks were fast becoming a reality. The bottom line was, that if they failed to secure the Stourley account, he could well find himself out of a job.

"I think we'll leave Mum and Charles to their talk and we'll have our coffee in the study." Amanda glanced in Kevin's direction, he was quiet tonight.

"That's the first time I've ever cooked a full meal," Amanda said as she filled their cups.

"It was a lovely meal." Kevin's mind was not on the food.

"Mrs Judd left everything ready," Amanda admitted, but was glad it was over.

"When *is* the over-forties weekend?" Kevin asked in an attempt to make conversation.

"In about three or four weeks. I don't know whether she'll be in time to book though, Jane's had a big response to her advertisement. It would do Mum good, she needs a break from her work. You know how difficult it is to think of anything else except enjoying yourself once you get to The Willows."

Amanda looked at him anxiously. Kevin was a million miles away and hadn't heard a word she'd said. "Are you OK, Kevin?"

"Sorry, I was just thinking . . . ."

"Problems?"

"Possibly."

"Share them?"

"It's the same old story, but you don't want to hear more of my nonsense."

It took very little persuasion on Amanda's part for Kevin to share his concern. Amanda could well believe that his firm was struggling, Coogan, Howard and Green's own profits had taken a bit of a tumble this year. It was a shame that Derby's were so dependent on one account.

"Looking on the black side, and I'm sure we are, what would you do if Derby's did decide to part with their best copywriter ?"

"I don't know, there are a lot more copywriters than there are jobs. But at least I have the comfort of knowing that my firm in Dublin will take me back. I had a letter from one of my friends there the other day. He mentioned that after all these months they're still having a real hassle finding someone else. My boss sent his regards and, according to Liam, said I could have my old job back any time – the sooner the better."

♥ ♥ ♥

Amanda almost didn't see the cyclist and swerved out of his way just in time. Since their dinner last night she could think of nothing but Kevin and dreaded the thought that he might return to Dublin. It had taken this crisis to make her realise that she was in love with him. She was sure that he didn't love her, but who knew what might happen in the future? Now the future looked bleak. Amanda was sure she'd never meet anyone as nice as Kevin – even at *Personal Agenda.* She'd wind up alone. As it was, she was probably the only thirty-three year old virgin left in London.

Amanda ate her sandwiches without realising that she had. Her book, which she'd been enjoying up until today, lay unopened on the desk. She ran her fingers through her hair, she was still not used to its silky texture. She curled a lock round her index finger then walked to her office window. She stared unseeingly at the silent rows of parked cars but could find no solution to her problem so she returned to her chair and swivelled it heedlessly from side to side.

"Ready?" Lois's voice startled her.

"Ready for what?" Amanda asked.

"For lunch?"

"Oh! It's Wednesday." Amanda clasped a hand over her mouth. "I can't believe that I mixed up the days."

"You've eaten, I see," Lois said accusingly.

"Don't worry, I'll have a coffee with you while you eat."

"Don't fret, I'll send out for a sandwich, all right to eat here?"

"Of course."

"So, what brought on this advanced case of senility?" Lois asked, her feet resting comfortably on Amanda's desk.

"The devastating thought that Kevin might go back to Ireland," Amanda said, enviously admiring Lois's slim legs.

"How come?"

Amanda didn't want to discuss Kevin's job at Derby's. She chose her words carefully. "I suppose he's a bit homesick or something . . ."

"I'm sure it's just a whim, he'll have forgotten all about it tomorrow," Lois said cheerfully.

"Maybe." Amanda was dubious. Kevin had succeeded in transferring his anxiety to her and Lois had a knack of worming things out of her. She wanted to get off the subject of Kevin. "What's happening in the great world of account handling?" Amanda asked.

"We're concentrating on a big lager account. It could revolutionise drinking – a hangover free lager – Imagine, you could drink yourself under the table and wake up as fresh as a daisy."

"Sounds too good to be true. Is it one of those alcohol-free lagers?"

"No, it's an ordinary lager with some added magic ingredient – a well guarded secret, naturally – seemingly that's what prevents any hangovers."

Amanda's ears pricked up, maybe she could find out how confident Lois was that Coogan, Howard and Green would land the account. "Are we the only one pitching for it?"

"Pitching and tossing." Lois frowned. "There's some other agency in the running, a smaller one, I can't remember who."

Amanda didn't volunteer Derby's name.

"When do you make the presentation?" she asked casually.

"End of next week, Friday I think. Don't worry you'll know all about it."

They both laughed. The agency was always chaotic when it came to presentation day. Amanda normally hid in her office until things got back to normal. That side of the business didn't concern her. The copywriters would be secreted in their office all this week. She could tell how things were going by the plastic sacks of discarded coffee cups and shredded paper outside their door. Amanda had almost tripped over a full one earlier and it was only mid-morning. Maybe later she'd have a nose around.

"I suppose I'd better be getting back, I'm not in the mood to work," Lois grumbled. "Next Wednesday, lunch? I think I'll send you an inter-office memo to remind you!"

"Today was really stupid. Wednesday's fine." Amanda felt herself flush. Thank goodness for her green concealer.

Chapter Forty-Five

Sasha sat on her bedroom floor with the wig-block clamped firmly between her knees. She pulled the brush carefully through the damp hair on the block, working on a small section at a time. She hadn't felt like going with Jane to Justin and William's tonight, she hadn't felt much like going anywhere lately. She wound a roller tightly round a strand of the nylon hair and struggled to understand her lethargy. She had oodles of energy so it wasn't that. She'd really looked forward to seeing Ray Parker last weekend. But he'd treated her more or less like an in-house-jester. Charles was the same, pleased to see her, to have a laugh for a moment, then she was forgotten. Sasha knew she was just as attractive as most of the women who came to *Personal Agenda*, and probably a lot more entertaining. She could find a witty retort with the speed of a whip, only Justin was faster. So why did men ignore her? She was used to being in the thick of things. The only time she'd felt that way in the past weeks was at the drama weekend.

Sasha jabbed the pin into the last roller. "There,

that'll do for now," she said as she looked at her watch. It was only five minutes to six. Perhaps she *would* go to Justin and William's, the walk would do her good.

"Of course you can change your mind, do you want William to go over and pick you up?" Justin asked when she phoned.

"No thanks, I'd like to get there in one piece," she teased. William was learning to drive but still very unsure of himself. "I'll walk over. I should be there in about twenty minutes."

"Be like that," Justin said airily. "See you soon."

Justin was planting the last of the shrubs as Sasha turned in the gate.

"You were quick," he smiled.

"The garden is really coming on," she said, bending to firm a wayward plant. "Justin, can I talk to you for a minute – just the two of us?"

"What's up? You look a bit down." He hooted with laughter at his own contradiction. "Come on, Jane and William are browsing through book catalogues. Let's go through to the back garden."

They sat on the new bench which was still in its wrapping.

"Talk to me," he commanded.

"I was thinking this afternoon, nobody seems to take much notice of me. I don't mean I want them to fawn over me or to dance round me like a maypole or anything. But they don't stop to talk or . . . take any notice of me, like I said."

Justin let her words sink in. He liked Sasha enormously, she'd become the sister he didn't have and William was extremely fond of her too.

Justin always enjoyed teasing Sasha and she could give as good as she got. They had the same sense of humour but, apart from the time he'd persuaded her to return to The Willows, they'd never had a deep conversation. It was difficult to take Sasha seriously at times. He thought back to the first time he'd seen her in that Victorian maid's outfit with the white face, it had been amusing but quite a shock. Now he was so accustomed to her crazy dressing up, it had little effect on him.

"Justin?" Sasha said querulously.

"I'm thinking about what you said," he replied. "I remember the first time we met, you were wearing a mini-skirt, striped socks and Doc Martens. You looked a scream."

"But what's that got to do with the price of fish?" Sasha asked impatiently.

"Wait, I'm coming to that. What I'm trying to say is, that when people meet you they see you only as a funny lady, a character that you've chosen to be. They don't see Sasha, the way you are now for instance."

"You mean dressing-up – they don't appreciate my talent?"

"No, I mean they don't get to meet the *real* you." Justin wondered if she was being deliberately obtuse.

Sasha pursed her lips. Perhaps Justin was right, it could be a bit off-putting she supposed. "So what you're saying is, no more dressing up?"

"Not exactly, it's fine at the right time and in the right place. But be yourself Sasha, you're a person in your own right and one worth knowing."

"Are you two coming in for a drink?" William called.

"In a minute," Justin said. "Why not give it a try next time you want to impress someone, see if I'm right?"

"But what about all those costumes? What about my acting?"

"Sasha, how many actresses do you suppose have such a wonderful collection of costumes? Theatres *provide* them, they'd be thrilled to get their hands on such marvellous wigs – if you sold them, and everything else, you could probably *buy* a theatre with the proceeds. They must have cost you the earth."

"Very little actually," Sasha said thoughtfully as she popped a couple of bubbles on the plastic sheet which protected the bench. "When I was younger I used to spend ages in a shop at home which specialised in costume-hire. I often helped the old lady who ran it. One day she told me to take whatever I wanted, she was closing the shop. She insisted that I took loads more than I could ever need. I ended up packing a taxi to the roof with all sorts of clothes, shoes, wigs and enough make-up to last me a life-time, she even gave me two rails to hang the costumes on. 'Treat them lovingly and with care and they'll see you through anything,' she said. When I went back the following week there was a 'To Let' sign on the shop, and the man from the newsagent next door told me she'd died the day after the shop closed its doors."

"How sad, poor old thing."

"*Justin, Sasha*, dinner's ready," William called again.

"Before I forget, would you like John Pritchard to give a talk one weekend?" Justin said.

"You mean the author?" Jane asked.

"Yes. He often comes into the shop and we know him well. I'm sure he'd be pleased to, he's going to stay at the cottage in about three weeks' time, he wants to do some research for his next crime novel. We thought Dornley would make a perfect background for his thriller."

"I'd love that, he's so well known I'm sure everyone would be delighted. Our ideas are a bit thin on the ground at the moment," Jane admitted.

"When I was driving home today, I was thinking . . ." William began.

"Is that what you were doing?" Justin interrupted. "It certainly wasn't driving."

Sasha and Jane grinned at each other. Justin had barely stopped crashing the gears himself.

"I'll ask around for our friends for ideas, you never know what we'll dredge up, or who," Justin said.

"When's the over-forties' weekend?" William asked.

"Two weeks' time. I hope it works out. I hope they won't be bored or find it too much." Jane frowned.

"Dear, dear, do you have a good stock of Zimmer frames?" Justin asked.

"You know what I mean." Jane gave him a light punch on his arm.

"I do. We'll come over and help you to take them up and down stairs."

"You're laughing at me, you horrible man. From now on I'm renaming it the fit-forties."

"What's on the programme?" William asked.

"We're making candles . . ." Jane stopped and waited for Justin to make a derisory remark but he was surprisingly enthusiastic.

"I'll definitely be over for that," he said. "It's always fascinated me – all that gooey wax which ends up in those wonderful shapes."

"Before dinner we're holding a wine tasting. That was Susie's idea, she bumped into the man we used to buy our wines from in London," Jane explained. "He's extremely knowledgeable. He was even more keen to come down when I explained that we use quite a lot of booze each weekend and that I was floundering a bit."

"You've really got it all worked out, haven't you? Good on you, I'm proud of you," Justin said, smiling fondly at her.

"We aim to please. By the way, I forgot to tell you, Amanda's mother has joined *Personal Agenda.* She wanted to come to The Willows for the over-forties' – fit-forties – weekend, but we're full. I promised Amanda that, if we had a cancellation, I'd contact her mother."

"How's Charles?" Justin hadn't heard his name mentioned recently.

"He's OK, he's coming down next weekend," Jane said.

"He's sulking because he's missed a couple of weeks," Sasha added. She'd decided that she wasn't in love with him any more.

"As I was going to say earlier before I was so rudely interrupted, how about hiring a boat?" William asked as he and Jane dried the dishes. "It would be very pleasant to cruise along the river. You could even have a picnic lunch. What do you think?"

"I think it sounds a lovely idea, but can we do that?"

"Of course, haven't you noticed the pleasure craft? There's always one or two passing The Willows."

"It never occurred me that they were hired, I suppose I took it for granted that they were privately owned. Where would I make enquiries?"

"Can you wait until the weekend, then I'll find out for you."

"That would be marvellous. I've also been trying to think of an alternative to the barbecues. With luck we might manage a few more before the weather turns cold but that's about all. They've been such a joy during the summer, but what about the rest of the year?"

"I don't know, a buffet I suppose or perhaps a barbecue-outside-eat-inside type of meal." William threw the tea towel into a bucket to soak and they joined Justin and Sasha in the high-ceilinged living-room. They'd been having a similar conversation.

". . . then you could invite people like John Pritchard – a journalist perhaps, people from different walks of life. At a push I could be persuaded to give a talk about the book business . . ." Justin said thoughtfully.

"Justin, what a marvellous idea, I didn't think of you," Jane enthused.

"Charming!"

"Anyway, don't let's spoil the evening worrying about it," Jane said firmly.

Chapter Forty-Six

Ray Parker's hands shook uncontrollably as he read the letter. All his fears and premonitions were there in front of him, spelled out in black and white. Rage gripped him with a physical force. Beamish and Chambers had effectively destroyed him in one single, dismissive page.

"Get Elizabeth Beamish for me," Ray barked at Linda Lou.

There was something in Ray's tone which warned her not to get smart with him. Ray might act like a lemon at times but he was usually polite. She dialled the number. I suppose I'd better get the paper on the way home tonight and have a look at the situations vacant, she thought as she waited to be connected.

"She's not available, her secretary said," Linda Lou relayed the message.

"Well she f-ing well better get available," Ray roared. "Send Donahue in to me."

Ray pointed to the letter on his desk, he was so choked with temper he could barely speak.

Donahue read the devastating words and shook his head. "I wish I could say I'm surprised, but I'm not. There've been too many questions lately, too many stumbling blocks put in our path.

All that work for nothing, so disappointing."

"Disappointing? *Disappointing?* Is *that* the best you can find to say?" Ray stormed.

Donahue shifted nervously. Ray's face was scarlet with anger, he'd never seen him in such a fury. There was no point in trying to talk to him while he was in this mood. Ray would give himself a heart attack if he wasn't careful. How was he going to get . . .

"Yes?" Ray snarled as he picked up his phone.

Donahue moved to the door as fast as he could, the phone call had given him the perfect out.

♥ ♥ ♥

Ray looked at the sleeping figure beside him. Who was she? How did she get here? He raised himself on one elbow and groaned as the pain shot through his head like an arrow. She turned over. A wave of disgust followed his pain. Her make-up was yellow and caked, her mascara smeared, it covered her cheeks with dirty, black uneven lines. She groaned and opened one eye. "Hello, Robert Hall," she mumbled as she attempted a smile. The smell of stale drink on her breath made his stomach heave. He turned his head away. Robert Hall? Why had she used that name?

"Would you mind leaving please?" he asked rudely. He didn't try to be polite or remember her name, didn't even attempt to ask where they'd met. He just wanted her out of the flat.

She glanced at his clock through bleary eyes. "It's only six o'clock in the morning," she wailed.

"There won't be no buses at this hour."

"Get dressed, I'll give you money for a taxi. There's a rank around the corner, there's always someone there."

She climbed into her laddered tights. The mini-skirt barely covered her ample bottom and her crumpled blouse had seen better days.

"How could you?" he asked himself as another ripple of nausea gripped him.

She swung a black PVC jacket across her shoulders and a waft of stale food assailed his nostrils. A vision of Evie, with her country-fresh complexion and ladylike manner, floated in front of his eyes.

"Please *go*," he gagged.

Ray clutched his head, then his stomach and staggered into the kitchen in his boxers to find some Alka-Seltzer. He prayed he could keep it down, he'd never had a hangover like this in his life. What *had* happened last night? How could he have picked up such a sleaze bag? He vaguely remembered two different pubs but, after that, everything was a blur. He must have given her Robert Hall's name instead of his own. Good. At least he'd had some sense. Had he slept with her? He prayed not. He pulled the sheets and pillow cases off the bed as fast as his throbbing head would allow and left them in a bundle on the floor, then took a shower. He longed for oblivion.

"I won't be in this morning." Ray's voice boomed in his head like a cannon.

"Right. Are we going to get the boot?" Linda Lou asked tersely.

"You'll *know* when you're fired." Ray crashed the receiver down. "Of all the stupid, rapacious, moronic, self-serving, avaricious bitches . . ." He collapsed onto the bed. "Not, *I'm sorry Ray. Can I do something to help, Ray?* Just *me, me, me*." Totally out of control, he ranted and raged for the next five minutes until he was exhausted, then fell back on his pillow in a deep alcoholic stupor.

He was covered in sweat when he woke. The small bedroom was stiflingly hot. Something unpleasant niggled at his fuzzy brain, then the full force of yesterday's event hit him again. "No, oh no!" he moaned and covered his face with his hands. He had to get some air, he was choking in the airless room.

"Anyone phone?" he asked Linda Lou.

"If you *mean* Beamish and Chambers, no." Linda Lou sounded vindictive.

"I'm at home if you need me." He didn't wait for an answer. "Sadist," he yelled as he slammed down the receiver.

The hot tea helped a little although even the sight of the milk carton made him queasy.

"Think!" he shouted at himself. "Get your act together." But it was hopeless, his mind was a sludge of questions and broken promises. His anger turned towards Elizabeth Beamish. It was easy for her to hide behind her lackey, Robert Hall. She hadn't returned a single one of his calls. Why should she when her toady was there to do her dirty work for her? Which of them was responsible for the decision? Was there anything CCC could have done to avoid this?

Ray drooped with despair, this agonising was futile. He'd have to find a way to prevent CCC from going to the wall, but how? And those bank loans, what was today's date? The next payment was due on the first of the month. He picked up the used tea bag and refilled his cup.

By the time he reached a solution, he didn't notice that the third cup was so weak it was almost colourless. He searched through his papers, his briefcase, he turned drawers upside down and scattered their contents on the bed. Again he was soaked in sweat. "Where did I put it?" He forced himself to remember, he was positive he hadn't thrown it away.

"What was I wearing? I know." He leapt from the bed as fast as his head would allow and found his jeans. One by one he tried the pockets, but they were empty. There was one last chance, his shirt. He yelled triumphantly, then cringed at the noise when his fingers located the tiny folded piece of paper.

Ray looked around him, then entered the seedy public house. The bar was smoky and badly lit. He made his way around the room and, satisfied that the man hadn't yet arrived, he sat at a beer-stained table in a dark corner and signalled for a waiter. He sipped his whisky slowly, anxious never again to repeat the hangover he'd suffered a few days ago. This was not the type of bar that Ray was used to. People huddled together at little tables, their conversation loud and punctuated by raucous laughter. Eyes rested on him suspiciously, strangers here were rare.

"You're here then," the man said.

Ray nodded. "I don't know your name," Ray said as he moved along the tattered bench seat to make room for him.

"It's not important – you know. Now, what can I do for you?"

Chapter Forty-Seven

Jane felt more nervous than she had since *Personal Agenda* first opened its doors. She couldn't rationalise her fears so she didn't voice them. Her pink crepe jacket and short chiffon skirt were stylish, and she was getting used to wearing the new higher heels. Sasha had teased her all week when she'd trotted round the house in her leggings and four inch stilettos.

It was fun to see glamour coming back into fashion.

Sasha had taken Justin's advice to heart. Even Jane did a double-take when Sasha slinked into the kitchen looking like a super model. She'd taken Nikki's make-up a step further and used her skill with brushes and colours. She'd twisted her hair into a feathered fantasy and the dress, which had taken her four days to make, was simplicity itself – an unadorned, magenta, sheath of velvet.

"The new me!" Sasha announced.

"It certainly is," Jane agreed. "I never realised what a super figure you have, that dress really shows and tells."

Sasha was pleased by Jane's reaction but not half as pleased as she was when she passed Charles in the hall and heard his whistle. Next week she'd go to London and flog *most* of the costumes and wigs which had played such a big part in her life. It would be a wrench but the more she thought about Justin's advice, the more convinced she was that he was right.

As Sasha placed the toppings on the canapés she planned how she would spend the money once she'd sold her possessions.

Jane relaxed and wondered why she'd been so apprehensive. They were a sophisticated crowd, intelligent and fun. She grinned to herself as she remembered Justin's remarks about Zimmer frames. She glanced at each of them in turn, what a conglomeration of careers were represented at her table. A market trader, a private assistant to a government minister, a chiropodist and Michael Gleeson, a fellow countryman, who'd just launched his own travel agency. Richard Fenway manufactured shoes, Lisa Bowers was in publishing and the prettiest of the women, Delia Conway, was a mature model. She must have been stunning when she was younger, Jane realised. Delia still had a wonderful bone structure and her eyes were as blue as her own. Since the death of his wife, Neil Drummond had spent the last three years immersed in his work and, on his doctor's advice, he'd left his drawing board for the time being and joined *Personal Agenda*. He'd made quite a name for himself as an architect but the all-work-no-play syndrome was what gave rise to his doctor's objections. She couldn't remember exactly what Nancy Green's occupation was – an administrative post in one of the big hospitals, Jane thought.

Nobody seemed to want to move from the table. She and Sasha served coffee in the dining-room so as not to interrupt the flow of conversation. Charles and Lisa Bowers, the sub-editor of a well established women's magazine, were discussing an article in one of the papers which had slated a newly opened restaurant.

". . . surely it would be fairer if a food critic visited a restaurant twice," he argued.

"I agree," Michael Gleeson cut in. "Anyone can have an off night."

"It doesn't work that way," Lisa assured them. "After all, you don't review a film twice, or a book."

"But that's not comparing like with like. A book, or a play, a film even, is a finished product. Food is a spur of the moment, one-off chance, to prove your skill," Michael argued.

"In theory, you're right. But when you visit a restaurant, you're dealing with professional people who offer a professional service," Lisa insisted. "Besides, restaurant reviews or crits – call them what you will – save you time and money."

Jane was thankful that *Personal Agenda* wasn't under the scrutiny of some jaded-palate foodie.

"Now, I have some news for Jane," Lisa continued. "Apart from the obvious advantages of being here, I've promised my editor to write an article about *Personal Agenda*, with Jane's permission of course."

"I . . . well . . ." Jane could feel Charles's eyes on her. Don't stutter and stammer, she warned herself. "I'm not sure, Lisa. Confidentiality is important to us . . ."

"Perhaps it should be discussed privately,"

Justin jumped in quickly; it was wrong of Lisa to put Jane on the spot like that, to discuss her plans in front of her guests.

"And she should be able to see any copy *before* it goes to print," William added.

"Why are they speaking for Jane?" Charles wondered jealously.

"What does everyone else feel about this?" Jane asked.

"I've no objection," Neill Drummond stated.

"Nor I." The woman on his left, Nancy Green, agreed.

"I would prefer if my name wasn't mentioned," Delia Conway said with a frown.

"I think that *must* apply to everybody," Jane said firmly. "And I want to read the *finished* article before it's published, as William suggested. You have my permission only if you agree to these conditions."

"I do agree," Lisa confirmed. She was deceptive, Jane Anderson. Mild-mannered and gentle but with a tough core. Attractive too and obviously on the ball, it couldn't be too easy running a business like this. I must organise a photographer, a picture of her and Sasha wouldn't hurt their readers' eyes too much. Bizarre set-up. *Personal Agenda*, where did Justin and what's-his-name fit in? A dating agency was an unlikely place for *those* two. Charles Graham seemed at home – cushy job he had. He's quite handsome, smooth without being too suave. I must pry him away from the crowd later, I wouldn't object to a little quiet bonking with him.

Charles looked at Jane with new respect. She was in total control now. He really had done her a great favour when he'd hinted that she must make her own decisions.

Jane was relieved when the conversation turned to the latest books, television, new films and the Lottery.

"What do you actually do when you win one of these vast fortunes?" Serena Smith asked.

"I think I'll wait till it happens," Justin laughed.

"I did the Lottery last year when I was in Ireland," Michael Gleeson said. "They have what you call a 'quick-pick', you don't have to even mark in the numbers. They punch a button on the computer and you're given a print-out – random numbers."

"Sounds easy enough. I do it every Saturday, I'm positive I am going to win." Serena's face was serious.

"You and several million others," Justin observed sardonically.

"Old folks tucked up in bed?" Justin grinned when Jane came back to the kitchen.

"You'll never let me live that down, will you?" Jane grimaced.

"Live what down?" Charles demanded. He hated being left out.

"I was a bit . . . Never mind, it's not important." Jane said. Why should Charles know she had doubts? She threw Justin a warning glance and he busied himself pressing the plunger on the coffee maker.

"What's not important?" he persisted.

"That's right, what's *not* important!" Jane teased.

Let her play her stupid games, Charles sulked.

"How's the cottage coming on?" he asked William.

"We're beginning to see daylight at last," William said. "Why don't you pop over and see it for yourself? Come after breakfast tomorrow."

"I'd like that. I'll walk over and take a lift back with you if that's OK?"

"Brave man," Justin grinned. "William's driving, he needs the practice for his test."

Again Charles felt he was out in the cold, he had had no idea that William was learning to drive. Did Amanda know? She must have forgotten to tell him.

"I think we'll leave you to it," Justin said, draining his cup. "See you tomorrow, if that's all right?"

"Need you ask?" Sasha replied, kicking off her shoes. "I'll walk you to the door."

William led the way down the hall to the front door. When he was out of earshot, Sasha tipped Justin's elbow. "How do I look tonight?"

"Gorgeous," Justin assured her. "See you tomorrow."

"What was Sasha whispering about?" William asked as they set off home.

"She wanted to know what I thought of her new image."

"What did you tell her?"

"That she looked lovely," Justin frowned. "I hadn't the heart to tell her that she still looked stagey; that hair piled up with those feathers and too much make-up for my taste. I may say something if she asks again, but for the moment she's doing OK."

"Justin Sadler, adviser to the stars." William

smiled as they turned into their road. "That woman Lisa didn't appear to approve of us."

"I felt the vibes too. She was a hard piece." Justin locked the car door and walked round to where William stood. They looked proudly at the cottage.

"Isn't it lovely, the lights shining through the trees? A real home at last." He put a reassuring hand on William's shoulder. "What does *she* call home, I wonder? I wouldn't swop with any of them."

"Neither would I." William smiled as they made their way up the little path which led to their freshly painted front door.

Chapter Forty-Eight

Charles walked slowly along the avenue. A wind had whipped up during the night and the first of the leaves had fallen. He tried to get a glimpse of the houses through the trees and hedges, everyone was so private in Dornley, the world and his wife could see *his* flat without any effort.

William was pottering in the garden when he reached the cottage.

"Come inside," William said. "Justin is making coffee."

Charles looked around the room in astonishment. The interior of the cottage was in total contrast to what he'd expected. It was light and airy, very hi-tech with all those built in speakers and hidden fanlight windows behind the ceiling beams. And yet they'd managed to preserve an air of cosiness with large comfortable looking chairs and sofas. They'd scattered colourful cushions wherever there was a place for them and the white walls, which could have been austere, were decorated with bright prints and paintings. Charles admired the bookcases, stacked high with what he assumed were valuable first editions and rare books. He wasn't much of a reader but he recognised that Justin and William must know what they were doing.

They smiled at each other when Charles, embarrassed, barely glanced at their bedroom. They'd spent a good deal of energy finding just the right material for the curtains and bed cover; an old Mexican design, vibrant yet subtle, colours which Jane adored.

When they'd finished their coffee Justin insisted that Charles must inspect the garden. "The real work when you have a house," he groaned.

"Come off it," William said. "You love it."

It was a small garden, tiny compared to Jane's, but they'd planned it well. Two beautiful old trees – an ash and a birch – formed the backdrop for the flower beds. They had done away with the lawns and added crazy paving instead and Justin's herb bed was already beginning to boast a fine crop of parsley and rosemary. "It's too late now for a lot of the herbs, but I can't wait for the spring," he explained.

Charles told them about the time he'd spent working in a nursery and immediately Justin plied him with questions about planting shrubs and fruit trees.

They'd kept the climbing rose which now clung to fresh wiring on the back wall of the house. Charles assured them that by next summer it would cascade on to the patio.

"That's the biggest bonus of all," William said, pointing to the patio. "It's utterly blissful to eat here at night, such a shame that summer's over."

Charles shared their regret. He'd enjoyed those Sunday barbecues at The Willows, the tranquillity of the garden no matter how many people were there, and the company. For a moment he envied

Justin and William. He'd never been at ease with their relationship but now, for the first time, he realised that *they* were happy, content in each other's company and their beautiful new home.

♥ ♥ ♥

"Go and watch them," Mrs Jones said. "I'll manage just fine."

Jane slipped into the garage. Liz Traynor, a plump blonde woman with a dimpled smile, was showing them how the paraffin wax was melted to make candles. It would be a while before the wax would be ready to start the dipping, there'd be time enough for Jane to pop back in about ten minutes.

Only the tip of Richard Fenway's chair could be seen sticking out from behind the willow tree. Did Richard enjoy his own company, or was he shy? He'd been quite sociable last night. Jane hesitated then walked across the lawn. She stopped suddenly, he was talking to someone and she didn't want to impose. As she turned to retrace her steps she halted again. He was talking about Serena Smith in a most peculiar manner.

" . . . Serena Smith. Arrived alone at Personal Agenda. *Apart from one man, Charles Graham, she appeared to know no one else. Charles Graham is employed by* Personal Agenda *to vet their clients."*

Jane heard a click, then a whirring noise. Richard Fenway must have been making a tape recording.

"Friday, seven p.m.," his voice continued. *"Subject introduced to other members of the party.*

Eight p.m. dinner, she spoke in general terms to the men nearest to her. Twelve minutes past one subject returned to her bedroom. Nobody entered the subject's bedroom during the night, and she did not leave it again until eight minutes past four a.m., Saturday."

Jane was rigid with shock. It had taken her a couple of minutes to understand what he was doing.

"Charles, I must speak to you." Jane said quietly. "Outside, not here."

She beckoned him to follow her away from the garage and the candle-making. He could see that Jane was extremely agitated.

Jane repeated what she'd heard.

"But how did he fool me?" Charles asked, he didn't blame her for being upset. "He told me he was the chairman of a small company which manufactured shoes. I phoned him at home, the address was genuine – in the phone book. We met, he paid me there and then as you know. I don't understand it, how did he slip . . ."

"Charles, it's not your fault and not important now. The question is, what are we going to do?"

"Chuck him out. He can't stay here. I'll go and tackle him."

"I'll come with you."

"Are you sure you want to?"

"He's not an armed robber, he's spying on someone."

"What the hell do you think you're playing at?" Charles asked as Richard tried to hide the tape machine.

"What do you mean?" Richard Fenway asked innocently.

"Come off it, Jane heard you talking into a tape recorder, the one you're trying to hide – Serena Smith, right?"

"It's just an exercise in reporting, journalistic practice, I got the idea last night from Lisa."

"And I'm Beethoven's younger brother!" Charles said scornfully.

"Just what are you doing here?" Jane's tone was icy. "Either tell us or the police, the choice is yours."

Richard's smile disappeared. "I don't think it's a police matter, do you? I haven't committed a crime, a minor deception perhaps . . ."

"That's a matter of opinion. Now, what are you up to?" Charles demanded.

"OK, OK. I'm here to make a report on Serena Smith."

"For whom? Why?" Jane snapped.

"For her ex-husband. That's all I can tell you," Richard Fenway said firmly.

"Why is her ex-husband spying on her?" Jane persisted. "I think you owe us an explanation."

"That's all I can tell you." Richard Fenway obviously intended keeping his mouth firmly shut.

Charles and Jane moved away. "What do we do now?" Jane frowned. "I suppose he's right, it isn't really a crime. And I certainly don't want the police involved, the publicity wouldn't do us any good. It will be easier all round if he just left quietly."

"Are you going to tell Serena?"

"I need to think about that, there's no rush."

"I'd like you to leave right away," Jane ordered.

Richard Fenway pulled a face. "Is that really necessary? I won't complete the report, you can speak to my agency if you like, tell them you've rumbled me. After all, I've paid for the weekend and frankly I've enjoyed every minute – up till now. "

"What a neck!" Charles exploded.

"Just a minute, Charles," Jane placated. "You can't stay, there's no way I will allow you to carry on your . . . . profession on my premises. Shoe manufacturer! How do we know that everything else you filled in on your brochure isn't a lie too?"

"I swear all the rest is true. I *am* single if that's what's worrying you."

"Everything about you worries me," Jane admitted. "If, at some future stage, you wish to return in a purely social capacity, then I'll re-think it."

"When will that be?" Richard asked.

"I hardly think that this is the time to ask, do you?" Charles replied.

"I suppose not. But I *would* like to come back," he assured them.

"Let's get this weekend over with first," Jane said anxiously.

Richard Fenway rose from the comfortable lounger and picked up his tape recorder. He hesitated for a second then placed it on the ground again. Jane watched as he carried the chair and replaced it with the others in the garden. He's trying to earn brownie points, she thought.

"I'd like to ask you something before you go, how did you know when Serena would be here? She booked a long time ago, so did you."

Richard Fenway gazed at her puzzled face. He didn't suppose it would do any harm to tell her that much. If the agency got stroppy he could always tell them that she'd threatened to call the police.

"Her son has an expensive lifestyle. Her ex keeps him supplied with cash, generously supplied, I imagine, in return for information. He lives with *her*. If you think *I'm* underhanded, how does that grab you?"

Jane's mouth formed a perfect O, even Charles's expression was one of horror.

"That's the most disgusting thing I've ever heard," Jane sputtered.

"I see and hear things that are *far* worse than that. Maybe someday I'll tell you about my job," Richard offered.

"If it's all like that I don't think I want to hear about it," Jane said.

"I'll leave you then. By the way, are you going to tell Serena about this?"

"I honestly don't know. I don't know if I have the right to interfere in someone's life. I wish I hadn't asked you that last question."

♥ ♥ ♥

It was too chilly to sit outside after dinner. Jane felt a swell of pride as she looked round her. The glow of the lamps in the big living-room cast soft pools of light, and the orange flames of the firelight reflected the contented faces of her clients.

When she'd first bought the house this was exactly how she'd imagined *Personal Agenda* would be. Somehow the summer and the garden had played such a big part in their weekends, that she'd lost sight of the long autumn and winter months which stretched ahead. Her gaze fell on Serena Smith sitting on the rug beside the fire how relaxed she was. How could she possibly spoil Serena's weekend by telling her the reason Richard Fenway was here? Charles had casually mentioned during lunch that Richard had suddenly been called away.

♥ ♥ ♥

After a poor night's sleep, Jane still hadn't made up her mind what to tell Serena. But there was no time to think about that now, they still had to get through breakfast and pack the picnic lunch for the boat.

Jane stood at the river's edge and waited until the boat reached the bend in the river and disappeared from sight. Sasha and Charles had gone with them and, for the first time in months, Jane and Mrs Jones had the house all to themselves on a Sunday. Justin and William had invited her to have lunch with them. William's brother and his wife were visiting the cottage for the first time. Tempted though she was, Jane felt she should stay at The Willows.

"We must have a picnic too. Let's go and sit in the garden while we still can," Jane urged. Mrs Jones had become part of the weekend family and she kept Jane and Sasha constantly amused with tales of her children and their pranks.

". . . and little Alice was almost expelled when she put that frog in the teacher's desk for safekeeping," she laughed. "We decided . . . Is that the phone?"

Jane dashed through the garden and grabbed the receiver through the open window. "*Personal Agenda*," she panted. "Hello? *Personal Agenda. Hello.*" The phone went dead, a wrong number no doubt. As she returned to her lunch it rang again, but again no one spoke.

"You can ring all you want," she said. "I'm going to finish my lunch."

They struggled off the boat, chattering and laughing.

"You missed a marvellous trip," Michael Gleeson told Jane. "The countryside round here is beautiful, and we felt like peeping Toms watching everyone in their gardens. And what gardens!"

"What I'd give to get my hands on a few sites like those," Neill Drummond sighed.

"You'll have to do what Justin and William did, find a derelict house or cottage," Jane said.

"Lucky them, do you think there are any more?"

"Could be, I don't know. Why don't you contact the local agents, I'll give you their number."

Jane waited until Serena Smith was ready to leave and asked if she could have a word with her.

"Is something wrong?" Serena asked.

"Not at all, but there is something I feel you should know. We can talk in my office."

Serena admired Jane's friendship rug then sat on the arm of a chair, her legs elegantly crossed.

Jane cleared her throat nervously. "Richard Fenway? He left *Personal Agenda* in a hurry yesterday?"

"I remember."

"I asked him to go. He was . . . well, he is . . . he was . . . a private detective. I found him taping a report . . ."

"Not again," Serena sighed. "That damned husband of mine, *ex-husband*, he never gives up. He must have wasted a small fortune having me followed. Would you mind telling me why I should go to a dating agency if I'm supposed to have a lover? He's utterly convinced that I have. And what's more, even if I had, it's none of his damn business."

Jane frown vanished, all those hours of worry dashed away in a few words.

"There's just one thing, how did he find out I'd be here and . . ." Serena watched a flush of colour heighten Jane's cheeks. "You know how, don't you?"

Jane wished she was wearing some of Amanda's green concealer. "I really think that's something you should discuss with your . . . husband."

"It's that son of mine, isn't it?" she asked.

"Honestly I think you . . ."

"Right, that's it, I've had enough. First thing tomorrow I'm going to see my solicitor and take out an injunction against that slimy snake. I've been very patient but now I've come to the end of my tether. He'll destroy Brian's sense of values with these endless bribes. I've had my suspicions for a long time, but now I know. It's got to stop."

In spite of her anger, Serena's eyes were sad.

Jane could only imagine how awful she must be feeling; her own son, a traitor.

"I'm really sorry that your weekend had to end like this, I really did think long and hard before telling you. But because you were followed here, I felt . . . honour bound."

"Please don't worry, Jane, I appreciate how difficult it must have been for you. However, I must say it hasn't spoiled my enjoyment one bit and I'd like to book here and now for your next *fit-forties* weekend. By the way, Neil Drummond is taking me to a photographic exhibition next week and then we're going out for dinner. Let my husband stew over that!"

♥ ♥ ♥

"They were good fun," Sasha announced, as she and Jane cleared the debris from the late afternoon tea. "I spent ages talking to Delia Conway, she gave me millions of hints and tips about how to dress, make-up and all sorts of interesting things."

"How come you're into all that? Are you thinking of becoming a model?"

"I'm a bit long in the tooth for that," Sasha said scornfully.

"I suppose twenty-three *is* very old," Jane laughed.

"Twenty-*four*," Sasha corrected. "No I was just making enquiries about how to spend my fortune when I get it!"

"You're sure that you'll be able to sell all those costumes and things?"

"Positive. The man at the costumiers gave me a

rough idea of what they were worth providing they were in good condition, and they are."

Sasha had spent endless hours checking her treasures. Everything was washed and neatly ironed, packed away for the journey to London and the costume hire firm. Nothing would persuade her to part with the ones they'd used for the drama weekend. Jane repeatedly offered to buy the costumes they'd used so that Sasha wouldn't be out of pocket, but just as often, Sasha refused. "I had such fun with that play," she pointed out. "This way we'll be able to do it over and over again. Don't mention it again, Jane."

"What time are Justin and William calling for you on Tuesday?" Jane asked.

"About seven-thirty. They're taking me to Dobbs' Costume Hire before they go to work. Justin is worried about what will happen if Dobbs' decide not to buy everything. I think he has visions of me trailing around London like a bag-lady."

"He's very thoughtful, isn't he?" Jane smiled.

"They both are. Right, that seems to be everything back in order." Sasha closed the cupboard door with a sigh of relief. "Come on, let's raid the fridge and watch the telly, we've earned it."

Chapter Forty-Nine

Alex took a taxi from Heathrow Airport to Kim's flat. He'd psyched himself up and was relieved when he heard her footsteps coming to the door. He'd decided that, if necessary, he'd jam his foot in the door and *make* her listen to him. He'd done his best to try to wheedle Kim's number out of Ros at the airline. She was friendly but firm in her refusal.

"May I help you?" The woman who opened the door was a total stranger. Just his dumb luck. "I'm looking for Kim Barrett," Alex said politely.

"Sorry, she left here months ago."

"Can you let me have her new address?"

"I'm sorry, I'm afraid I can't help you."

"That's too bad, I'm supposed to meet her tomorrow but I've got to leave for the States in the morning and I don't want her to drag all the way to . . . Brighton for nothing," Alex adlibbed. Brighton was the first place he could think of.

"Flying Concorde are you?" the woman asked.

The question caught him by surprise, how did she know that Concorde left London in the morning?

"Yes, that's right."

"Have a good journey," she said and closed the door.

Susan French listened as his footsteps faded. He must be the man Kim mentioned – tall, large-framed, reddish-brown hair.

During a coffee break on one of their flights, Kim told her that she'd finally taken the plunge and bought a flat. Susan's own lease was about to run out and she'd been delighted when Kim offered to recommend Susan to her landlord. Susan was happy here, it was a nice flat in good condition, and well situated for shopping and transport. In return for the favour, Kim made her promise that if anyone came looking for her – Alex Travis in particular – she wouldn't give him Kim's new address. Susan had heard rumours that Kim had had a bust-up with some American. She must phone Kim and tell her that some guy was looking for her.

Susan left a message on Kim's answering machine and got on with her ironing, she had an early flight tomorrow.

Alex went back to his hotel and phoned Samantha. She recognised his voice immediately and, before he could manage little more than hello, she slammed the phone down. What was he supposed to do now, camp at the airport until Kim appeared? It would be almost impossible to spot her in those crowds. He wouldn't know where to begin looking for her. The phone book! How crack-brained he was, he hadn't thought to look in the most obvious place.

He ran his finger down the list of names. "Barrett, A . . . A . . . Ann . . . Alan, here we are,

. . . Karen, Karim, Kathleen, Kenneth . . ." Alex threw the book down with a bang. There were two K. Barretts, one a dental surgeon, the other a garden designer.

Alex wasn't in the mood to sit in a restaurant, he'd eat here in his room.

"Room service," a pleasant voice answered.

"I'd like to order dinner," Alex said. "An omelette please and send me up a bottle of Johnny Walker, Black Label."

"Certainly Sir, what kind of omelette? Mushroom, mixed herbs, cheese, ham?"

"I don't care, you decide," he said dejectedly.

"Cheese?"

"Whatever."

"Would you like some rolls or bread and butter with it?"

"If you like."

"Oh dear, you don't sound very hungry."

"I'm not in the mood to eat."

"I'll tell the chef to make you a mixed omelette, would you like some coffee or tea?"

"And spoil good Scotch?" he asked.

"Oh dear," the voice repeated. "It sounds as if you haven't *had a good day.*" Tracy liked that expression which she'd picked up from Americans staying at the hotel.

"I haven't."

"Sorry I can't help with that," she laughed.

"No I'm afraid . . . Hang on, maybe you could."

There was silence on the other end of the line. "Are you still there?" Alex asked.

"What are you suggesting, *Sir*," her tone was suspicious.

"Don't worry, nothing illegal or immoral. What

time do you get off-duty?"

"I'm married."

"But I don't want to *marry* you." He smiled for the first time that day. "All I want you to do is make a call for me. Could you meet me in the lobby and I'll explain the whole thing? It's complicated. One call, that's all and there's twenty doll . . . pounds in it for you."

"Twenty pounds for one phone call?" she asked.

"That's right. What I do for love."

"OK," she said, her tone still a little sceptical. "I'll be off-duty in an hour. I'll wait at one of the tables near the reception desk." It was all very strange but she was intrigued, and she couldn't come to any harm in the foyer with all the other staff around.

"Fine. How will I recognise you?"

"Dark hair, a red suit – and a husband who's a policeman."

The girl at the table nearest the desk looked up apprehensively.

"I'm Alex Travis."

"I'm Tracy."

"May I sit down?"

"Yes." She indicated the chair furthest from her.

"Let me explain about the call," he said immediately. "But first, would you like a drink?"

She shook her head vehemently.

"OK, the phone call. I arranged to take my girlfriend Kim out for dinner last night, it was her birthday. I was badly delayed so I called her and we arranged to meet at the restaurant. By the time I got there, an hour later than I promised, she'd gone. The waiter said she was mad as hell when she left. You see it was her birthday."

Tracy sucked in her breath and shook her head. "Nice one!"

"So why didn't I go to her apartment or call her you're wondering?"

She wasn't, but now that he mentioned it . . .

"That's where the problem started. The piece of paper she gave me with her number on it had vanished. I must have pulled it out of my pocket when I paid the cab. And here's the real rub, she moved to a new apartment this week and I don't even know the address."

"That's awful," Tracy agreed sympathetically.

"I tried to contact her girlfriend, she and Kim are air stewardesses, but she's out of town." Alex looked sorrowfully into her eyes. He'd rehearsed his story well.

"So who do you want me to call . . . to phone?" She thought his girlfriend must be round the twist, fancy getting *that* annoyed just because he was late. Alex Travis was such a nice-looking man.

"I want you to call her friend, Ros – at the airline. I tried myself but Kim is so mad she's already told her not to give me the new number. You gals really stick together don't you?" he said ruefully. Alex had tried to leave a message with Ros months ago, when he and Kim first broke up, but she refused point blank to talk to him.

"So you want me to phone this girl Ros and ask for Kim's number?"

"Exactly, Kim Barrett is her name. Say that you're meant to meet her tonight and you can't make it, OK?" He would have liked Tracy to ask for Kim's address but that might make it sound suspicious.

"That sounds simple enough. What name will I use?" She asked.

"Mmm . . . your own name."

"There are phones round the corner, follow me." It's good fun playing Cupid, Tracy thought.

"It's ringing," she said with her hand over the mouthpiece. "Hello, Ros?"

Alex leaned his head next to hers.

"Hello, who's that?" Alex could hear Ros's voice ask.

"Ros, can you give me Kim Barrett's number please. I'm supposed to meet her tomorrow and I'm at in the airport now and I've forgotten my address book."

Alex admired her inventiveness.

"That you, Samantha?"

Tracy looked at him questioningly. Alex nodded.

"Yes Ros, I'm in an a awful dash."

"You got a cold? You sound funny."

"A bit of a throat," she coughed loudly. Alex grinned and rubbed his ear. Tracy was quite an actress.

"Hang on a mo," Ros instructed.

"You're doing fine," Alex encouraged her in a whisper.

"I've got a contact number for her, she's away until tomorrow morning. You got a pen?" Tracy repeated the numbers aloud while Alex wrote them down.

He covered the receiver with his hand and told her to ask for Kim's home number.

"Ros, can you give me her home number?"

"No point, like I said, she's away."

Tracy frowned at Alex. "Will I keep pushing for it?" she mouthed.

"Try again," he whispered.

"Samantha, are you there? What's going on? Is that you, Samantha?"

Alex could hear the doubt in Ros's voice. If she became suspicious she might warn Kim. He shook his head at Tracy and signalled with his hand to end the conversation.

"Ros I'm deathly late, thanks a million, you're a pal." Tracy banged the phone down before Ros got a chance to reply.

"You're a real pro," Alex said.

"Not the most tactful expression," Tracy laughed.

"You did well. Here's the twenty pounds I promised you."

"I can't take it, to be honest, it was fun, I enjoyed it. Oh dear, I'm sorry, I didn't mean . . ."

"It's OK. But please, we had a deal, take the money. Buy yourself some flowers or something."

"No, really. Call it a favour, for love's sake. But one thing you can do, phone down tomorrow and let me know what happened."

"It's a promise," Alex said.

He sat on the bed in his room and punched out the number.

"*Personal Agenda*," a voice answered.

He didn't speak.

"Hello? *Personal Agenda* . . . hello." It certainly wasn't Kim's voice. He cut off the call. There was nothing listed under that name in the phone book. How was he going to find out what

Personal Agenda was? Or where it was? Maybe the time had come to call it a day, this obsession with Kim was ruling his life. But on the other hand, perhaps he'd have one last try.

"I'm sorry Sir, we are not permitted to give out addresses," the directory enquiry operator said. Alex's emotional plea fell on her deaf ears.

"This is crazy," he told himself. At least tomorrow my time will be more sanely occupied. Thank goodness for work.

♥ ♥ ♥

At one minute to six the next afternoon, Alex slipped into the florists just as the girl was placing a closed sign on the door. If the owner hadn't been there he wouldn't have got into the shop. The surly assistant showed no interest as she wrapped the huge bouquet of flowers.

Tracy wasn't on duty. He left them at the reception desk for her with a note of thanks and wandered into the hotel shop. He bought an evening newspaper and a large bar of chocolate. His colleague wasn't picking him up until eight o'clock, he'd never last until then without something to snack.

Alex lay on his bed and read the paper. The news was as bad here as it was in the States; burglaries, rape, people on the take. He flipped through the advertisement pages and threw the paper aside. It was still only seven o'clock. Alex looked at his book and wondered whether to start it. Maybe it would pass the time. He leaned forward to pick it up and his eyes caught a heading in the personal column.

"PERSONAL AGENDA"
An invitation to relax and share a luxurious weekend break in the company of other bright, single professionals.
For brochure write to Box 1034 or telephone 5555 7203

So that's what *Personal Agenda* was all about. A singles' weekend. The phone number Tracy read out to him was the same, he remembered the first four numbers. He was totally on the wrong track, it wasn't a training course as he'd imagined. But a singles' weekend – that was the last place he would have expected to find Kim.

"I'd like to apply for a brochure," Alex said.

"Certainly," replied the bright voice on the other end of the line. "May I have your name and address?"

Alex hesitated, there was no reason why he should use a false name. "My apartment isn't ready yet so you can send it here to my hotel."

"Oh! I'm not sure we can do that, we usually require a permanent home address."

"I perfectly understand, but that won't be for several weeks. You could check here at The Terrapin, they know me well."

"I'll have to talk to the owner of the agency but I doubt that she'll break the rule."

"I'll wait to hear from you. Before you go – where are you situated? I don't have a car yet, I'm waiting for delivery."

"We're in Dornley-on-Thames."

"Heavens to Betsy! I have friends there. Now

let me think – Primrose something or was it . . . Rose? Do you know where I mean? Which street is yours?"

"I can't help you, I don't know either of those names. Contact us again when you have a permanent address, we'll send you the brochure."

"Thank you," Alex said gratefully.

He'd almost succeeded in getting the address, but even with his slight knowledge of small English villages, he was sure that *Personal Agenda* wouldn't be difficult to find.

Chapter Fifty

Amanda mooched around the house feeling miserable. Kevin's phone call yesterday cancelling their date had upset her. Surely he didn't have to work on Sunday? Was his excuse genuine or was he fed up with their relationship? Had she been too eager, pushed too hard? She didn't think so. He'd sounded really out of sorts, distracted.

She searched through the kitchen cupboard for something sweet, she had a sudden longing for a biscuit or a piece of cake. Then Amanda remembered she'd asked Mrs Judd not to buy anything that might tempt her. She shut the door in disgust and wondered if she should go to the garage and buy a load of her favourite snacks. There should be a box of chocolates from last Christmas somewhere, maybe in her wardrobe.

Amanda tore the wrapping from the box and opened the lid. The chocolates were covered in a white bloom. She was sure that wasn't harmful, a bit stale maybe. She bit one gingerly, it tasted perfectly OK.

Tears flowed from Amanda's eyes as she watched a father saying goodbye to his dying son. She blew her nose loudly on a tissue and scavenged around in the box without taking her eyes off the television. As the closing credits scrolled Amanda still cried. She searched for another chocolate but all she could feel were the crinkly wrappers. She looked at the box in horror. "I've eaten the lot," she groaned. "White bloom and all."

Full of remorse and furious with herself for her greedy self-indulgence, Amanda tied a light cardigan round her waist and left the house to walk off the damage.

Emma Brown was home by the time Amanda returned.

"I saw your car and was wondering where you were." her mother said.

"I walked round the block a few times to get a bit of air." She had no intention of admitting that she'd walloped through a whole box of chocolates, her mother would never be tempted by anything like that.

"How was Kevin yesterday? I didn't want to disturb you last night, you must have been asleep by the time I came home."

"We didn't go."

"Oh?"

"Kevin had to work."

"That's too bad, but I suppose his work must come first."

"I s'pose."

"And *I* suppose I'd better get off to bed. I'm going to Glasgow tomorrow and I've still got a report to finish. Don't wait dinner for me. If the meeting drags on, I may stay overnight."

♥ ♥ ♥

"Why is everyone so crotchety?" Amanda muttered irritably.

"That's all right for you to say, your office is like peace on earth compared to that jungle out there," Lois said. "I've come here to hide and have my sandwich. OK with you?"

"Sure, do you want coffee? I was just going for get one for myself."

"When is the presentation?"

"Friday morning, I'll be glad when it's over. It'll be nice to walk around again without tripping over papers. There's a pre-pre-presentation meeting going on now, and another on Wednesday."

"What time on Wednesday?" Amanda asked.

Lois looked at her quizzically, Amanda never took any interest in the presentations, they weren't even in her domain, she was only interested in the company's finance. "Why do you ask?"

"I . . . I thought it might interfere with our lunch, that's all."

"Oh, I see. No, it won't. It doesn't start until three o'clock. Even we can be back by then!" Lois laughed, their lunches often lingered well past the hour and a half they allowed themselves. But then neither of them really needed to punch a clock.

Chapter Fifty-One

"Ready?" Lois asked as she stuck her head round the door.

"On my way," Amanda replied.

They decided on a small sandwich bar round the corner from Coogan, Howard and Green. "I have to watch the time today," Lois warned.

"Don't worry, I'll remind you."

"I've decided to apply to your dating agency," Lois said when they'd ordered their lunch.

"It's not really *mine*," Amanda laughed.

"You know what I mean." Lois's voice was edgy. "Sorry, I didn't mean to snap, this Stourley account has us all worried."

"Why?" Amanda asked.

"Because each time I speak to them, they seem to take a sadistic delight in hinting that the other agency has a very good campaign. It would be a brilliant feather in anyone's company-cap to grab the account. Their budget is huge and they really believe in advertising."

Amanda chewed thoughtfully on her sandwich. Judging from what Kevin had told her, Derby's were anything but happy with their campaign.

Amanda couldn't remember a time when

everyone was so nervous and up-tight about a potential client.

"I think I'll have another sandwich, how about you?" Amanda asked.

"No thanks, this one is sticking in my throat. I wouldn't mind some more coffee to wash it down."

"Aren't the copywriters pleased with their work?" Amanda probed.

"Sort of. It's the old story, last minute nerves, the usual doubts until the client says yes. Or no. I don't want to think about *that* possibility."

Amanda knew better than to ask for any more information. The storyboard was top secret – even within the agency.

"So have you written to *Personal Agenda*?" Amanda asked.

"Not yet, I keep meaning to."

"Would you like me to phone Jane Anderson for you?"

"Would you? I never seem to find the time."

"I'll do it as soon as I get back to the office. And talking of the office, we'd better move or you'll be late."

Coogan, Howard and Green was humming with activity. The boardroom door was open. The art director, the creative team, and the media planners were milling about in last minute panic. Lois took her seat just before the chairman, Bill Coogan, strode briskly into the room. The buzz of conversation stopped. As they took their places around the table, each member of the teams surreptitiously glanced towards the three empty seats. Tomorrow morning they would be occupied by the Stourley Chairman and his two advisers.

There was an expectant hush as the sound of a jingle filtered along the corridor. Amanda leaned against the frame of her office door. The tune was catchy. What Kevin would give to be a fly on *that* boardroom wall, she thought. Her heart began to thump uncomfortably as she watched Tim Reed leave the tiny studio next to the boardroom. He was clutching a sheaf of papers and a remote control.

The corridor was empty and silent as Amanda slipped into the studio. The tiny, dark room was packed with high-tec recording and video machines. One wall was completely lined with videos and audio tapes, their spines clearly labelled. She moved noiselessly to the small window which allowed her a clear view of the boardroom. Scarcely breathing, she listened to Bill Coogan making his opening remarks to the phantom client.

The large screen on the wall behind him flickered into life and the music began again. The film started as two doors opened simultaneously, and from behind each, a man appeared; one was bearded, tousled and unkempt, the other bright-eyed, groomed and well-shaven. He was the *Stourley* man, the narrator announced.

Amanda's eyes were glued to the screen, the advertisement seemed to last far longer than thirty seconds. It was amusing and to the point. In her opinion, it didn't fall into the trap of being either visually or audibly irritating.

Amanda could hear footsteps running along the corridor and she froze. Had someone discovered that she wasn't in her office? She had no reason to be in the studio, no right to be here. The boardrom door swung open and Amanda, shaking like a jelly, waited for the running figure to denounce her presence in the adjoining room.

But the copywriter quickly placed a leaflet in front of each of the team, took his place at the table, and Amanda breathed again. She turned the handle of the studio door and opened it a crack. She could hear them laugh as Bill Coogan talked about the click audience, those low-boredom channel-changers with their dreaded remote controls. She would wait to hear the radio version of the advertisement, then sneak back to her office.

Chapter Fifty-Two

Kevin read the message on his desk. Amanda wanted to talk to him. He looked at his watch and decided to phone her later. He was beginning to regret this claustrophobic relationship. Amanda was a very nice person but her manner was a bit cloying. There were too many phone calls suggesting that they go here or go there, too many tickets for the theatre or concerts that had suddenly fallen into her lap. He'd hidden behind his workload last weekend and felt rotten when he heard the disappointment in her voice. Guilt gnawed at him. When they'd first met he'd encouraged the friendship in the hope of gleaning some information about Coogan, Howard and Green. Even after he realised that she couldn't help, he allowed their relationship to drift on. He couldn't deny that he was pleased to spend an odd evening with her, it passed the time. And he couldn't deny he'd been the one to suggest it. But at dinner in her house last week, he began to notice that she looked upon him in quite a different light. He didn't want to get involved romantically with Amanda. Kevin shook his head as he pictured Meriel with her flaming hair and seductive figure. Amanda was not his idea of a dream girl, and never would be.

"Can we meet?" Amanda asked when Kevin finally called.

"When? Is it something urgent?" Kevin tried to curb the sharpness of his tone.

"It's not *urgent*," Amanda replied, "I . . . it's something that will interest you, that's all." The hurt in her voice was plain.

Guilt washed over him again. "How about tomorrow night?" he said. What did Amanda mean? She'd piqued his interest.

"Where do you suggest?" she asked tersely.

Now she was annoyed with him. He really didn't need this hassle. "It'll be fairly late before I'm finished, how about that bistro near your office, the one you said was quite good? That would be handy for both of us."

"You mean, Tratter's?"

"That's the one. Say about eight-thirty?" Kevin was aware that she'd have to fill in a few hours after she finished work, but there was nothing he could do about it.

"OK. I'll phone and book a table, they get very busy."

Amanda stared moodily through her bedroom window into the growing dusk. The beautiful white ash had shed almost half its leaves and the ones left on the branches were curled and withered. "Just like my life," she said aloud to her silent room.

This room had held such bitter memories until she'd joined *Personal Agenda* and met Kevin. All summer long it had been a haven for her thoughts and dreams. On the spur of the moment, she'd decided to redecorate it herself in soft pinks and wildly extravagant white fabrics, light as a summer breeze. Emma encouraged her to buy new furniture and they'd chosen it together. The result was frivolous and feminine, and she loved it. Now, as autumn's chilly grip took hold, her own *joie de vivre* began to fade as surely as those leaves on the increasingly bare branches. Kevin *is* engrossed in his work, she told herself. It *is* taking up all his time, his whole career is at stake. So why did she feel uneasy, so unsure of him, she wondered.

♥ ♥ ♥

Amanda dressed with care. Both Lois and Emma had approved of the long-jacketed, red suit with its red and black tartan skirt. She liked the neat black, low-necked 'body' that the girl in the shop said was perfect with it. As good as her word, Amanda always wore earrings now. From her worn pink velvet jewellery box she chose matt, square, gold discs with a matching lapel brooch. She was determined to leave the house with a positive attitude. When Kevin heard what she had to say, their romance would be back on track in no time.

"When do you make your presentation?" Amanda asked as soon as Kevin was seated.

"What . . . you mean Stourley's?"

Amanda's hair fell across her forehead as she nodded.

"In a couple of weeks' time."

"How's it going?"

Kevin regarded her quizzically. Why the sudden interest? Had Coogan, Howard and Green had a response already? Surely not. "It's OK. It's coming along." His reply was cagey.

"I presume you aren't going to use the – *one man bright and breezy the other half-dead* – image? The – *one man, surrounded by hangover cures, practically asleep at his desk, the other hobnobbing intelligently with his boss* – routine? The thinking man's lager-lout image?" Amanda's stare was unwavering.

Kevin sat back in his chair. What was she telling him? His stomach began to twist with tension. "Amanda, what are you saying?" he demanded.

"I just wondered if that's the kind of thing you intend to do?"

Kevin wouldn't dream of discussing Derby's campaign with her, but his copy wasn't too different from what she'd described. Had someone in Derby's leaked information? He needed another drink, needed to think all this through.

Kevin gulped the scotch down in two mouthfuls. Slowly but surely in a roundabout way, it began to dawn on him. Amanda had spelt out the details of Coogan, Howard and Green's campaign. Kevin could hardly believe his ears. This information was money in the bank for Derby's.

"Don't you think that using *men only* in advertising is sexist? Why preclude half the adult population? After all, women enjoy lager too," she mused. "I think cartooning this sort of advert could be fun. Why not make it outrageous?"

Kevin was withdrawn on the journey home. Amanda hummed quietly to the tape and didn't attempt to make conversation. At the restaurant she'd watched his face pale and knew she'd stumbled on *his* storyline. But now, thanks to her, Kevin knew exactly what not to do. In her roundabout manner she'd given him Coogan, Howard and Green's storyline.

"See you around," he said absently as he got out of the car.

Amanda's heart plummeted. "Will you phone me and let me know how you are getting on? By the way, I have two tickets for a concert on Saturday, would you like to go?" She'd sworn that she wouldn't ask him out. She could have choked herself.

"I'd love to," Kevin said. "But I can't make any arrangements for the moment. You do understand?"

No I *don't* understand, she raged to herself. I've just given you a passport to success and that's the thanks I get. "Of course I understand." Her voice was even although she was seething with indignation.

Chapter Fifty-Three

Alex Travis smiled at the women sitting behind the counter. If there was one thing he'd learnt about English village life, it was that the people who ran the local shops knew more about their customers than the customers did themselves.

"So you're from America?" Mrs Reid asked breathlessly. "My sister went to America for her holidays, she sent me a lovely postcard from Nigeria Falls."

Alex opened his mouth then closed it again.

"They are quite majestic," he agreed.

"Well she really wanted to go to see the Grand Cannon, but with her husband's grout and everything it would be too long for him to sit on the plane."

It took all Alex's will power just to nod solemnly. He pictured the woman's brother-in-law sitting on the wing of the plane, his bandaged foot stretched out in front of him.

"I'd love to go to America myself." Mrs Reid's eyes had a faraway look.

"Can't you manage a vacation there?" Alex asked.

"I'm so busy here I'd never have time." Mrs Reid made herself more comfortable on her chair and settled down for a chat. "Where do you live in America?"

"Washington mostly."

"I heard it's lovely there. Did you ever meet President . . . Clin . . . Clingon?" she remembered triumphantly.

Alex choked. "I think you mean Clinton."

"That's him."

"Yes we've met a couple of times. At business dinners."

Mrs Reid's innocent face beamed with delight. It's not every day she met someone who had dinners with a president. "And did you meet his wife?"

"No, Alex admitted, "she wasn't there."

"I suppose she must have been worn out from making the dinner, poor soul." Mrs Reid's eyes shone sympathetically.

"You're probably right. I wonder if you can give me some help?" Alex asked, terrified that he would laugh and hurt Mrs Reid's feelings.

"If I can, I will, and if I can't, I won't," she said in a sing-song voice.

"I'm on my way to . . . *Personal Agenda* but I've lost the address, can you direct me?"

It was a long way for him to come to join that new-fangled dating thing, Mrs Reid thought, but it took all sorts.

"I can, and I will. It's approximately, exactly three miles from here."

Alex couldn't take much more of this.

"First, you go out of the shop – well you'd have to wouldn't you?" she cackled at her own wit. "Then you go left . . . or is it right? No, left, . . . left. Go round the pond. Aren't the ducks lovely? I prefer the swans myself, I love it when the little cygnals are born. Anyway, from there you go past the house with the white front door and keep going straight till you get to the D junction. Are you with me?"

Alex assured her that her instructions were exceptional.

"After that you . . ."

Alex was still smiling broadly when he reached the leafy road where Mrs Reid said The Willows was situated. Her somewhat garbled instructions were correct. Dornley was a glorious part of the countryside, it reminded him of New England in the fall. He turned into the driveway of the sprawling house and parked his car next to Jane's.

Jane frowned as she heard the sound of the bell. She wasn't expecting anyone to call. Through the tiny coloured glass panes she could see the distorted figure of a tall, heavily built man. Be careful, she warned herself as she called out.

"Personal Agenda?" the muffled voice enquired.

"Yes," Jane answered cautiously. If Sasha was in the house she would have opened the door immediately, but Sasha was in London.

"Can I speak to you?" an American voice asked.

Jane quietly slipped the chain on the door and opened it to its limit. The man was tall but not as heavy as she'd imagined – athletically built. He had a rounded face and a friendly smile. "I'm sorry to disturb you, but I'm trying to trace a friend of mine, Kim Barrett. In one of her letters she mentioned that she'd been here with you. I'm ashamed to say I've lost her letter and don't know where to contact her." Alex had lost count of the number of times he'd told that same lie.

While he explained his predicament, Jane took stock of the American. He was neatly dressed, obviously a gentleman and most apologetic. But even if Mel Gibson himself – Sasha's latest heartthrob – asked for an address she wouldn't give it to him.

Alex shuffled his feet slightly.

"I'm Jane Anderson, owner of the agency. I'm sorry but we never give out clients' addresses."

"I can understand that, but a phone number will do just fine."

Jane shook her head and pursed her lips. "Same thing. I'm afraid not."

Should he try this attractive woman with a big sob story? His gut feeling told him he wouldn't succeed. Alex had made up his mind before he left London that this would be his last attempt to contact Kim.

"Well, I tried," he sighed. "Thank you for your help anyway, I apologise again for disturbing you. I'd better get back to London. At least it gave me a chance to see your great countryside." He looked sad as he began to turn away.

"Just a minute," Jane said.

Alex hid his look of triumph and turned to face her.

"Would you like to come in and have a cup of coffee? I'll telephone Kim now. If she's not at home, you can leave your number with me and I'll pass it on to her." She felt a little embarrassed as she closed the door in order to take off the chain.

"That's very kind of you, I'd really appreciate that." Alex was willing to bet a dollar to a dime that, the moment Kim heard his name, she'd either give Jane a tough time or slam down the phone. But at this stage he'd nothing to lose.

Alex stepped into the hall and was captivated by its airy elegance. "This is wonderful," he enthused. "And hey, look at that planting by the stairs. What a wonderful interior designer you must have had."

"All me, I'm afraid." Jane was pleased with the burst of colour from a display of bronze and yellow chrysanthemums. They flourished in their warm, indoor bed.

"Don't apologise. It's very impressive. May I?" Alex walked forward a few paces and stood in the entrance to the living-room.

"It's big when the doors are opened back like this, isn't it?" Jane said.

"Big, yes, but tasteful. I think you missed your vocation." A bit of flattery may soften her up.

"Would you like to come through to the kitchen? I have something on the stove."

It reminded him of his childhood. There was a wonderful smell of . . . what?

"What can I smell?" He sniffed.

"Caramel, or it was. I've burnt it. Never mind, it's only sugar and water."

"Now I know what it reminds me of, candy apples. Hallowe'en."

"That's exactly what I was trying out," Jane smiled. "Not apples on sticks but an apple and toffee dessert."

"I'd forgotten Hallowe'en is only a few weeks away."

Jane moved the pan from the heat. "I can do this again later. Let me put the kettle on. It won't take a minute."

Alex sat at the table which was covered with a colourful confusion of recipe books, pencils and notes. Jane took a biscuit box from a cupboard and put it in front of him. He lifted the lid and an aroma of lemon filled the air.

"Please help yourself," Jane said as she spooned the scoops of coffee into the plunger jug and waited for the water to boil. "How did you meet Kim?"

"In a restaurant during a snow storm, I was on my way to Seattle," he said.

Alex munched on the biscuits and told Jane of their meeting.

"Sounds positively romantic." She placed the coffee jug on the table.

"How long were you marooned in New York? I'd love to visit the States," she admitted.

"We were snowed in for a day-and-a-half." Alex crunched another biscuit. "These are great, did you make them?"

"Uh huh. It must be maddening to get stuck like that. Were you able to find enough to do?"

"I was lucky. Kim and her friend Samantha kept me entertained. We had a fun game of poker, played solitaire, talked and ate. Kim and I even took a quick walk in the snow. The time passed all too quickly."

She pushed the biscuit tin nearer to him. There was a wistfulness about him. "It must have been difficult to keep up the . . . friendship. I know Kim is in New York a lot . . ."

"It *was* frustrating. You see I live in

Washington and commute to New York. We have a branch there."

Jane didn't like to ask what he did for a living. "I'll go and phone Kim now, we might be lucky enough to catch her."

Jane went into her little office and looked up Kim's number. "It's ringing," she called.

Jane squealed with fright as his big hand appeared over her shoulder. He reached forward, pressed the receiver button and cut off the call.

"I didn't mean to startle you. Please don't be afraid, it's just that I haven't told you the full story."

Jane backed away. How could she reach the alarm's panic button without him stopping her? If she lived to tell this tale she'd never allow a stranger into the house again.

"I'd like you to leave immediately," her voice quavered.

"*Please* may I tell you what happened? Don't be alarmed, I won't harm you in any way. You seem to be an understanding person and, selfishly, it would do *me* good."

Jane shrugged, she had precious little option. Alex seemed to fill her tiny office and she doubted if she could push past him even if she tried.

"Come back and sit down. I'll pour *you* some coffee." He left the office and Jane looked longingly at the phone. Could she ring the police without him hearing her? She thought not.

"We met for the second time . . ." Alex's eyes were glazed with memories as he relived those months; the wonderful time they'd shared in London, Kim's trip to Canada, and the phone call from his wife that ended their idyllic few days.

Jane caught her breath. "Your wife?"

"Please wait. It isn't what it seems." A guilty look crossed Alex's face, "Oh dear," he muttered.

"What's wrong?" He was probably going to ask her if he could phone his wife too, Jane thought angrily.

"I'm afraid I've eaten all your biscuits."

She couldn't help it. Jane burst out laughing at his contrite expression, "There are plenty more," she said. She opened a cupboard and produced another tin.

Jane's sympathy for Cassie Travis, Alex's wife, was wholehearted. But it wavered a little as he explained her unwillingness to do anything to help either of them to get over the tragic loss of their little daughter. She could understand his wife's reluctance to have another child. But to shut herself away and not communicate with him must have made his life all the sadder. Jane knew only too well how lonely he must have felt. She remembered those empty nights spent reading or watching television while Hugh cavorted with his *friends.*

". . . and that was the last time I saw Kim. On the drive home from that Harvard lecture, I realised that I couldn't face the rest of my life without her. It wasn't an easy decision to make, divorce was the only answer. But then I wondered, could I go through with it? Would Kim marry a man who'd divorced his helpless wife?" Alex paused as if he was still trying to find the answer.

Jane shrugged. "I don't know. I don't think I'd be able to live with myself if I'd been the cause of a sick woman's divorce," she said honestly.

"I was riddled with guilt, but, as I said, Cassie lived in a world of her own, a world where I couldn't reach her. I knew that Kim was dreading our parting as much as I was. Just thinking that we could be together eventually made it a whole lot easier.

"I saw the police cars as soon as I turned the corner to the beach house. Their lights were flashing and their sirens still shrieking. They blocked the street and an ambulance was parked directly in front of the house. I almost freaked, something had happened to Kim. I left my own car in the middle of the street and dashed through the yellow cordon."

Jane pictured the scene with a shudder.

"I remember asking a cop if there'd been an accident. He wouldn't answer me, said something like – he wasn't in charge, I'd have to ask someone else. A detective appeared and asked me who I was, then took me inside the house. It was like walking through quicksand. Every step I took brought me nearer to news of Kim which I didn't want to hear. There was a trail of minute, neatly cut pieces of flimsy black fabric from the bedroom to the patio door. It was as if I was dreaming, each one was identical in size to the others.

"It took me a few minutes to recognise those squares of chiffon-confetti. It was material from a nightgown I'd bought for Kim. It must have taken patience to cut it like that, but why had she done it? I didn't understand. I looked at the closed bedroom door and all I kept thinking was that I couldn't go in. Cops came and went and then I found out that Kim wasn't inside the house, she was outside, in the ambulance. The detective insisted that I identify her. I felt sick. Then came the biggest shock of all. It wasn't Kim lying there, it was Cassie, my wife." Alex's voice faltered, but Jane sat quietly and waited for him to recover.

"I'm not proud to admit that a great wave of relief swept over me and almost knocked me off my feet. But then I was even more puzzled. Why was Cassie here? How had she avoided her nurse? Why hadn't the nurse contacted me? Had Kim taken the call while I was at Harvard? I had no answers."

"I'm sure if Kim knew that she'd . . . escaped, she'd have phoned you," Jane said.

Alex nodded. "You're probably right. My reactions were fuzzy. But even so, I began to realise that the detective's questions were extremely accusative. Where was I at the time of the accident? . . . What time did I leave my lecture? . . . It might be easier if we 'went to the station,' then I could make a proper statement. He wouldn't tell me anything about what had happened, when it happened, or even where. He countered each of my questions with one of his own. Naturally I was scared – he was treating me like a suspect. Shocked though I was, I asked if I could call my lawyer. Too many hours spent watching TV, I suppose. I could *prove* where I'd been. Lots of people could prove where I'd been, but the surly detective just kept saying that it would all be sorted out at the station.

"All the love and happiness of our week together was wiped out in one terrible moment. And then something far more sinister struck me. When the cops realised that I wasn't alone at the house, Kim would be even more of a suspect than I was! But not for a single second did I think that Kim could have harmed Cassie. It was the most terrifying experience of my life. I was being dragged along by a force over which I had no control."

"I know that feeling only too well," Jane said bitterly.

Alex's eyes narrowed but he didn't ask why. "They didn't cuff me – which surprised me. I sat in the car and kept asking them what had happened to Cassie. But they still wouldn't say a thing. Just as we were about to leave, a cop came running up to the car. The detective got out but I couldn't hear what they were saying. My lawyer promised to have a substitute at the station."

Jane was thankful that she'd escaped all that when Hugh died.

"The detective opened the car door and told me I could go back into the house. He sent one of his uniformed men to stay with me. I don't know how long he was gone but it seemed like a lifetime. Then, as suddenly as the nightmare began, it was over. The detective came back, told me that I was off the hook. My neighbour had given him all the answers he needed and if I wanted the full story of what had happened, I should talk to her. He wrote down the address of the hospital where they'd taken my wife and then they all left. I was shocked and totally confused."

"I'll bet you were. Did your neighbour see what happened?"

"Yes she did. At least – to Cassie. We'd never met before, my neighbour and I. She was a timid person in her fifties and confined to a wheelchair. When I went into her house, she was obviously very shaken by her experience. Her daughter was with her and she urged her mother gently to tell me what she'd seen.

"She'd been sitting by the open window when the sound of footsteps on the wooden stairs attracted her attention. She said she always enjoyed fashion and the woman who came down our steps was pretty and elegant, and wearing a lovely mint-green suit. Then the woman picked her way carefully over the sand to the water's edge. She took out a mirror – my neighbour said she knew it was a mirror because it glinted in the light – then combed her hair. Then, she used a lipstick. Although my neighbour couldn't exactly see it, she judged it was that by the woman's movements. Then she appeared to replace everything in her bag. She straightened her shoulders, held her head high, and walked into the sea. And she just kept on walking until finally she disappeared under the waves." Alex's eyes were dull and his voice lost its strength.

"How awful," Jane shuddered. "How unhappy she must have been. Poor you, poor both of you. I've never heard anything so sad."

"And my poor neighbour too. She was distraught because she couldn't do a thing to prevent Cassie . . . She phoned the police, and prayed it wasn't too late."

"Can you imagine how helpless she must have felt?"

"I can. I was an expert at feeling helpless. To tell you the truth, in some ways I blamed myself for her . . . Maybe if I'd have been there . . . But the doctors all insisted that it would have happened sooner or later."

"You said before she'd tried several times."

"She had. And although I grieved for her irrationality, I couldn't mourn for Cassie. The girl I'd loved and married died the day we buried our daughter, only Cassie's shell remained."

Jane bit her lip, she couldn't think of anything to say that would make him feel better.

"The day after the accident I tried every hour on the hour to contact Kim, to tell her what had happened and to find out what had passed between them, if anything. My neighbour did say she'd heard the sound of a car arriving at the beach house and it left a little while later. I worked it out that Kim must have left in the same car Cassie used to get to the house. A cab I suppose."

"Could the police not have checked with the taxi companies?"

"There was no point, they couldn't tell me what went on between them in the house."

"That's true. So you phoned Kim?"

Alex nodded. "If Kim was at her flat, she didn't pick up the phone. I left messages on her answering machine but she didn't respond. My life seemed to come to a full stop. I left the house and moved into a hotel. I couldn't bear to spend another moment at that beach house. By the time I boarded the plane for Washington, the . . . arrangements were under control and the beach house was on the market. I vowed that I would never step foot in it again. I tried to push those tragic few days to the back of my mind. But it was impossible."

"I can understand that," Jane shuddered.

"I became *obsessed. I had to speak to Kim.* What had Cassie done or said to make Kim pack up and go without leaving a note? By then I was convinced they'd met."

"It sounds likely," Jane agreed.

"Cassie's nurse was waiting for me when I got home. She was aggressive. She was sympathetic . . . but nevertheless she launched into a tirade about Cassie. She accused her of being devious and cunning."

"That was a horrible thing to say. What was the point of upsetting you even more?"

"She was afraid of being blamed, I suppose. The best means of defence . . . do you have that saying?

"Yes. I'm sorry, go on, I interrupted you."

"Seemingly, the day she disappeared, Cassie was in one of her black moods. Cassie's bedroom was locked when she'd taken up her breakfast. She put the tray on the little table outside Cassie's door and left her to get over her tantrum in her own good time . . . I didn't want to hear any more. There was nothing more to be said. I told her to pack up and go."

"I don't blame you."

"The minute I went into my study I discovered how Cassie knew where I was. My desk had been forced with a knife . . . or a screwdriver. All the details of my travel arrangements, my lectures, Kim's address, were scattered across my desk and slashed to ribbons. This was a side of Cassie I didn't know existed. To me she was like a zombie, living – if you could call it that – in a constant trance.

"After it was all over, there were so many decisions to be made. But I really needed to talk to Kim. Whatever the future held for me, it wasn't going to be in that house either. I put it in the hands of a realtor and found myself a rented apartment. And that's about all I can tell you. As you'll gather from my . . . unorthodox arrival here, I still haven't succeeded in talking to Kim."

"So you still don't know what happened between her and your wife?"

"No." Alex shook his head.

"Maybe they didn't meet. Perhaps Kim didn't like goodbyes and left early for her flight. You said that she was upset you had to part."

"That's possible. Anything's possible. You wouldn't believe the endless possibilities I dreamt up during those months of sleepless nights."

"It must be a comfort that at least your wife and your daughter are together now."

"No, they're not. Cassie is in a different place."

Jane could see that reliving all this had distressed Alex.

"So how did you find out about *Personal Agenda*?" Jane asked.

Alex explained the subterfuge he'd used to con the information out of Ros, Kim's friend at the airline. How he'd all but given up when he saw the advertisement in the paper. Shamefacedly, he admitted that he'd wormed the name of the village out of Sasha. Jane remembered an American had phoned and asked if he could join *Personal Agenda* but, as he had no permanent address in London, Sasha had told him to apply again when he had.

"The end of my quest was in your village shop. The woman, Mrs Reid?"

Jane nodded and a smile spread across her lips.

"Mrs Reid . . . was an education!" Alex laughed for the first time since he'd set foot in the house. "She's something else. I found it very difficult to keep a straight face."

"Isn't she funny? But she means well and loves to be in the thick of things. I don't think I've ever met anyone who enjoys her job as much as Mrs Reid."

"I believe you." Alex glanced at his watch. "I've taken up too much of your time, I'm sorry."

"Don't worry, it's a fairly relaxed day for me. But back to Kim. Obviously she doesn't want to talk to you and you're anxious to pick up where you left off?"

"No. It's finished, over."

"No!" Jane spluttered. "Why . . . what . . . are you doing here? You say you love Kim, I really don't understand."

"I know I must sound crazy, but before I explain, let me make it up to you, may I at least take you for lunch?"

Jane was wrestling with Alex's logic, or lack of it. She was lost. "I can make something here," she said vaguely.

"I thought I saw a pub in the village, am I right?"

"The Drake's Inn, yes."

"Let's go there."

Alex piled his plate with hot crusty bread and concentrated on the cheese board. "Those cheeses look superb," he told the landlord. Jane smiled as she watched him cut a piece of each one for Alex.

"Yes," Alex said, "I'll definitely try the pie. No, I've never tasted pickled onions before."

The bar was quiet and they sat at a table in front of the fire. "This is wonderful, a real fire. You can say what you want about gas logs, to me there's nothing like the smell of wood burning."

Jane watched as Alex demolished the bread and cheese. He reminded her of a schoolboy in a sweet shop, not knowing which to eat first. Just as she was about to ask him to explain why he didn't want to continue his . . . romance . . . with Kim, the landlord returned with another basket of bread and the cheese board. "I like a trencherman," he said.

"A *trencherman*?" Alex had never heard that expression before.

"You were going to tell me why you've gone to so much trouble to contact Kim and why it's . . . all over between you."

"Have you ever really loved someone, Jane?" he asked.

"Yes, a long time ago."

"Kim and I really loved each other, or I thought we did. She knew all about my wife, of course." Alex detected a look of surprise in Jane's eyes. "I was totally up front, told her everything. But now, after all those phone calls I made, and getting the bum's rush like that at Kennedy Airport, I knew that she couldn't love me. How can you say you adore someone one day and condemn them without a hearing the next?"

"I don't know," Jane admitted.

"After a couple of months, my heart hardened.

But I still wanted to tell her, needed to tell her, my side of the story. She doesn't even know that Cassie is . . . "

"So what do you want me to do now?"

"If you don't mind – call her. Ask her if she'll speak to me – which I doubt. If she won't, tell her exactly what happened. Maybe she'll tell you about Cassie."

"I'll phone as soon as we get home. She owes you that." Jane's tone was very definite.

Kim's answering machine purred its message. Jane left her own message and asked Kim to phone her as soon as possible.

"Could I take a look at the garden?" Alex asked as he looked through the office window. "I love that river, it looks so inviting."

They walked across the leaf-strewn lawn to the river's edge. "Just look how it winds and curls," he said enviously. "When I was a kid I used to go fishing with my Dad. Do you have a boat?"

"I don't have one. But we hired one for the day a few weeks ago. We always try to put on some sort of entertainment for our clients," Jane explained.

"Sounds fun. What else do you do?"

Jane told him about the drama weekend, the colour-consultancy, the wine tasting and all the various speakers and hands-on events of the past few months.

"What made you decide to start a dating agency?"

"I ran a secretarial bureau . . ." Jane stopped abruptly and began to shiver. "I'm sorry, you must be frozen too. Come back inside and I'll make some coffee."

The fire in the study grate burned brightly and the light began to fade. He sat quietly as she found herself telling him about Hugh. He nodded sympathetically as she described how she received news of his death from the police. "You see I do understand how you must have felt that day."

"We certainly have a lot in common, don't we?" he asked bitterly.

"I dreamt of opening the dating agency quite a while before Hugh died. Then suddenly it seemed as though the time was right. Like you, I couldn't bear to stay in my house. I was very lucky to find a house like The Willows, it was almost as if it was meant to be. An omen."

"It's a wonderful house, and the village is picturesque. Maybe when I come back to London in a couple of weeks I'll *genuinely* apply to become a member of . . ."

They could hear the telephone. "Come with me," Jane instructed.

"Hi Jane," Justin's voice said.

She shook her head, and Alex's face fell.

"What's new with you? Are you cancelling our dinner?" Jane looked forward to their Wednesday nights. They took it turns to visit, it was Justin and William's turn tonight.

"No, no. I just phoned to say we've been slightly delayed. Come over at seven thirty and you can have a drink while we cook."

"That's lovely. I have someone with me at the moment anyway."

"Would you like to bring them with you?"

"I . . . I don't think so," Jane said awkwardly.

"Well, if you change your mind . . ."

"Thanks, Justin. See you later."

"I'm sure I've overstayed my welcome." Alex heaved himself out of the comfortable chair and stretched. Kim still hadn't returned Jane's call. "Will you let me know what Kim has to say?"

"You haven't imposed, and I'll let you know the minute there's anything to tell you. How long will you be in London?"

"Till Saturday. Let me give you all the numbers where I can be reached and please, call collect. I think you call it reversing charges," he explained.

As they left the cosy study, they could hear the rain beating unmercifully on the big window behind the staircase. "It's bucketing down, you can't drive in that. At least wait until it stops."

Alex opened the front door and was forced backwards by the rain-soaked wind. "I've seen better weather," he agreed.

By six-thirty the storm showed no sign of abating.

"I have a suggestion, why don't you come with me to my friends. They'll make you very welcome. It makes no difference whether you go back now or later, it's almost dark anyway."

There was something compelling about this serene woman. Talking to Jane had been cathartic, he felt better now than he had since . . . since he could remember. He felt light-hearted, ready for anything.

"I'd love that, if your friends wouldn't mind. Besides, I'm hungry as usual."

Alex's sheepish grin was infectious.

"We'd be delighted, by all means bring him

along," William said generously. "We're having lamb so there's loads of food."

Theirs was open house, and most Sundays, they had a steady stream of visitors.

"Thanks, William." Jane looked over her shoulder and then whispered into the receiver, "Don't mention Kim Barrett if you can avoid it. I'll explain later."

"No problem," William whispered back. "Why am *I* whispering? What's your friend's name?"

"Alex Travis, he's an American."

"OK. See you soon. Drive carefully, it's skiddy out there on those fallen leaves."

Alex didn't argue when Jane suggested that she should drive. She steered around the fallen branches and piles of leaves which had formed themselves into little hillocks at the side of the lanes. Jane told Alex how they'd met Justin and William. She made him laugh as she described Justin's reaction to Mrs Grundy. Alex was looking forward to meeting them. He'd like to meet Sasha too, she sounded a real character. He glanced towards Jane and, in the dimness of the car, he could just about see her pretty face, taut with concentration. In spite of Jane's wretched marriage, she appeared to be very much together now. Very attractive too. At least she had endless opportunity to meet new people. He hoped that she would meet someone else and be happy. She was a nice person and deserved a second chance.

"Here we are," Jane announced.

Alex manoeuvred himself awkwardly out of the small car. He held the umbrella over Jane's head as they dashed up the little path to the cottage. The door was opened almost immediately. "Come in, come in," Justin urged. "What a rotten night. A night to be in front of your own fire."

Jane introduced them and they followed Justin into the kitchen where William was chopping herbs.

He wiped his hands on the big apron, shook hands with Alex and gave Jane a peck on the cheek. "Sit yourselves down. Justin, I'm sure they need a drink."

While Justin took over the cooking, William showed Alex round the cottage. His admiration was genuine. "It's perfect," he declared. "From outside it looks as though it's been here since the flood."

"A most apt comment tonight," William laughed.

Alex thought of the house on the Cape. That too had been deceptive. Forget about it, he rebuked himself sharply.

"You don't mind if we eat here in the kitchen?" Justin asked. "I like to hear what's going on."

A few minutes later he served the soup, a rich broth full of vegetables and pulses.

"Just perfect on a night like this," Alex licked his lips.

"Help yourself," Wiliam said taking the lid off the soup tureen.

"If you don't mind," Alex grinned sheepishly. "I have a disgustingly healthy appetite."

As they ate, Alex told them a little about his business and his travels, but he was just as interested in hearing how William and Justin ran their shops and how they managed to cram so much into their days.

"It must be very satisfying when you discover a rare edition," Alex said.

"Marvellous! But it doesn't happen too often these days. People are far more aware of the value of their possessions now. My brother is an antique dealer and he finds exactly the same thing," William said.

"Talking about dealers, what do you hear from Sasha?" Justin laughed.

"She's having a ball," Jane said. "Once she unloaded all her costumes, she launched a one woman assault on the shops."

They explained Sasha's trip to Alex.

"I'll miss those crazy outfits of hers all the same," Justin smiled.

"Don't worry, there are plenty of them left. You should see some of the grotesque Hallowe'en masks lurking in her room," Jane shuddered.

"Are you full that weekend?" William asked.

"Absolutely jammed."

"We're very proud of Jane. *Personal Agenda* is madly popular, people can't wait to get back to The Willows." Justin leaned across and patted Jane's hand.

"Justin," Jane objected, the colour rising in her cheeks.

"Come on Modest Mary, it's quite true," Justin teased.

"I'm sure Alex doesn't want to hear you eulogising *Personal Agenda.*"

"I certainly do," Alex assured her.

William carved another couple of slices of lamb for Alex, and he helped himself from the huge dish of garlicky, herbed potatoes. As he ate he listened to them discussing the forthcoming weekend.

"That was to kill for. If I had a hat I'd take it off to you," Alex said as he wiped his mouth on his napkin. Even he couldn't eat any more. "I cook every now and again but nothing like that."

"What about dating agencies in the States?" William wanted to know.

"There are thousands of them I'm sure. Also singles' bars, singles' shopping nights, singles' this and singles' that. The personal columns are bulging with people who want to meet their ideal partner but there are other ways too. A lot of people join night classes to meet partners with similar tastes. Some of the higher income groups volunteer to work on prominent charities. That way they mix with the wealthy donors, there are even night classes on how to meet and marry a millionaire."

"Are any of them residential?" Jane asked.

"That I don't know, but there are singles' weekends at hotels and ski-resort inns. But I think the big thing now is dating by electronic-mail. That's world-wide. But some people never get that far. Only last week I read about a couple who'd met when they went to an agency to find out how the e-mail dating worked. Neither of them were computer-minded so they gave up and went for a drink together instead!"

That appealed to Justin's sense of humour.

Alex was quite disappointed when Jane announced it was time to leave.

"It's been a lovely evening, thank you." Alex shook hands with Justin and William. "I hope we meet again."

"We hope so too," Justin said.

Jane listened to the messages on her answering machine. Three clients wanted to book places at *Personal Agenda*, and Kim had returned her call.

"It's Kim. Sorry I missed you, Jane. I'll be out fairly late tonight but will be at home until ten-thirty tomorrow morning."

As they left her little office, Jane pulled a face. "I'm sorry we missed her. I promise I'll phone first thing in the morning."

"I know you will. And now I really must be on my way. It will take quite a while to drive back in this weather. I've really enjoyed my day. Thank you for everything, Jane."

"But I haven't done anything," Jane objected.

"Trust me, you certainly have. Goodbye, Jane."

"Alex . . ."

"Yes?"

"This is probably crazy, but why don't you stay at The Willows until tomorrow. The weather is appalling and, before you leave in the morning, you can hear for yourself what Kim has to say. That is, unless you have an early appointment."

"My first appointment isn't until three o'clock. It's very tempting – weather-wise. I'd really like to stay, I don't relish the journey."

"That's settled then. I hate to think of you driving

through that awful rain. Do you fancy a nightcap?" Jane asked.

"A nightcap. What are you suggesting?"

Jane immediately began to regret her words. Had Alex misunderstood her act of kindness as an invitation?

He saw the look of dismay that flashed into Jane's eyes. "I mean what *drink* do you suggest?"

"Oh, brandy or . . . something." She felt foolish.

"The reason I asked is because I'd *love* a cup of hot chocolate. I see a tin on the shelf over there." Alex removed his coat and hung it over the back of a chair. "I haven't slept well for months and I find it very soothing."

"We often have one ourselves at night." Jane found a small pot and poured some milk into it. "How do you find the food here? Is it very different from the States?"

"Not really. Although that lunch today was fantastic. And the meal Justin and William cooked was wonderful, the best. They're very protective of you, aren't they?"

"They're super. I liked them enormously from the day we met." Jane told Alex about the invasion of ants on the morning of the house-warming party and how they dashed to her rescue. ". . . and especially as we hardly knew Justin and William then."

"You found their cottage for them, didn't you?"

"Yes. It's terrific having them so near by."

"They obviously spend quite a bit of time here too."

"They enjoy some of the activities. They know

they're welcome any time."

"Do your clients ever find it strange that two gay men take part in the weekends?"

Jane's eyes narrowed, she would be surprised if Alex had a problem with Justin and William's relationship.

"Don't misunderstand me," he said hastily. "I only ask because it's unusual to find a couple, and a well-matched one at that, at a dating agency."

Alex had Sasha's unnerving ability to read her mind. Was her face so revealing?

"They're very popular," she defended.

"I'm quite sure they must be, they're very good company. Have you had any problems with guests . . . clients? It's a big undertaking to have people stay at your home." Alex was anxious to get off the subject of Justin and William. The last thing he wanted was to upset Jane.

"Touch wood, we've been lucky so far." Jane said tapping the side of her head. "We had one guy who was a private detective and he was following a client, or spying on her, whatever the expression is. We've had a couple of difficult people, I think they expected to find someone and marry them within a few days! I doubt if we'll see them again."

"What did you do about the private eye?"

"Sent him packing. I was doubly annoyed with him because there was a candle-making session going on when I discovered what he was up to and I really wanted to watch it."

"I can see now why it's good to have Justin and Wiliam around."

"I handled the situation myself." Jane's voice was haughty.

"Expertly no doubt."

Why am I so touchy, Jane thought? That's the third time in a few minutes I've got the wrong end of the stick.

"I'm sorry, Alex, I didn't mean to sound snappy. Before I set up *Personal Agenda*, I met with a lot of scepticism, a lot of advice *not to attempt anything so foolish.* And for a time, my friends did sway me. So, if I sound defensive, I apologise. It's taken me quite a while to build up my confidence. I was burgled the day Hugh died and later that afternoon I had an offer from one of my friendly competitors to buy out my secretarial bureau. It was an opportunity to make a new life for myself against all the odds . . ."

"I think you're very courageous and I admire you."

Jane blushed. Now I'm acting like a stupid twit. "Thank you," she said regally, then burst out laughing.

"What's funny?" Alex demanded.

"I'm not laughing at you. One minute I'm full of doubts, the next I'm . . . cool! One of our clients is an American girl and *cool* is her favourite expression."

"American client, so I won't be your first foreigner?" he teased.

"Our fame has spread far and wide! Well, as far as London to be honest. Dale, our American, lives there."

"So I *will* be the first foreigner."

"Are you applying?"

"Yes, I'll become a part-time member."

"Bit of a journey to get here for a weekend?"

"I'll get Mrs Reid to plan it for me."

They both laughed.

"Seriously, if you're in London over a weekend and we have room, you'll be very welcome."

"I *am* serious. I'll be here quite a few times on business over the next couple of months and I can't think of anywhere better to spend my weekends. From all that I've heard tonight, it sounds like the place to be. Would you give me a form to fill in?"

"It would be a terrible waste of money for you. Besides, you wouldn't want to bump into Kim, would you?"

"You've changed your mind already."

"No I haven't. You'd be welcome, but as a friend, not as a client. Even better, if you do come to *Personal Agenda*, I can add the words *international clientele* to my brochure."

"It's a deal."

"I'd better show you to your room, it's late." Jane picked up Alex's damp coat. "I'll put this in the airing cupboard for you."

They stood inside the doorway of the bedroom. "You'll be comfortable here," she said.

"It's a lovely room, I'm sure I shall. Thank you again for everything, goodnight."

"Goodnight, Alex."

Alex climbed into bed, his thoughts occupied by the strange day. Tonight he would cope calmly with his insomnia. The search for Kim suddenly seemed to have lost its urgency. Jane would handle things beautifully, he was sure.

What date was he due back in London? Was it . . . Alex slept.

Jane quietly turned the key in her bedroom door. There was no point in taking chances. She removed her eye make-up and slapped a dollop of cleansing cream on her face. How could Kim have walked away from Alex without giving him a chance to explain himself? She knew that he was married. It was unfair to judge her. How did anyone know how *they'd* react in the same situation. Alex seemed to be such a sincere person. And had he fallen out of love with Kim, or was that *his* defence mechanism working overtime? How many times would she have forgiven Hugh if he'd shown even the slightest sign of contrition? Dozens probably. Jane looked at her shiny face in the mirror. Her skin was creamy and fresh, her eyes as bright as ever. How long would it be before the wrinkles started to appear and her blue eyes to fade? Would she tire of *Personal Agenda*? Were the dating agency and other people's lives enough to fulfil her own, or would she meet someone and remarry? How would I avoid making the same mistake again? How does anyone know? What would it be like to have a child? Jane loved children.

She replaced the lid on the jar and tissued off the cream. She poked a finger into the silky moisturiser and absent-mindedly dabbed it all over her face in little white blobs. She'd promised Alex that she'd talk to Kim, but would Kim resent her interference? Jane hoped that Kim would relent and talk to Alex herself. That would let *her* off the hook. Why did people seem to be hell bent on tormenting each other? Jane tried to think of any couple she knew who hadn't been through some sort of major crisis – and failed. As she climbed into bed and pulled the duvet up snugly under her chin, she was still trying to think of one.

Jane sat at the table and read her paper. She glanced at the clock on the kitchen wall, nine-fifteen and there was still no sign of Alex. He must have had a really bad night, she thought sympathetically as she started the crossword. She was completely engrossed in the clues when he came into the kitchen.

Alex smiled widely. "That was the best sleep I've had since Lincoln was a boy," he announced.

"And there was me thinking, poor Alex, tossing and turning all night. I take back my sympathy!" Jane smiled at the big athletic man. "Breakfast?"

'Wonderful, I'm starving."

Jane added another few sausages to the grill pan. She poured him some orange juice and asked if he'd like coffee or tea.

"Whatever you're having is fine."

The eggs spluttered happily in the pan. She divided the sausages, bacon, mushrooms and tomatoes between the plates. Alex was still smiling as he read the paper. Jane put half her portion on to his plate and took it to the table.

"You certainly look happy this morning," she said as the toast popped from the toaster.

"I feel it. I feel terrific."

They talked about the latest government scandal, the break up of the Wales's marriage, the difference in taxes between their two countries, crosswords and the frustrations of solving that last clue. They talked about everything except the phone call that needed to be made – and soon. Kim said she'd be leaving the flat at ten-thirty.

"I'll ring Kim now." Jane was reluctant to leave the table.

"Kim? It's Jane."

"Sorry I missed you yesterday."

"That's OK. Kim, I have a friend of yours here, Alex Travis."

There was silence at the other end of the line.

"Kim, are you there?"

"Yes, I'm here."

"He'd like to speak to you."

"I don't want to speak to him."

"Kim, he really *needs* to talk to you," Jane persisted.

"Jane, *I don't want to talk to him.* I don't know what sort of sob story he gave you, but it's over, *finis*, kaput, F-I-N-I-S-H-E-D, finished."

Jane pulled a face and shook her head. "She's adamant," she mouthed.

"Ask her will she speak to you then?"

"Kim, if you won't speak to Alex, will you tell me what happened?"

"There's nothing to tell, I found out he's a liar and a cheat. End of story."

Jane fought desperately to avoid hurting Alex. "Excuse me a moment, Kim."

Jane placed her hand over the mouthpiece. "What can I say? She doesn't want to talk to me either."

"There's nothing more you can do. Thanks for trying."

Jane stood for a moment looking at the instrument in her hand.

"Kim? I'll be in town next Tuesday, will you meet me for lunch?"

"I'd be delighted to meet you, Jane. But on your own."

"Absolutely, I give you my word. If you don't want to talk maybe you'll listen."

"Where do you want to meet?"

"How about the lounge at the Carlton Tower? It's comfortable and I hate a midday lunch, a sandwich, that OK with you?"

"That's fine. I have some shopping to do anyway."

"How's twelve-thirty?"

"See you then, Jane. And Jane, don't forget your promise."

"I won't."

Chapter Fifty-Four

Jane handed the keys of her car to the porter and made her way into the hotel. Kim was already at a table in a corner of the lounge.

"Lovely to see you," Jane said nervously.

"And you. It's really pleasant here. Great to get the weight off my feet."

Jane slid her sensibly shod feet out of sight. How did Kim walk in those heels? The waiter asked if they'd like a drink but they both settled for mineral water.

"What do you fancy?" Kim asked.

Jane looked at the menu. "Soup, I think. And cottage cheese and fruit salad."

"Kim, let's get this over with, then we can enjoy our lunch."

Kim nodded with a sigh.

"The first thing I want to say is that Alex isn't trying to pick up where you left off. It's over for him too." Jane saw the surprise in Kim's eyes.

"Then why has he been chasing me for months? For God's sake he even showed up at Kennedy Airport. Did he tell you that?"

"Yes he did. Perhaps I'd better tell you *exactly* what he told me. When he arrived back from his lecture the day you were due to leave Cape Cod . . ."

Kim's eyes opened wide as Jane described what Alex's neighbour had seen. "So she really was nuts."

"She was *mentally ill,*" Jane reproved. "The nightie Alex bought you?'

"Yes?"

"Did you cut it up?"

"Of course not! I couldn't get out of there fast enough once she showed up."

"Well then, Cassie Travis cut it up into hundreds of pieces before she left the house."

"That's sick," Kim said.

"I think that's the point Alex was trying to make. But most of all, I think he deserves to know what happened between you, and you're the only one who can tell him." Jane felt better now that she'd got it all out.

Kim sat quietly. Jane's news had obviously jolted her. Jane wondered if hearing the truth would change Kim's feelings, send her back to Alex.

"Can you imagine how I felt when this so-called *irrational* woman arrived on the doorstep. She was beautifully dressed, totally in command of herself –and me – and patronisingly sympathetic . . ."

In a flat voice devoid of any emotion, Kim repeated every minute detail of her meeting with Cassie. "So you see, you couldn't blame me for running away, could you?"

"No, I don't blame you one bit. I might have done the same thing myself. The only thing I don't understand is why, when Alex refused to give up, you wouldn't hear him out? After all what harm could there be in a conversation between two people three thousand miles apart?"

"What *good* could it do?"

Jane shrugged, they were obviously seeing things from two different points of view.

"Do you come from a happy family background?" Kim asked suddenly.

"Yes . . . I suppose I do." Jane didn't feel like discussing her parents' shortcomings with Kim.

"I didn't. I know how lousy men can be. I know what lies they tell, how they use women – children, anyone and everyone, to get their own way. And one thing I've learnt, you don't hang around for the inquest, you get out and stay out." Kim's tone was bitter.

Jane didn't know how to answer that and mumbled, "I'm sorry."

The waiter brought their soup, served in pretty flowered china bowls. They chose a roll from the large selection in a basket.

"This soup is good," Jane said. She hoped that she hadn't offended Kim, she'd been very quiet for the last few minutes.

"As a matter of interest, how did Alex know where to contact me?" Kim asked suddenly.

"I . . ." Jane was lost for an answer.

"But who told him, surely not my friend Samantha?"

"I'm sure not. I don't suppose it matters," Jane said evasively. If Kim wanted to know, then let her ask Alex.

"I'm curious, that's all," Kim said peevishly.

"Why not ask Alex?"

"No thanks. Obviously all he wants from me is information."

So Kim was hurt, or at least her pride was.

"You think I was wrong, don't you?" Kim demanded after a lengthy silence.

"Not wrong, a bit unfair perhaps," Jane said honestly.

"Maybe you're right."

"Have you seen anything of Jonathan?"

"We've been out a few times, once to his hospital dance, but I think I told you that. We had dinner together and went to a show one night. Our timetables don't match too well. We're both looking forward to Hallowe'en."

"Me too. There'll be loads of people you know. Dale, Amanda, Kevin, I think. And who else – oh yes, Evie – you remember Evie?"

"I do, she was a sweet person."

"Charles will be there and one of the Ainsley brothers – Tony. We've doubled up some of the rooms now so we're able to fit more people without being crowded. And we've asked an extra thirty clients for Saturday night."

"Sounds terrific." Kim's answer was mechanical. "What did you think of Alex?"

"I liked him. He seemed very genuine, a very nice man. Justin and Wiliam invited him to dinner – they were extremely impressed." Jane could see no reason to tell Kim that Alex had stayed overnight at The Willows, she'd had enough trouble with Sasha. When Sasha returned from her shopping spree, she was shocked that Jane had allowed a stranger into the house, let alone invite him to stay.

"He can be *very* charming," Kim said acidly.

While their coffee was being poured, Jane looked round the room. She particularly liked the huge flower arrangements, she couldn't use anything so big but she could certainly copy them on a smaller scale. There were friends having lunch, just like Kim and herself. Plenty of business meetings. From her seat Jane could see the comings and goings in the foyer. One woman was laden with glossy carrier bags from well-known designer shops and a man followed her carrying almost as many from the men's shops. As the couple passed close to their table, Jane could hear them arguing loudly in Italian.

"That would ruin any day out," Jane said quietly.

"I'd put up with a lot of grief for a day's shopping like that," Kim said.

Kim looked very attractive in a short black A-line skirt and fashionable cropped jacket and white sweater. Jane noticed that her shoes and bag matched beautifully.

"More coffee?" Kim asked as she grabbed the bill from the waiter and put it in her pocket.

"I'd love to but I promised to call in on a friend before I go home. It's been lovely seeing you. Before I go, won't you change your mind and phone Alex?"

"There's no point. You can tell him what happened. Please don't give him my number."

"You should know better than that, of course I won't. Thank you for lunch. I'll look forward to seeing you at Hallowe'en."

Somehow their meeting was soured. Suddenly

Jane was anxious to escape the warmth of the cosseted luxury and walk in the cool autumn air. As she strolled along Sloane Street towards Knightsbridge, she was aware of the people milling about her, the traffic fumes, noise. How quiet Dornley-on-Thames was by comparison. She thought of the serene duck pond, the curved terrace of quaint shops, the Drake's Inn. She glanced at the shop windows but kept on walking towards Harrods. She needed to replenish her spices, order pumpkins for Hallowe'en and have a quick look at their novelties for her flower arrangements and table decorations.

Jane dashed back to the hotel to collect her car. She tipped the porter, locked her parcels in the boot, then eased her way into the stream of traffic. She was really looking forward to seeing Susie again. They spent far too little time together these days. As far as Jane could tell, Susie and Matt had settled their differences and seemed to be happy again. The after-effects of Matt's affair had rekindled their dying marriage. Susie regarded her husband in a new light and Matt treated her like a china doll.

Susie's face was glowing. She hugged Jane. "If you hadn't come to town I'd made up my mind to drive down and see you."

"I never thought I'd say this but, apart from you and Matt, I don't miss living in London one bit. My feet are aching like mad," Jane grumbled as she took off her shoes.

"You're not used to the pavements any more," Susie said. "Go and make yourself comfortable. I'll make us a nice cupper then we can have a good chat."

"How are things with you and Matt?" Jane asked when Susie was curled up in a big easy chair. Jane was in her favourite spot on the rug beside the fire.

"Better than ever," Susie smiled. "He's unbelievably contrite and clucks around me like a mother hen. He is thrilled about the baby and will barely let me move."

"I'm pleased. I know it was difficult in the beginning, but you look radiant, Matt must be doing something right."

"He is, everything. Now tell me what brings you to our neck of the woods. You sounded so mysterious on the phone I was itching to know what you're up to."

Jane told Susie about Alex, but didn't tell her who the woman was. And Susie didn't ask. She was fascinated that any man would travel half-way across the world just to tell someone that their romance was over. Her mouth fell open when Jane explained that Alex's wife had committed suicide and that the woman she'd met for lunch today was probably the last person to see his wife alive.

"You've really aroused my nosiness." Susie admitted.

"You don't know her."

Susie and Kim *had* met but her name was better kept out of it.

"So what happens now?"

"I promised to phone him, he's back in the States."

"And?"

"And what?"

"When are you seeing him again?" Susie's eyes shone with mischief.

"Susie, you're incorrigible. I've known the man for one day."

"And one night!"

"How can you make something out of nothing? Pregnancy has warped your mind."

"Maybe, but not my hearing. Alex has made quite an impression on my protesting little friend." Susie winked her eye as she clamped her lips together.

"I'll find out all about him from Justin and William at Hallowe'en."

"Please Susie, don't. They know nothing about Alex other than that he's a friend."

"OK, I'm just teasing. But if he proposes– let me know."

"You'll be the first, I promise."

"So tell me all the news. How's the cottage coming along?"

Jane described the cottage, told her about the previous weekend and about their plans for the coming weekend. "Caroline is coming to give her talk about *cooking on a time budget*, and *power eating* – I think she calls it. It's ages since we arranged it, I hope things don't go wrong this time. We've also got a graphologist coming on Sunday, that should be fun. She's promised to do an analysis of everyone's handwriting."

"How do you think these things up?"

"I didn't, one of our clients shares a flat with the handwriting expert and she suggested it."

"I like the sound of that. What's on the cards for Hallowe'en?"

"Liz Traynor is coming back, remember, the girl who makes those fantastic candles? I'm looking forward to watching her, I missed it all last time."

"Oh yes, your snoopy detective spoilt that for you. Did you ever hear from him again?"

"Yes, he's coming to stay and volunteered to give a talk about his work. I think that could be very interesting."

"But you still haven't told me what's happening at Hallowe'en?"

"And I'm not going to! Just come in fancy dress, or black and white."

"You're full of mysteries today."

"Aren't I just! And with that, I'd better be getting back home."

"So soon? It seems like you've just got here."

"My keeper will be worried. She's totally disgusted with me, thought I was mad to let Alex stay at The Willows."

"So do I! Never mind, you've lived to tell the tale. But it was a bit dangerous."

Jane reluctantly left her cosy spot by the fire. She promised to keep in touch by phone. "Now that you're only working part-time, come down any time you feel like it."

"I may well do that. But if not, we'll see you at Hallowe'en," Susie said.

Sasha was peering anxiously into the dusk when Jane's car swept up the drive. "I was getting worried about you," she said as she helped to unload the parcels from the car.

"I'd forgotten how bad the traffic can be. I spent longer than I planned at Susie's and ran slap into the rush hour. She sends her love by the way."

"Thanks. Dump your coat while I put away the perishables. I've lit the fire and made a nice casserole, we can eat in the study."

"Sounds wonderful. But first I must phone Alex. Will dinner wait a few minutes?"

"No problem."

Jane sat in her office and dialled his number. It was the first time she'd made a call to the States and she was tickled by the strange ringing tone.

"Alex? It's Jane."

"Hi, Jane, how are you?"

"Fine, thank you. And thank you for the beautiful flowers, you really shouldn't have sent them. I've written to you but I'm sure the note hasn't arrived yet."

"It was my pleasure."

"I met Kim today, Alex. Now I can tell you what happened . . ."

Alex listened without comment until she'd finished speaking.

"Cassie must have been most convincing. I still find it astonishing that she could be so devious. And Kim? How did she react when you told her what happened to Cassie?"

"She . . . was surprised, obviously. Sorry." Now that Jane came to think about it, Kim hadn't expressed any regret.

"Well, that was nice of her."

"Yes. I think she was quite taken aback that you didn't want to continue the . . . friendship."

"That still stands. I've thought about it a lot over the last ten days. I feel as if my demons have been laid to rest. And now that you've given me the final pieces of the puzzle, I can close the book."

"I'm pleased that you have peace of mind, Alex."

"And it's all down to you. How do I thank you?"

"You already have."

"I'll be back in London at the end of next week, would you let me take you to dinner – after the weekend?

Jane hesitated. She felt uncomfortable. What about Kim, would she mind? Would she feel that Jane was being disloyal? "I don't know, Alex."

"I see, is there a problem?" he asked.

Jane played for time as she tried to find the right answer. "You're in London for the weekend?"

"I thought I'd go to London a few days earlier than I need to. If you weren't so packed all the time I'd have asked you if I could spend the weekend at *Personal Agenda.*"

That wouldn't be too difficult to arrange. Justin and William had offered her the use of their spare bedroom. And Mrs Jones's neighbour said she was always happy to let Jane have a room if she was stuck. It could do no harm to invite Alex to The Willows. That way she wouldn't be treading on anyone's toes.

"We'll always find you a room if you'd like to come. Justin and William's spare room is usually free, if not, I know someone else close by."

"That would be wonderful. I'd be very pleased to stay anywhere that you say."

"Maybe Mrs Reid would be glad of your company!"

"Don't scare me like that."

"Just testing. We'll expect you when we see you, Friday afternoon I suppose?"

"Yes. Can I get anything in the States for you? Name it, and it's yours."

"What a tempting offer! But no thanks, I can't think of a thing."

"OK. But if you do, you have my numbers, just call."

"Are you going to stay on the phone all night or what?" Sasha asked peevishly.

"I'm finished, sorry I've been so long," Jane apologised.

"Come on then, the casserole is beginning to look like a burnt offering."

While they ate, Jane told Sasha about her lunch with Kim, and what had transpired between her and Cassie Travis. Sasha's reaction was the same as Susie's – open-mouthed astonishment. "It's hard to take in," she said. "What a tragic mess. He must be a very sad man."

"I don't know what he is, but you can judge for yourself, he's coming to stay next weekend." Jane waited for Sasha's retort.

"Again?"

"Again! Don't sound so surprised. He'll be backwards and forwards quite a bit for the next couple of months. He is doing business with a client in London. He asked if we could find room for him and I said we could."

"Where are we going to put him?" Sasha demanded. "We're packed to the rafters."

"It's OK, Justin and William offered us their spare room, remember?"

"Oh yes, I forgot."

"I'll give them a ring tomorrow to make sure they don't have any of their friends staying." Jane yawned and turned her attention to the television.

Chapter Fifty-Five

Charles Graham dozed lightly and woke just in time for the interval. He'd seen the play already and it had bored him the first time. The couple he was with, two delightful but naive sisters from Connecticut, waited for him to tell them what to do next.

"I've ordered drinks in the bar," he explained. "They'll be ready for us."

"Do we go and get them?" Clarissa Bone asked.

"Yes, it's a chance to stretch your legs."

"We'll follow you if that's OK?" Jenny Bone said nervously.

Charles longed to ask them to follow him out of the theatre.

"Have you enjoyed the play so far?" he asked as he handed them their drinks – an orange juice for Clarissa and ginger ale for Jenny.

The sisters looked at each other and Clarissa spoke for them both. "It's very nice, thank you. But to tell you the truth, we really don't understand it."

Charles's eyes twinkled. "You're very honest. Now I'll tell *you* the truth. I've seen it before and I can't make head nor tail of it either."

Relief crossed their chubby faces. They were

the least likely people he'd ever escorted. Neatly dressed in black dresses with hand-crocheted collars and cuffs, Clarissa wore a cameo brooch at her neck and Jenny a golden locket. With their rosy-red cheeks and unlined faces, Charles thought that the sisters would have been more at home at a country fair than in the heart of London's theatreland.

Should he ask if they'd like to leave, he wondered?

"Does the play get better?" Jenny Bone asked timidly.

"No!" Charles laughed.

"Oh dear, oh dear me," Clarissa floundered.

"Would you like to leave now before the second act? We can go and eat a little earlier than we planned."

"Do you think the actors and actresses would be insulted?" Jenny fretted.

"I don't think they'd notice," Charles said gravely. He wished he had a pound for every time his clients had left half-way through a show. But the Bone sisters were the first ones to be concerned about the feelings of the cast.

They left the choice of meal to Charles. They weren't used to eating so late or ordering food in restaurants, except for their local pancake house. They rarely ate out.

"Shall we tell Mr Graham our secret?" Jenny asked Clarissa as if Charles wasn't there.

"I think we can trust him, don't you?"

"I'm sure we can." When she smiled, Clarissa's eyes sparkled with mischief and her mouth turned up at the corners making her cheeks plumper still.

"You see, we won the Lottery." Now they were both smiling.

He'd be smiling too if he'd won the Lottery, Charles thought. Those American Lottery prizes were enormous even if they didn't get all the money in a lump sum. That explained a lot about these two ingenuous women. "That's *wonderful*," he said and meant it.

"We still can't believe it, can we, Clarissa?" Her sister nodded her head in agreement.

"We can't," she confirmed. "Two-and-a-half million dollars."

Charles whistled softly. "That's incredible. No wonder you can't take it in."

As they ate their seafood crêpes the sisters told him the story of their life before their spectacular win. It was much as he'd imagined; they'd led a quiet uneventful existence in a small town in Connecticut. Neither of them had married but the rest of their brothers and sisters had. There were eight of them in all. Their parents had lived to a ripe old age and Clarissa and Jenny had devoted their lives to looking after them. Now they were on their own they decided to sell the house that was theirs, and bought a tiny farmhouse. One of their brothers had insisted that they sold off the land, which they did, and he invested their money for them. As a reward from the real estate broker they were given lottery tickets to fill in.

"We'd never gambled in our lives," Clarissa chuckled.

"Except the lotto at the church hall," Jenny reminded her.

"But that was in a good cause, dear."

"We decided that we must see something of the world before we're too old," Jenny continued. "It's been very exciting. We've been to New York, and to Disneyland in Florida. Now here we are in London, England."

"What made you contact our agency?" Charles asked.

"Our brother," they chorused.

"He made all sorts of arrangements for us, doesn't trust us to be sensible, I think." Clarissa gave one of her big smiles.

"He told us not to tell anyone we'd won so much money or we'd get kidnapped or mugged," Jenny said gravely.

"He's quite right," Charles agreed. "There are plenty of unscrupulous people about just waiting to take advantage of . . . of unsuspecting, kind ladies like yourselves."

Charles refused dessert but encouraged the sisters to indulge their fancy. As they examined the dessert-trolley, Charles's mind wandered forward to the rest of his week.

He was due to escort an Italian woman and her young daughter to the opera tomorrow night, and on Thursday he was meeting Amanda for a snack. He hadn't seen her for a while although they spoke on the phone once a week. She'd sounded distant the last time they talked, troubled. But she'd brushed off his concern. "I'm fine, very busy at the office."

He was looking forward to spending an evening with her again.

Charles wasn't going to The Willows at the weekend. Three of his favourite clients, a family from New York, would be in London on Friday. They'd refused to take no for an answer when Charles declined to escort them round their favourite haunts. His weekends were sacred now. But he'd agreed in the end. He liked the family enormously. Ed Korchek was a short, stocky, bluff New Yorker with a fund of incredible stories. He had a wicked sense of humour. His wife, Marti, was tall and emaciated with a long pointed face. "A salad and water gal," she claimed. Marti was well able to deal with her husband's idea of fun. Her own laconic wit and her razor-sharp retorts kept them all amused. They bickered constantly with a good-natured exchange of banter. Their teenage daughter was dragged along with them because, as Ed explained, "We don't trust Mary Jo on her own especially with those bums she hangs round with in New York."

Mary Jo's winks, nods and asides added enormously to Charles's enjoyment of their outings.

♥ ♥ ♥

Amanda brushed his cheek with her lips and dumped her parcels under her chair.

"It's ages since we've had a night out," she complained smilingly.

"Whose fault is that?" Charles challenged. "You're so busy with Kevin you've no time for me these days."

Amanda's face clouded.

"What's up?" Charles demanded. Amanda couldn't fool him for a minute.

"Nothing. Really." Her green concealer wasn't working, Charles thought as her cheeks turned fiery-red.

Charles didn't want to add to her discomfort by pushing her for more information. He told her about the two American sisters and their win. Then they took it in turn to decide what *they'd* do with the money if it was theirs. Charles spent his imaginary fortune twice over. Amanda had difficulty thinking what she'd do with hers. He could see that her attention was wandering, so he tried to amuse her by repeating some of Ed Kochek's anecdotes. The stories fell flat.

"Come on, let's get the bill," he suggested.

"I wouldn't mind, if you don't. I haven't been very good company tonight, I'm sorry, Charles."

Amanda felt sick. Sick with fear. With each successive mile her stomach churned with fear and trepidation. A car coming from the right blasted its horn, she'd gone through a red light. Amanda slowed to a crawl. She had enough to answer for already, she didn't want to add reckless driving to her list. Deceiving the company that employed her was bad enough.

Amanda had always prided herself as being law-abiding. She wouldn't even park her car on a yellow line. But in her despair she had committed one of the biggest business sins possible – espionage. Her stomach heaved. What would Coogan, Howard and Green do when they found out that she'd sabotaged their efforts? And Amanda had now convinced herself that they *would* find out.

It was ten days since Kevin had phoned. Her hand had strayed to the phone more than once. It took every ounce of willpower she had just to sit back and wait. There were ten more days before Hallowe'en, at least she'd see Kevin then.

Chapter Fifty-Six

Ray Parker was driving him mad. Donahue Reilly waited for his door to close and then scrolled down the document on his computer again. Thanks to Ray's interruptions, he'd totally lost his concentration. Ray was going to Dublin for a weekend – not manning an expedition to the moon. Such a fuss for a couple of days' holiday.

Linda Lou looked up from filing her nails. What was the matter with Ray? He was behaving like a hyperactive kid – up and down, in and out. He'd been like that all day.

In the big open room with its row of computers Ray stood behind Katie, their youngest programmer, and watched as her fingers flew over the keys. She began to falter. Spelling errors appeared on the screen as her nervousness increased.

"*That's* not right." Ray said. He bent over and jabbed a finger at an offending word.

Katie didn't feel she could tell her boss to go away. She'd been working perfectly well until he arrived, but with him breathing down her neck, her fingers and her brain refused to co-ordinate.

Ray wandered along to the coffee machine, poured himself yet another cup of the stewed, sludgy liquid and carried it back to his office. It was no wonder he was so jumpy, he must have drunk at least ten cups of coffee today. He flicked open his travel folder and checked the flight times again. Just another hour and he'd be out of here and on his way to the airport.

"Ready?" Ray asked Donahue.

Not again! Donahue felt like clocking him one. It was only ten minutes to five. "I want to finish this," Donahue said irritably.

"Can't you do it on Monday?" Ray asked. "I don't want to be late. Leave it for now, it's your *personal work* isn't it?" Ray's comment was accusing. Donahue wished that his own computer was repaired then he wouldn't have this hassle. Then he'd be only too delighted to leave early.

"Just give me another ten minutes," he pleaded.

"Too long. Come on, shut down. I really have to go."

Donahue cursed silently as a stack of papers fell and fanned themselves on the floor.

"Come on, *come on.*" Ray paced impatiently. "I've got to lock up now."

"Let me make a back-up of this and I'm out of your hair."

"Leave it, switch off now. You'll have all the time in the world on Monday."

More's the pity, Ray thought ruefully. There was so little happening at CCC at the moment they'd be lucky to keep going for more than another week.

Another two weeks, Donahue judged, and his own system should be finished. Then all he had to do was find a software house that would market it for him.

Donahue pressed the save button on the machine then searched amongst the debris on his desk for his diskettes, but couldn't find them. Furiously he shovelled his papers into his tattered hold-all, then unhooked his jacket from the clothes-stand in the corner. "I'm done. Satisfied?" he asked sharply. It wasn't in Donahue's nature to be spiteful but, as he banged the little office door with a crash, he didn't even bother to wish Ray a safe journey nor did he utter any of the usual platitudes. Frankly he was glad to see the back of him.

At last the building was empty. The computers in the main room were shrouded in their plastic dust-covers. The printers, photo-copiers and fax machines were silent as were the phones. He switched off the lights then checked the alarm, it was switched off too. Even allowing for heavy traffic, he should have plenty of time for a snack at the airport before the flight.

Kevin O'Hanlon had been very helpful when Ray phoned him. He gave Ray a telephone-tour of Dublin; places of interest, the beauty spots, restaurants and night-clubs. Kevin also gave him his friend Aidan's phone number. Kevin recommended several hotels and Ray's travel agent arranged an excellent weekend package at Jury's Hotel on the south side of the city.

♥ ♥ ♥

Ray watched eagerly through the rain-spattered windows as the bus made its way from Dublin

Airport through the city towards his hotel. There was a real buzz in the foyer as he waited to register. His room was comfortable and overlooked the main entrance. Ray pulled aside his curtain and in the forecourt below he could see a constant flow of cars, people coming and going. Suddenly he wanted to be part of it all. He unpacked his few belongings then phoned Kevin's friend, Aidan. There was no reply.

The bar was full of bright, laughing Friday-nighters – Dublin was no different from London. Why was there always a more relaxed, anticipatory atmosphere everywhere on Fridays? Pay day? A long weekend of leisure ahead? But, just as in London, he was alone.

Ray grabbed the table as a group abandoned it. Tonight he was content just to sit and have a drink. Watch and listen to everyone around him. Later he'd go to the Coffee Dock and have a meal. Ray decided that the song was right – Dublin girls *were so pretty*. He loved that soft Irish accent. Some of the girls sounded just like Jane Anderson. Jane! She was really something. He wouldn't even *dare* to invite her out. There was almost a force-field of aloofness round her. And yet she was friendly, charming and kind. Jane spent her time trying to get other people together, but of all the women he'd met at *Personal Agenda*, *she* was the one he fancied most. He was looking forward to Hallowe'en, it would be fun. He needed to organise some sort of costume for the fancy dress, but he could worry about that after Monday. In the meantime, he'd have another Scotch.

He waited till after breakfast before he tried Aidan's number again. But it just rang and rang. He consulted Kevin's list and decided to take the Dublin Bus tour. Perhaps he would meet someone interesting on that.

He was disappointed that the seat beside him on the tour was vacant. There were times he felt he was destined to spend his life alone.

Ray had heard of many of the places before; Phoenix Park of course, and Guinness's Brewery naturally – who hadn't? But Kilmainham Jail was new to him. It no longer served as a prison and had become a major tourist attraction, sometimes used for filming. Not far away was the Royal Hospital, a seventeenth century building which started life as a home for retired soldiers. It had been totally renovated and was now the Irish Museum of Modern Art. Perhaps he could visit the National Gallery tomorrow, it was a most imposing building. But after lunch today he'd go to Henry Street and Moore Street, Saturday was the best day of the week to see Dublin life, Kevin said.

Kevin was right. Ray loved the language – *gab*, Kevin had called it – of the Moore Street traders as they called out to the passers-by. They didn't allow anyone to handle the goods. The locals gave the traders as good as they got, back-answering in the same cheery manner.

At a stall which sold fish, Ray stopped to watch the owner weigh the largest piece of plaice he'd ever seen. The customer paled at the size of it. She was a slim little woman who looked as though the slightest breath of wind would blow her away.

"There ya' are, luv, a pow'ind." The trader slipped the monster fish into a plastic bag.

"Oh dear, that's far too much for me," the woman apologised.

"OK darlin'," the kindly trader said, "we'll call ih' fifty pence."

♥ ♥ ♥

There were so many places to choose from in Temple Bar. Kevin said it was definitely the most up-beat place in the city, a warren of narrow streets full of bars, cafés, galleries, shops and music. A haven for young people. He'd take Kevin's advice and eat at the Bad Ass Cafe, but first he'd have a drink.

"Anni'one sittin' here?" The girl didn't wait for a reply as she settled herself on the plush seat opposite him.

"Help yourself," Ray replied. Things were looking up. She was fresh-faced and pretty, dressed in the *mini-skirt, opaque tights* and *short jacket,* fashion must. Even though she wore quite a lot of make-up her natural beauty shone through. He stole a glance at her sweet face but her attention wasn't focused on him.

"Hi'ya, Maria," she said as another girl joined her.

"Howa'ye, Therese. Were ya' long here?" Maria was almost her clone. Their clothes were practically identical. Therese's short cropped-hair was black instead of brown, but otherwise they might have been twins. Ray wondered if they were.

"Jus' legged ih' in through the door."

"What'ya buy?" Maria wanted to know.

"A smashin' pair'a tights. Com'ere, take a look." Therese opened the bag. Maria stuck her hand in and drew out the packet.

"Smashin'," Maria agreed.

Ray's face fell, he hoped they would talk to him. But he might as well have been invisible. He glanced at the *Evening Herald* but didn't have the inclination to read it.

"Would'ya looka' tha'!" exclaimed Maria.

Ray looked up at the source of their amazement. A statuesque girl with white-blonde hair paused for effect just inside the doorway of the pub. She carried a flower-decorated crash helmet and wore a black leather jacket, shocking-pink Lycra leggings, with lipstick to match.

"Ah, here she comes, Feels on Wheels!" Therese snorted.

"Mother O'God! Wha's she done ta' her hair?"

"I dunno, but I beh' her Ma's still lookin' for the lavatory bleach."

"Watch, Therese, watch. Off wit' the jackeh'." All three pairs of eyes were riveted on the blonde.

"Greah'! Wouldn'ya know she'd be wearin' a crop top tha wouldn' fih a Barbie Doll."

Ray presumed that the short black top stretched to straining point across the girl's large breasts was called a crop top. The black blouse covering it was as transparent as glass.

"Little slapper! I heard in the fact'ry tha' she uses Velcro on the backa' her bras to save the fellas time."

As the "slapper" came towards their table Ray could see the misshapen slogan on the black top which read: *Many Have Tried.*

"Would'ya *look'a* tha'," Maria scoffed. "She shoulda' puh'; *None have failed*, on the back."

The blonde stopped at their table. She stood so close to Ray he could feel the heat of her body. "Howa'ya, Therese? Howa'ya, Maria?"

"Howa'ya, Sharon, we were jus' sayin' how grea' ya look." Therese smiled beatifically.

Ray almost choked on his drink.

"Feelin' greah' too. No dates tonigh' girls?"

"A' *course* we have," they answered in unison.

Ray could feel their eyes boring into him.

"Actually, Maria and Therese are with me," said Ray. He was as surprised as they were to hear it. The two girls looked at each other and sniggered with satisfaction.

"Wit' *you*?" Sharon asked.

They looked at her pityingly. "Have ya trouble wih' yer ears?" Maria smirked.

"Takes *all* sorts." Sharon shrugged dismissively. But she gave a Ray a sexy smile anyway.

Sharon jiggled her way to a table further down the room.

"Ta very much," Therese said to Ray. "Lihhle rip, she is, anni'one could geh' a date wih' a reputation like hers."

"I bet ya they're sellin' raffle tickets ah' tha' table. The loser gehs Sharon," Maria bitched.

"There's a fella in accountin' tha' says, she's a miracle of gen . . . geneh . . ."

"Genetic engineering?" Ray volunteered helpfully.

"Gene'hic *interfeerin* more like ih'," Therese sniffed. "Ih's a wonder wit' them boobs she can stay uprigh'. Mind'ya, she doesn't have much call for ih'." They shrieked with laughter and Maria had a look to see where Sharon was.

"You mean she's horizontally-prone?" Ray had to butt in quickly while there was a break.

"You're a greah' one for big words." Maria gave him a look. But at least she'd acknowledged his existence again. "Anni'way I knew that'ya were clever."

"How did you know that?" Ray asked.

"Because, ya big eejit, yer readin' yer paper upside down." They both roared at Maria's remark and, not wanting to be stuffy, Ray joined in.

"Can I buy you a drink?" he offered.

"Yeah, ta. Mine's a lager an' Therese's is too."

When Ray returned to the table they were arguing about where they would spend their evening. Maria wanted to go line-dancing but Therese was pushing for the disco.

"Sure we've ages ta decide. Shurrup an tell me about yer man the other nigh'," Maria instructed taking a hefty swallow of her drink.

Ray was trying to decide whether he should ask them to join him for a meal but decided to hold off for a while. Once again he'd been sidelined.

"Y'mean Sean Byrne?" Therese asked.

"Come off ih' ye chancer, how many men d'ya *know*?"

"Ih' was Tuesday nigh' . . ." Therese chose to avoid the question.

"I know *tha*," Maria scoffed.

"Are'ya goin' ta listen or gab?" Therese demanded.

"Gowon." Maria's eyes were glistening with impatience.

"Well, I was over ah' the pub and who walks in, only yer man. I wouldn' even give 'im a look. An' *no* sign of the wife, a'course. I was after ladderin' me tights on the way an' had'ta go ta the shop an' buy new ones. I was *ragin'* and nah'in the besta' humours. 'Can I buy ya drink?' says he. 'No ya can't,' says I, and turned me back on the little tyke."

Without warning, Therese turned to Ray and explained that, *yer man, Sean*, had made Mary-Margaret the supervisor instead of her. The job should have been *hers*, but Mary-Margaret never slapped his hand away when he tried to cop a feel. And he was *always* at it. Therese, seemingly, wasn't into that.

Then, like a cloud passing over the sun, Ray was blotted out again.

"I gave 'im me best ignore for the resta' the nigh'. He was swillin' pints wih' his crowd an' I was jarrin' wih' my lot."

Therese looked at her empty glass. "If ya wan' ta hear the rest, geh's a half," she said to Maria.

"Go on with your story, I'll get them," Ray said. "Same for you Maria?"

"Ta."

Ray felt involved at last. He attracted a barman's attention and ordered the drinks.

"So anni'how, ih' comes to closin' time, an' ih's lashin' outta the heavens. Yer man comes over on his way ouh' an' asks, 'D'ya wan' a lift home, Therese?' He musta been feelin' *dead* guil'hy.

"'Y'dirty ould devil, ya' can shove your lift,' I says."

"You were righ' too," Maria approved.

"Waih' now! – 'Ih's a filt'y nigh', Therese,' says he. 'And I'm only t'ree doors away from ya.'

"The others were ah' me noh' to be so stupih'.

"'Alrigh',' says I. 'But, lay a hand on me Sean Byrne, and you'll make tha' fella Bobbitt look like a Chippendale.' Ouh' to the car we went, he was dead *pol'iet.*" Therese stuck one finger down her throat and made a choking noise. "He opened the door on my side and closed ih' again when I was in. An' off we went. An' tha's when i'happened. I remembered the laddered tights in me bag." Therese stopped and took a noisy slurp of her lager.

Ray felt it was his turn to urge her to go on.

"I took them outta me bag an, din' I drape them over tha' pockeh' thing in the door on my side. Ih' was pitch black and Sean couldn' see them. Buh' he gives the wife a lift to work every mornin' . . ."

Maria squealed with delight. "Ye maggoty eejit, thah'll fix him. Go'won, tell us wha' happened next."

Ray was transmogrified.

"I dunno. Well, I sorta' know, because she goh' inta the car next mornin' and two minutes later she goh' ouh' again, yellin' and screamin' at 'im ah' the top of her lungs. I was listenin' ta' them ah' the bus stop.

"He told me ah' work he'd geh' even wit' me for tha'. I told him if he tried annithin', the wife would hear abouh' Mary-Margaret."

"Yer *terrific,*" Maria said proudly. 'A few more stunts like tha' an' we'll all be safe."

The girls found someone else to shred and this time Ray did read his paper. Or tried to. With or without a date, these two girls were having fun. They didn't need his company and, much as he'd enjoyed their acerbic wit, they were too young for him.

Was this the way he was meant to spend his life? Alone in a crowd? A fierce wave of loneliness gripped him, so strong that tears stung the back of his eyes. He lowered his head even more. How long had it been since he'd felt a loving arm around him, someone who really cared about him? Probably not since he was a little boy. Even then his parents had never been affectionate. In fact, he couldn't remember his father hugging him. He could just about recall an awkward kiss on the head from his mother. Why should it be so difficult to find someone he liked and who liked him in return? Even at *Personal Agenda*, he often felt he was on the outside looking in. Evie was nice, but not really enamoured with him. There was Jane of course, but she was beyond his reach. Sasha could be great fun. But if he did ask her out, she'd probably turn up in one of those crazy costumes of hers. Maybe things would be different at Hallowe'en. Perhaps then he'd find the right person for him. Once next week was over, he'd be able concentrate more on his social life. He must organise that costume for the fancy-dress. Next week. A shiver ran through him.

Maria's raucous laughter brought his maudlin thoughts to an abrupt end. He needed to get out of the pub, have a walk, have something to eat. The walls were closing in on him.

"Nice to have met you," Ray said to the girls as he stood up to leave.

"End yoo!" Maria mimicked his English accent.

"Thanks for tha' gargle." Therese was more polite.

As he left them he knew he'd be next on their hit list.

The Bad Ass Cafe was lively and noisy. He'd have liked to sit at a table in the gallery which overlooked the restaurant, but it was packed with regular customers. The floor was flagstone and the decor extremely Americanised – red, white and blue, the food a mixture of Mexican, steaks, pizzas and salads. Kevin had told him that their ice creams were special.

The couple at his table were deeply engrossed in conversation. He glanced briefly at the menu. The drink had dulled his appetite so he settled for a pepperoni and pineapple pizza and a salad.

The waitress took his order and placed it in a small metal cylinder. She clamped it on to its metal head, then tugged a wooden handle. The cylinder glided smoothly along a cable towards the kitchen. As he watched the tube swaying on its way it took him back to his childhood. The thrill of being allowed to stand on a shop-counter and pull the handle of a cylinder just like the one above his head.

The waitress returned with his Coke and a demijohn of wine for the other couple. He listened to her explain that the jug held twenty-four glasses of wine, they would only be charged for what they drank.

The man filled their glasses and looked briefly at Ray.

"A glass of wine for you?" he asked.

"No thanks." Ray pointed to the glass of Coke. An hour ago he would have jumped at the chance to talk to them but now he couldn't be bothered to make the effort.

His pizza and salad arrived a few minutes later. He picked at them both uninterestedly. He refused a dessert and asked for his bill.

Ray walked down the narrow street and through the arch which led to the river. He stopped for a moment, facing him was the famous Ha'penny Bridge. A taxi coming towards him slowed and he hailed it impulsively. He gave up the idea of going to a club.

♥ ♥ ♥

Early next morning for lack of anything better to do, Ray dialled Aidan's flat once more. To his surprise his call was answered. Aidan was pleasant, eager to hear about Kevin – but busy. He said that if Ray came to Dublin again he must give him a few days' warning and he'd be delighted to show him the sights.

He pottered around the hotel, ate a far bigger breakfast than he wanted, and decided to explore the city on foot. He walked through Stephen's Green and along Dawson Street. He stopped to look at the attractive Mansion House then went on towards Trinity College. He was delighted to be sidetracked by a branch of Waterstone's. That took up the rest of his morning.

Ray lost all sense of time as he became absorbed in the paintings in the National Gallery. In the end the day passed all too quickly, and his spirits had lifted a little. He walked back to the hotel to collect his case. His flight to London was due to leave at seven-thirty and he'd timed it nicely.

♥ ♥ ♥

"This is Donahue. Ring me any time up till midnight. It's urgent."

Ray glanced at his watch. It had just turned ten o'clock. He switched off the answering machine, turned on the television, and settled himself down with the remote control and a can of Coke.

Chapter Fifty-Seven

When the phone rang at midnight, Ray Parker pressed the volume button on the television remote control and increased the sound.

"Donahue again. Thought you might be back by now. See you tomorrow."

Ray lowered the sound. Tomorrow would be soon enough.

They all stood together in the empty room; the programmers with their shocked looks, Donahue red-faced and agitated, Linda Lou and Ray. Dozens of wires trailed forlornly from the wall sockets and ended abruptly in tangled confusion on the anti-static carpet.

"You're a key holder?" The detective broke the silence.

"Of course I am, you phoned me didn't you?" Donahue's reply was sharp, bordering on insolence.

"And you, sir. You're a key holder too?" The policeman turned his attention to Ray but his jaw muscles were chomping with anger.

"Yes. CCC is my firm." Ray's face was pale, his voice was low and controlled, well-practised.

'We weren't able to contact you?"

"No, I was away for the weekend – in Ireland."

"And what about you, do you have a key?" he asked Linda Lou.

"Not me. I'm only a secretary, strictly a nine-to-fiver."

The detective took his time. He questioned each of them in turn. As he noted their replies, Ray watched another man moving from room to room. He brushed dark powder on the damaged outer door, the interior doors, the desks, the alarms, the light switches and the window sills. Bag in hand, he came back to the denuded computer room and shook his head. "Nothing," he said to the detective.

"Do you have a list of the missing items?" A uniformed sergeant took over.

"Yes. I'll get it for you," Ray said faintly. "If you don't mind coming into my office – I . . . I'd like to sit down."

The sergeant followed Ray along the corridor to his office.

Ray picked up an overturned chair and offered it to the policeman. "If you've finished with the others I'll tell them to go home."

"Yes, I don't think they can be of any further help."

"There's nothing we can do for a couple of days," Ray said calmly to the little group. "I suggest you all leave now. Come in on Wednesday morning, unless you hear otherwise. It'll take me a day to get over this, to get myself together. In the meantime I'll try and organise some temporary computers. Don't worry about your pay packets, they'll be taken care of as usual. You might as well look on this as a couple of days' paid holiday. Donahue, hang on a moment, I'd like a word with you."

Linda Lou's frown vanished. She was relieved to hear that they'd be paid. She led the programmers from the room. Ray heard their footsteps on the stone steps outside. "I wanted to know . . ."

"Where the hell were you last night?" Donahue interrupted angrily.

"I got back to London fairly early and decided to call in on a friend . . ."

"Didn't you get my messages?"

"I did, but I didn't think you'd appreciate a call at two o'clock in the morning. Besides, what difference would it have made, we couldn't have stopped this, could we? It happened on Saturday night, the policeman said. I must get back to the sergeant. Wait here till he's gone then we'll talk." Ray shook his head as he looked at the desolate wires, all that was left of a fully equipped high-tech computer centre. "By the way, did they ask *you* for the list of items that were stolen?"

Donahue shook his head, his face sullen.

Ray sat on his desk, the sergeant occupied the only remaining chair.

"I wonder why they left this desk and chair?" Ray asked.

"Maybe they were disturbed," the sergeant suggested. "So that's all you can remember for the moment?"

"Off hand, yes. Sixteen, or was it seventeen, computers, two fax machines . . . without my documentation . . ."

"I understand, it's been a shock. You can ring the station if there's anything else . . ."

"You know, I can understand them stealing the filing cabinet, but what use are the files? All our receipts were in that cabinet, our records, our contracts . . . everything. Every bit of paper work . . ." Ray rubbed his hand over his face and groaned. "Where do I begin? . . . "

The sergeant rose to his feet. He certainly didn't envy the fellow his task, but it wasn't nearly as bad as some robberies he'd seen. Apart from one smashed door, there was no damage. Mr Parker could count himself lucky there. He'd seen buildings reduced to a shambles, every window and door smashed, walls defaced, furniture chopped into little pieces. This wasn't the worst by a long way.

"We'll be in touch if we have anything to report," he told Ray.

"Why are *you* so angry?" Ray asked Donahue.

"Why am *I* so angry? Thanks to you and your rush on Friday, I've lost *months* of work, *that's why I'm angry*. Weeks and months of working all night. *That's* why I'm angry. My diskettes have been stolen. My system gone. You couldn't wait *three* more minutes, could you? Three miserable, sodding minutes while I made copies. And now it's all gone. You lousy selfish, bastard, they're *gone*." Donahue's voice ended in a roar.

"But surely you must have back-ups at home?" Ray reasoned.

"They're completely out of date. Both sets of diskettes were here, I told you that on Friday. My back-ups were here."

"I'm sure you'll be able to remember what you did."

Donahue snorted derisively. "Are you? Well I'm *not.* That's probably the most ignorant statement you've ever made. And believe me, you've come out with some beauts in your day."

"I'm really sorry, Donahue."

"Sorry won't make up for it." Donahue's voice was almost inaudible.

At least he'd stopped shouting. Ray wondered what he could say to diffuse Donahue's fury. "I've lost my diskettes too. I've lost computers, printers, faxes, photo-copiers . . ."

"I know what you've lost. Well I've got one more item for your *lost* list – me. Add that to your bloody list."

"Don't be ridiculous, you're just upset. When you've calmed down it won't be so bad."

"Oh, go to hell."

"Donahue, do you think for one moment I would purposely put your work at risk? After all these years together can you look me in the eye and say that?" Ray struggled to find something that would calm the man.

"I didn't say that you did it deliberately, but three more minutes, Ray."

Donahue looked beaten.

"You can walk out of here now if you can honestly say that I don't appreciate your loyalty, your competence, your ability. You *know* how much I value you." Ray was sincere in this. It was too late now but he wished he'd let Donahue have those extra few precious minutes to make his copies.

Donahue didn't reply. He slumped in the chair, dejected.

"I'll tell you what, why don't we hire a

computer for you today – now. Have it delivered to your house. Take a week off, or however long it takes and spend your time on your own work. How does that sound?"

"A week? You must be out of your mind, it'll take months, more – if ever."

"The quicker you start the fresher everything will be in your mind. I'll come round and help you if you like."

"You couldn't help, no one could."

"So what do you say? I'll phone right now on my mobile."

"I suppose so," Donahue sighed.

Ungrateful bastard, Ray thought, but kept his mouth shut. He'd be in a sorry state if Donahue left.

"It will be delivered to your house between four and five this afternoon," Ray confirmed.

Donahue dragged himself off the chair and started for the door. Ray's offer was better than nothing, especially as he'd been informed that his own computer was still not ready. And it was beginning to look as though it never would be.

"Just a minute, I'll give you your pay-cheque now. Save you a journey at the end of the week."

Ray took his personal cheque-book from his inside pocket. He added a hundred pounds to Donahue's normal salary. "That will pay for any extras you need."

"Thanks," Donahue said glancing at the amount.

"Off you go. Keep in touch."

"Will you manage here?"

His question was music to Ray's ears, Donahue's threat to resign, avoided.

"You just concentrate on yourself. That's your main priority at the moment." He tried not to sound obsequious.

Ray spent the next hour on the phone. He spoke to his insurance broker, talked to a company who agreed to let him rent three computers at an exorbitant rate. He hired a photo-copier and fax from a reluctant supplier with whom he'd tangled in the past. A carpenter agreed to board up the door temporarily. Ray's final call was to the service department of the alarm company although the last thing he needed at the moment was the protection of an alarm.

Now all he had to do was to go home and wait for the phone call from the man in the pub, the man he'd christened, *You Know.*

♥ ♥ ♥

By eleven o'clock Ray was sure he'd made the biggest mistake of his life. He'd trusted a stranger. All his elaborate plans had come to nothing. His heart began to race alarmingly, and he could feel the blood pounding in his head. Everything he owned was in that building and he was probably going to lose a packet on the insurance as well. He would have to 'embroider' the list considerably . . .

He was on his feet in a flash when the phone rang.

"Hello, it's er, you know," a muffled voice said. "I phoned to tell you that *Aunty is over the operation and it was a success.*"

"I'm very pleased to hear it," Ray said calmly. "Tell her I'll pop in and see her as soon as I can."

He slipped his hand into his pocket, the folded cheque crackled as he touched it. He'd had no problem finding a taxi and within minutes he was on his way to their prearranged meeting spot.

A man stepped from the shadows. Ray stayed where he was until he was sure it was *You Know*.

The man said, "Have you got the cheque?

"What kept you?" Ray asked.

"Things. Have you got the cheque?" he asked again.

Ray gave it to him. *You Know* handed him a key and a scrap of paper. Ray glanced at the address.

"That's it then," he said to Ray. "Good luck." Within seconds he'd disappeared back into the shadows, Ray could hear his footsteps echoing in the darkness.

Ray did a little jig in the dark, quiet street. As he reached a lamppost he held the piece of paper under its dingy light and memorised the address *You Know* had given him. He slipped the key of the lock-up into his pocket and, as he walked, he shredded the paper, threw it into the air then watched the tiny scraps drift away on the breeze. What a shame he couldn't give Donahue his precious diskettes back, but he daren't risk it. All that was left to do now was fill out the claim forms and he was home free.

•

Chapter Fifty-Eight

Alex Travis slowed his pace until the digital counter gradually returned to zero. The fitness-centre and swimming pool on the lower ground floor of his apartment block had proved to be a real bonus. It was usually quiet at night. He liked to start with a work-out on the treadmill then enjoyed a swim. More often than not, he had the azure-tiled pool all to himself.

Still in his terry robe, he took the elevator to his seventh-floor apartment. He was satisfied that he'd made the right decision. He showered and sat at his desk to revise his schedule, a mug of steaming hot chocolate in front of him.

Jane had sounded genuinely disappointed when he phoned to tell her that his trip had been postponed until the following week. He could have spent the extra week in London, he was sorely tempted. It troubled him that he could so easily tumble from one relationship to another. A relationship which, so far, was all in his mind. He tried to rationalise his feelings for Jane, but couldn't. He'd spent *one* day with her. Was he impetuous or just plain crazy? He'd asked Jane if he could take a rain check until the following weekend.

"Hallowe'en . . . you know Kim will be here?" Her voice faltered.

"I understand – it was just a thought." Alex allowed the silence to hang between them.

"Are you still there, Alex?" she asked.

"I'm here."

"As I said, I'm really sorry you can't make it this weekend."

"I am too. Perhaps I could call you?" He didn't say when.

"I'd like that."

Their conversation ended abruptly. He felt deflated. What could Jane do? Why should she jeopardise her business, risk losing a client for his sake?

Alex's perfect formula for sleep deserted him. The combination of exercise and hot chocolate failed as his thoughts fluttered restlessly. Maybe he should phone Jane again. What time was it in England? That was another thing, the time difference between their two countries was infuriating. As the dawn light filtered into his room, Alex finally slept.

♥ ♥ ♥

"Why are you so crabby?" Sasha asked unceremoniously.

"I'm not crabby," snapped Jane. But Sasha was right, Alex's phone call had left her in turmoil. She'd been looking forward to seeing him again. She'd flown through her work, planned to have her hair restyled and treat herself to a new dress for Friday night. She could still have done all that the following week, but then there was the problem of Kim Barrett. She and Alex couldn't be at The Willows together. Blast her anyway. Kim would be with Jonathan, how many men did she want?

"Come on, spit it out. There's something wrong, I can smell it," Sasha insisted.

"Smell what? Oh, the cake! I forgot the cake." Jane dashed into the kitchen and grabbed a cloth. She practically threw the burnt-offering, still in its tin, onto the sink top.

"A cinder-cake, how interesting!" Sasha said.

"Belt up, anyone can make a mistake."

Sasha took the cloth from Jane's hand and led her to the table. "Sit down," she commanded. "Now, let's have it."

"Alex has cancelled for this weekend."

Sasha waited.

"He wants to come next weekend instead." Jane pulled a face. "How can I do that to Kim?"

"But Kim . . . she'll be with Jonathan. She's not interested in Alex, so what's the problem?"

"You are dim at times."

"You mean she *is* still interested?

"How can a . . . romance, affair of that intensity end just like that? I'm not saying that she is dying of a broken heart, but, let's face it, the air needs to be cleared between them. I think she'd have a pink-fit if she arrived at *Personal Agenda* and found Alex here."

"I see. So what you're saying is, that although Kim doesn't want him, you shouldn't have him either? Good thinking, Jane. What a great martyr the world has lost." Sasha's voice was tight with disgust.

"And what would *you* know about love affairs?" Jane retorted, stung by Sasha's sarcasm.

"Enough to know a fool when I see one."

"My God, how can you stand there and say that after the ridiculous spectacle you made of yourself over Charles?" This was turning into a full scale row and Jane hated rows. "This is getting us nowhere. That was unforgivable, I'm sorry Sasha."

"I asked for it. Why are you apologising? Why won't you learn that there's a difference between sensitivity and sensibility? *You're* entitled to a life too. If having Alex here makes you happy, to hell with Kim. And if your long face is anything to judge by, you'd like Alex to be here that weekend, right? And Jane, now that we're into home truths, I must say that I'm not surprised that you lost the battle with Hugh . . ."

"Sasha!"

"Let me finish! I'm only going by what you told me. You didn't even fight for him. You just sat there passively and watched him living a life in which there was no place for you. You didn't *make* a place for yourself. You let him walk all over you, fill your house with people you couldn't stand. And what did you do? Ask them to leave? Tell Hugh to ask them to go? No! You hid yourself away, behaved like an intruder in your own home . . ."

"*That's enough*, Sasha," Jane lashed out.

"Ah! Now you're talking."

Jane rose from the chair, she couldn't trust herself to say anything more. She'd put up with a lot from Sasha over the months but this was intolerable.

Jane sat on the edge of her bed seething with anger and indignation. Of all the low, mean unfeeling remarks . . . how could Sasha say those terrible things? How could Sasha possibly understand the heartbreak she'd felt, waiting, hoping that Hugh would realise . . .

"Jane?" Sasha tapped lightly on the door.

"Go away, Sasha."

"Please, Jane, open the door. I'm the one that should be hiding, not you. Maybe now you see what I mean?"

Sasha was right. She was the one who should apologise, the one who should have had more feeling, more tact.

"Jane, *please* may I come in?"

"The door's open," Jane said wearily.

"I had no right to speak to you like that," Sasha gulped, tears streaming down her face. "Please forgive me. There's no one in the world . . . you're the one person . . ."

"How could you say those terrible things?" Jane couldn't bring herself to look at Sasha.

"I couldn't bear to see you throw away a chance to be happy . . ." Sasha sniffed then dashed away the tears on her sleeve. "I'm afraid I'll say the wrong thing again."

"Then don't say anything."

"What I mean is, you . . . you *like* Alex. Whether you admit it or not, there was a song in your voice after his visit. A gleam in your eye that wasn't there before. And that's why it was so hard to hear you say 'no' to him because of that hard little piece Kim." Sasha had been appalled when she learnt how Kim had walked out on Alex.

"I appreciate your sentiments," Jane said stiffly. "But that doesn't excuse the awful things you said about Hugh, about me."

"I spoke without thinking, tactlessly. What I meant was that *you* were right, but you allowed Hugh to make you feel the guilty one. You made it too easy for him."

"Have you ever really loved someone? Made excuses for them when they were at fault? Turned a blind eye because you didn't want to see what was under your nose? Loved someone so much that you'd walk over hot coals for them?"

"No, I haven't. And I don't think I ever could go on loving someone who hurt me so much. But that's the way I am. I wouldn't hang around for more."

"You're probably more sensible than I am, but, to quote you – *that's the way I am.* That's the way I felt about Hugh. In time I learnt not to care. But it took a long time. Maybe you are right and I was wrong, it's academic now."

"No, Jane, it's not. Invite Alex, give yourself a chance to get to know him. Kim wouldn't give *you* a second thought."

"I'll think about it."

"Am I forgiven?" Sasha asked in a plaintive voice.

"I suppose so," Jane said unenthusiastically. Sasha deserved to suffer too.

It took Jane all her courage to phone Kim. She'd made up her mind that if Kim was there well and good, but if not, she wouldn't leave a message. Kim answered after the third ring.

"I'll come straight to the point," Jane said with false bravado. "Alex was due to come to The Willows this weekend but can't make it. Would it upset you if he was here at Hallowe'en instead?"

The silence at the end of the line seemed endless. "No, it wouldn't bother me. As long as *he* doesn't bother me," Kim added quickly.

"I think that's highly unlikely. He knows you'll be here and is unconcerned," Jane said bitchily. "I wanted to check with you first. We've had a cancellation and he might as well avail of it."

"If it doesn't worry him, I'm happy."

"I'll let him know that there's a place for him. See you Friday week?"

"See you then."

Jane waited until Sasha was out of earshot. Her hands were shaking as she lifted the receiver to phone Alex. His secretary put her on hold. Music jangled in her ears and after a few minutes she lost her nerve and hung up.

Alex phoned back five minutes later.

"I'm so sorry you were kept hanging on like that. A client was leaving and I went outside to say goodbye."

"We were cut off," Jane fibbed, ashamed now that she'd been so cowardly. "I've just had a cancellation for next week and wondered if you'd still like to come to The Willows?"

"You bet. But, what about Kim? You seemed anxious about her."

"I've spoken to Kim. There's no problem. She

is seeing someone that she met at *Personal Agenda*. Jonathan will be here too. Is that OK with you?"

"I told you, it's over. A closed chapter."

Jane waited until they were having dinner before she told Sasha the news.

"I'm glad," was Sasha's only comment. She'd said more than enough for one day.

Chapter Fifty-Nine

Derby's was buzzing with anticipation. People scurried around with armfuls of paper, phones rang incessantly. Everyone was on edge.

Kevin O'Hanlon followed the Art Director and the rest of the teams into the boardroom. The pine table was set out with notepads, pens, bottles of mineral water and glasses. In one corner there was an elaborate floral arrangement and opposite, at eye level, a television set on a wall bracket had been swung into place.

Kevin was introduced to Stourley's Chairman, Walter Cox, and his two advisers. When they were all seated Kevin tried not to let his eyes stray in Cox's direction. But he couldn't resist the odd glance or two as Derby's Art Director, Stanley Gibbs, began the presentation.

Walter Cox was all-powerful and he knew it. His body language was aggressive. Kevin could sense it and it made him uneasy. Stanley Gibbs began the pitch with facts and figures but Kevin barely heard him. Finally it was his turn. His hands were clammy and his throat felt dry. Take your time, don't blow it, he told himself sternly as he took a sip of water.

"We've decided to avoid the obvious, the

banal," he began. "Two men, one hungover, the other, the Stourley man . . . You get the picture, the bright and breezy Stourley man chats with his boss, the other one is half dead at his desk . . . routine," Kevin said dismissively. He spoke slowly and deliberately, punching home each point – the very essence of Coogan, Howard and Green's storyboard. Everything at which Amanda had blatantly hinted.

Walter Cox scribbled furiously in his slim leather notebook. Kevin slowed even more. He noticed the look which passed between the three men and was satisfied that his message had hit home. He caught a glimpse of Stanley Gibbs's face out of the corner of his eye and could imagine his impatience. What Derby's decided not to do was of little importance, a negative approach. But then Stanley Gibbs didn't have access to the information that he did.

What the hell was Kevin playing at, why was he wasting time? Stanley Gibbs fidgeted uneasily with the remote control. Cox was taking notes and that made him nervous. The sooner they got on with this the better. "Kevin, gentlemen, if you're ready?" Stanley Gibbs took advantage of the lull. "I'll switch on now, lights down please, Kevin."

Walter Cox nodded his balding head. No emotion showed on his pinched, bony face. His eyes, glacially-grey, were chilling and the narrow lips on his downturned mouth reached almost to his chin; a cold, unfeeling automaton, full of his own sense of importance. If the bags under Cox's eyes were anything to go by, a workaholic too. Kevin disliked him on sight but he put his own feelings aside, Walter Cox was still the man he needed to impress.

The opening scene of the advertisement flashed onto the screen in the darkened boardroom – a cartooned party in full swing. Music played and cans popped. Cans of Stourley's hangover-free lager were clearly visible in the foreground. The scene changed. The party was over and the cartoon guests, with rubbery legs and rumpled party clothing, stumbled and staggered into taxis and cars.

Kevin had taken good care that only the sober guests were shown driving cars, otherwise there'd be a flood of objections from viewers. Catchy modern-rock music echoed round the boardroom. It was daylight on the screen. A glamorously-drawn woman with jet-black hair, an impossibly tight red dress and a five inch waist, swayed seductively to the rhythm as she vacuumed the floor. In an upstairs room, the cartooned walls expanded and contracted to each beat of the music. The figure of a man who was obviously suffering emerged from beneath the bedclothes. His head swelled and shrank in sympathy with the walls. Each painful step he took was accompanied by the dull thump, thump, thump of the bass. He finally made it down the stairs and tapped the swaying woman on the shoulder. His eyes, in close up, were crackled and bloodshot. The light was glaringly bright and, here too, the walls were moving. She switched off the vacuum cleaner. He held his head and collapsed into the nearest armchair. The screen was silent. The walls were still. She looked at him compassionately and shook her head. In close-up and with a rock-steady hand, she poured a glass of Stourley's hangover free lager from a can, and handed it to him. From beginning to end not a word was spoken.

The radio advertisement used the same musical theme, but this time with a well-worded script.

Kevin felt like the man in the ad, used and broken. Had he pulled it off? Would Walter Cox like it? It was impossible to read Cox's expression, the faces of his two companions were equally inscrutable.

"Interesting concept." Walter Cox shook Kevin's hand. Cox's hand was cold and damp.

"Thank you," Kevin replied but Cox didn't appear to hear him.

"We'll be in touch," Walter Cox told Stanley Gibbs.

"Kevin, can I have a word?" Stanley Gibbs frowned.

Kevin followed him towards his office. He was going to enjoy this, and so would Stanley.

Chapter Sixty

The car that screeched to a halt at the front door was a growler. Long, low, red and powerful. Jane watched from behind the curtain as the driver got out. The woman was tall and skinny with a mane of fiery auburn hair that glinted in the rays of the late afternoon sun. Adelaide Sydney McCall whom, Charles said, liked to be called Lady, was a model turned fashion editor. She was casually dressed in a cream jacket under which Jane caught a glimpse of a caramel coloured waistcoat and trousers. The long scarf draped round her neck picked up the cream of her blouse and toned perfectly with her waistcoat. Even her luggage matched the ensemble. "Three, four . . . five. Five cases for a weekend! What on earth does she think this is, a fashion parade?" Jane said aloud in amazement. "My God, now I'm talking to the curtains!"

"Welcome to *Personal Agenda*," she said, taking one of Lady's cases.

"I have three more," Lady confessed.

"I'll give you a hand," Jane offered.

They brought them inside and just as Jane was about to close the front door, Alex's car turned into the drive. Jane's heart gave a little skip of pleasure.

"Would you excuse me a moment?" she said to Lady. "Leave your cases here and help yourself to a drink. There's tea and coffee through there." Jane pointed to the open living-room.

They greeted each other warmly, Alex took both her hands in his own.

"What are in all those bags?" Jane asked Alex. Everyone was weighed down with luggage today.

"Wait and see. Help me carry them?"

The coloured paper-bags were light and Jane took hold of all six of them at once.

Alex smiled at her, she looked so pretty with that new short hairstyle, gamin.

"Did you have a good flight?" she asked as she set down the bags in the hall.

Alex nodded but didn't answer, he was looking at the pumpkins with their carved faces.

"Sorry, yes, the flight was fine. I was admiring the art work, they look terrific."

"Sasha and I had great fun doing them. Here's Sasha now."

Jane introduced them and noticed a tiny smile lift the corner of Sasha's lips. She approves of him, Jane thought.

Sasha busied herself with coffee for Lady, while Jane poured a drink for Alex.

"Would you like to open the bags now while you have a quiet minute?" Alex asked when Sasha and Lady disappeared upstairs.

Alex spread them in a row at her feet.

"I'm really curious," Jane admitted as she delved inside.

She gazed at the contents spread out on the floor. Witches' faces and hats, large and small, wonderfully frightening masks, gold stars and new moons, full-length cardboard skeletons with moveable arms and legs. "Oh Alex, they're fantastic, how thoughtful. We can use them all."

"I had a ball buying them. Hallowe'en is a big thing in the States, I used to love it as a kid, trick-or-treating. Do you do that here?"

"I did – in Ireland. Here Guy Fawkes night is more popular, the fifth of November."

Alex nodded. "I remember that now. Would you like me to help you put any of these things in place?" he asked.

"You go and unpack, I'll manage."

Sasha joined them. She waxed lyrical as she examined the goodies. "They're brilliant," she exclaimed as she danced round the room with one of the skeletons. "Look at those moons and stars, wouldn't they be fantastic on the curtains in the dining-room. There are so many of them we could put them in every room."

"Just peel the little sticker off the back and they'll cling to fabric. They won't damage anything." Alex was pleased she liked them. Sasha was dressed quite normally in jeans and a sweater, he'd expected someone far more bizarre.

"You show Alex to his room," Sasha said. "I'll get started on these."

Jane danced downstairs on light feet. It was going to be a terrific weekend. She was sorry that she wouldn't have a lot of free time to spend with Alex, but he was here and she was glad.

Her heart sank as the car drew up. Kim and Jonathan had arrived.

Jane handed the funny little witch to Sasha. "Put it over there, I'll open the door for Kim and Jonathan."

"Stay cool!" Sasha instructed as she watched the light in Jane's eyes die. "Just listen to me, two minutes in Dale's company and I've already picked up her expressions."

Jonathan, much to Jane's surprise, hugged her warmly. "I can't tell you how much I've been looking forward to this. Two and a half blissful days – and not a phone or a pager in sight."

"Nice to see you both again," she said. Well, it was nice to see Jonathan.

They knew the ropes by now. Jonathan poured himself a Scotch, Kim preferred tea.

Dale and Tony Ainsley chattered as they came down the stairs and Amanda and Charles followed behind with Ray Parker in their wake.

"Quite a reunion," Tony said. "Has Evie arrived yet?"

"Not yet," Jane said.

Alex and Lady met on the stairs.

"Lady McCall," she said. "As in short for Adelaide."

"Alex Travis."

"Nice to meet you. Where's home for you? London, I suppose."

"Washington DC."

Lady's eyebrows rose but, before she could reply, the mobile phone in her shoulder-bag bleeped. She followed Alex down the remainder of the stairs and into the living-room, firing instructions down the line as she walked.

"There, sorry about that. Washington DC you said? So what brings you here?"

"Would you like a drink?" Alex asked, avoiding her question.

"I'm far more interested in hearing about you."

"Oh, I'm not very interesting. What do you think of this lovely house?"

"Lovely," Lady said without moving her eyes from his face. "What do you . . ." Her phone rang again.

Alex escaped to the other side of the room and stood apart from the others as he sipped his drink. He'd met Lady's type before and knew exactly how to deal with her.

"Charles Graham – you must be Alex." The two men shook hands and out of the corner of his eye Alex could see Lady crossing the room.

"Do me a favour," Alex said, "Hang around for a minute."

"There you are!" Lady gushed. "Terribly sorry about the calls, there's a panic on at the magazine. Fashion editor – never off duty."

"Hello, Lady," Charles said.

"Charles." She acknowledged him briefly. "Now, Alex, what were we talking about?"

"Alex, let me introduce you to one of your fellow-countrywomen, or should that be countryperson?" Charles steered them both over to where Dale, Amanda, Tony and Ray were standing in a group. Lady struck Tony and Ray off her eligibility-list. The handsome American was more her type.

Tony welcomed Evie with a hug, and Lady went to find Jane. She'd ask Jane to put her next to Alex at dinner.

"I'm sorry, Lady," Sasha said. "But the table has already been planned."

"It won't take a second to change it. I'll do it for you if you like," Lady offered.

"Sorry, I'm afraid not." Sasha said firmly.

"Where is Jane? I'd like to speak to her," she asked in a cold voice.

"I shouldn't bother, Jane leaves the table arrangements to me."

Lady left the kitchen in a huff.

Boy she's pushy, Sasha thought. Jane will have her work cut out with that madam. Not that she blamed Lady, Alex was a lovely bear of a man. She'd liked him the instant she met him. Imagine being thoughtful enough to bring those Hallowe'en masks and decorations all the way from America, and not a crushed one amongst them. It's no wonder Jane was disappointed when he couldn't make it last week. Now she was delighted that she'd bullied Jane into inviting him.

Jane refused to go into the living-room. She didn't want to be there when Kim and Alex came face to face.

"It would be better if you did," Sasha insisted. "Anyway, Kim is the least of your worries from what I can see. Lady's hanging on to him like a limpet mine – in between phone calls. She came floating in here a few minutes ago and asked me to change the table plan. What a neck. But Alex isn't interested. Every time she catches up with him he runs the other way!"

"Hello, Alex." Kim's face was pale.

"Hi, Kim." Alex answered calmly.

"I was sorry to hear about your wife, sorry the way things turned out. I hope there are no hard feelings between us." There, that was over and done with.

"None. I don't think either of us would be here if there were." Alex hadn't been looking forward to this moment, unsure of his emotions when he saw Kim again. But now that he stood facing her, he had no regrets. It was finally over.

"I'd like to introduce you to someone." Kim's tone was tentative.

"OK," Alex said affably.

"Jonathan Campbell-Smith, Alex Travis." Kim watched the two men shake hands. Alex appeared to tower over Jonathan's slight frame although there were only two or three inches difference in their heights. Alex was slimmer than she remembered and, if she was honest, better looking too. Even though she knew Alex would be here, it had given her quite a jolt when she saw him again. For a moment she wondered what would happen if she gave him any encouragement? Had he really recovered from their affair? Had she?

"What do you think of this hideaway?" Jonathan asked Alex.

"Wonderful," Alex said. "I love the village, the whole area."

Their conversation was interrupted by Jane as she introduced Robert Gill to the three of them. Jill Wells was the last to arrive, a serious-faced girl with a shy manner. Jill reminded Alex of one of those old black and white movie heroines. Remove her glasses, unpin her hair, and she'd turn into an absolute beauty.

Lady made her entrance in a sensational white and gold suit. Her hair was twisted and coiled into a sophisticated knot. She looked as though she'd just stepped from the hairdresser's. Her gold jewellery was just right – not too little, not too much. Jane had to hand it to her, Lady certainly knew how to make the best of herself.

As Ray edged his way to her side, Lady deliberately moved away. She made her way over to Kim and Jonathan. Jonathan looked quite interesting, a possible alternative to the American.

♥ ♥ ♥

The table was fully extended and looked magnificent. It had taken Jane the whole of the previous afternoon to create the centrepiece, a cascading autumnal arrangement of lemon, orange and gold flowers intertwined with fruit and nuts. In front of each place setting was a floating candle in a crystal glass. Tucked here and there were the stars and moons which Alex had brought.

As they waited for Sasha to serve the first course, Lady's mobile phone rang again. Jonathan's hand automatically went to his belt. He smiled with relief – it wasn't his problem.

Alex studied Jane's face. If she was angry with Lady, it didn't show. He couldn't see the need for a phone on an occasion like this. He loved Jane's hair, it was so stylish. Her blue beaded blouse sparkled in the candlelight but no more brightly than her eyes. In spite of her sophisticated blouse and elegantly draped skirt, she looked about nineteen.

No sooner had Lady put the phone at her feet, than it rang again. Now Jane *was* becoming agitated.

"Why don't you tell her to switch it off?" Alex asked in a quiet voice.

"I'm going to. I don't think this is necessary, do you?"

Where was Sasha? She was taking an unusually long time. Jane left the table. As soon as she was out of view, she dashed to the kitchen. "What's up?" she asked.

"The stupid soufflés have stuck to the dishes, they've all collapsed," Sasha wailed. She and Mrs Jones were dicing lettuce as fast as they could. "We'll have to use tomorrow night's pâté instead."

While they made up the plates Jane decorated them with some radishes and cherry tomatoes. Suddenly she remembered the flowers outside the back door. Quickly she broke off the stems and placed a large petalled chrysanthemum on each plate.

When Jane returned to the table, Lady was questioning Jonathan.

"Exactly *what* in the medical profession?" she persisted.

"A trainee nurse," Jonathan said, straightfaced.

"A *nurse*?" Lady repeated.

"I'm a late starter. You see last year – when I was a porter – I decided that nursing was what I *really* wanted to do."

Kim stifled a giggle. Jonathan was having fun winding Lady up.

Jane waited for Lady to finish yet another call. "Lady, you are so dedicated," Jane said evenly, "but you're here to relax. Why don't you switch off your mobile and forget the magazine for tonight."

"I can't possibly be out of touch. You never

know from one minute to the next what emergency might arise."

"I understand. But surely you deserve a couple of days off."

"I don't mind – unless it worries anyone else."

Jane could feel Charles's eyes on her.

"I think perhaps it would be more relaxing for all of us if you switched off. Why don't you tell your office you'll be out of touch for a couple of hours at least?"

Dale, flanked either side by Robert Gill and Ray Parker, was in her usual sparkling form. If ever anyone saw the funny side of life it was her. She'd had a bit of a run-in with her landlord and was devising ways to get her revenge. Soon everyone joined in and, probably because it was Hallowe'en, several methods of medieval torture were suggested.

"The only answer is to buy him out." Ray teased.

"Yes, why not get Daddy to buy the place." Charles's tone was sarcastic.

Jane coloured and glared at Charles. His remark was barbed and uncalled-for.

"What a wonderful idea, Charles. That's just what I'll do." Dale winked slyly at Jane.

So she's not just a barrel of laughs, Jane applauded her silently.

The house was quiet. Jane and Alex sat by the dying fire in the living-room.

"So how do you rate your first official visit to *Personal Agenda*?" Jane asked when they were alone.

"The best. I had a really good time tonight –

after I'd off-loaded Lady. She's on Jonathan's case now." Alex rolled his eyes.

"Don't be too sure of that. Jonathan is with Kim, even Lady is no match for her." Jane clapped her hand over her mouth. "I'm sorry, Alex, that was nasty."

"Don't apologise, it's true," he said without rancour. "But I hope you're wrong about Lady."

"Jonathan enjoyed ribbing her, didn't he?"

"Why is he so reluctant to say what he does?" Alex asked.

"Because as soon as someone finds out that he's a cosmetic and/or a plastic surgeon, they plague him with questions."

"In the States they're not so reticent."

"It was a bit like a reunion here tonight. I hope you didn't feel left out. How did you find the others?"

"They're a good bunch. Dale is a smart cookie for all her kidding around. That guy Kevin is very likeable. The girl who was sitting beside him . . . Amanda?"

"That's right." Jane nodded.

"She was a bit out of the loop. Does she have a thing going with Kevin?"

"Well . . . yes, sort of. They've been out together. Why do you ask?"

"Gut feeling. He spent a lot of time talking to Jill. I don't think that scored too many brownie points with Amanda."

Now that Jane thought about it, Amanda had been subdued.

"Tell me what else I missed," she demanded.

Jane could have sat and talked to Alex all night but Saturdays at *Personal Agenda* were always hectic. Although Alex claimed that *watching* was one of his hobbies, he was quite a conversationalist too. She *did* notice that. When Alex had something to say, they all listened intently. Obviously she wasn't the only one who thought him charismatic.

Chapter Sixty-One

Liz Traynor walked across the garden to the garage with her pots of wax. A magpie, totally uninhibited by her presence, strutted up and down. His black wings were neatly folded back, his chest gleaming white. Like a maître d', he examined the bird table and the ground underneath. Satisfied, he turned, and began to inspect the rest of his domain.

"I'm all set up." Liz said cheerfully as she joined Jane and Sasha in the kitchen.

"We'll start about eleven o'clock. I'm really looking forward to watching you this time." Jane handed her a cup of coffee.

"I hope you're both going to try your hand this afternoon," Liz said.

"We will if we can. Justin certainly will . . ."

"Justin certainly will what?" Justin bounced into the kitchen and William trailed behind. He was carrying an enormous bundle of tightly twisted newspapers.

"'Morning everyone, where do you want these firelighters?" William asked.

"Not in the garage," Liz advised. "My gas burners can be temperamental."

"Dump them in the shed," Sasha suggested.

"Who's the fashion-plate in black and taupe talking into a mobile?" Justin asked.

"Lady McCall," Jane said.

"Lady as in 'Lady'?"

"No, that's her nickname, Adelaide Sydney McCall," Jane explained.

"Sounds as though her mother was frightened by an Australian map-maker," Justin chuckled.

Liz held up a long piece of waxed string. "This is the wick," she explained. "I thought you might like to see what the paraffin wax looks like before it's melted and coloured."

They passed the bowl between them.

"It looks like coarsely granulated sugar," Sasha said as she trickled the white grains between her fingers.

"It does. And, to complete the meal . . ." Liz held up something that resembled a block of honey-coloured cheese. "Pure beeswax," she said. "People often ask what it looks like so I brought a little piece along. As it's Hallowe'en and because I know that Jane has chosen black and white as a theme, I have also. And gold too. The pots you see behind me . . ." Liz stepped sideways to allow them to see the three large steaming containers. "They work on the same principle as a double boiler. The wax is melted by steam, it never touches the water. In order to save time, I've already done that and it's cooled off slightly. That allows the wax to stick to the wick. Now, I'll use these tongs and we'll start dipping." With a practised hand she dipped the wick into the cooling tub of white wax, then dipped it into the black container.

"See how to alternate the layers?" she asked. She placed the fat, perfectly rounded black candle on a table.

With a small sharp instrument that resembled a scalpel, Liz made a firm, deep cut into the side of the candle. "You cut it from the top to about half-way down. Make sure the wax is still firmly attached by its base to the candle." Deftly she eased it away and then divided the cut section in half.

"You need to work fairly rapidly at this stage." Quickly Liz twisted the two pieces, then looped them back onto the candle. The twist revealed all the black and white layers. Without any apparent effort, she made four more loops.

"Now we do the same thing again, but this time working from half-way down almost to the bottom. Don't forget, the piece you cut must be teased away gently, otherwise you'll be left with a piece of wax in your hand and a gash in the candle." She scooped out small petals between the curled loops and the candle became more beautiful with every cut and fold.

"Now, that's not difficult, is it?" Liz grinned.

"Easy as falling off a log!" Dale groaned. "I think I'll go back to the house and have a Mexican breakfast."

"What's that?" Kevin asked.

"A cigarette and a glass of water!"

"I think I'll join you – and I don't even smoke," Justin said.

"You'll all have it down to a fine art in no time," Liz assured them as she dipped the next candle, this time in gold and black. She chose an even more complicated design. The result was stunning.

"At least you'll have no problem with the scalpel," Kim said to Jonathan.

"Don't bet on it . . ."

"Why should a nurse use a scalpel?" Lady asked Jonathan. She'd managed to elbow Amanda aside so she could stand beside him.

"Sometimes when a surgeon feels like a cup of coffee, we nurses operate instead."

Lady gave him a withering look. "Couldn't you come up with something more original than that?"

"I'll try."

Lady's eyes narrowed. They were having a laugh at her expense. She slipped out of the garage and pulled her phone from the pocket of her long black coat. "Sophie? It's Lady. Jonathan Campbell-Smith – medical, can you get me any info on him? Ring me back."

It took Sophie less than half an hour to discover that Jonathan Campbell-Smith had indeed been the subject of a lengthy article in a rival magazine's beauty section. Lady listened as Sophie gave her a synopsis. Not for a moment had she believed his story – a nurse, huh!

By the time they'd finished lunch and gathered again in the garage Liz had re-melted the wax.

"That's excellent, Kim," Liz said as she watched Kim twist the pliable wax into a loop and stick it firmly in place. "Now do the same thing again but lower down."

Liz walked the length of the trestle tables and commented on each candle. "It needs to be more evenly divided, Amanda."

"Who the hell cares," Amanda said when she'd gone. She threw down her paring blade and marched out of the garage. She couldn't give a damn about this stupid pastime anyway.

Evie and Tony were doubled up with laughter. Their candle stood drunkenly, the wick protruding from its side. The more lopsided it became, the more they laughed. They were never going to earn their living as chandlers, and Liz left them to their fun.

"You're a natural, Jane." Liz was astonished how quickly Jane had learned to loop and twirl the black and white wax.

Alex gave up before he began. "I'll advise Jane," he declared.

Justin elected himself supervisor. He marched along the line behind Liz, mimicking her comments. Evie dabbed some of the spare wax on his nose and soon everyone followed suit.

"One is disgusted at such a display of bad manners." Justin's high-pitched voice was the one he'd used to play the part of Lady Bracknell.

"When are we going to do *The Importance of Being Earnest* again?" he asked Jane as he peeled the wax from his forehead.

"When I get these loops right," she said concentrating on a twist.

"That's original!" Dale's candle had three wicks poking out from the top. "Three wicks, how come?" Liz asked.

"Three candle power – better than one," Dale said, as if the reason was obvious.

Liz wondered if that was true.

When they declared they'd done all they could with their masterpieces, Liz encouraged them to try the gold wax. Jane would have adored to have spent the rest of the day fiddling and carving, but she had go and help Mrs Jones. Sasha was supervising the bonfire.

♥ ♥ ♥

Alice and Peter Jones, Mrs Jones's children, stood quietly at their mother's side watching her put the sausages onto the metal barbecue racks.

Mrs Jones said the children had talked of nothing else but Hallowe'en for the last two weeks.

"Hello! I'm Jane," she said.

Alice dimpled prettily. She was the image of her mother, especially with those round, rosy cheeks and that ready smile. Peter, the shyer of the two, mumbled a quiet hello.

"Do you like sausages?" Jane asked them, as she broke the ice gently.

"I do," Alice nodded.

"Me too," Peter said in a whisper.

"There'll be all sorts of lovely things to eat," Jane said. "Let's see. There's hot cheese . . ."

Alice clamped her lips tightly together and shook her head.

"No cheese for you?" Jane asked. "Well how about chicken on sticks?"

Alice thought about that for a moment. "Do we have to eat sticks?" she whispered to her mother.

Mrs Jones laughed uproariously. "Bless you, no," she assured her daughter. Alice's little face flooded with relief.

"Would you like to help me with these apples?" Jane asked them.

They both nodded solemnly. Jane cored the apples then showed them how to thread them with string. While they worked, Jane told the children all about Hallowe'en when she was a little girl.

Alex stood unnoticed in the kitchen doorway. The three of them were sitting at the table surrounded by apples and masses of coloured string. He felt a sudden tug of sadness as he watched them. Although Alice had dark hair, she reminded him so much of his own daughter. Alice's innocent face, with its intense concentration, tore at his heart. How natural Jane was, what a shame she'd never had children of her own. As he looked at the scene before him he was certain she'd make a wonderful mother.

"Hi!" Jane said as he finally came to join them. "This is Alice and this is Peter."

Alex smiled at the children. "I'm Alex," he said.

Alice edged nearer to Jane. Alex must have looked like a giant to the little girl. "What are you up to?" he asked.

"'Fredding apples," Peter volunteered much to his mother's surprise.

Alex sat down and was given the job of tying the strings.

"What are you going to do with the apples?" he asked Alice.

"You have to tie them on the line and bite holes in them . . ."

"Jane says you must keep your hands behind your back," Peter added.

". . . And you must only take little bites or you'll choke," Alice warned him.

"I'll remember that," Alex said gravely.

"Quite a production line," Charles said when he came into the kitchen. "Have you seen anything of Amanda?"

"Isn't she in the garage?" Jane asked.

"She was, but she left a while ago."

"She may be in her room, shall I go and see?" Jane asked guiltily. After Alex's observation last night, she'd intended to keep an eye on Amanda. But the morning had flown and she'd quite simply forgotten.

"Amanda," Jane called as she tapped on the door. She thought she heard a noise in the room. "Amanda," she called again. "It's Jane. Are you there?"

"Yes," Amanda replied in a muffled voice.

"Are you OK?"

"Yes," Amanda said.

"May I come in?" Jane thought Amanda sounded a bit odd.

"I'm OK."

"You don't sound it, please, Amanda, can I come in?"

Amanda didn't answer. Was it her imagination or was Amanda crying? Jane turned the handle, the door was unlocked. Amanda was curled up in a ball on the bed. Her eyes were red and swollen. "Oh, Amanda, what's the matter, what's wrong?" Jane sat on the bed and took Amanda into her arms. Jane's kind sympathetic manner made her cry even more.

"Don't cry, tell me what's wrong, maybe I can help."

"No one can help," she sobbed.

Jane stroked her hair and waited for Amanda to explain.

"Is it Kevin?" Jane asked.

Amanda nodded.

"Has he upset you?"

Amanda nodded again.

"Can you tell me what he did?" Jane caught a glimpse of the time, it was almost five o'clock and she still had a fair bit to do.

"He didn't do anything, didn't say anything. That's the trouble."

Amanda was talking in riddles. "I don't understand," Jane said.

"I thought we were friends, more than friends," Amanda sobbed. "I helped him with his work, gave him good advice. After that he was too busy to even bother with me. I've hardly spoken to him for weeks. Last night – and today – he practically ignored me. Spent all his time chatting up that girl Jill." Amanda spat out the name.

Jane's heart sank. There was nothing she could do about that. Kevin was free to talk to anyone he chose. But she could well imagine how that upset Amanda.

"I don't know what to say, Amanda," she said truthfully. "Perhaps tonight . . ."

"I'm going to stay here in my room tonight. I've had enough humiliation for one day."

"You can't give up like that." Sasha's accusation was still fresh in her mind – how easy she'd made life for Hugh. "If you want him, Amanda, fight for him."

After a couple of minutes, Amanda stopped crying. Jane was right, perhaps she should try again.

"You'll try?" Jane asked patiently.

Amanda sniffed. "I'll try."

As Jane left Amanda's bedroom she heard shrieks of laughter coming from Evie's room. The door was open and she peeped in. Evie, Tony and Dale were huddled together, back to back, in a huge piece of black material. On their joint heads was the most enormous pointed hat Jane had ever seen. They were completely oblivious to her presence.

Jane dashed down the stairs two at a time. There were forty-eight people to be fed tonight, fifty if she counted Peter and Alice. Justin and William had volunteered to look after the mulled wine. The barbecues were ready and waiting and a huge cauldron of soup was slowly heating. She and Sasha had made hundreds of snacks on sticks. During the week they'd agreed to cook them in the regular oven leaving the barbecues free for the sausages.

Jane glanced at the clock on the wall, twenty minutes left before the rest of the guests were due to arrive. She dashed round the house and lit the candles. Light shone through the cut-out faces of the pumpkins which cast eerie shadows in the hall. She turned off all the electric lights and the big square hall became ghostlier still. The multi-shaped candles from Liz's class would wait until later.

"Oh no!" Jane groaned as the front door bell sounded. The other guests had started to arrive and she wasn't even dressed yet. She ran her fingers through her short hair and opened the door.

Jane drew back a little when she saw the bent old woman. The woman was obviously in pain and leant heavily on a gnarled stick. Her face looked grotesque in the flickering light and, when she spoke, her breath rasped in her chest.

"Please help me, I feel faint," she gasped.

Jane just stood and looked at her. She couldn't turn her away but couldn't ask her in either. "Oh dear," Jane fluttered helplessly.

The woman swayed. "Just a drink of water, please."

Jane fled to the kitchen and grabbed a mug which she filled from the tap.

The woman was sitting on the chair in the hall. She was almost bent double, her body wracked with coughing. "Thank you," she said and put out a shaking hand to take the mug.

Jane watched her trembling body, then she reached forward and gave the woman a hefty wallop on the arm.

"You *devil.*"

"Ooh! What have I done?" the woman wheezed.

"Sasha!"

"How did you know it was me?" the old woman demanded, straightening up.

"Because sick old ladies don't wear black lace tights with Doc Martens, that's how I knew."

"Hell, I didn't think they'd be seen. Other than that, Mrs Anderson, what do you think of the state of play?"

"In a word – brilliant. I really wouldn't have recognised you. Those warts – they're disgusting, and your teeth – ugh!"

"They look like real cavities, don't they?" Sasha grinned widely.

"They do. How did you get so wheezy?"

"I'm an actress aren't I?" Sasha asked in an imperious tone.

"Yes, but that's way and above . . ." Jane rescued herself with a compliment.

"Don't say anything to the others will you? I'll just – appear."

Jane had decided not to wear fancy dress. Not everyone was comfortable dressing up. When Jane sent the invitations, she'd given them an alternative, *Fancy Dress*, or *Black and White*. She'd bought two outfits for the weekend, the beautifully beaded blouse with its matching draped skirt and, for tonight, a pair of black, fine wool palazzo trousers which she'd teamed with a stunning black and white sweater.

There were witches, skeletons, ghosts and monsters all over the garden. There was a human pumpkin lit from within by a miner's lamp. Several people had opted for black and white, and Alice and Peter made wonderful little elves, the bells on their hats tinkling as they moved alongside their mother.

The bonfire crackled brightly and Justin and William served the hot wine. From within the house a figure appeared, dressed in black and silver. Everyone stared as it glided across the lawn. Lady approached the bonfire, shimmering with every step. Her dress was magnificent; tight-fitting, it glittered with silver beads, on her head she wore a crown. The facets of the stones twinkled in the light from the bonfire.

"Lady, the wicked queen! That collar must have needed a suitcase all of it's own," Sasha said to Jane as they poured soup into the plastic cups.

"I'm sure it had one," Jane retorted picking up the tray.

The night was sharp and frosty and everyone was glad of the heat from the bonfire. A wonderful smell of burning wood wafted across the garden. Ray and Kevin had volunteered for "sausage duty," and Jill helped too. Alice and Peter's delighted squeals as William and Mr Jones set off the fireworks made everyone laugh. Jane put down the empty tray and went to stand beside Alex. He too preferred black and white. Jane adored fireworks, loved the showers of colour as they exploded against the black velvet sky. She felt a little hand clutch hers. Alice smiled up at her. Jane bent and scooped the little girl up into her arms. "Aren't they beautiful?" she asked as another cascade of colour lit up the sky. Peter stood at her side. She nudged Alex.

"Would you like to be the tallest person here?" Alex smiled at Peter.

Peter thought for a moment then nodded. With an easy movement Alex swung the youngster on to his shoulders.

Evie stroked Alice's hand and was rewarded with an impish grin.

"Isn't she gorgeous?" Jane asked.

"Wouldn't little David love all this?" Tony said.

Evie smiled as she thought of her young son. "You know him, he'd be into everything, probably want to set off the fireworks himself."

"He's a very bright little fellow, he just has an enquiring mind," Tony objected.

Jane couldn't help overhearing their remarks and was surprised. She knew that they'd been out together, but Tony seemed to know the child very well. They'd certainly been inseparable this weekend – even if Dale was a part of their three-headed-witch.

The fireworks were finished and the bonfire

had almost burnt out when Mr Jones came to collect the children. They thanked Jane in piping voices. "Can I have a hug?" Two sets of arms wound themselves around her neck as she knelt down. "Will you come back and see me soon?" asked Jane.

"I'll come back soon," Peter said in a grave voice.

"An' me," Alice squeaked. They were tired out from all the excitement.

"Don't be too long," Jane said to Mr Jones. "We'll be eating soon." Their neighbour had promised to look after the children until Mr and Mrs Jones got home later on.

"They're cute, aren't they?" Jane cocked her head on one side as she watched the two elves trotting along beside their father, their bells still ringing as they disappeared from sight in the darkness.

Alex slipped his arm around Jane's shoulder, pulled her to him and kissed her tenderly. Kim watched, her face immobile.

Jane was shaking when he released her. She wasn't sure whether it was the surprise or the kiss. But she was sure that she'd like Alex to do it again. She no longer felt the chill of the October night, for her it might as well have been midsummer night.

The dining-room table was covered with a black sheet. With Alex's help they'd managed to replace the centre-piece without too much damage. The gold moons and stars glittered between the leaves. Witches peeked from the folds of the curtains and a skeleton sat in a chair in the corner lit by the light of a pumpkin.

"I'm sure you're all longing to get out of those costumes, so before we eat I'll announce the winner of the fancy dress prize," Jane said. Lady smiled in anticipation. "The prize – the prizes – go to the three-headed witch."

Everyone cheered loudly. Tony, Evie and Dale shuffled forward awkwardly. Their costume was ingenious; whichever way the witch turned, a hideous face greeted the onlooker.

"Just my luck!" Jane laughed. "All *three* of you get a free weekend at *Personal Agenda.* I think there should be one special mention – Sasha."

Again everybody whistled and cheered. Lady swept from the room in disgust.

Jane had tried hard to find food that fitted the black and white theme. Huge steaming dishes of black spaghetti brought gasps of surprise. She'd been thrilled to find the pasta – dyed black with cuttlefish juice. They'd made a delicate white sauce for that. She'd really thrown caution to the winds and bought several black truffles for the white pasta sauce. The salads were mostly white, she did have to cheat a little there and left the mayonnaise on top to be mixed later. The Black Forest gateaux, meringues chantilly and cheese cakes were in keeping. Jane left the cheeses in their black wax coating and chose Wensleydale and Brie as a contrast.

Several people had discarded their voluminous costumes. They sat about comfortably in their casual clothes, drinking coffee. Spectral shadows played on the living-room walls.

Sasha gave *herself* a fright when she saw her reflection in the oven door. She took advantage of the lull and went upstairs to remove the warts and restore her teeth to their natural pearly beauty.

Lady got over her sulk and found herself a new outfit. Dressed in black cashmere, draped with a white and black scarf, she was deep in conversation with a man in public relations. Susie sat contentedly talking to Justin. Jane smiled at her friend, the bump was certainly beginning to show. One more batch of plates for the dishwasher and she too could relax for a while.

Jonathan and Kim sat on the couch by the window.

"It's so relaxing here," he sighed.

Kim wished she could agree. She was coiled as tightly as a fully wound spring. The day had been difficult enough, but when she'd seen Alex kissing Jane, she felt a sharp pang of jealousy. All the attraction she'd felt for him bubbled to the surface again. All the things she'd found so attractive about him . . . still were. But Alex had made it more than plain that *his* love was a thing of the past.

"What are you thinking about?" Jonathan asked as he noticed her fierce look of concentration.

Kim chewed her lip. "I was thinking about how nice you are." She rubbed her arm along his sleeve and smiled at him.

"I'm pleased to hear it. You've been awfully quiet today."

"It must be the strain of all those twists and loops!"

It was too late now, there could never be a future for her with Alex. Jonathan was a nice man, kind, considerate and a gifted surgeon. Kim knew it would only be only be a matter of time before he proposed to her. She'd longed for children of her own as she'd watched Alice and Peter Jones today. She didn't have too much time to waste. Jonathan was so tender with his young patients, Kim felt sure he'd make a marvellous father.

"We've had so little time on our own this weekend," Jonathan complained.

Kim took a deep breath. "Why don't you come to my room later?"

Jonathan was taken aback, "You mean that?"

"Yes, Jonathan, I do."

The skeletally thin man entered the room quietly. Sasha led him to a chair next to the fire. He wore a tattered old raincoat, loosely-tied, and walked with a stick. No one gave him more than a passing glance.

Jane asked everyone to take a seat. They grouped on couches and chairs, on the floor and anywhere it was possible to sit.

The room was quiet now and the man whose cadaverous face was accentuated by the leaping flames of the fire began to speak. His voice was deep and lyrical. He told of the witches who lived in the wood, the monsters who dwelt in the forest . . . There was hardly a sound as he told his stories, just the odd sharp intake of breath. There were ghosts who haunted houses – just near here. They could imagine the howl of the wind and the creak of old timber doors. His voice rose to a crescendo. Jane clutched Alex's knees and reminded herself they were only stories.

He paused to take a sip of the drink at his arm,

then began again. Modern stories this time, even more scary and frightening.

Justin and William smiled at each other as they watched their friend and the reaction to his tales. He was as gifted a storyteller as he was an author.

Sasha had done a wonderful job of his make-up, his clothes too. John Pritchard, a fine healthy young man, looked as though he was about to expire any moment from consumption.

When his last story drew to a close, the applause was thunderous.

"I'll certainly lock all my windows and doors tonight." Kevin shivered. "I loved listening to ghost stories when I was a kid, but they were never as terrifying as these."

"I've never heard one before, and I don't think I want to again." Ray Parker shuddered.

Charles Graham didn't want to admit that the stories spooked him. He was glad to learn he wasn't alone. A grown man afraid of fairy tales!

John Pritchard accepted their praise graciously. Derek Smith, the public relations agent, made his way to John's side. Within minutes he was offering to represent him. "John, you have a great future as a narrator too," he insisted.

After one o'clock people began to leave. As usual Jane was inundated with requests for weekend stays. Their bookings already stretched well into the new year.

Alex followed Sasha and Jane into the kitchen.

"There's quite a bit of work here. Let me give you a hand," he said looking at the mountain of glasses and cups. Jane had insisted that Mrs Jones and her husband must leave things as they were and listen to John Pritchard.

"We're used to this. A couple of machine loads and it'll all be done," Sasha said. "We usually start by making a cup of tea."

"Alex likes hot chocolate," Jane told her.

"Don't worry about me. I'll make you a *cupper*." Alex's American accent made the word sounded strange.

They sat at the table and gossiped about the day while the machine rumbled through its cycles.

"My God! Amanda! Did either of you see her tonight?" Jane stopped unloading the dishwasher, a deep frown creased her forehead.

"I saw her in the garden earlier. But . . . not after that," Alex said.

"I didn't see her at all tonight. Is something wrong?" Sasha knew that look of Jane's.

"She wasn't too happy this afternoon. We had a talk . . ."

"Do you want me to pop up and see if she's OK?"

"Would you mind?" Jane couldn't face another session with Amanda, she was too tired.

Sasha returned to the kitchen carrying a piece of paper. "You'd better read this," she said.

Tried my best. Have gone home. I'll phone you on Monday. Thanks for everything. Amanda.

Jane read the note then passed it to Alex.

"Kevin?"

"Kevin."

"I reckon we saw that coming."

"I don't understand. They were inseparable last time they were here . . . I talked to Amanda today, she didn't understand either."

"There's no use worrying, Jane. There's nothing you can do now even if you wanted to." Alex yawned and stretched.

"Why didn't I keep an eye on her?" Jane chastised herself.

"Probably because you had so much else to do," Alex said reasonably. "I suppose I'd better be off to bed. See you both in the morning."

Jane wished that Sasha wasn't there. She longed for Alex to kiss her again, to feel his arms around her.

Alex wished that Sasha wasn't in the kitchen. He wanted to kiss Jane again, feel her sweet mouth on his own. As he got ready for bed he thought about the day, it had been marvellous. Jane certainly knew how to create an atmosphere of well-being. Not that poor Amanda would agree with his sentiments.

He climbed into bed and pulled the soft duvet around him. The long, silent night hours were no longer his enemy.

Jane trudged upstairs, her face white with exhaustion. As she reached her room she heard the sound of a door closing on the floor below. She looked over the banisters but there was no sign of movement. Too tired to care, she went into her room, removed her make-up and fell into bed.

♥ ♥ ♥

Kim rubbed the perfumed cream into her skin. She brushed her dark hair vigorously until it shone. She stepped into the white satin nightdress then examined herself in the mirror. Her figure was lithe and trim. Satin, she knew, was a very cruel material, it could pounce on flab with the accuracy of a heat-seeking missile. She slipped her feet into the swansdown slippers and sat on the edge of her bed to wait. Was she being foolhardy? Could she be happy with Jonathan? Alex would fade from her mind – in time. Their paths would probably never cross again once she left *Personal Agenda*.

Kim could just see the outline of Jonathan's sleeping figure. She knew now she would never feel the love or the abandon she'd experienced with Alex. Memories of Alex had got her through the night. This was insane, lying in one man's arms thinking about another. But Jonathan loved her. He'd told her so repeatedly. Could she live a lie and tell him that she loved him too?

Beads of perspiration pearled her forehead and she could scarcely breathe. She slipped out of bed and groped her way around the darkened room towards the open window. She stood silently in the cold morning light, between the window and the quilted curtains.

Jonathan asked Kim to marry him at lunch-time on Sunday, and she accepted. Kim would have preferred to keep the news to themselves for the moment, but Jonathan was far too excited. "I'll die on the spot if we don't tell someone."

Kim smiled, Jonathan's idea of someone meant everyone.

Jane managed to hide her astonishment. She insisted they must celebrate *Personal Agenda*'s first success immediately. She was a little ashamed that she thought of their announcement that way – now had it been Evie and Tony . . .

She and Charles eased the champagne corks from the bottles and poured the frothing liquid into crystal flutes.

Alex raised his glass in salute. Kim's cheeks were bright with colour. Was that mockery she could see in his eyes? She clinked glasses with Jonathan and they drank a little of the champagne – her gaze firmly locked onto Alex's eyes.

Jane was troubled by the look that passed between her and Alex. Kim might be engaged to Jonathan, but she was positive that it was Alex Kim wanted. Poor Jonathan! He deserved better than that. But then so had Alex, Jane thought.

♥ ♥ ♥

Lady McCall thanked Jane effusively for a fabulous weekend. "I enjoyed it immensely and I'll recommend your agency to all my friends," she promised. She hesitated for a moment at the door. "Would you mind giving my card to Alex Travis, if he finds himself at a loose end in London . . ." She let the end of her sentence trail as she picked up the last of her suitcases.

Jane pulled a face at her retreating, white-coated back. She must give Lady's card to Alex, tempted though she was to tear it up. She waited until Lady's car roared out of the drive then gave the front door a hefty slam. Talk about persistence . . .

"Thanks, but, no thanks. Throw it away, Jane," Alex grimaced as he read the card. "Two days of her and her mobile are more than enough for any man to bear."

Tony and Evie were almost the last to leave.

"It's been wonderful," Evie said. "The best weekend of our lives."

Jane looked from one to the other.

Evie nudged Tony's arm surreptitiously.

"I can see you won't be happy until you've told Jane," he said smiling fondly at her.

"We're going to be married next spring," Evie burst out, her eyes shining with happiness. "You're the very first person to know. But it's a secret until we tell our folks."

Jane hugged them both with delight. "That's the most wonderful news. I know that you'll be happy together." As she looked at Evie's radiant face she thought how cold and stiff Kim's had been.

"I think Kim's still in love with you." Jane said bluntly when they were alone.

"I doubt it. But, even if she is, that's her problem," Alex said firmly. "I'm not in love with her."

Jane handed him a plastic sack. Enough of Kim, she'd had little enough time with Alex this weekend.

"What a pity to have to throw these in the trash." Alex held up the pumpkin and made an ugly face.

"Never mind, we'll be able to use all those lovely decorations again next year," she assured him.

"Next year? I wonder where we'll all be this time next year?"

Jane looked at him sharply. It was unlike him to be so rueful.

Jane walked with Alex to the car. They'd arranged to meet in London on Wednesday, he was anxious to take her to a show, then they'd have dinner.

Jane would have happily settled for a meal, that way they could talk.

He took both her hands in his and kissed her lightly on the lips. "I'll phone you tomorrow."

Jane meandered round the flower beds nearest to the house reluctant to go indoors. She didn't know why, but somehow, the weekend which started with all the energy of a fire-cracker had ended like a damp squib.

Chapter Sixty-Two

Emma Brown was troubled about her daughter. She didn't believe Amanda's story – that she'd been bored and left The Willows early because of it. A whole day early? Emma couldn't accept that. Something or someone had deeply upset Amanda, and Emma had a good idea who that someone was.

Amanda's door remained firmly closed for the rest of the day. Emma was tempted to knock but decided not to. Amanda was a big girl now, old enough to make her own mistakes, and Emma was determined not to say anything that could spoil their precious relationship.

"I hope you feel better soon." Howard Martin replaced his receiver. If his memory served him correctly this was the first time Amanda had ever missed a day. She certainly sounded wretched, those flu bugs could be devastating.

Amanda crept back into bed. She couldn't care less whether Howard Martin believed her excuse or not. She'd often thought that nothing in her life would ever be worse than the day her father walked out, but she was wrong. Kevin had coolly and calmly destroyed every ounce of the self-confidence she'd so slowly built up. If only she hadn't tried to win him back by giving him that information about the advertisement, what an idiot she'd been.

Amanda pulled the covers tightly around her and pretended she was asleep when Emma knocked to say that Jane was on the phone.

"I probably shouldn't ask, but what happened last weekend? Amanda hasn't left her room since Saturday night," Emma said to Jane.

"I think you'll have to ask Amanda that, I'm really not sure myself."

"She's pretending to be asleep. Amanda can keep that up for days."

"Ask her to give me a ring when she feels like it, will you? I won't bother her again." The more Jane thought about the way Amanda had left The Willows the angrier she felt.

Charles had spent ages on Sunday trying to phone her. He was extremely upset that he too had failed to notice Amanda's distress. They were supposed to be friends, why hadn't she talked to him?

Jane reluctantly told him what was wrong with Amanda.

"But you mustn't say anything about this, Charles," she insisted.

Apart from Amanda's feelings, her sudden and unnoticed departure wouldn't do *Personal Agenda*'s reputation much good either.

"I'd like to give the bastard a good thump," muttered Charles furiously. "Still, if you say so, I'll keep quiet."

Jane left a message on Charles's machine. Amanda had arrived home safely but Jane hadn't spoken to her. She left the name of a new applicant to be vetted, and said she'd speak to him in a couple of days.

Kevin had known that Hallowe'en was going to be a difficult weekend for him. He'd felt guilty when he refused Amanda's offer of a lift. He felt guilty about Amanda. No one understood the feeling of rejection more than he did. But he knew that if he was weak and continued to encourage her, he could find himself in another mess. Possibly even a second unsuitable marriage. He'd chosen the coward's way out; a mumbled half-hearted excuse about working late. Then he made it worse by arriving at The Willows before Amanda did.

Amanda's fury on Saturday when she slammed out of the candle-making session made him feel like a heel. Kevin knew it was because he'd barely spoken to her. Anyone else would have taken the hint by then. Amanda had been positively rude at the fancy dress party in the garden that night. She'd snapped at Jill. Then she stood firmly between himself and Jill cutting off their conversation in the middle. He'd really been a cruel sod. He'd stretched his hand across Amanda and moved Jill to his other side.

On Sunday morning, Kevin suddenly realised he hadn't seen Amanda since that incident in the garden. Was it his paranoia or had Jane answered him sharply when he asked where Amanda was?

"She has a bad headache." Jane's eyes didn't meet his with their usual candour.

Amanda hadn't appeared for the rest of the day. He asked Sasha if Amanda was better when he and Jill were leaving. Either she didn't hear him or she didn't know. Either way, he got no answer. But it made it easier all round that Amanda wasn't about.

Next time he visited *Personal Agenda* he'd make sure that Amanda wasn't booked in. If his date with Jill went well on Thursday, he mightn't need *Personal Agenda* any more. He really liked Jill. She seemed to be very solemn at first but then he discovered that this was just a front. Behind those glasses was a keen mind. She had a lively sense of the ridiculous. She was obviously interested in him, and was content to let him do the chasing.

♥ ♥ ♥

It was four o'clock on Monday afternoon before Derby's learned they'd won the Stourley account. Kevin was dizzy with delight. Everyone congratulated him. For the second time in two days he drank champagne. The story of his coup sped around the office like wildfire.

"What a dream! Coogan, Howard and Green's presentation handed to you on a plate – how did you manage that?"

"Pity the poor sucker who gave you all that information – they've committed advertising suicide."

Successes are rarely hidden in the advertising world. Kevin knew that it wouldn't take too long before the news reached Amanda's bosses.

He owed it to Amanda not to reveal her name. So far, he hadn't.

Chapter Sixty-Three

Donahue Reilly traced a finger down the directory of companies in the foyer. Timpson's were on the fourth floor. As he waited for the lift he thought about the job he had to do. The work should take about a week. He'd been pleased when Ray phoned to tell him about the new contract.

"A definite, for a change." Ray sounded quite positive, chipper even.

"Things are looking up," he told Donahue. "There are lots of bits and pieces in the pipeline now. We have two new leads, both promising."

Donahue wouldn't have given tuppence for Ray's chance of survival a few weeks ago. When Ray did phone, Donahue expected that it was to give him the bad news.

He'd spent the last three weeks working in isolation at home. He fought hard against a gnawing sense of frustration. He was ashamed of the times when he snapped at his wife Alison for no reason at all. Times when he couldn't remember how he'd found solutions to the problems facing him. He'd had it all at his fingertips – until the night of the robbery. Where were the diskettes now, lying at the bottom of a tip? Dumped in someone's dustbin or on the bed of a river? He absolutely had to get out of the house, work on something else for a while. But he couldn't bear to think of his work, his dream, discarded like a piece of old rubbish.

Timpson's was a similar set-up to their own. The offices were respectable, not plush or luxurious. The receptionist waved him to a chair while she answered the constantly ringing telephone. At first he was impressed but then he realised that she was employed by all the firms on the fourth floor.

Jeremy Timpson shook his hand then led him along a narrow corridor to a sparsely furnished office.

"We don't use this office very often," he said by way of an excuse.

"It's good to have the extra space." Donahue wondered if Timpson's couldn't afford to furnish the room.

"I gather that Ray Parker has told you exactly what we need from CCC?"

"Oh yes, I'm well used to setting up these systems," Donahue assured him. I can do this with my eyes closed, you silly fool, he wanted to say. There was something about Timpson that reminded Donahue of Ray; a man struggling to keep his business alive.

"I'm delighted to have up-dated the computer." Jeremy's eyes rested almost lovingly on his new machine. "The one I had was hopeless, gave me problems all the time."

Donahue could sympathise with that.

"I'm in the same boat," he said ruefully. "My own computer has been out of action for weeks.

No one can find the fault and I'm beginning to wonder if they ever will."

"That's a shame, they're so expensive to replace."

"True, but I haven't given up hope yet."

"I'll leave you to it," Jeremy Timpson said. "Call me if you need me. I'm only next door."

Donahue took off his jacket, settled himself in front of the screen and logged on. His first task was to check the space available to install his software – a quick directory listing would do that.

As the contents scrolled, his eyes opened wide. There on the screen with its flashing cursor was *his* system, the Beamish and Chambers' system.

Donahue jumped up from his chair. "What the hell is . . ." It took less than ten seconds to register the information in his brain. This was his work, one of CCC's stolen systems and therefore one of CCC's stolen computers.

This was marvellous. Whoever sold this machine to Jeremy Timpson would probably lead them to the rest of the stolen goods.

In a flash he was out of the office.

"Can you tell me where you bought that computer?" His voice was calm.

"Which computer?" Timpson asked stupidly, his face beginning to pale.

"The machine I'm using." What was wrong with the man? Maybe . . . maybe I know what's wrong with him – Jeremy Timpson was aware it was stolen.

"I think it would be as well to tell me where you got it," Donahue said sharply.

"I bought it from Ray Parker – paid him a fair

price," Jeremy added hastily. "Why, is there something wrong?"

Donahue's mind was working feverishly. So that was Ray's game. He'd have to be careful not to arouse Jeremy Timpson's suspicions or he'd be on the phone to Ray in a second.

"No, if you bought it from Ray, that's fine. For a moment I thought it was a machine that I'd used before and had given me trouble. But it can't be, Ray got rid of it ages ago." That was the best explanation Donahue could think of on the spur of the moment.

Jeremy Timpson's face brightened. "I'm relieved to hear that."

Donahue forced himself to walk slowly to his temporary office. So many things began to make sense now; Ray's sudden holiday in Dublin, his refusal to allow Donahue, or anyone else, to lock up the premises that weekend – Donahue had done it dozens of times in the past. Ray's calm acceptance of the robbery, his need to know if the police had been given a list of stolen items. The look of relief on his face when he learnt that Donahue hadn't talked to them about it. Ray's magnanimous gesture in hiring a computer for him was out of character. Yes, it all made sense now.

Ray's insurance claim for the stolen machines was due for payment soon. Donahue could just imagine how that must have been padded.

But above all, Donahue could never, *would* never forgive Ray for costing him all those months of work. Somehow, Ray was going to have to pay for this . . .

Donahue made copies of everything he'd

previously created. For a wild moment he prayed that his own system could be here. But he knew in his heart that it wouldn't be. He'd used an older model, a 286, and this wasn't it.

Donahue telephoned CCC. "Let me speak to Ray please," he said to Linda Lou.

"Hello, Donahue, what's up?" Ray's cheerful voice asked.

"I phoned to tell you I'm leaving CCC. I can't concentrate on my work, you'll have to find a replacement."

"Don't be foolish, Donahue, you've been overworking at home. You'll soon get into the swing of things again," Ray said dismissively.

"You're not listening, I've made up my mind, I'm leaving. Find someone else." Donahue replaced the receiver on a sputtering Ray.

He slipped the diskettes into his briefcase and left the building quietly without speaking to anyone. He walked for a few minutes until he saw a taxi.

"Where to?" the driver asked.

"The nearest police station," Donahue replied.

Chapter Sixty-Four

Jane watched the slender black hands of the clock anxiously. It would be wonderful to have Alex all to herself for two days. This would be his last trip to London before Christmas. Goodness knows how long it would be before he came back to England again. But she wasn't going to let that spoil their time together.

"I'm ready, Jane," Sasha called.

Sasha was going to London to do her Christmas shopping and planned to stay with Susie and Matt. Now that she knew Alex, she approved of him wholeheartedly.

Jane waited with Sasha until her train arrived.

"Be good," Sasha warned as she hugged Jane.

"I'll try," Jane grinned.

Jane stopped in the village to collect her groceries. She was tempted to tell Mrs Reid that her favourite American was coming down today but decided against it.

Alex liked the Drake's Inn so much she'd take him there for lunch. Then they could go for a long walk, something else they'd never been able to manage during the packed weekends. Justin and William had invited them for dinner but Jane refused.

"We'd love to, but another night perhaps. We've spent hardly any time together."

"Then I take it that you find Alex more attractive than me?" Justin teased.

"Absolutely not," Jane assured him, "but you're spoken for!"

"Ain't that the truth." Justin laughed.

They walked companionably along the country roads.

"The last few days have been hectic. Lots of meetings and prolonged meals. I'm so thrilled to be free for a little while."

Jane asked him about the meetings and he tried to explain some of the complications of transatlantic investment.

"I'm sure I'd never get the hang of it," Jane groaned. "It used to take me all my time to work out the differences between the pound sterling and the Irish punt."

"Do you miss Ireland?" Alex asked.

"Not so much now that I live in Dornley. I've very few friends left in Dublin, most of them live in London. Unfortunately since I started *Personal Agenda* I've hardly seen them either – except Susie and Matt of course."

"They're a charming couple and mad about you."

"They've been wonderful friends. They were really good to me when things went wrong with my marriage . . ." It was the first time Jane had thought about Hugh for weeks.

Alex shook his head. "What a foolish man he must have been."

"I'll take that as a compliment."

There were a lot of compliments Alex would like to pay her, a lot of sentiments he'd like to express. They were good together, he and Jane. Alex was certain now that he loved her. Last time he'd visited The Willows he'd made up his mind to tell her how he felt, but the timing was wrong. Jane had been up to her eyes as usual.

"It's lovely to have you all to myself," he said as they lingered over their wine.

"I must confess that's exactly what I thought this morning." Jane coloured prettily.

Such endearing qualities, her honesty and her directness.

They left the table and sat by the fire. "You choose some music," Jane said dreamily.

The soft strains of a Chopin étude matched their mood. They sat quietly by the flickering firelight. At peace with one another and the world.

"Jane, will you have dinner with me at Christmas?" Alex asked.

"But I thought you'd be in the States at Christmas?"

"I will, but I'd like you to be there with me."

"My goodness! I . . . I don't know . . . I've never been to America."

Alex laughed at her confusion. "Wait a moment," he said.

He returned with a slim package beautifully tied with a big bow.

The packet contained an airline ticket. "London, New York, London," Jane read. "On Concorde! Oh, Alex, Concorde."

"So will you say yes?"

"It sounds incredible. It's such a long way away . . . I've never been to America before . . . I suppose you think I'm being ridiculous."

"If you want an opinion, I think that you're wonderful. Honest, funny, compassionate, intelligent and lovely. I think I've just run out of superlatives."

"I can make do with those until you re-stock. But you're pretty wonderful too," she said shyly.

They made love on the rug by the fire. Alex aroused in her an almost forgotten fire, the half remembered sweetness of total love. How gentle his hands were, caressing then demanding. His kisses soft, then probing. Their bodies cast a single shadow on the wall as they experienced the joy of surrendering mind and body to tenderness and desire.

They slept in each other's arms in Alex's bed. When he woke next morning he was alone. For a moment he thought he'd dreamt it all. He put out his arm lazily and could feel the dent in the pillow beside him.

Jane stood dreaming while the toast burnt. She didn't know if she was on her head or her heels. She couldn't remember when she felt so happy.

She started at the sound of Alex's voice. "Are you going to make an honest man of me or what?" Alex stood in the doorway, his hair still damp from the shower.

"Hello, Alex."

"Hello, sweetheart." In two strides he crossed to her and lifted her off the floor into his arms. "Now, as I was saying last night, do I eat alone at Christmas?"

"No, you don't."

"That's incredible! I'll make it an enchanted Christmas," he promised. "We'll do all the sights in New York, then catch the shuttle to Washington on the twenty-third. We'll spend Christmas at my apartment, then you can decide what you'd like to do with the rest of the time. How does that grab you?"

"I can't take it all in. But don't forget I'll only have about ten days."

"All you have to do is pack, close up the house, and go to the airport. I'll see to all the rest."

A wicked sparkle lit Jane's eyes.

"What are you thinking?" Alex asked.

"Wouldn't it be poetic justice if Kim was on the flight? I'm so bitchy!" Jane giggled. "I shouldn't be, if it wasn't for Kim I'd never have met you. Come and sit down. I've already burnt one lot of toast I'm in such a state."

Jane tearfully said goodbye to Alex. She lay in her bed that night, and lived the day again in her mind. She couldn't remember if she'd eaten breakfast or not, lunch escaped her too. But she blushed as she thought of their sensuous afternoon of love-making. They'd dreamed aloud and talked about their plans for the holidays.

"You'll need one formal dress," Alex said. "We've been invited to a special dinner in New York, at Senator Norton's apartment. It's a wonderful place, you'll enjoy it."

"A senator? But I won't be invited . . ."

"You certainly are. I've told him all about my sweet Irish girl with the laughing blue eyes."

"How did you know I'd say yes?" Jane didn't think she was that obvious.

"I didn't. I just hoped you would."

Sasha was thrilled to hear Jane's news.

"I'm so happy for you, really I am. I hated to think of you here all alone at Christmas. Now you'll have the most exciting holiday with someone . . . you love?"

"If you're fishing . . . you're right. I do love Alex. And it will be exciting, we're invited to a senator's apartment for dinner – in New York. Then Alex said . . ."

Sasha listened to Jane's excited chatter. Suddenly she began to see the black side. Jane and Alex loved each other. If Jane's trip went well, Sasha had no doubt that Alex would ask her to marry him and that would be the end of *Personal Agenda.*

She'd been happy here at The Willows, Jane as dear to her as her own sisters. She and Jane were closer perhaps now that the girls lived very separate lives. Justin and William had become a very important part of her life too. But she mustn't spoil Jane's excitement with her own worries. Jane gave so much to others, she was entitled to a little happiness of her own.

"We'll have to think about what to pack. You'll need your most seductive clothes – or will you need any clothes at all?"

"Sasha!" Jane hugged her friend. "You're an idiot but I love you."

Chapter Sixty-Five

Amanda immediately understood the seriousness of his tone. Martin Howard had never spoken to her like that before. She dragged herself from her chair. Now that the call had finally come she felt a strange sort of relief.

The boardroom was cold and unwelcoming, but not nearly as frigid as the faces of the people gathered around the table.

"Sit down, please," Martin Howard commanded.

Amanda walked to the nearest chair. Lois Hayes and Martin Howard both avoided her glance as she sat at the table.

"Would you like to explain your relationship with the copywriter from Derby's?" Martin Howard wasted no time on niceties.

"I have no relationship with anyone at Derby's."

Lois's head shot up. "Martin means *Kevin O'Hanlon.*"

"I have no relationship with Kevin O'Hanlon."

"Amanda, that's not true," Lois insisted.

Amanda stared hard at Lois. Some friend she'd turned out to be.

"Yes, Lois, it *is* true. I don't have any contact with Kevin O'Hanlon."

The heads of department were content to let Lois sort out the mess. They all liked and respected Amanda. They found it difficult to believe she'd behaved in such a treacherous way.

"You mean he used you to get information, then dumped you?" Lois didn't bother to mince her words. Thanks to Amanda and her bruised self-esteem, Lois's job was on the line – all those months of toadying to that horrible little creep, Walter Cox, the Stourley chairman. She shook with rage.

"No, he didn't *dump* me. And what makes you think I gave him any information?" Amanda's cool reply infuriated Lois even more.

"Because I had lunch with their Accounts Director today. He told me *exactly* how Kevin made his pitch. In case you're in any doubt as to why we *know* it was you . . ."

"Stop, Lois," Amanda snapped. "You've had your pound of flesh. I resign."

"Just one moment. That's not good enough." Martin Howard's face was red with anger. "How *dare* you do such a thing. You've jeopardised our integrity, your own good name," he sputtered. "You'll never get a job in advertising again – I'll see to that myself. Apart from that, you've put other people's jobs at risk and lost us one of the biggest accounts in advertising today. And you tell *Lois* to be quiet?" He wanted to hit her. "What made you do it, Amanda?"

Amanda returned his stare insolently. She could imagine their reaction if she told them the truth – she'd given Kevin the information so that *he* wouldn't lose his job. That would really go down well.

Her truculent silence infuriated Lois even more. "I'll tell you why, it was the only way she could get Kevin O'Hanlon to pay her any attention. She tried to buy his affection, popularity at a price. She dangled the Coogan, Howard and Green carrot in front of his . . ."

Amanda picked up Martin's glass of water and flung the contents in Lois's face.

"You're insane," Lois gasped as the water dripped from her hair into her eyes and over her suit.

"Be thankful it wasn't coffee," Amanda threw the empty glass back on the table with a crash.

There was nothing she wanted from her office except her jacket and her handbag. Without a backward glance, Amanda marched along the corridor, her head held high. She swung through the doors of Coogan, Howard and Green's and into the street – for the very last time.

She kept her composure until she reached her car then, where no one could see her, she began to weep. If only I could turn back the clock, start again, Amanda sobbed. I hate Lois Hayes's guts – *"Buying his affection . . ."* How *dare* she say such . . . but, Lois was right. That's exactly what I tried to do, buy his love with something far more valuable than money – information. And now I've lost everything – my job, my integrity, my self-respect and Kevin. *Kevin! Poor down-trodden Kevin.* I was everything his wife wasn't, I cared about him, worried about him. But the moment he got what he wanted, I was forgotten, cast aside like yesterday's newspaper.

♥ ♥ ♥

Emma Brown was fed up with Amanda's silence. Frightened by her behaviour.

"Please Amanda," she begged, "tell me what's wrong. Let me help you."

"I've been fired and I don't want to talk about it. Please, Mum, go away, leave me alone."

Well if Amanda wouldn't discuss it, maybe Martin Howard would.

Emma's face paled as she listened to his high strained voice. If what he was saying was true, she couldn't blame him for his bitter attitude.

"I'm really sorry, Mr Howard. What you've told me about Amanda's behaviour is very distressing. There must be a reason for what she did, she's a very loyal person."

"That's what we thought too, Mrs Brown. And it makes it worse. We believed in her and she betrayed us. There's no excuse for that. Amanda will never work in advertising again if I have anything to do with it."

"Thank you for talking to me," Emma said quietly.

I need time to think, Emma told herself. She cancelled her lunch appointment and walked sadly out of the office.

The autumn leaves crunched under her feet as she made her way along the well-worn path in the park. She huddled into the collar of her coat and pulled her scarf tightly round her head. After two circuits of the park she stopped walking and sat on one of the wooden benches, deep in thought. An hour later a rueful smile twitched her lips. Perhaps Amanda's disgrace would prove to be a blessing in disguise.

♥ ♥ ♥

"Amanda, I want to talk to you," Emma marched firmly into her daughter's room. She drew in a deep breath. Amanda's hair was a mess, her face grey. The bed was strewn with empty biscuit cartons and chocolate wrappers. The room – Amanda's pride and joy – looked like a slum. Her clothes littered every surface and the stench of sour milk made Emma gag. She climbed over the debris and opened the window wide.

"Leave me alone," Amanda said rudely.

"You've been alone long enough. I am your mother in good times and bad. And now we're going to sit together and talk this out – like adults. But first, you're going to get out of those filthy pyjamas and have a bath. I'll give you ten minutes then I'll be back. Hop to it, Amanda, or I'll bath you myself."

Just as Emma was about to go upstairs Amanda came into the study dressed in a clean nightdress. Emma's heart turned over. Amanda looked just like the bewildered little girl who'd stood in front of her all those years ago, once again seeking a mother's comfort. This time Emma held her arms out to her daughter. Amanda rushed towards her sobbing bitterly. Emma stroked her hair and let her cry until her sobbing became convulsive. Gently she released Amanda from her hold and poured a small brandy for them both.

"Have a little of this, darling."

Emma took a gulp and shuddered as the drink hit the back of her throat.

"I spoke to Martin Howard this morning."

Amanda shrank from her mother.

"No, no, it's all right. I know something awful must have happened to make you do what you did. Whatever it is, I'm on your side. Tell me why Kevin upset you so much?"

Emma listened to her daughter without surprise. Amanda made no excuses for her misguided actions. She'd tried to hold Kevin's interest the only way she knew how. She was wrong and didn't deny it. But she'd sacrificed everything she'd worked for, betrayed her principles for someone who'd taken her affection and trampled it into the mud. "After all Kevin suffered from that dreadful wife of his . . ." Amanda's tears gushed again.

Emma wiped away her daughter's tears with a gentle hand. "Believe it or not, I do understand your motives. I know what it's like to be cast aside. All I can say is that the hurt *will* pass. You'll get over Kevin, find another job and your life will come together again. But it will take time. Perhaps a holiday would do you good – somewhere warm."

Amanda shook her head.

"Have you talked to Charles?" Emma asked quietly.

"Once."

"Why not phone him? You two have been good friends, don't punish him for something Kevin did."

"I'll see. I'm not in the mood."

"That's the most difficult thing – making the effort to pick up the threads of your life again. Will you try?"

The last time she'd been told to try, she'd made a total fool of herself. But her mother was right, it wasn't fair to blame Charles for Kevin's behaviour.

"I'll phone him later." Amanda promised.

"Are you up to discussing your career?" Emma asked tentatively. So far she'd succeeded in calming Amanda.

"What career?" Amanda said bitterly.

Emma's courage was ebbing. "Have you thought about what you'd like to do?"

"Advertising is the only business I know."

"You know there's always a place for you at Leland's with me, there's nothing I'd love more."

"Oh, Mum, you don't need an accountant."

"I certainly *could* do with an accountant. After all these years, figures are still a headache for me. Just think, you and I together . . ." Emma's dream was hovering on the horizon.

"It wouldn't work."

Don't push her, Emma warned herself. "Think about it. There's no hurry, no hurry at all."

Amanda rose from the sofa and looked at her mother with tears in her eyes. "You're a wonderful mother," she said, then fled from the room.

What magic those words held, Emma thought as her own eyes filled with tears.

"I spoke to Charles," Amanda said as they ate dinner.

"I'm glad." Emma smiled.

"He was very understanding too . . . He's going to pop over tomorrow, he's working tonight."

It will do her good to have some company, she's locked herself away for long enough, Emma approved silently.

Chapter Sixty-Six

Jane kicked off her shoes the moment she got home. "Never again," she groaned as she rubbed one foot against the other.

Sasha looked at the packages and boxes strewn about the hall. "I take it that you've had a successful spree."

"To think people shop as a hobby!"

"Come on, let's have a look at the spoils." Sasha dashed upstairs carrying as many parcels as she could. Jane trailed behind with the rest. The soft carpet was already soothing her throbbing feet.

"I don't know how Susie did all that walking."

"She's got boundless energy. Even I was exhausted last time we shopped together, she was as fresh as a daisy," Sasha admitted. "Hurry up, Jane. I'm dying to see what you bought."

Jane unwrapped the tissue paper which protected an exquisite brocade jacket.

"It's heavenly," Sasha said as she gently touched the material. "And your favourite colour blue."

"I fell for it the second I saw it."

"To be worn with what?"

"This dress." From another bag Jane withdrew a slinky crepe dress in the identical colour.

"Wow! You'll knock their eyes out with that."

"You don't think it's tarty, do you?"

"Oh for heaven's sake, since when did you ever look tarty?"

"I'll try it on tomorrow, then you can see for yourself."

Sasha sat cross-legged on the bed while Jane opened the parcels. There were trousers with matching sweaters, a smart hip-length jacket which could be worn with anything. There was a gorgeous black blouse that made Sasha whistle. "Now that's what I call sexy. What do you wear under that, if anything?" she leered.

"This," Jane said, throwing the bag on to Sasha's lap.

"Scrummy." Sasha held the black satin-bound slip against her jumper.

"This was my mad moment. The slip cost more than the blouse," Jane said.

"I don't care, it's perfect. You could wear the slip without the blouse, it would make a brilliant camisole top."

'I never thought of that," Jane said. Lots of the tops she'd rejected were scantier.

"What do you think of this for Alex?"

Sasha examined the padded jacket. "I think he'll love it," she announced. "It's warm but not bulky."

"And this to go underneath?" Jane waited for Sasha's verdict.

Sasha held the sweater against the jacket. "They're perfect together. You have very good taste."

"Funny, that's one of the first things Alex said when he came to the house." Jane's eyes had a faraway look.

"Come on dreamer, let's see the rest."

Jane could hardly believe there were only ten days left before her holiday.

She wished that she didn't have to face another weekend. She'd always enjoyed the fit-forties, they were entertaining, never dull. But after that, she'd have two weeks all to herself, no cooking, no cleaning, no guests, just Alex and herself. Never mind, she told herself philosophically, just one more weekend.

Once the weekend got under way, Jane forgot her earlier reluctance. Richard Fenway, the private detective, more than made up for his first visit. Jane was fascinated by his tales of espionage. Eight of the ten guests were either divorced, separated or widowed. At first Jane was a little uncomfortable that Richard might be stepping on someone's toes with his stories. But they were as engrossed as she was if their intent faces were anything to go by.

She was pleased to see that Emma Brown had struck up a rapport with Neil Drummond. He looked ten years younger than when he'd first come to The Willows. He too had spellbinding tales to tell. His reduced workload allowed him to pick and choose the buildings he wanted to design, but houses, he said, were his first love.

"How long would it take to design and build a house?" Emma wanted to know.

"Difficult to say, the last one I did took about two years, give or take a few weeks," he said in answer to Emma's question. "My clients came to the site every day. They added a room then extended another. Finally, the house was finished. I like to have a bit of a celebration when I hand over the keys. The man of the house took the bottle of champagne and the key from me. To my horror and embarrassment, he handed them to his wife, and simply said, 'I'm leaving you. It's all yours now.' "

Jane knew she'd never forget his story. That's probably the sort of thing that Hugh would have done.

"Why on earth did he go through all that if he was going to leave her?" Emma didn't understand.

Richard shrugged. "I don't know. Especially as building a house can be so traumatic. After the wife recovered from her shock, she moved in. The subject of her husband's callous behaviour wasn't mentioned again. As far as I know they're still apart."

"I wouldn't have stood for that." Kitty Smith was one of the two singles at the table.

"How would you've prevented it?" Richard Fenway asked.

"I would have demanded that he move in, then discuss . . ." A ripple of laughter stopped her.

"I'm sure that would've made all the difference!" Delia Conway, the model, snorted at Kitty's naiveté. If that's how her mind worked, no wonder Kitty was still single.

The more Jane got to know Emma Brown, the more she admired her. They'd promised to get together this afternoon for a chat. Charles had kept Jane in touch with Amanda's news. Jane felt really sorry for her. Amanda hadn't been back to *Personal Agenda* since Hallowe'en, and Jane hoped that her bad experience wouldn't sour her feelings about the agency.

"I hear you're off to the States for Christmas," Emma said when they finally escaped to Jane's office.

"How do you know that?" Jane asked.

"Charles told Amanda."

"How is Amanda?"

"Not too bad, considering. It was very kind of you to write her such a lovely letter. She appreciated your support."

"In a way I felt a little responsible. Amanda did meet Kevin here."

"Nonsense. She could have met him anywhere."

"Has she decided what she's going to do now that she's . . . left her job?"

"Not yet and I don't want to push her. I was hoping she'd join me in the business, but she's reluctant – to say the least." Emma gave a wry smile.

"She may change her mind."

"Tell me about your trip, are you very excited?" Emma didn't want to talk about Amanda any more.

"Absolutely. I'm going to New York first – on Concorde." Jane's whole face lit up as she spoke. "Then after that, to Washington. I've never been to the States before."

If Jane Anderson isn't in love, then I'm a pink lizard with red spots, Emma told herself. How wonderful to love someone so much. Jane's face was lit from within, her blue eyes shone with delight.

"He must be a marvellous man to have such an effect!" Emma smiled.

"He is," Jane said vehemently.

Emma knew that Jane's marriage had been an unhappy one. She was pleased that Jane had been given a second chance.

"What will happen to *Personal Agenda*?" Emma mused aloud.

"Wait a minute, I'm only going for two weeks."

"This time!"

"Alex and I only met a couple of months ago." Jane ran her finger up and down the seam on her sleeve. Emma had already married her off.

"I predict that by . . . February, you'll be making wedding plans."

"Then you know something that I don't."

"Have a bet on it?" Emma asked.

"OK. A bottle of your favourite perfume – smallest size."

"I accept! This is one bet that's going to cost you."

Emma looked through the window at the deepening gloom. "I hate these dark afternoons, don't you? It's been a really super weekend. I forgot all my problems for two whole days and that's miraculous."

"Neil Drummond wouldn't have anything to do with that, would he?" Jane teased.

"What do you mean?" Emma asked.

"Now who's being coy?"

"We have arranged to meet next week," Emma admitted.

"Maybe we can make it a double wedding." Jane laughed heartily at Emma's discomfort. "Now you know how I felt."

"I asked for that."

Emma sat silently for a minute or two. "Jane, promise me something. If you should decide to emigrate . . . no, wait, I'm serious. Will you let me know?"

"If I do, then . . . yes. But why?"

"I might be interested in taking over *Personal Agenda* myself. Not a word to anyone, particularly Amanda. Promise?"

"I promise," Jane agreed. "But you already run one high-powered company, could you tackle another?"

"Let me worry about that."

Jane stood at the door long after Emma's car disappeared from view. The one thing Jane hadn't really given any thought to was marriage. Emma's banter made her realise that it wasn't such a remote possibility. She and Alex loved one another – now. She'd once loved Hugh and look how that turned out. What was to stop the same thing happening again? If they did get married and the marriage fell apart, she would be all alone on the other side of the world. What about The Willows? Sasha couldn't run *Personal Agenda* single-handed, no one could.

It was only a short time since she'd established the agency, but Jane was proud of what she'd achieved. Evie and Tony, Kim and Jonathan, two marriages – or one marriage and a sham, depending on how you looked at it, she shrugged. With Sasha and Charles's help, she'd proved the sceptics wrong. And what about Justin and William? She'd come to love them dearly. Matt and Susie? These people were her surrogate family, the people she was leaving behind. A flutter of fear ran through her.

Sasha's voice broke through her morbid

thoughts. "Why are you standing there in the cold?"

"Sasha, do you think I'm foolish to get involved with this trip?" she asked.

"What brought that on? Come inside, Jane."

They sat at the table in the warm kitchen as they had done countless times before. "Now tell me what's upset you?" Sasha said.

"I suddenly realised I'm going half-way across the world to be with a man whom I hardly know."

"Is *that* all?"

"Isn't it enough?"

"You're going to spend two fabulous weeks in one of the most – *two* of the most exciting cities in the world. And in those two cities is the man who put enough sparkle in your eyes to power a generator, a man you're crazy about and who's mad about you. If you can find anything wrong with that set-up, tell me about it."

A look of relief crossed Jane's face. "When you put it that way, it does sound good. It's just that I suddenly thought about leaving you, and Justin and William – and all this." Jane glanced about her.

"You mean the washing up, the laundry?"

"Idiot! America seems so far away."

"Less than four hours by Concorde. It will take me longer than that to get home at Christmas."

"You're always so . . ."

"Jealous?" Sasha interrupted. "Too right I am. I'm green with envy. If you don't want Alex I'll have him, so make up your mind. Besides, I've promised Alex that I'd send him some of my famous mince pies."

"I didn't know you were famous for your mince pies."

"I'm not, but it sounds so positive."

"You're totally nuts, do you know that?"

"Yep, but you like me just the same."

"You're right, I really do."

Chapter Sixty-Seven

Apart from Donahue's resignation, Ray couldn't think of a time when CCC had fared better. They had five current jobs on hand. It would only be a matter of days now before he received his insurance cheque. Everything had gelled beautifully. There were still five computers to be sold but he'd have no trouble getting rid of those.

Ray swivelled the thickly upholstered leather chair to face the window. The tree-tops were bare, which made him think of winter. He closed his eyes and a vision of warm Caribbean sands, swaying palm trees and blue- lapping water filled his mind. Grass-skirted girls with leis round their necks floated towards him. It didn't disturb his fantasy that they were Hawaiian.

The men from the fraud squad didn't bother to knock at his door. His dream faded as he swung his chair back to reality.

Ray frowned. "What can I do for you gentlemen?"

"Ray Parker?" One of the men stepped forward.

Ray nodded warily.

"You are under arrest . . ."

Ray didn't hear the rest, didn't hear the caution.

Odd words lodged in his brain . . . *fraud* . . . *theft* . . . *insurance claim*.

He lost track of the hours he'd sat in that cold interrogation room. He could imagine the headlines in the tabloids. With a sinking heart he thought about his parents. No scandal had ever touched them, crime was something that happened to other people. His questioning seemed to have gone on forever. Finally he gave them the address of the lock-up garage where the stolen machines had been hidden. Sweat trickled down his neck onto his back. The sweat of fury and frustration. How many times did he need to repeat himself – he didn't *know* the name of the man who'd carried out the robbery.

"He refused to give me his name," Ray repeated for the tenth time. "I had a phone number, that's all."

"We have that," the detective said. "It's a public pay phone."

Ray wondered whose fax number *You Know* had used.

A solicitor was appointed for Ray and he arranged bail. Ray's flat looked as though it had been hit by a hurricane which had blown through on its way somewhere else. He couldn't even afford the rent now. How had the police found out? How?

Ray kicked the mattress which stood to attention against the bed. The sheets lay in a tangled heap with his clothes and books. Drawers had been opened and left that way. The diskettes – where were Ray's diskettes?

Could he sue the police for this intrusion, he wondered hysterically.

♥ ♥ ♥

Ray sat hunched in a corner of the carriage; the clack of the wheels on the track made his nerves jangle. With each passing mile he became more and more depressed. In his mind he could see the look of shock on his parents' faces, almost feel their sense of shame.

He trudged up the path of the semi-detached house. He stood at the door for a moment, he could hear someone moving around inside. Ray took a deep breath and pressed the bell.

"Ray! What a wonderful surprise! Come in, son, come in. Johnny, Ray's here," Mary Parker called excitedly to her husband.

Ray wanted to run away. He wanted to spare them the hurt and humiliation that would surely follow. But he had nowhere else to go, no money, no future, not even a life to look forward to.

"How are you, son?" Ray's mother asked.

"OK, Mum," he replied in a flat voice. How was he going to tell them? How?

"What are *you* doing here?" Johnny Parker asked his only son.

"Hello, Dad." Ray could barely meet his father's eyes.

"What's wrong, Ray?" Mary Parker had always known when Ray was worried or troubled.

"It's nothing – really."

"What's the matter?" she repeated stubbornly.

Ray told them the truth, the whole story. His eyes blurred with remorse as he saw the shock cross their faces just as he had feared it would.

But there was no point in trying to lie to them. He'd rather they learnt the truth from him than read it in the newspaper.

Ray sat and stared at the blank television screen in the little parlour. It used to amuse him when his mother insisted on calling it that. But today the memory didn't bring even the vestige of a smile to his worried face. How had the police found out? When had it all started to go wrong? The day after Donahue had resigned? Donahue? No, Donahue didn't suspect a thing. The only thing he whinged about or cared about were his bloody diskettes.

Mary Parker put the mug of tea on the table beside her son. They didn't speak. She shambled back to the kitchen and poured a mug for herself. She hadn't seen the neighbours recently, Ray did all the shopping now – it was the least he could do. In the room up above she heard her husband get out of bed. Poor Johnny, he hadn't been the same since it happened . . . after the way they'd brought Ray up . . .

Chapter Sixty-Eight

The four of them plus Jane's luggage barely fitted into the car. Justin and William had taken the morning off; Jane was not taking a taxi to the airport while they had a say in the matter.

"Be careful of that case," Sasha warned.

"Yes, madam," Justin bowed.

"What's in it that's so precious?" William asked as he leant against the door and watched Justin heave the case into the boot.

"My mince pies. They're for Alex."

"You should have put a label on the case, fragile, mince pies, handle with care," Justin puffed and panted.

"And let everyone know about its precious cargo?" Sasha asked.

"Stop fighting you two," Jane begged. "I'm nervous enough."

Tears glinted in Jane's eyes as she said goodbye to them.

"Don't forget J A – phone home," Sasha called.

The Concorde lounge was situated in a three-storey atrium in terminal four. It was already buzzing with passengers. Jane settled into a gold-coloured tub chair and looked nervously about her. Everything was hushed and calm in the lounge. Her eyes followed the Greek key pattern on the carpet, then wandered to the soothing pictures on the walls. The effect of the subdued lighting was restful and calmed her fears. Nobody else seemed to be unduly harried or concerned. They were obviously all seasoned travellers. She sipped the champagne she was offered as nonchalantly as she could.

The aircraft cabin was divided in two. Jane's seat was half-way down the aisle in the rear cabin. A pretty stewardess helped her to settle in. "The seat beside you is empty, so once we're airborne you'll be able to spread yourself out."

Jane smiled at her. Just as she was about to ask if Kim Barrett was on board, the stewardess's attention was distracted by a group of passengers whose seat numbers needed sorting out.

She gripped the arms of her seat and braced herself as the supersonic jet hurtled along the runway. Miraculously the plane lifted off the ground and soared into the air.

"It's only an aeroplane, not a rocket," Jane heard the man in the seat behind say to his companion. She was in sympathy with his partner.

They climbed steadily at a steep angle and, after what seemed the length of two lifetimes, the plane levelled out.

Jane was impressed with the service. She'd promised Sasha that she'd keep any interesting menus she came across on her trip, and if the stewardess didn't object, this one would start the collection. Jane watched the mach counter reach the legendary '2'. A couple of passengers stood either side of it while a stewardess took their photograph. Twice the speed of sound, Jane thought, it felt just like any other plane. She opened the magazine that Justin had bought her, put on her headset and tried to relax until lunch was served.

The canapés were beautifully decorated, some with aspic, others under a glossy coating of mayonnaise. Sasha would really appreciate these, Jane thought, as she bit into a tiny pastry case filled with caviar. The chicken with lemon-grass fragrance was interesting but Jane just picked at it, her appetite had deserted her. She refused the wine and asked for another glass of champagne instead. There would be no point arriving with a headache or, worse still, a hangover.

She leafed through the in-flight magazine, twiddled the switches on her CD player. She thought she heard her name and opened her eyes.

"Kim!"

"Hello, Jane. I saw your name on the passenger list. I must have been in the cockpit when you came on board."

Jane felt a flush creep up into her cheeks. Kim must surely know that she was going to see Alex.

"Are you going to spend Christmas in the States?" Kim asked.

"Yes, Alex has invited me." There was no point in beating around the bush.

"Your first trip, isn't it?"

"Yes. I've always wanted to go there." This was embarrassing.

"You'll have a wonderful time." There was no hint of irony in Kim's tone.

"How's Jonathan?" Jane asked.

"He's fine, run off his feet as usual."

"Have you set the date yet for the big day?"

"First of April."

All Fools' day, how appropriate, Jane thought uncharitably.

Kim's arm was casually draped on the empty seat in front. Jane could see the glint of a ring. "Is that your engagement ring?" she asked.

Kim held out her perfectly manicured hand for Jane to see. The ring was beautifully set, a ruby surrounded by diamonds. "It's gorgeous. I'm sure you're thrilled with it."

"I am. It was Jonathan's grandmother's originally. It was a little old-fashioned, the stones unsafe in their setting, so we designed this new one together."

"It's lovely," Jane assured her again.

"How's everyone – Sasha, Justin and William?"

"They're well, they brought me to the airport this morning."

"What do you think of the bird?"

For a moment Jane looked puzzled. "Oh, Concorde. A very glamorous way to travel. I'm afraid I've pinched a menu for Sasha."

"Take it with pleasure, I'll see if I can find you a couple of different ones. We give them to the passengers as souvenirs."

"Thanks. Will you be in America for the

holidays?" Jane would hate it if they ran into Kim in New York.

"I'm off duty after the twenty-third. We're going to spend Christmas with Alex's parents . . . I mean, Jonathan's parents." Kim's face blushed redder than her ring.

"They live in Surrey, don't they?" Jane muttered. Kim's faux pas hadn't escaped her.

"What a good memory you have," Kim babbled.

"Why don't you sit down for a minute – if you have time."

Kim glanced towards the forward cabin. "Just for a second or two," she said warily.

"Kim, are you really over Alex?"

"Yes . . . yes, of course." She was flustered by Jane's bluntness.

"Forgive me, I know it's none of my business. But I do know what it's like to be trapped in a loveless marriage. In my case it didn't start out that way. Don't talk yourself into something that isn't right for you. Be sure that you love Jonathan before you commit yourself – or him."

Kim opened her mouth to speak then closed it again. They sat in silence.

"But I do love Jonathan," Kim said defensively. "He's everything I've ever wanted in a man, kind, considerate, thoughtful, handsome, talented and, yes, a comparatively rich man."

"I'm sure he is all those things. But, Kim do you love him for himself or for his attributes, is the chemistry right?"

Kim bit her lower lip, her eyes dark as storm

clouds. "We're happy together. We get on extremely well. I think we'll have a good marriage. After all, as you said yourself that day we met in London, even when you love someone madly, things can go wrong."

"I hope you're doing the right thing, Kim."

"Let me ask you a question. Are you in love with Alex? Does he love you?"

"Yes, I think I do love him. And yes, he says he loves me."

"Are you going to marry him?"

"He hasn't asked me to."

"He probably will. He'll make a wonderful husband, Jane. Grab him and don't let him get away."

"Oh? Why do you say that? You let him go."

"Look, it's a very long story, but I'll cut it short. I know how cruel men can be, not from my own experience – someone else's. I've always been wary, over-cautious if you like. Against my better judgement I did fall in love with Alex. I knew it wouldn't lead anywhere but I accepted the folly of it. We spent a magical week together, almost too good to be true. So when his wife showed up that day in Cape Cod, I thought, this is your punishment my girl, your comeuppance. You can't claim someone else's husband. She was so plausible, Jane, so much in control. The 'irrational' wife was nowhere to be seen. I know now that I should have listened to him, trusted him, given him a chance to explain. But at the time I was so incredibly hurt I could only think of my mother . . . yes, it was my mother that I saw abused, mentally and physically. Then one day, along came the kindest man I'd ever met. He treated my mother like a queen. He made her happy.

"I was only a youngster and he was marvellous to me too. And Jane, she is still happy. Jonathan is so like him. Alex was too. But I lost Alex because of my own stupidity. I don't want to lose Jonathan. I think I can make him happy, he deserves nothing less. And you and Alex – well, you hardly need my advice." Kim stared down at the picture in Jane's magazine. She'd never voiced her feelings like that before. Suddenly it was very important that Jane should know that she intended to do everything in the world to make Jonathan a good wife.

"I have to confess, I really misjudged your motives and I apologise." Jane's blue eyes blazed with sincerity. "You seem to know where you're going and I truly wish you every happiness."

"And I, you."

"That's a long way off."

Kim rose from the seat and smoothed her skirt. "I know what Alex is like. He's very impetuous and once he makes up his mind . . ." Kim leaned forward and touched Jane's arm. "Be happy, and don't be afraid to trust him. Will you let me know what happens?"

"I will."

Jane sat quietly. At least now she understood Kim's behaviour a little better. Hugh had probably been as cruel as most men but he'd never abused her physically. But then neither had Alex abused Kim . . .

"Ladies and gentlemen, we are now making our approach to Kennedy . . .

Jane shot up in her seat. " . . . local time nine-twenty."

Where had the hours gone? She couldn't believe they were going to land so soon.

Alex's tall figure was the first one Jane saw when she came through into the customs hall. What a noise! His face broke into a huge smile when he saw her. She returned his kiss shyly and took comfort from the warmth of his arm around her waist as he propelled her out of the building.

"I have a car waiting, we'll go straight to the hotel."

The Savoy-Carillon on Park Avenue was definitely a most luxurious hotel. It had a club-like atmosphere and Jane looked about the suite with fascination. The Regency decor of the living-room was a little stiff and formal for her taste but the tightly upholstered wine and grey striped fabrics with their tasselled cushions were impressive. She loved the tall bookcase crammed with the latest novels. There were several well-placed lamps by the arms of the striped satin chairs and there seemed to be acres of pale grey carpet, yards and yards of drapes – swagged in the most intricate design. Her eyes drank in the huge vases of flowers, their musky perfume blending with the smell of new wood. The porter told them that they were the first people to occupy the suite. The bedroom, with its kingsize, two-poster bed, was magnificently carved and draped. Jane was thankful that she didn't have to dust all the folds of the canopy which hung above the bed. There were several chairs in the room and a couple of small tables. The size of the room astonished her, such space. The bathroom, not surprisingly, was grey and wine also. She loved the fittings, a deep shade of wine, the towels, bathrobes and carpets all pale soft greys. She noticed that even the soaps and tissues were carefully colour matched.

"It's fantastic," she said.

"I thought a suite would be nicer," Alex admitted. "The jetlag will catch up with you tomorrow, you'll need a place to veg out."

"Veg out?" Jane asked – she'd never heard that expression before.

"Vegetate – sit in front of the television and fall asleep," Alex laughed.

Jane was worried that he'd gone to such expense to impress her. First there was the chauffeur driven car, now this.

"I hope I don't fall asleep, there's so much I want to see."

"And so you shall. I'll tell you what I've planned." Alex had been his usual thoughtful self. "I suggest we take the car and give you a tour of Manhattan. I haven't booked for a show or anything tonight – it'll take you all your time to stay awake. Tomorrow we can spend the day shopping and perhaps do a museum if you'd like – you name it, Jane, it's yours. We'll go to dinner in Chinatown tomorrow night, I think you'll enjoy that. The next day is yours to command and then, of course, there's the Nortons' Christmas bash that evening. The following morning we leave for Washington. How does that sound to you?"

Jane smiled up into his anxious face. "That sounds like quite a programme."

Alex relaxed. "It's so good to have you here." He held her tightly in his arms.

Locked in his warmth, Jane wondered why she'd ever doubted her love for him.

"I'd better let go of you, otherwise we'll never leave the hotel," he said reluctantly.

Jane craned her neck to see the top of the imposing skyscraper. Travis Inc. occupied one floor of the building on Wall Street. The reception area was manned by four girls, each dressed in a pastel-coloured Armani suit. Their sole job was to answer the phones. The enormous square room was wood-panelled and furnished with honey-coloured suede chairs. There were gigantic coffee tables with immaculately arranged magazines and daily papers. The walls were covered in tasteful corporate art, a couple of paintings familiar in style. As she passed it, Jane touched a leaf on one of the plants. The plant was so perfect she wondered if it was real. Jane was positive the whole ground floor of The Willows would fit into the reception hall, with room to spare.

Alex led her along corridors and introduced her to his vice-presidents. There were rooms everywhere. She met countless bright young investment councillors, lawyers, accountants, women and men from the typing pool and Alex's private secretary. She was a stylish woman in her early fifties, who apologised to Jane for leaving her holding the phone the day she'd rung.

"It's a bit bewildering at first, I must admit," Alex said as they sat in his office. It too was ridiculously large.

"It's all so huge. Is everything built on this scale in New York?"

"Compared to English companies I suppose it does seem very spacious. Prestigious office suites are part and parcel of our particular business. But the firm owns the building so we don't have to pay rent." Alex's tone was diffident.

"Would you like to go to a real New York deli for lunch?" Alex asked as he finished signing his papers. "There, the rest of the day is all ours."

"I'd love to try that," Jane admitted.

The Carnegie Deli was packed to the doors. Jane was sure she was being rude as she stared at the mountainous sandwiches on people's plates.

"Do you think I could order a small one?" she asked Alex when they finally found a table.

"Eat what you can – don't worry, this place is known for its generosity."

Jane managed to do justice to about a quarter of her meal. The chicken noodle soup was appetising and the pickled gherkins pungent and sharp. "Don't worry," Alex reassured her, "we'll take the rest home in a doggy bag."

Jane smiled. No doubt Alex would make short work of the rest. She knew by now that he was always hungry.

They drove along the avenues and streets of midtown Manhattan. There were so many of them. Then there was Greenwich Village, with its amazing variety of restaurants, SoHo with its cast-iron façaded buildings.

"This used to be the home of artists and writers. But when Greenwich Village was no longer hip, people began moving here. Now owning a loft in SoHo is very fashionable, the 'in' place to live, but very expensive," Alex explained.

"There are loads of antique shops around here," Jane noticed.

"Yes, but again very expensive."

After a couple of hours the names and places began to swim in her head, TriBeCa – Triangle below Canal Street, Alex translated. There was Little Italy, Chinatown, east this and west that. She'd never come to grips with directions here. They crossed the Brooklyn Bridge and drove through Brooklyn and Brooklyn Heights, a residential area with well-kept streets and houses. They drove through Queens, a neighbouring borough.

Jane struggled to take in all she saw and heard.

"How are you feeling?" Alex asked.

"A bit muddled, I think that jet lag is knocking at my door."

Alex asked the driver to take them back to the hotel.

Jane was happy to "veg-out" as Alex suggested. She curled up in the big chair and waited for tea. By the time room-service knocked at the door, she was sleeping soundly. Alex dragged a quilt from one of the beds and covered her.

♥ ♥ ♥

"Alex?" Jane called.

"Here," he answered from the bedroom.

"I'm sorry, I must have fallen asleep."

"You went out like a light."

"What time is it?"

"Almost seven-thirty."

"Why didn't you wake me?"

"Because you looked so peaceful and happy."

Jane held up her arms to him. Alex knelt down beside her and she wound them round his neck. "I'm so happy to be here," she said and smothered his face with kisses.

"Not as glad as I am. But, don't stop . . ."

"Shall I cancel the car for tonight, we can eat here if you like?" Alex asked.

"It's a very tempting offer but I think I'll just fall asleep again."

"What scintillating company I must be," Alex pouted.

"There's no one in the world I'd rather be with," Jane said quickly, then realised he was teasing.

"Where would you like to eat?" Alex asked.

"I don't mind. Somewhere informal?"

"OK. Go and have a shower it will refresh you. I'll book a table."

The wind was bitingly cold and Jane was glad of her long cosy coat.

In order to enter the restaurant they had to pass along a frosted window in which hung every kind of cut meat. Jane peered through the frosting.

"Don't worry, it's a real restaurant," Alex reassured her as he watched her puzzled reaction.

The room was long and narrow. A bar ran down the length of one side, and tightly packed tables took up all the floor space at the other.

"Gallagher's serve the most wonderful steaks you'll ever eat," Alex said. "It's always jumping from five-thirty onwards. People stop off here for a drink and sometimes a meal on their way home. It's near the theatres too."

Alex selected an enormous prime rib from the tray. Jane pointed to the smallest filet mignon she could find.

"They won't take long." The waiter asked if they wanted salads with their French fries or did they prefer baked potatoes? A barman took their drinks order, a Diet Coke for Jane, Alex ordered beer.

"Look at this," Jane turned her fork sideways and used it to cut the steak.

"Amazing isn't it?" Alex smiled.

"This must be a perfect breeding ground for half the coronaries in New York!"

"Could be, but what a way to go."

Alex wanted to hear all the news from Dornley. "How's my friend Mrs Reid?' he asked.

"Blooming," Jane laughed. "She doesn't change."

"I sent her a Christmas card," Alex said.

"That was thoughtful, she'll be thrilled. No doubt she'll tell me all about it when I get back."

"What happened between Amanda and Kevin? Did they ever sort out their problem?"

Jane paused for a moment, she didn't think it would do any harm to tell Alex the full story.

". . . and then she resigned – just before they fired her," Jane concluded sympathetically.

Alex's expression was grim. "You're far too soft, Jane. I'm afraid I can't share your feelings. There is no possible excuse for that kind of disloyalty, you can't buy popularity at other people's expense."

"I suppose that's another way of looking at it."

"And where did it get her? She's destroyed her career and lost Kevin anyway."

Jane wondered if he was hers to lose in the first place. "I suppose I feel sorry for her because I know what it's like to have been betrayed," she said honestly.

"We can all claim that. But character comes into it too. Imagine if everyone did what she did . . ."

The last thing she wanted to do was have an argument with Alex about Amanda. "Before I forget to tell you, Justin and William send their regards. Sasha said to give you a big hug – I'll give you that later," she promised.

"Did she send my mince pies?" He was glad to talk about something else. Jane was too soft for her own good.

"She certainly did. They're triple tin-foiled and cocooned in miles of bubble-wrap. Why do you think I needed two suitcases?" she grimaced. She made Alex laugh as she described how Sasha stood guard while they loaded Jane's luggage into Justin and William's compact car. The Willows and *Personal Agenda* seemed a world away now.

They lay languorously in each other's arms, she could become addicted to this.

"I think we'll stay here all day," Jane laughed as she watched the first flurry of snowflakes dance past their window.

"What a lovely thought, but we've got work to do," Alex said. "We've got to go and add our charitable contribution to the stores. There's a bare, lonely Christmas tree in Washington waiting to be decorated, I thought you'd enjoy selecting the trimmings for that. And I'm sure you'll want to buy something for yourself, some gifts for Sasha and the others."

Jane stared at the festive decorations in the stores. There were more glittering trees per square foot than anywhere in London. Never had she seen more marvellously wrapped packages. "Even if they were empty they'd be beautiful," she said.

Alex smiled at the wonderment in her face at the sheer size of Macy's.

"It's the largest department store in the world," he told her.

"And I think we've covered every inch of it, and I think I've been sprayed with every perfume known to woman."

At every counter's end there was a promotion of some fragrance or other.

It was a luxury to hand her purchases to the driver and then start again empty handed. Alex had made her buy so many decorations for the tree, Jane was sure they'd be able to decorate all the neighbours' trees too. He took her to a bookshop which specialised in second-hand books. She was thrilled to find a beautifully bound Harriet Beecher Stowe first edition for Justin and William. For a Washingtonian, Alex certainly knew his way about New York. Jane agonised between two sweaters for Sasha, then bought them both. They spent far longer than necessary in FAO Schwarz's toyshop on Fifth Avenue. She chose the latest Barbie doll for Alice Jones and a box of colourful painted cars for Peter.

There were Santa Clauses in their bright red suits tolling bells on every street corner. Jane was grateful to step into the car and be whisked away from the jostling crowds fighting each other for taxis. In heated comfort she remembered Christmases in London, happy at first then increasingly miserable. She tucked her arm into Alex's and hugged him to her. He smiled and kissed her. Perhaps he too had bad memories of wasted years and unhappy holidays.

Chapter Sixty-Nine

Jane stood nervously at Alex's side while they waited for the elevator. He looked so distinguished in his tuxedo. Two other couples, also in evening dress, joined them. They were obviously in a party mood and their friendliness broke Jane's tension.

The apartment, overlooking Central Park, was staggeringly large. Jane was now beginning to accept these vast, spreading buildings. Cecil Norton and his wife were accomplished hosts.

"Welcome to New York." Cecil Norton held out both his hands in greeting.

"We're delighted that Alex brought you," Ellie Norton said warmly.

"It's very kind of you to invite me," Jane said.

"You look gorgeous, Jane," Ellie Norton said approvingly. "Cecil, look after Alex while I introduce Jane to the other guests."

After the first fourteen or fifteen handshakes people's names escaped her. Jane could see Alex's head above the crowd as she was steered deeper into the massive reception room with its Christmassy decor. She admired her hostess's artistry. There were two trees in the room, one decorated in red and gold, the other, Jane guessed, for their children. It was temptingly bedecked with striped sugar-canes, candies and all sorts of edible gold and red ornaments. The sober cream monotone of the room was relieved by the cheerful decorations. Vases as tall as Jane were filled with gold-tipped twigs and tied with red bows. Jane could appreciate how long it must have taken Mrs Norton to achieve that effect. Over the thickly carved door lintels and along the fireplaces – one each end of the room – great boughs of fir tapered artistically. Fir cones sprayed with seasonal gold added their own bright splashes of colour. Ivy trailed down either side of the doors and miniature red bows hung with tiny tassels of gold were attached to the shiny, green leaves.

"Your decorations are exquisite, it must have taken you days to do all this," Jane said.

Ellie Norton laughed uproariously. "I wouldn't know where to begin. My florist takes care of it all."

Jane felt gauche. "I'm sorry . . ." she began to apologise, then stopped. "It's a hobby of mine, I just assumed . . ."

"I'm afraid I have neither the talent nor the time for this kind of thing," Ellie Norton sighed. She excused herself and left Jane to greet some new arrivals.

"I'm Ellie's sister." The woman who stood beside her looked nothing like her sister. She had a sharp pointed face, and eyes that were almost squinting with concentration made her look vindictive. She probably needs glasses, Jane thought, but is too vain to wear them.

"Alex Travis brought you along, didn't he?" She

narrowed her eyes and had a long look at Jane's dress.

"Yes," Jane said uncomfortably. The woman made her feel like an appendage.

"How did you meet him?" she asked.

"We met in London." Jane's reply was curt.

"Tragic news about Cassie, wasn't it?"

Jane nodded, she didn't know where this conversation was leading.

"You knew Cassie?" Her eyes had now reached Jane's hair.

"She died before I met Alex."

"Hard to believe that was less than a year ago. Made a rapid recovery, didn't he?"

"Would you forgive me, there's someone over there I need to say hello to."

Jane moved purposefully to Alex's side.

"How are you doing?" Alex put a protective arm round her shoulder.

"Not too well, I think. That woman – Ellie's sister . . ."

"Patty? Don't take any notice of her. She's a real flake. Likes to make something out of nothing and that's exactly what fills her mind – nothing."

"Alex, aren't you going to introduce us?" A tall white-haired man held out his hand to Jane.

"Lee! What a nice surprise," Alex said. "This is Jane Anderson, Lee Norton."

Jane could see the resemblance between Lee Norton and his brother the Senator.

"A pleasure," he beamed. "I heard Alex had netted himself a beautiful mermaid. But my word, I'd no idea just how gorgeous."

Jane flushed, she wasn't used to such extravagant compliments.

"As long as she doesn't disappear back into the sea, I'm all right. Lee and I are old fishing buddies from way back," Alex explained.

They reminisced for a moment or two until Lee apologised for their bad manners. "How did you two meet?" he asked.

Let Alex answer that one.

"I landed on her doorstep one day," Alex said easily. "From then on I was hooked."

A muffled gong sounded in the distance. Lee Norton crooked his arm and Jane, not wanting to appear churlish, slipped her own arm through his.

Yet another surprise greeted her; the dining-room must have been sixty feet long. Jane counted six separate curtained windows. The table appeared to be fashioned from a single piece of highly polished wood and ran almost the full length of the room. Jane wondered how it would be possible to pass anything across its width. Perhaps it was made from one of those giant sequoia trees. She couldn't imagine anything smaller would do. She stifled her laughter as she pictured herself crawling along its top in an effort to decorate it. The elaborate centrepiece stretched from one end of the table to the other. Jane wished she had a camera. Sasha, Justin and William would love this. This made their dinner parties look a doddle.

When the forty guests were seated, the Senator, who told her to call him Cecil, smiled benignly at her.

"Do you work?" he asked.

"I run a dating agency, *Personal Agenda*," Jane said.

"How interesting. All done by computers now I suppose?"

"No, we are residential. Each weekend . . ."

Several people stopped talking and listened to what she had to say. Jane wasn't used to being the centre of attraction and found herself quite enjoying it.

"What do you charge?" one man asked.

Jane was taken aback at the blunt forthright question.

"What a shame you are so far away." An attractive dark-haired woman saved her from having to answer. "It sounds like a whole lot of fun."

"Surely you must have similar agencies here?" Jane asked.

No one knew of any. When their attention was diverted, Cecil Norton whispered that if they did, they wouldn't admit to it anyway.

From the far end of the table, in his place of honour beside Ellie Norton, Alex watched Jane's face light up with laughter. He was too far away to hear her conversation, too polite to let his attention wander from his companions. How beautiful Jane looked, how assured and natural. When she'd walked into the sitting-room of their suite tonight dressed in that wonderful blue dress, it had taken all his strength of will not to propose on the spot. Earlier he couldn't wait to introduce her to his friends and acquaintances, now he could barely wait to take her home, keep her all to himself.

The meal was professionally served by an army of white-gloved waiters. The turkey, perfectly carved in identically sized pieces, looked attractive but secretly Jane thought it lacked taste. She much preferred her own crisp roast potatoes to the sweet potatoes they offered but she was probably being over-critical.

All conversation came to a halt when a waiter dropped a magnificent fruit platter with a crash. Scarlet-faced, he escaped from the room and the anguished frown of his employer. Jane felt sorry for him. They'd been remarkably lucky, she and Sasha. Apart from the wayward soufflés and undercooked beef, their other disasters – like the caramel she'd burnt the day she met Alex – could be righted.

"Why are you smiling?" Cecil Norton asked, anxious to get the conversation back on an even keel.

"I was thinking about the day of our housewarming party . . ." Jane told him the story of the ants.

It was the first time Jane had been to a dinner party where the men remained at the table and the women congregated in the living-room. It seemed strangely old-fashioned in this day and age.

"Hi! I'm Marcie." An attractive woman, roughly her own age, joined Jane on the sofa. "I noticed your look of surprise when the men stayed in the dining-room."

"It seems odd. I thought that kind of thing went out with smoking!"

"This is when the real purpose of the dinner begins."

Jane was puzzled.

"When the deals are done. There's a heck of a lot of serious money in that room tonight," Marcie assured her.

Jane's eyes wandered towards the women. They were expensively and fashionably dressed, and several of them wore quite a lot of jewellery. Their ages differed considerably. Some were around her own and Marcie's age, most of them older.

"I don't think I met your husband, did I?" Jane asked.

"Come back after New Year's and you will," Marcie smiled – smugly? "Did you notice the man about three seats away from you? Salt and pepper hair?"

"Yes, I know who you mean now," Jane said. She recalled the man, he'd been very quiet, just smiled a lot.

"He's my husband-to-be. It's under wraps for the moment – please don't say a word. He hasn't told his wife yet, poor sucker. He wants to wait until after Christmas."

Marcie's candour shocked Jane. "His wife, is she here?"

"Sure. That's her over there, in pink. Not her colour!"

Jane's eyes rested on the group of women sitting across the room from them. Marcie was right, that insipid flesh-pink was not the most flattering colour for her rival. But Jane felt an overwhelming sympathy for the wife who was to be "dismissed" after Christmas.

"And she doesn't know about . . . you and her husband?" Jane couldn't help asking.

Marcie shrugged. "I dunno, maybe."

Jane wondered why Marcie was here. Was she a friend of the Nortons?

"I'm Jimmy's personal assistant." Marcie solved

the mystery. "He needs me at these dinners. If he strikes a deal, I need to take notes for him."

Jane presumed that could be necessary. She warned herself not to get involved.

"So you and Alex are an item?" Marcie winked.

"We're friends, yes."

"He vanished for a little while after Cassie popped her cork. A real mess *she* was. He wouldn't allow anyone to attend the service or the cremation. I suppose with their daughter's grave being there . . ."

Jane couldn't be bothered to correct Marcie, Alex had told her that Cassie and her daughter weren't buried together. Jane hadn't liked to ask why.

"It was tragic losing his little girl like that."

"Sure was. I hear that he was besotted with her. I only saw the kid once, she was a real doll. I think even way back then, he had more time for the kid than he did for Cassie."

"I didn't know his wife," Jane said for the second time that night. Marcie wasn't the kindest person she'd ever met. "Do you know Alex well?" Jane didn't really want to talk about Alex but her curiosity got the better of her.

"Not as well as I would have liked to!" Marcie's grin was cheeky. "Anyone that good-looking, and that rich, has my undivided interest."

Jane made no comment.

"So he turned up in your pool!" Marcie observed.

"As I said, we're friends."

"Well honey, I'd do something to cement that friendship if I were you. He's got to be one of the best catches around."

Pool or no pool, Jane thought, I'm getting out of my depth. She was relieved when they were joined by Ellie Norton.

Jane was pensive on the short journey back to the hotel. Alex took her silence as tiredness and sat quietly holding her hand. Marcie, with her matter of fact approach, had given Jane plenty to think about.

♥ ♥ ♥

Everyone in New York seemed to be heading for the airport. Their driver complained that traffic was grid-locked for miles around. But somehow, despite all the odds, they finally arrived at their destination on time. Alex's tall figure protected her from the milling throng. With surprising ease he checked in and they escaped to the sanity of the departure lounge. Jane wasn't used to having someone look after her like this.

The Washington shuttle was cleared for take-off and Jane relaxed in her seat. "I never thought we'd actually be sitting on a plane today," she admitted.

"Christmas Eve is probably a rotten day to travel. But we should be at the apartment by noon."

At five minutes past midday Alex put the key in his front door. He stood aside to let the driver take the cases into the entrance hall.

"I won't need you again today, John. Have a good holiday." Alex slipped an envelope into the driver's pocket.

"Thank you, Mr Travis," he said. "Hope you have a good holiday too."

"Is he your own driver?" Jane asked as she followed Alex into the apartment.

"Yes, he is. John's been with the firm since he was a boy," Alex said. "My father never drove and, although I enjoy motoring, there are times when I need to get from one place to another in a hurry. Parking isn't as bad here as it is in New York but it can still be pretty difficult. Take a look round the apartment while I dump the bags."

The first thing Jane noticed was the big Christmas tree. Alex was right, it did look forlorn and lonely, and so did the rest of his rented apartment. It was warm, well-furnished but totally impersonal. What a colourless place the living-room was. There were two bedrooms with en suite bathrooms and a well-equipped kitchen. Jane smiled to herself, only she could get excited about a trash compactor. The living-dining-room was about thirty feet square, a similar size to or maybe bigger than the one at The Willows. In one corner there was an attractive round table and six comfortably-upholstered chairs. The rest of the room was furnished with featureless but soft large chairs and two sofas. Alex could never be happy in a small, confined space.

On a small table beside a lamp were two mother-of-pearl-framed photographs. Jane's face broke into a smile. She recognised Alex instantly, a gangly teenager, leaning against a boat and proudly holding up a fish. The second photo was also of Alex but this time with a little blonde-haired girl of about two years old. Her face rested on his shoulder and her hands were tiny compared to Alex's.

"She was so pretty, wasn't she?" Jane said gently.

Alex nodded silently, his face sad.

"What do you think of the apartment?" he asked as he cradled her in his arms.

"I think it's . . . lovely," she said lamely.

"And needs a woman's touch?"

Jane laughed. "You're as bad as Sasha, she can always read my mind too."

"Let's get unpacked and see what the day brings."

By the time Jane had hung up her clothes and extricated the mince pies from her case, the phone had rung a dozen times.

"News travels fast around here." Alex frowned. "After that dinner last night I suppose people have found out that I'm back in circulation, and invitations are flooding in thick and fast."

Jane's face fell. She began to worry if she'd brought the right clothes with her and whether she could cope with more parties.

"I hope you don't mind but I've refused most of them. I said yes to a couple of my old friends who would love to meet you. But don't worry, if you don't like the idea, they'll understand."

"I'd love to meet your friends. As long as their wives aren't like Marcie and Ellie's sister."

"Marcie! I had other things on my mind last night." Alex grinned lasciviously. "I forgot about her. What did *she* have to say?"

"She said I should cement our relationship before someone else got their claws into you, and that I'd hooked a seriously-rich man."

Alex shook his head. "What else did she say?"

"That she was going to marry Jimmy . . . I

don't know his other name. It's supposed to be confidential but she obviously didn't care. Can you imagine her telling me that, a stranger, while his wife was sitting there? He's going to give his wife the good news after Christmas." Jane's voice was bitter.

"That all?"

"Just about."

"Half of it's right, the other half wrong. You should definitely cement our relationship!" Alex's eyes twinkled. "You never know who's behind the curtains waiting to grab me."

"And the other thing?" Marcie's marriage no doubt, Jane thought.

"The other thing is . . . yes, I suppose I would be considered to be . . . comfortably off. When I was younger that meant a lot to me. I wanted to prove that I could earn a lot of money. But I was so involved in what I was doing, that became unimportant. When my life fell apart, work was my saviour, not my money."

"And what about Marcie?"

"Marcie and Jimmy? I guarantee that Jimmy has no intention of marrying Marcie. I've seen him with five or six Marcies in as many years. In a couple of hours from now, she'll be clutching some wildly extravagant gift and a letter containing Jimmy's heartbroken lies."

"But that's terrible, I mean . . . I thought . . . she was so sure. Why did he take her to the dinner?"

"That's his way, conceit perhaps – Marcie's not bad looking, much younger than his wife. He's a very generous and influential man. But there's no way he's going to leave Helena for Marcie.

Helena is well used to his affairs, we all are. But everyone turns a blind eye – including his wife."

"I think that's disgusting . . ." Jane stopped as the bell rang.

Within minutes people were swarming all over the apartment. Florists delivered flaming red poinsettias, greenery for decorations, an armful of brilliantly coloured birds-of-paradise and two boxes of choice winter blooms. There were containers and wires and all the paraphernalia of flower arranging.

Caterers followed hot on the heels of the florists. A plump, uncooked turkey rested on the kitchen counter beside a bag of ready peeled potatoes. A woman was filling the freezer and, a man carrying a huge plastic container, asked Alex where he should store it. There were bowls of salads, wickedly-rich chocolate desserts and foil containers everywhere. It reminded Jane of the day-of-the-ants.

Soon everything was quiet again. "Let's explore," Alex said eyeing the boxes of food.

"Are you having a party?" Jane asked bewildered.

"No party, just the two of us. You do enough catering all year round, this is your vacation. I'll cook the turkey tomorrow, everything else is ready to eat."

"You really are a thoughtful man, Alex Travis." Jane stood on her tiptoes and kissed his cheek.

"Is that the best you can do?" he asked as he caught her in his arms.

By mid-afternoon they were ready to start trimming the tree. Jane couldn't remember when she'd enjoyed herself so much. Alex's height was a boon. Jane just stood back and showed him where to hang each of the coloured ornaments. In the end the boughs were so laden with baubles that she was afraid the tree would topple over.

Alex looked at the room.

"What a difference. You really are talented, Jane."

The birds-of-paradise in the plain tall vases added touches of exotic colour to the insipid room. Jane had massed the plants in great drifts of scarlet. In the centre of the dining table she'd placed a festive arrangement of flowers and ornaments. "Now it's beginning to look like Christmas," she agreed. Anything to do with flowers was a pleasure to her.

"Would you like to phone Justin and William? Sasha perhaps? I'm sure you'd like to wish them Merry Christmas," Alex suggested, looking at his watch.

"I'd love to," Jane said enthusiastically.

"What a lovely surprise," Justin said. "It's Jane," she heard him call to William.

"Are you having a wonderful holiday?" William wanted to know. "Where are you?'

"I'm having a brilliant time. We're in Washington – New York was amazing. How are you both?"

"Fine. We have a cottage full here. We miss you."

"I miss you too."

"We popped into The Willows this morning just to check around. No problems there."

"Thanks, Justin. I've almost forgotten what Dornley looks like. Everything here is so vast, you should see the height and the size of the buildings. But I'll tell you all about it when I get home. Can I have another word with William? Happy Christmas, Justin."

William was delighted to hear Jane sound so eager. He too said they missed her. They'd have a belated Christmas dinner when she and Sasha got back.

"I'll really look forward to that. Hold on a moment, William, Alex wants to say hello."

Alex spoke to both men and promised not to let too much time elapse before his next visit to England.

"Send Jane home soon," Justin instructed.

"That's one promise I can't make. I'd rather not send her home at all."

Sasha was equally happy to hear from Jane and Alex. Jane told her as much as she could about New York, about the Nortons' dinner party.

"Yes, my outfit was fine, it was admired by quite a few of the women."

"And all of the men," Alex called in a voice loud enough for Sasha to hear.

". . . yes we are, Alex is cooking it. I'm barred from the kitchen. We've had a lovely afternoon trimming the tree, and you should see the flowers Alex ordered."

Jane could hear Sasha's sisters in the background. "Have a lovely Christmas, Sasha. See you soon."

♥ ♥ ♥

Jane slept until eleven o'clock. She dashed out of bed and rushed to find Alex. "Happy Christmas," she called.

"Happy Christmas, darling." He kissed her and said, "Go back to bed and I'll bring some coffee."

"I'm going to get thoroughly spoilt," Jane said chewing a piece of hot muffin.

"Stay where you are." Alex left the room and came back with a pile of beautifully wrapped gifts. Jane was captivated by the coffee-table cookery book of American recipes. There was a set of American spoons and measures in a flowered box. She loved the fragrance of the latest perfume from Estée Lauder and also the delicate spider's-web scarf in her favourite blue.

Jane took Alex's gifts from her drawer. He tried on the padded jacket and refused to take it off. The sweater he thought perfect for cold winter days, and he was delighted with the woody-scented aftershave.

"Don't forget the last one," Alex reminded her.

Jane frowned. Then suddenly remembered, Alex and his appetite. Jane handed him the parcel from Sasha. Only three of the pies were damaged and he popped one of them into his mouth there and then. "No point in making crumbs!" he said convincingly.

The day passed in relaxed contentment. Alex made a good job of cooking the turkey but he did ask for advice now and then. He relented and allowed Jane to roast the potatoes. While they ate she told him of her childhood Christmases in Ireland. The seasonal fun of the earlier days of her marriage. She loved all the preparation, the fuss. But she didn't speak of later years. Years when she sat alone, too ashamed to admit she didn't even know where Hugh was.

Alex's Christmases were spent at the Cape Cod

house. Beautiful crisp and frosted days, often feathered with snow. Church on Christmas morning. The roaring log fires, all the sweeter for having chopped the wood. Neighbours coming to call. Egg-nog and punch. And after enormous lunches, they sat by the tree and opened their gifts. Although he didn't say it to Jane, this was the first time he'd talked about the beach house without shuddering.

"I wonder was it as magical as we imagine?" Jane asked.

"I think so. Kids were more innocent in those days. The pleasures more simple. I remember being thrilled to open a box of fishing-flies, a jigsaw that kept me busy for days."

"You and me both. I love jigsaws. I was lost to the world with my book of paper dolls and their cut-out clothes. A world of paper dreams."

"I have some jigsaws in the cupboard, would you like to try one?"

They pored over the wooden pieces, far more beautiful than any Jane had seen before. Each piece, in the shape of an animal, was extremely difficult to put together. When they finally completed the puzzle, the resplendent figure of a lion emerged.

"Do you want to try another? This one is even more difficult."

The second one was made up of different shaped trees; when those pieces were linked correctly, a beautiful chestnut tree appeared on the table.

They made love that night with a tenderness and poignancy Jane would never forget. As she listened to Alex's deep even breathing she wondered how she could leave him and go back to her normal life at The Willows.

But Alex wasn't asleep. He lay quietly thinking how empty his life would be when Jane returned to England. How much longer could he go on taking time off to visit her? A love affair by phone with snatched visits? Tomorrow would be their last day together – maybe forever.

Chapter Seventy

John, Alex's driver, collected them early on New Year's Day. They drove through the wide streets then headed away from the city towards the Virginian Hills. Jane had seen quite a lot of the capital city and she liked the slower pace of Washington compared to the frenzied, churning movement of New York.

"Tell me about your friend," Jane said as she watched the passing landscape.

"He was really my father's friend. I've known him since I was a boy."

They drove along a winding path and stopped outside the door of a long rambling house sheltered from the chill winds by the hills behind.

"It's gorgeous," Jane exclaimed. "This must be heavenly in summer. Just look at those creepers growing on the walls." The stone house was barely visible under its coat of gnarled, twisting creepers. A shutter had broken loose from its moorings and was flapping against the wall. Jane wished she had a hammer so she could tack it back into place.

Bill Brigham greeted Alex affectionately. His snow-white hair was in marked contrast to his startlingly black eyebrows. His green eyes burnt bright in his face, his skin paper-thin with a gentle network of blue veins. A man at ease with himself. He kissed Jane's hand in a delightfully old-fashioned gesture. He ushered them into his sitting-room and sat them by the fire.

"I am pleased that Alex has brought you to see me. It's time he had the company of such a beautiful young woman. Not good for him to be all alone and brooding."

Alex smiled at the man. "You don't believe in beating around the bush, do you?"

"One of the few privileges of old age," Bill retorted.

"What a lovely home you have here." Jane left the chair and walked to the window overlooking the garden.

"Would you like to see the rest of the house?"

"I'd love to."

Bill Brigham relived aloud the times they'd spent in the spacious reception rooms. The parties they'd had when his wife was alive and the children were all there.

"It's not used any more," he said sadly. "The rooms are all closed up, stuffy and forgotten."

Jane glanced at Alex, his face was sad too. But in spite of the faded paintwork, the well-worn carpets and furniture there was a warm, homely atmosphere about the house. A lick of paint and a few bright fabrics would work wonders.

"Let's go and have a cup of coffee," Bill said. "Martha? Martha, are you there?"

A grey-haired woman appeared from the kitchen carrying a tray. "Mr Alex, it's so nice to see you again. It's been a while since you came to visit."

"Hello, Martha. It's good to see you too." Alex spoke softly to the woman as his eyes searched the tray. "You've made my favourite chocolate brownies."

"A visit wouldn't be a visit without them. Don't eat too many at once," she admonished. "I'll give you the rest to take home."

"You have quite a reputation, I see," Jane teased.

"Mr Alex has always had a sweet tooth. It's a wonder he isn't the size of a mountain." Martha smiled fondly at Alex.

Bill and Alex talked about the old days, the people who'd come and gone. Alex asked about Bill's sons and their families. Jane felt her eyes beginning to droop in the warmth of the pleasant room. It was a shame that the house was so unlived in, too big for one person . . .

"I think we'd better head back," Alex said. He noticed that Bill was beginning to tire and Jane looked positively sleepy. Suddenly he didn't want to share any more of their last precious hours.

Just as in New York, it was attempting to snow. Large flakes of melting white. Wouldn't it be wonderful if they got snowed in, he thought, then Jane wouldn't be able to go home. The last time he'd been caught in a blizzard was the night he'd met Kim. He felt no bitterness towards her now, after all, it was thanks to Kim that Jane had come into his life.

Alex hadn't asked her what she'd like to do on her last night in Washington. They'd spent fourteen wonderful days together. And fourteen even more wonderful nights. Jane alternated between happiness and despair. Happy to be together, sad that they must part. There'd been no talk of parting or when they'd meet again. Perhaps Alex would say something tonight. Jane peered through the steamy car window at the buildings which had become familiar. She recognised the round dome of the Capitol, much more beautiful from inside. They'd covered miles walking leisurely about the museums. It would take half-a-lifetime to cover all the exhibits thoroughly. Jane had met several of Alex's friends. All of them expressed delight in one way or another that he'd finally come out of the darkness. They were friendly people, laid-back and easy company just like Alex himself. Jane had taken to two of the wives instantly, and one she found reserved but sweet.

"Betsy is very shy," Alex told her. "The more you get to know her the nicer she is."

Jane was quite willing to believe whatever Alex said was true. She trusted his judgement totally.

They spoke very little as they prepared dinner. Alex read the cooking instructions on the caterer's carton of veal, while Jane made up a salad.

Halfway through the meal Alex put down his fork and pushed his plate away.

He poured more wine into their glasses and sat moodily swirling the liquid round and round. Jane too had lost her appetite and was glad of an excuse to leave the rest.

"Come and sit down, I need to talk to you," Alex took her hand and led her to the other side of the room. She sat facing him and waited for him to speak.

Alex put a blue velvet box into her hand.

Jane looked at the sapphire nestling in the silk-lined box. "It's so beautiful, Alex . . ."

"Jane, you know that I love you with all my heart. I would like you to be my wife."

Now that Alex had actually uttered the words they came as a shock. She loved Alex with every fibre of her being. The last two weeks had deepened her feelings for him, if that were possible. When she'd woken in the mornings or lain awake at night she tried to imagine how she would answer if he asked her to marry him. Each day that passed made the thought of life without him intolerable. Alex was everything she could ever desire. He was the kindest man she'd ever known. Thoughtful, funny, serious, responsible – everything that Hugh hadn't been. He was a wonderful lover. The only negative thought in her mind was that she would have to move to the United States to be with Alex.

Alex moved to her side. "I know it would be a big change for you – to move away from all your friends to a strange country. But I'll look after you, Jane." For a moment his serious look vanished to be replaced with an impish grin. "As Marcie said, you'll be well looked after financially too, so that wouldn't be a problem."

Jane held out her hand to him. "Money doesn't enter into it. I love you more than I've ever loved anyone in my life. You're the nicest man I've ever met. But I'm scared by the thought of moving away from everyone I've ever known."

"I understand that, Jane. You would be throwing your lot in with one person, leaving everyone you care about. But Jane, that one person will do anything in the world to make you happy."

"Move to England?" she asked with a wan smile.

"I would if it was possible. But I'd have to sell Travis Inc. . . ." Alex's expression had become serious again.

"Would you really do that for me?" Jane's voice was incredulous.

"If that's the only way we can be together, then, yes."

His answer was totally unexpected. He was willing to give up so much for her. "Oh, Alex, I can't ask you to do that. I will marry you, I'd be honoured to marry you."

The rest of the night went by in a blur. Alex, beside himself with delight, insisted they must celebrate by opening a bottle of warm champagne. He'd thought earlier of putting a bottle in the refrigerator, but didn't want to tempt fate.

Jane wasn't sure whether she was tipsy from the bubbles or the excitement.

"First thing tomorrow morning we'll take the sapphire to the jewellers and have it made into a ring for you." Alex planned.

Jane was shocked then excited, she hadn't realised that the beautiful stone wasn't a ring.

"I thought it was a ring," she giggled.

"If you'd refused to marry me I was going to have it made into a pendant for you instead," Alex explained. "There's something else, you must have thought it odd that our last full day together was spent with a friend of the family?"

"Not really, he's a lovely man. Lovely hou . . . sse." Jane slurred her words slightly.

"That's why I took you there, to see the house. Bill wants to sell the house. It's too big for him now. I've always loved it and I thought if we did get married and you liked it too . . ."

"I *adored* it, it would be a wonderful house to live in. Alex, would you like to have children?"

"I'd love to have children." He looked away for a moment. Jane put her hand under his chin. "No secrets, no hidden feelings?"

"I agree. But sometimes I feel very sad when I think about my little daughter."

"Why shouldn't you?" Jane stroked his arm.

"Why did I wait so long to ask you to marry me? Now we'll have to talk about everything on the phone. I'm so mad at myself. But I wanted you to be sure, give you time to get to know me."

"Couldn't you come home with me tomorrow?" Jane wove her arms round his neck.

"How can I? I'm stacked with . . . No, wait. If you stay a day longer I should be able to reschedule things here. How would that be?"

"Put it there." Jane laughed slapping Alex's palm. "I'm getting tiddly."

"Enjoy it, you don't get engaged every day."

"We should get engaged every day. We'll have to let Justin and William know I'll be home late," Jane said dreamily.

"I don't think they'd appreciate a phone call at this hour. The second we wake up tomorrow we'll phone them."

Alex laughed as Jane pulled a face. "But I want to tell them the news, now."

"Would you like to send a fax?"

"Yes, send a fax."

"Do you have the number?"

"Over there." Jane waved an arm in the vague direction of her handbag.

"I'll do it now."

"Then come to bed." Jane crooked her finger, picked up the empty champagne bottle and left him to type the fax.

By the time he reached their bedroom, Jane, fully dressed, was sound asleep cuddling the empty champagne bottle.

Chapter Seventy-One

Jane turned in her sleep, something was digging into her face. As she began to wake in the darkness of the early morning, she knew that something good had happened. She and Alex were going to be married. She moved her arm and discovered that she was clutching a bottle. Of all the nights to get tipsy! Her face flamed with embarrassment, she must have fallen asleep fully dressed – and with a champagne bottle. She'd be lucky if Alex hadn't changed his mind.

She was far too excited to stay in bed, there was so much to think about, so much to decide. Jane moved silently about the kitchen and waited for the coffee to percolate.

She sipped the hot liquid and tried to think where to start. There was The Willows, of course. Was Emma Brown really interested in buying the house or was it the idea of *Personal Agenda* that attracted her? *Personal Agenda*. What would happen to her clients, to all those weekends that were booked? And what about Sasha, would she stay on with Emma Brown?

When Alex came into the kitchen an hour later, Jane was thoroughly panic-stricken. He kissed the top of her head and smiled at her lazily.

"How's my bride-to-be this morning?"

"Embarrassed, ashamed, in a panic."

Alex tilted Jane's face and saw the alarm in her eyes. "What's the matter, Jane? You haven't changed your mind, have you?" he asked.

"No I haven't changed my mind, I thought you might have, and I wouldn't blame you."

"Is that all? You got a bit tipsy, what's wrong with that?"

"It's not just that, although I am disgusted with myself. I don't know what to do about my clients, the weekends. And there's Sasha, what'll happen to her? And The Willows, how do I know what it's worth? Now that I want to sell it, will Emma Brown still want to buy it or was that something she said on the spur of the moment?"

Alex took Jane's cold coffee and tipped it away. He refillled her mug, poured one for himself then sat beside her at the narrow counter.

"You've overlooked one thing," he said.

"What else have I forgotten?" she groaned. There were probably dozens of things she hadn't thought of.

"You've forgotten that you're no longer alone. I'll be there with you, we'll be together. We'll work things out *together.*"

Jane looked into his compassionate eyes. Together. She'd forgotten what is was like to be part of another person, to share, to belong. Tears misted her eyes. "What have I done to deserve you?" she asked.

"Or I, you?"

Chapter Seventy-Two

Sasha was waiting for them at the door. She and Jane hugged each other as if they'd been apart for years.

"Don't I get one too?" Alex demanded.

"Of course you do." Sasha stood on tiptoes to embrace him. "Come inside, you'll catch cold standing there," she fretted.

Jane and Alex had wasted no time on their flight home.

"I've drawn up a list of all we need to do," he said. Ideally he would have loved to have taken Jane back with him when he left in a week's time. But he doubted that even he could make that happen.

They'd agreed from the start that Jane should use a firm of solictors recommended by his own lawyers. "That would make the legal end of things much simpler," Alex's lawyer assured him. By the time they were ready to leave Washington the following day, he had already set the wheels in motion.

Sasha watched Jane's expression and listened to her excited voice as she told Susie her news. Jane laughed as she held the receiver away from her ear.

"I gather Susie is delighted?" she smiled.

"You gather correctly." Jane rubbed her ear and replaced her earring.

"I have a present for you, let me get it and then we'll sit down and I'll tell you everything."

Alex knew when he was beaten. He left the two of them talking and went for a walk. Being back at The Willows made him realise how much Jane loved the place, it would be a big step for her to leave it. But he could make her happy, *would* make her happy. He must wipe Cassie from his mind, Jane would be his wife now.

Sasha was obviously thrilled for Jane, but he thought he could discern an underlying sadness in her eyes. He wondered what would happen to her when Jane left? It *would* be lovely for Jane if Sasha, Justin and William could come to the wedding. He must see if he could arrange something. Surprise her. His long strides took him towards the village. He made his way to the newsagents to say hello to Mrs Reid, a smile on his rugged face.

♥ ♥ ♥

"Of course I was serious," Emma Brown said. This could be exactly what Amanda needed. "I'll talk to Amanda tonight and see how she feels about it. Providing we can work things out, you need look no further for a buyer. I'll phone you tomorrow."

Emma Brown replaced her receiver thoughtfully. Jane had kept her word and given her first refusal. She had no doubt that *Personal Agenda* would be a good investment, but that wasn't her prime concern. The whole set-up could be just what Amanda needed, an opportunity for her to recover her self-esteem, her confidence. There would be no problem as far as price was concerned, naturally she'd drive as hard a bargain as she could. Jane didn't strike her as being particularly tough or materialistic.

Emma flipped her pen over her fingers like a magician practising sleight-of-hand. She was pleased that Jane had come to her first but disappointed when Jane told her that Sasha didn't want to stay on at The Willows. Perhaps she could offer her an incentive, but instinct told her that wouldn't make any difference to Sasha's decision. Sasha would have been perfect for Amanda, she was an excellent cook, was well used to coping with clients and was quite a personality in her own right. In spite of her forthright manner and often bizarre appearance, people liked Sasha. But it wasn't the end of the world, they could hire staff; a cook and a housekeeper. That would leave Amanda free to attend to the running of the agency. And Charles, would he stay on? Emma's eyes narrowed – Charles Graham, now there was an ambitious young man if ever there was one. He would make the perfect partner for Amanda – if the price was right.

♥ ♥ ♥

"Charles? Emma Brown. How are you?"

"Fine, thank you." Charles was surprised to hear from her.

"Good. I wonder if we could meet in a few days' time? I have a proposition to put to you."

"What sort of proposition?" What was Emma Brown up to now, he wondered, when she refused to elaborate.

"I'll explain when I meet you. Please don't mention our meeting to Amanda."

Emma Brown had already made up her mind, if Amanda didn't want to run *Personal Agenda*, she would take it on purely as a business investment. Either way Charles Graham would be more than useful.

Chapter Seventy-Three

Jane's was the second unexpected call that morning. Charles stretched the telephone cord to its limit and sat on the arm of the chair near the window. As he listened to Jane he didn't notice the beauty of the sky, the fast moving clouds of white, pink and gold tinted by the sun's rays.

"Congratulations, I'm very pleased for you, Jane."

"Thank you, Charles. I must admit that I'm over the moon, I'm sure that this time I've picked the right partner."

"Alex is very . . . charming."

Jane heard the hesitation in his voice. "Don't you approve?" she asked quickly.

"Of course I do," he assured her. Jane hadn't changed, always seeking approval. How could he tell her what was spinning around in his mind?

This would end his comfortable arrangement with *Personal Agenda.* He would miss the commission, the luxury of a weekend retreat. But more than anything he'd miss the company, not just the clients but Jane and Sasha, Justin and William also. "I was thinking how sad it is that after all your hard work, *Personal Agenda* will just fizzle out."

"That might not happen," she said mysteriously.

"How come?"

"I'm thinking of selling The Willows as a going concern." Could she tell Charles that Emma Brown was interested? Why not? It wasn't a secret. "To be truthful, Emma Brown, Amanda's mother, is coming to see the house and she's keen to keep the agency."

So that's what Emma's call was about. This could be a lifeline for him. "I'm so pleased, Jane. I mean that all your hard work in *Personal Agenda* won't die after all," he said hastily.

"I'd like to think it will continue, but we'll have to wait and see."

"Obviously you haven't advertised the . . . house, there could be plenty of other people who'd be delighted to buy a thriving dating agency."

This was a much brighter picture; when Jane had first told him her news, he had taken it to be the end of *Personal Agenda.*

"When will you know if you have a deal?" he asked keenly.

"I don't know yet. I'll let you know if there's any news."

"Good luck, I'm rooting for you."

"Thank you. I'm sure Alex will know how to handle things. Bye, Charles."

Charles sat and stared at the carpet unseeingly. Jane's news had surprised him, probably because of his own ostrich-like refusal to believe that life could change. He should have realised that Jane wouldn't have gone haring across the Atlantic to visit Alex unless she felt very deeply about him.

But he'd pushed the thought aside as if by doing so, everything would remain the same.

His thoughts wandered back to the night of the house-warming party, that kiss which he'd "bestowed" on Jane. What an arrogant fool he'd been. At the time Jane's insecurity had irritated him and he'd made a grave mistake by letting it show. It had been difficult to worm his way back into her affections. If he was totally honest with himself, things had never been quite the same since. It was too late now, but if he'd made a greater effort, turned on some of his "stock-in-trade" charm, how differently things might have turned out. What an opportunity he'd missed and he had only himself to blame.

Chapter Seventy-Four

"They'll be here on Thursday with their architect, Neil Drummond!" Jane said as she returned to the kitchen.

"Oh, yes? Success story number three?" Sasha's eyebrows rose with her voice.

They explained to Alex that Emma Brown had met the architect at *Personal Agenda.*

"Two members of *Personal Agenda*? That could certainly work in your favour. Don't worry, the final figures will be ready by then," he said. He had volunteered to sort out the accounts leaving Jane free to attend to her own work. It had taken him a while to persuade her to cancel the next few weekends. "It's just not practical," he said. When Jane stubbornly refused to let people down, he appealed to Sasha to help him. After a long struggle, they succeeded.

Jane wasn't looking forward to Emma and Amanda's arrival. She wasn't good at being forceful. With her usual honesty she wondered if that was the true reason, or was it the finality of handing over The Willows to someone else? She must stop thinking like this, it was unfair to Alex. She pushed the thought from her mind and concentrated on the inventory of the house's contents.

♥ ♥ ♥

Alex did all the talking. Emma was very much in control as she swept through the house, Neil Drummond and Amanda trailing in her wake.

"It's larger than I thought," she commented as they sat round the dining-room table. "There's also plenty of space for expansion."

"Would that not make it more difficult to run?" Jane ventured.

Alex tapped her ankle with his foot.

"Expansion is always healthy," he encouraged. Jane's honesty had no place at this meeting. "The price of the house and goodwill of the business are here." Alex slid a piece of paper towards Emma. "Naturally we are not open to negotiation. I think it's fairly priced."

Jane glanced at the sheet of paper and paled. Alex had written a huge figure under the heading, goodwill. He'd been quite vague this morning when Jane asked him what that figure should be. Now she knew why. She'd never have agreed to such an amount.

Emma's expression didn't change. Did that mean she accepted their price? Jane looked anxiously at Alex. She couldn't read his expression either.

"This is a very hefty price," Emma finally said.

Alex shrugged. "Please don't feel any obligation. Jane is in no hurry to sell The Willows . . ."

Jane giggled inwardly, that's not what Alex had said in bed last night when he threatened to buy the house himself and give it away to a charitable organisation.

Emma looked at her daughter standing by the window. When she told Amanda what she planned to do, Amanda had reacted so enthusiastically that even Emma was astonished. Her lethargy had vanished and soon she was planning weekends for years to come.

"We'd like a few minutes to discuss this, if that's all right with you?" Emma said.

"Of course," Alex replied amiably. "We'll leave you to talk about it." Alex held Jane's chair.

"I'll send you in some coffee," Jane said as she followed him from the room.

"Why did you nudge me?" Jane asked Alex as the door closed behind them.

"If they want to extend The Willows that's their problem. I imagine that Emma intends making *Personal Agenda* less personal, more of an agenda!"

"Do you think she'll buy it?" Jane asked, too worried to smile at his comment.

"Yes I do. She'll kick a bit at the price, but don't worry, she'll agree in the end."

"They look pretty grim," Sasha said when Jane asked how things were going in the dining-room. "They stopped talking when I came into the room."

"Relax," Alex instructed. "Think how long it took you to make up your mind to buy the house."

Jane had visited The Willows four times before she made her decision. But she hated this waiting.

Amanda came into the kitchen to tell Jane and Alex that her mother was ready.

"We like The Willows very much, like the whole concept." Emma sat stiffly upright on the chair, her hands clasped loosely in her lap. "But I'm afraid the price is too high. I am, however, prepared to offer you ten thousand pounds less than your asking price."

Alex let his gaze wander to the window where Amanda stood slightly hidden in the shadows. He met Emma's eyes steadily. "We understand your dilemma but I'm afraid that is the price. As I said before, you musn't feel obligated."

Emma began to twist her hands. She's biting, Alex noticed with satisfaction.

"There is no *dilemma*, Alex, just a question of value for money." Why should Alex think that she couldn't afford to buy the house?

"Whatever the reason, we obviously have no common meeting ground. Now if you'll forgive me, I have some calls to make." He sprang lightly to his feet. In her muzzy disappointment Jane thought how easily Alex moved for such a tall man.

"Wait," Emma's voice rang. "Will you accept five thousand less?"

Alex moved the chair back to its place at the table. "I'm sorry I don't seem to have made myself clear," he said apologetically. "There can be no reduction of the price. None at all." He held out his hand. "Sorry we couldn't work things out. I've enjoyed meeting you, Emma, nice to have seen you again, Amanda – Neil."

"You drive a hard bargain, Alex Travis," Emma sighed.

"For someone who was ready to give the house away you took a heck of a chance," Jane said.

"It was in the bag."

"How do you know? she demanded.

"By Amanda's face, her body language. Unlike Sasha, she's not a very good actress. She wanted The Willows so badly you could smell it. When she came to call us back she was totally unperturbed and she stayed that way all through the meeting. She knew Emma would buy it in the end. All I had to do was keep an eye on Amanda and wait."

"You drive a hard bargain, Alex Travis!" Jane laughed as she repeated Emma's words.

Jane packed the last of her clothes into the crates. Everything was ready for the shippers. She sat back on her heels and breathed a sigh of relief. Emma had agreed to buy the entire contents of the house with the exception of some of Jane's mementoes. This time Alex had been much more flexible. He seemed to know instinctively when to push and when to draw back.

She would miss Alex terribly when he left tomorrow. But Jane had given her promise, she would stay with Amanda and show her exactly how everything worked. Luckily Amanda was used to working with computers, that would make things so much easier for her. There were so many things that she needed to explain to Amanda, things that she and Sasha took for granted. She must show her how to work the household machines, how to keep track of the linens, give her a list of people who supplied food and wines and she musn't forget to give her the phone number of the builder. But she would tackle that tomorrow, after Alex was gone.

Jane wasn't looking forward to the evening. Justin and William were making a farewell dinner for Alex. They'd also invited Susie and Matt as well as Sasha. She couldn't bear to think of their goodbyes. Naturally she'd see the others again, but Susie . . .

In spite of her earlier reservations, Jane thoroughly enjoyed the evening. Unknown to Jane they'd all decided to keep the evening free of *do-you-remembers*. It would serve no purpose and upset them all.

Sasha reverted to her old habit of dressing for the occasion. Her crinolined gown and bonnet totally blocked Alex's rear-view as he drove. Full of remorse and, as a compromise, she'd promised to remove the hoop before they started the journey home. Two oval red-cheeks, painted eye-lashes and a red, rosebud mouth, completely altered the shape of her face. She walked with jerky movements, her white starched pantaloons crackling as she moved. Now Alex knew why they'd always considered Sasha a trifle eccentric. She reminded him of a wooden doll and told her so.

"Thank goodness I haven't lost my touch," she'd beamed at him as she swished her skirt up the cottage path.

Everyone was in a jolly mood and once Jane got into the swing of things she kept them entertained with her description of the Nortons' party.

"I'm beginning to wonder if we were at the same place," Alex said. "I must lead a very blinkered existence."

"You were wheeler-dealing in the dining-room," she accused.

"Jane thought it highly sexist that the men remained behind in the dining-room after dinner and that the women *withdrew to take coffee.*"

"What on earth for?" Sasha asked.

"Ostensibly to complete business deals but mainly to have a quiet cigar without their wives nagging them!"

"I thought there was more to it than business," Jane said triumphantly.

"It sounds very interesting all the . . . " Susie shifted in her chair and gave a little yelp.

Matt's face was full of concern. "Susie, what's the matter?"

"Nothing's the matter, the baby has started playing soccer again. Oops, it's just scored an own goal."

"Can I feel the baby kick?"Jane asked.

"Sure, just put your hand here and wait."

Susie placed Jane's hand flat on her tummy. Jane's face broke into a beautiful smile. "It kicked, I felt it," she said in wonderment.

Jane stood beside William while he measured the coffee into the percolator. "How I'll miss you both – all of you."

"Our lives won't be the same without you, either." William squeezed her arm affectionately. "But Jane, do you want to stay with us, live your life without Alex?" William's calm reply soothed her.

"I worry about Sasha." Jane's brow was creased in a deep frown. "What will she do? I wish she'd stay on at The Willows for a while, at least until she . . ."

"You don't need to worry about Sasha," William interrupted. "We have some exciting news for her. We decided to wait until after dinner to tell her."

"That's marvellous, what is it?"

William smiled at her impatience. "You'll hear in a minute."

Justin cleared his throat and held up his hand for silence. "We have some more good news tonight," he began.

They stopped talking and looked at him expectantly.

"*This* good news is for Sasha."

Sasha stopped pleating the material between her fingers.

"What good news?" she demanded.

"A friend of ours, he owns the Cormorant Theatre, is looking for a make-up artist *extraordinaire*," Justin said dramatically. "Look no further, I said . . ."

The rest of Justin's speech was interrupted by great shouts of joy from Sasha. She grabbed him by the arms and waltzed him round the room. Never one to miss the chance of some fun, Justin followed her dancing feet. Eventually he stumbled and they ended up on the floor in a laughing heap.

"Tell her the rest, William," Justin said gasping for breath.

"Can you hear me, Sasha?"

"I hear you. Quick, tell me more."

"The job is very exacting. It needs someone like you, someone with talent. And that you have. We've arranged an interview for you on Monday. You'll have to do three make-ups; two faces and one body. If all goes well, the job is yours."

Sasha sat staring at William, her skirt-hoop sticking up in the air at the oddest angle.

"That sounds too good to be true. I don't need to tell you how much I'd adore a job like that."

"You certainly should have no problems. The job would start in about a month's time and *will honour all holiday arrangements*," William said pointedly. Sasha's beam grew even wider.

"I'll tell you what," Justin said, still puffed from his dance, "we'll come over in a couple of days and I'll let you practise one of your make-ups on me."

"I'll be a model too," Jane promised.

"That's a terrific idea. William, are you game for the body make-up?" Sasha asked.

"No fear, find someone who's less ticklish."

It was after midnight before Susie and Matt left the cottage. Jane hugged Susie as tightly as her bump would allow and they both shed copious tears. Alex tugged gently at Jane's arm. Alex and Matt exchanged glances, the longer the friends stayed like this, the more upset they'd be. When the men prised them apart, Susie and Jane tearfully promised to speak to each other every night before Jane left The Willows.

Jane appreciated Justin and Wiliam's low-key farewells to Alex. They quietly shook his hand, wished him *bon voyage* and good luck in the future.

Surprisingly they'd made little fuss about the wedding. Neither did they hint at what would happen to Alex if he didn't look after her – none of the teasing she'd come to expect. But then she didn't know that on her wedding day they'd be there, standing beside her.

As they drove along the dark roads, Jane said, "I don't understand why parting is described as sweet sorrow. I think it's unutterably miserable." Alex held her hand with his own.

"I have to agree with that," he said as he thought of his own journey home next day.

Chapter Seventy-Five

They talked of everything except the reason for this meeting. Emma found herself enjoying Charles's company. He was well mannered, charming without being gushing, attentive but not sycophantic. It was easy to understand why he was successful at his job with the escort agency.

"I have asked you to come here because I have a proposition to put to you." Emma Brown replaced her coffee cup carefully on its saucer.

Charles Graham had kept his word and not mentioned anything about this to Amanda.

Amanda had been so excited, on such a high, when she rang to tell him about *Personal Agenda*, that Charles pretended that he knew nothing about it.

"I hear from Jane that you've agreed to continue vetting clients for *Personal Agenda*. I'm glad." Emma said. "But what I have to offer is more than just that. I'd like to offer you a full partnership with Amanda – fifty, fifty."

Emma had a habit of taking him by surprise. But people didn't give away partnerships for no reason. Here comes the crunch, Charles thought. Anyone with a bit of common sense could do what he did.

"That sounds very interesting. In return for . . . ?" he asked.

"You must live at The Willows. Help Amanda run *Personal Agenda*. You get on well together, don't you?"

"Yes we do. I'm extremely fond of her."

"That brings me to the rest of my . . . suggestion. If after a year, if you feel the same way about her, you ask her to marry you."

Emma's *suggestion* took his breath away. "Does Amanda have a say in all this?"

"Amanda knows nothing about this, *nothing*. And that's how it must remain for all time. Even if it comes to nothing, you must promise me that."

"I promise," Charles replied automatically. This woman was amazing.

"If she ever finds out, if you hint or breathe a word to her or anyone, the arrangement is off. I don't need to tell you she's hurting badly. Kevin O'Hanlon all but destroyed her. She's very fond of you and, I know Amanda, it wouldn't take too much to make her fall in love with you. That is if you're willing to try."

"And what about me? What if I don't love her?"

"That's up to you. But you must be absolutely sure before you get involved. I couldn't bear to see her hurt again, won't tolerate it."

"And if I do ask her to marry me, and she accepts, then what?"

"Then you'll have half of everything, the business, the house and the sum of . . ."

Charles stared at her stupidly. He realised that Emma Brown was a very comfortable woman but this was an astonishing offer. He would never have to worry again. To live at The Willows would be the fulfilment of his dreams, running *Personal Agenda* would be simple. Could he care enough for Amanda?

"What if Amanda refuses to marry *me*, doesn't love me?"

"Come now, Charles. With your charm? Men aren't exactly knocking down her door. I'm sure that *love* will find a way." Emma lowered her eyes. She was not proud of what she'd done. But this was her chance, an opportunity to make up for all those lost years. To see her daughter happy again was worth everything. She'd seen the look of greed in Charles Graham's eyes, but from what she'd seen and knew of him, she was convinced that he was honourable.

"May I suggest that you sleep on it. Think it over very carefully. Whatever you may think, Charles, I love Amanda and will to do anything in my power to make her happy. I think that you are the one person who could help to achieve that. By the way, if you do marry Amanda you will have to sign an agreement that everything reverts to her should there be a divorce. I must protect her. I'm sure that you understand."

Charles understood perfectly.

He stayed at the table and ordered a brandy, he needed it for the shock. Emma had offered him a lift home but he refused. Her words still rang in his head. He had met many tough, hard women in his day but Emma Brown was the most calculating of them all. She knew how he felt about *Personal Agenda*, they'd talked about it the night he'd had dinner at the house. She'd found his Achilles heel and had used his fondness for The Willows to bribe him.

♥ ♥ ♥

Jane heard Amanda calling her.

"I'm here, what's all the excitement about?"

"It *is* exciting, Jane. Mum has just phoned, Charles has agreed to run *Personal Agenda* with me. He'll live here at The Willows and work from here."

"Oh, Amanda, that's marvellous. I hated to think of you here on your own. That's a perfect solution. You'll need help if you're going to go ahead with your extension plans."

"We are, *definitely.*"

"I hate to bring you back to earth but we should try and finish these accounts. There aren't too many more left and then you'll be up to date."

Chapter Seventy-Six

Jane sat back with a sigh. She'd covered every aspect of *Personal Agenda* that she could think of with Amanda. Amanda's natural aptitude for figures, her ability to find her way round a computer, had made Jane's task easier.

It was strange to see her office without the friendship rug. It was one of the few remaining mementoes of her childhood. Where were they all now, those schoolfriends who vowed not to lose touch? Who would be her friends in Washington? The people Alex considered *his* close friends had been very nice to her, but would she make friends of her own?

The phone interrupted her reverie. She glanced at her watch, too early for Alex to ring.

"Hello, Jane, it's Kevin," Kevin O'Hanlon said.

She recognised his voice immediately.

"Hello, Kevin," Jane answered coldly.

"I was wondering if I could book in for a weekend?"

"*Personal Agenda* has changed hands, Kevin, if you'll hold on a moment I'll put you on to the new owner." Jane said.

Jane could hear his questioning voice as she went to find Amanda.

"Amanda Brown, speaking."

"Amanda? May I speak to Jane?" Kevin asked, uncertain whether he had heard correctly.

"I can help you. What is it you want to know?" Amanda's voice was even, her tone impersonal.

"I . . . I just . . . wanted to book for a weekend."

"I'm afraid not, Kevin. You see *Personal Agenda* belongs to me now. Frankly you will be unwelcome here, both now and in the future."

Jane couldn't hear his reply.

"No, there'll be no refund of fees – you've had more than your money's worth already. Goodbye." Amanda crashed the phone back onto its base. "And that's the end of him."

♥ ♥ ♥

Sasha packed the last of her shoes into her grip. Under any other circumstances she'd be dancing with excitement. She'd passed her audition with flying colours. Justin phoned minutes before the theatre owner rang to give her the news officially.

Sasha had revelled in those few hours she'd spent at the theatre. She knew that she would enjoy doing make-up artist almost as much as being an actress. What a wonderful opportunity to do something she loved and to get paid for it too, she smiled to herself smugly.

Her lips twitched even more at the thought of the evening they'd spent helping her with her make-up practice.

"Keep still, Justin," Sasha instructed as she painted deep black shadows under his eyes.

"I *can't* keep still, the brush tickles." Justin wriggled in the chair and, unable to stand the itch any longer, he wiped the back of his hand across his face and smeared his eyes.

"Justin!" Sasha wailed. "You look as if you've been in a prize fight – and lost."

"If my services are no longer needed, say the word." Justin sulked.

"You don't get off that lightly, stay right where you are." Sasha repaired the damage to Justin's eyes. With a steady hand she drew a line from his nose to his mouth. Justin sneezed. Patiently Sasha cleaned the blurred line and began again. Justin sneezed again, twice.

Jane and William began to laugh.

"It's not funny," Justin said and he too began to giggle.

"You're all rotten," Sasha complained as she repaired the latest damage. "Now Justin, just forget about those idiots and concentrate. This is my living at stake here."

Justin sat up straight and told Jane and William to shut up. Amanda sat quietly watching. They were acting like idiots, she agreed with Sasha. Sasha glowered fiercely then took up her brush. The line she drew was perfect – a deep, wide line which made Justin's mouth seem to droop on one side. Justin hiccupped.

Jane and William choked with laughter. Sasha threw down the brush and burst into tears.

"Oh Sasha, please don't cry," Jane begged. "Justin is obviously allergic to the paint."

"Come on, Sasha, I'll sit for you instead,"

William offered, he hated to see Sasha upset.

"Tricking comes to licking," Amanda said scathingly as she got up from her chair and made for the door.

All four of them stuck their tongues out at her back as if it had been prearranged. They looked at each other and began to laugh again. Sasha, the tears still wet on her cheeks, laughed loudest of all.

William looked like a man in his eighties. He had no problems with the make-up. Jane's face looked marvellous. She'd been anxious to make up for her bad behaviour and sat stock still for the twenty minutes it took to paint the colourful butterfly. It was a work of art and Justin, also eager to atone for his sins, praised Sasha endlessly.

"It's OK, Justin, I get the message," Sasha said and laughed as Justin sneezed again.

They sat round the kitchen table, drank beer and ate curry. No one said anything, but they were all relieved when Amanda announced that she was tired and was going to bed. Neither did anyone say anything about the fact this would probably be their last night together before Jane left for the States. Alex had warned them that Jane was dreading the goodbyes.

Justin and William had begun to treat Sasha like a helpless child. They fussed over her, fretted about her and checked every day to make sure that she was all right.

"I love them dearly." Sasha grinned as she replaced the receiver after another of their calls.

"But all this fuss and attention is driving me nuts. I'm a big girl now, I can manage."

"Don't knock it," Jane said severely. "They worry and care about you. I'm being selfish I know, but I'm delighted that they're there for you."

"You're right of course, and I owe them so much."

Susie and Matt had invited Sasha to stay with them for as long as she liked. She was very grateful, she'd come to love them dearly, but she needed to have a place of her own. Now at least she could take her time and look around for something suitable.

Sasha sat back on her heels and thought about Amanda. Amanda had been quite snooty with her all week. She couldn't understand why Sasha wanted to leave The Willows.

"Never mind," Sasha told herself as she folded the costume carefully and put it into the trunk. "Just another couple of days and I'll be out of her hair for good." But just another couple of days and Jane would be gone too. Jane, how she would miss her, their good and bad times together. She smiled as she thought how surprised Jane would be when they arrived on her doorstep in Washington. She would rather miss her own wedding than Jane's. "Jane will be happy with Alex. Pity he doesn't have a brother for me."

Jane had forgotten all about Kim. She slipped into the office and dialled her number.

"Amanda? Amanda Brown? How come?" Kim asked when Jane explained the agency was changing hands.

"Alex and I are getting married," Jane blurted out.

"That is good news. I can't pretend to be surprised. I told you, didn't I, once Alex makes up his mind he's a fast worker."

Jane wasn't sure what to say next.

"When's the big day?"

"Next month," Jane didn't elaborate.

"I wish you both every happiness. I'm sure Jonathan does too."

"Everything going well with you both?"

"Perfect. That was dreadful news about Ray Parker wasn't it? I could hardly believe my eyes when I read it."

"What about Ray, has something happened to him?"

"Didn't you see it in the paper? He's been charged with fraud."

"I didn't see that – none of us did. What did he do?"

"Apparently or – allegedly, as they say – he arranged to have his business premises robbed. After the burglary, the thief returned the goods to him. Then he made a big claim against his insurance, about twice as much as he should have done even if the theft was genuine. Seemingly he made a fatal mistake when he sold one of his so-called 'missing' computers to a customer. When his own programmer was sent to do some work for the customer, he found some of their own systems already installed. He twigged immediately and reported Ray to the police. The programmer seemingly had some beef of his own, I can't remember the details. But Ray will almost certainly be sent to jail. The insurance company is suing him as well as the fraud squad."

Chapter Seventy-Seven

Jane told Sasha about Ray. They were sitting in their usual late-night spot at the kitchen table.

"How did he imagine he'd get away with that?" Sasha asked, horrified.

"Search me. He must be crazy. Do you remember the weekend he went to Dublin? That's when it happened, Kim said, when he was out of the country."

"I wonder how long he'll serve in jail?"

"I don't know how all of us missed that," Jane frowned.

"It'll be a while before *he's* back at The Willows," Sasha yawned. "I think I'll go to bed. Suddenly, I feel drained."

Jane couldn't resist the urge to get up and hug Sasha to her. Dearest Sasha – she'd been such a good friend, and a loyal one.

"Goodnight Sasha, sleep well. Be successful, be happy in everything you do," Jane said and turned her head away. She didn't want Sasha to see the tears glistening in her eyes.

"You too, Jane." Sasha fled from the kitchen, she'd promised Alex no tears.

Before she turned out the lights for the last time Jane placed three envelopes on the kitchen table. She couldn't face goodbyes. Sasha would give the letters to Justin and William.

"If you really can't take it, Jane, just leave a letter for each of them, leave a day earlier. There's no point facing such a long journey when you're upset, they'll understand," Alex had said.

Jane felt like the biggest coward in the world. But it would be much easier this way. She had changed her ticket and was leaving in the morning instead of Wednesday as she'd planned.

She walked quietly through the silent rooms. What changes would Amanda and Emma Brown make? Would Charles settle down to a country-life existence or would he miss living in a city? Saying goodbye to him hadn't been too difficult. She'd wished Amanda luck earlier today but, try as she might, Jane couldn't warm to her again. She'd felt so sorry for her when Kevin acted up but having been in Amanda's company for the last couple of weeks, she just didn't like her. Perhaps I'm jealous, Jane thought, jealous that my home will be hers soon, all that I fought for, worked for, will be handed to her on a plate – a reward for being a bad girl.

Jane looked at the case standing in the corner of her bedroom. This was the last night she'd sleep in her cosy single bed. A shiver of anticipation ran through her. By this time tomorrow she'd be on the other side of the world, and in Alex's loving arms.

♥ ♥ ♥

Amanda heard the sound of footsteps crunching over the gravel. She jumped out of bed and went to the window. Through the partly open window Amanda could see the taxi and could hear its engine ticking over.

From behind her curtain she watched as Jane walked towards the gate. The taxi-driver came up the path and took her case from her.

Jane stopped at a flower bed, bent down and broke off two sprigs of heather. She held them to her cheek, they would be part of her bridal bouquet. Jane walked towards the gate but she didn't look back. Her life was in the future.

Epilogue

Each morning when she woke Jane uttered a little prayer of thanks. Never had she known such happiness, such peace of mind. Alex was the most thoughtful person she'd ever met. She smiled as she thought of her husband. He'd been positively miserable yesterday at the idea of leaving her for a night.

"I'll still be here when you get back!" Jane laughed.

"Couldn't you come with us?" Alex pleaded.

"Oh, Alex, you don't want your wife along on a one day business trip. Besides, what will I do all day when you two are in meetings?"

Alex agreed she was right. He and Tom Merryweather did have a full schedule.

"I'll phone you tonight," Alex promised as he kissed her goodbye for the second time.

Jane was just about to leave the apartment when the phone rang.

"Hello, darling." Alex's deep voice still gave her a thrill.

"Where are you?" Jane asked.

"I'm at the office, we're due to leave in about five minutes. I phoned to tell you I love you and that I'm going to miss you."

Jane smiled, Alex was impossible.

"I love you too," she assured him.

"Oh yes, there was something else, your credit cards have arrived, will you stop by the office and collect them?"

"I don't really need them today, but of course I will."

"I'll leave them with the relief secretary. Peg is home sick with a bug of some sort."

"OK, Alex. Have a safe flight."

"Have a good time today, talk to you later."

Jane made her way to the waiting car. John always greeted her with a cheery smile.

"Can you take me to the office first?" Jane asked.

"Sure. No problem," he said.

John glanced in his rear view mirror. He really liked Alex Travis's wife. She was a gentle person, a happy person, always smiling. He too smiled as he thought back to the day before their wedding, the day they'd tricked Jane into going to the airport to meet a client and friend of Alex's who was flying in for the wedding.

"How will I recognise him, Alex?" she asked dubiously.

"Don't worry," he replied, "John will be there with you, he's met him before. I know you're busy but it would be nice if one of us could be there to greet him."

John had purposely stayed back out of Jane's line of vision. He watched her as she peered anxiously at the arriving passengers. He couldn't see her face but he heard her squeal of delight quite clearly when two men and a woman came through the door. She rushed forward and threw her arms around them, tears of surprise and happiness pouring down her face. He wouldn't admit it to anyone but his own eyes were moist too.

"I was thinking about the day your friends arrived," he said to Jane.

"Wasn't that incredible? I thought I'd collapse on the spot. You don't have any more surprises for me today, do you?" she asked.

"No, not today," John laughed.

"And wasn't the wedding wonderful?" she said dreamily.

"It certainly was." He peeped at Jane again. She had a faraway look in her eye.

The only tinge of sadness she'd felt at the time was that Alex's sister wasn't able to come back from Australia for the wedding. She'd thought that none of her friends could be with her for the Great Day either. But Alex, darling Alex, had taken care of that. She would never forget the sight of Sasha, Justin and William coming through that door, their faces glowing with mischief. How she'd hugged them.

"I'm squashed to bits," Justin complained, lovingly.

That day passed in a haze as John whisked them around Washington on a whirlwind tour. They'd have plenty of time to see the sights after the wedding but Jane was eager to share their first impressions. Dinner that night had been such fun. They'd broken with tradition.

"I know the bride shouldn't see the groom before the wedding," Alex admitted. "But I'm not going to miss out on tonight."

She and Sasha sat on Jane's bed and talked until they were hoarse. Alex booked a room at the hotel for her too, he thought she would enjoy spending her last night as a single woman with her closest friends. "I've moved out of The Willows and I'm staying with Justin and William. Amanda was so horrible to me the morning you left, I just phoned for a taxi and left."

Jane knew how determined Sasha could be but also how sensitive she was.

"What did she say to you?" Jane asked.

"She said, *'You don't need to bother looking for your precious friend, she's done a bunk without saying goodbye.'*"

"That was nasty," Jane said, feeling guilty again.

"Don't worry, I gave her one in the eye. I told her we *had* said goodbye, but that it was only for a short time anyway. We were *all* invited to Washington to the wedding. You should have seen her stupid mouth drop open. And then I asked her 'innocently' if she'd been invited too!" Sasha smirked.

"Well said! Tell me all about Susie, how does she look, is she all right?" Jane asked. Sasha still knew nothing about the break-up.

"Susie's fine, she's *absolutely* fine, I saw her last week. She's beginning to waddle slightly but is blooming. Mind you, she doesn't look as blooming as you do!"

"I'm really happy, Sasha. Alex is a wonderful man, I'm so lucky."

"He certainly is and you don't need a magnifying glass to see how he adores you."

"I can't believe this," Jane said. "Here we are

sitting on a bed in Washington when just this morning I thought how much I missed you all and was so sad that you wouldn't be here tomorrow."

"We couldn't *wait* to see your face." Sasha yawned.

"You must be exhausted! I've been so excited I forgot you had a long journey today. Let's make our plans for tomorrow morning, what are you going to wear? Flowers, you need . . ." Jane stopped her excited chatter. Sasha was sitting back against the pillows fast asleep.

The wedding had been small, elegant and the happiest day of her life. She walked down the short, flower-decorated aisle of the hotel room, Justin one side, William on the other.

One of Alex's friends had taken her to a boutique in Georgetown called *Caprice*, and she'd been spoilt for choice. In the end she'd chosen a long, simple cream dress which showed her slim figure to perfection. She wore an intricate skull cap made from fresh flowers on her short shining hair. Sasha followed her solemnly, she took her duty as maid-of-honour very seriously. She too wore cream; the only touch of the old Sasha was a ten-string necklace of pale coffee-coloured beads which almost covered the jacket of her suit.

The reception was perfect – as far as she could remember. It passed in a blur of congratulations, popping corks, good wishes and hugs and kisses. She'd cried when she said goodbye to her friends but Alex reminded her that she could go and visit them whenever she wanted.

"You'll always be welcome, both of you," William insisted.

"Absolutely," Justin echoed in a choked voice.

The honeymoon was the stuff that dreams were made of, Jane thought. The sadness of saying goodbye was soon forgotten as they explored the beautiful Hawaiian islands. It was blissfully warm and everywhere they looked flowers bloomed in profusion. They swam in the ocean, lazed on the beach, toured the islands. They made love in small hidden coves on the beach, and giggled like guilty teenagers fearing they'd be discovered. They loved the wonderful food. Jane groaned that she'd get fat but couldn't resist the exotic dishes. Alex just said "I don't care, I love it."

Jane smiled as she thought of her husband's voracious appetite. It wasn't fair, she frowned, Alex could eat and eat and he never added more than a couple of pounds.

"We're here." John spoke quietly reluctant to disturb his smiling passenger.

"Oh! Thank you, John, I was miles away."

He watched her slim figure as she walked jauntily into the building. Alex had made a good choice, picked a winner this time.

Jane smiled at the girl behind the desk in the reception hall. "I'm Jane Ander . . . Jane Travis." Jane felt foolish, she wasn't used to her new name yet.

"Mr Travis said you'd be . . . Excuse me a moment." The girl turned her attention to the switchboard's flashing light. A frown furrowed her brow as she struggled with the switches. She looked relieved when she heard a voice.

"Yes, yes. No, I'm sorry Mr Travis is out of his office today. No, I can't contact him." The frown returned. "I'm sorry I can't help you . . . but just one moment please." The relief secretary put the caller on hold.

"There's a personal call for Mr Travis, do you think you could take it?" The girl looked so worried Jane felt sorry for her.

"I don't suppose I can help any more than you can, but OK."

"Jane Travis speaking," she said in a businesslike voice.

"There's no cause for alarm, Ms Travis," a man's voice said. "We wanted Mr Travis to know that his wife slipped earlier this morning and bruised some ribs. She's been X-rayed and there's no real damage. She's back with us now in The Tranquil Care Centre."

What was he talking about? There must be some mistake. "I don't understand, who are you?" Jane asked.

"I'm the director of the mental health facility, The Tranquil Care Centre? You are related to Mr Travis, aren't you?"

"Yes," Jane said hurriedly. "But who are you talking about?"

"Mr Alex Travis's wife – Mrs Cassie Travis."

ALSO BY POOLBEG

Intrigue

by

Anne Schulman

From the fabulous marinas of the South of France to the mansions of Washington; Dublin's top hotels to Kildare's stud farms; the casinos of Las Vegas to the beauties of Paris.

Five strangers meet, each with their own guilty secret. One of them is going to pay with their life for something in their past.

Is it Gaby? High-flying, attractive Gaby. An accident for which she is unfairly blamed alters her life. Does her need for revenge make her a target?

Is it Edward? Cutting corners while building a career in the casinos of Cannes and Las Vegas has produced formidable enemies.

Is it Rachel? Beautiful Rachel from her poor background. Shy determination spurs her on, but is fulfilment all that it seems?

Is it Claude? From childhood he worked, struggled, scrimped and saved to build the perfect hotel of his dreams. But walking the hard stony road on the way to success did he step on someone's toes?

Or is it Laura? Plain, down-trodden Laura. Manipulated by her conniving brother and her bed-ridden mother. She grasps a once-in-a-lifetime opportunity, but does the devil want his due?

ISBN 1-85371-336-8 £4.99

ALSO BY POOLBEG

Sins of Omission

By

Gemma O'Connor

In one fateful month Grace Hartfield's uneventful life falls apart. First her husband leaves her suddenly and brutally. A few days later, out of the blue, she is declared next of kin and only beneficiary of two unknown women.

In trying to untangle the enigma of these mysterious relatives and their sudden and fearful deaths, Grace is plunged backwards into her own terrified and violent childhood.

SUICIDE OR MURDER?

Two women, Grace in London, the other in Dublin and one man – the wealthy head of a Dutch development company. No apparent connection between them, yet their lives are destroyed by one searing incident, resolutely buried.

Bid Lacey, younger and more trusting is caught up in this web of secrecy and half truth which leads to three violent deaths. Or is it four?

Sins of Omission is a breathtaking psychological thriller.

ISBN 1-85371-534-4 £4.99